CW00919721

A Widow In Waiting

A Novel Out of Africa

Samantha Ford

Published on Amazon Via KDP
All Rights Reserved.
Copyright © 2022 Samantha Ford
(ISBN 9798353137023)

No part of this book may be reproduced or transmitted in any form or by any means, graphic, electronic, or mechanical, including photocopying, recording, taping or by any information storage or retrieval system, without the permission in writing from the copyright holder.

The right of Samantha Ford to be identified as the author of this work has been asserted in accordance with the Copyright, Designs and Patents Act 1988 sections 77 and 78.

This is a work of fiction. The characters and their actions are entirely fictitious. Any resemblance to persons living or dead is entirely coincidental.

******

Also by Samantha Ford

The Zanzibar Affair

The House Called Mbabati

A Gathering of Dust

The Ambassador's Daughter

The Unexpected Guest

Amazon Reviews

"A wonderful story which kept me intrigued from the first page to the last, the characters are rich and unforgettable. The storyline twists and turns and you are unsure what is going to happen next. A truly outstanding read and loved every page. And the ending blew me away. Highly recommend a truly wonderfully written book."

"I may have mentioned before, I hate novels. The author, Samantha Ford has changed all of that. Now I am hooked and will be looking for the remainder of her novels on Africa as soon as I am done here.

Taking the reader to the African destinations is done to perfection. To an extent you also get to meet the African people. Some good and some not so good. This story could easily be true as it kept me spell bound with descriptions and actions. For one who hates fiction, I can't not give this a 5-Star rating. Well-deserved Samantha"

"It's not just a novel. It's an adventure. A journey we long for. Travelling down dirt roads you can feel the dust in your throat. The cool cocktails and beers quenching your parched throat. The excitement of human interactions. The raw emotions. You will laugh. Get riled up at injustice AND you will CRY. My soul this is not just a book. So real you will feel you have made friends with the characters. Samantha Ford may your light shine bright."

Acknowledgements

I would like to thank the following for their unswerving support on this long and lonely road called writing.

First, and foremost, to all the people who have read my books and put up over five thousand reviews – every single one of you are special and I thank you for your support. Sorry about the tears…

To be compared to John Gordon Davis and Wilbur Smith, is a massive, and humbling, tribute. It would not have happened without you, my dear readers.

To my sister, Jackie, who spent so many hours reading, and re-reading the manuscript. What would I do without your input, even though you rolled your eyes a few times…well, more than a few times actually.

To Mark, my dear friend of so many years and designer of all my front covers – you leave me breathless with your talent. How you encapsulate my story into a stunning cover is beyond me…
(marknoujaimbaldwin@gmail.com)

To Gail, my formidable editor with the ability to pull me up short, and drop me to my knees in tears and laughter. She takes no prisoners…
info@gailbwilliams.co.uk

To Brian Stephens for taking away the pain of formatting and preparing my books for publication. Another great job – thank you.
brian@moulinwebsitedesign.com,

Captain Trevor Jones – and his unbelievable knowledge of flying around the Kenyan bush. Trevor, you can fly me around out there any time. Thank you.
tdfjones@gmail.com

I am fully aware that there is no British Embassy in Kenya, however, in this particular story I have elevated the High Commission to an Embassy…sounds better.

Finally, to you the readers, thank you for all the fantastic reviews on Amazon. Without reviews an author will struggle to sell their books. To be compared to John Gordon Davis, one of Southern Africa's most loved authors, and to Wilbur Smith, is indeed a huge compliment.

Thank you for purchasing this book, I hope it brings back wonderful memories to all of you who have ever had the privilege of living in Africa.

Through the long nights she walks beside you in your dreams.

In the distance of this other place, you hear your childlike voice, echoing through the bush as you run wild, free and barefoot chasing your dreams.

The sky so high and blue, the whispering grasses brushing against your sun-kissed legs.

You may have left this place, and travelled to another country you now call home.

But from far away you hear her voice, seducing you with a beauty you can never forget. The sounds of her, the fragrance of her, the unchanging essence of her, as she waits.

Because she never left you – she is waiting for you here to come back.

To this place called Africa.

Chapter One
1997 Kenya

There was a stillness and silence to the bush that day. The parched landscape was a dusty brownish yellow, the water holes and rivers drying up as herds of impala, zebra and buffalo searched for water.

The massive Baobab trees with their strange but distinctive shape, were scattered over the acacia scrubland. Their branches spreading widely above their bulbous trunks.

The hills were dotted with hard edged boulders, glinting white in the harsh sunlight. In the evenings when dusk fell, they would turn grey before melting into the darkness and becoming one with the bush.

A lone giraffe, oblivious to the heat, feasted on the dry leaves of a tree. His mouth moving rhythmically, his long thin tail flicking over his mottled hide against the irritating flies and insects on his body, where ox-pecker birds provided some relief by collecting the ticks.

Tsavo. One of Kenya's oldest national parks, was a peaceful place on that defining day – no tiered safari vehicles dotting the landscape, sending up clouds of dust behind them, only the animals sheltering where possible from the brutal heat.

In the distance a small speck came into view. The giraffe ceased his foraging. His mouth stilled as he watched, his ears twitching.

The ox peckers flew off. Sensing something.

The speck now took shape, the faint drone of something coming closer.

Without warning the shape in the skies seemed to drop, the noise increasing in volume. The plane throwing a brief shadow over the wilderness beneath its wings as it plummeted towards the ground.

The pilot knew these would be the last images he would see of this land he loved.

It would be quick.

*****

The aircraft hit the outcrop of rocks and with a screeching of metal, gouged a deep wound in the silvery white boulders which had been there for hundreds of years. The plane tipped over and burst into flames.

The pilot died with her name on his lips.

The giraffe, panicked by the explosion and the fiercely burning ball of fire, turned and made an ungainly canter through the dusty bush to the shelter of some trees, then turned and looked back.

At an elevated distance he watched the fireball sending flames up into what had been a peerlessly blue sky. The clouds of billowing grey smoke threw shadows across the bush where a few moments earlier there had been none. Then a veil of black acrid smoke briefly blotted out the sun.

Animals lifted their heads then bolted in panic, thundering their way through the bush, away from the fiery intrusion.

Then there was silence.

The animals, trees, chalky coloured rocky outcrops, the grasses and the burning sun would go on. The sun would set, darkness would come and paint the sky with a spectacular showcase of glittering stars. The land would cool and the predators would come out.

Life would continue as it had always done in Africa.

Chapter Two
A few days before…

The aero club at Kenya's Wilson Airport was relatively quiet for a Sunday afternoon.

There was a panelled restaurant, a terrace overlooking the airfield and a garden with a modest swimming pool. The bar was thatched in East African style, with a Spitfire engine perched in one corner and a Pratt & Whitney engine in another. The walls were plastered with memorabilia from a golden age of the past: faces of the magnificent aviators of that time. Finch-Hatton, Hemingway, Carberry and Beryl Markham amongst them, then newspaper cuttings of terrible crashes and the obituaries that followed…

Pilots were busy loading and unloading safari bags as the sun beat down, their crisp white shirts and shorts with the occasional glint from their epaulettes easily identifying them from the khaki safari wear of their passengers.

Alongside the runway bright billboards advertised hotels, bars and restaurants, amidst sun bleached older ones, with their Coca Cola signs or advertising some product which would enhance your life and how you looked and hopefully last longer than the faded product being advertised.

Sir David Cooper watched all the activity going on, drained his glass of beer and stood up. Reaching for his Panama hat he turned and walked out of the bar, glancing briefly again at the planes coming and going. Wishing there was an alternative to what he had to do.

*****

The next morning, David filed his flight plan then waited on the apron for the tower to give him clearance to take off for his flight to

Mombasa. He looked up at a cloudless sky; the other aircraft parked outside their hangers shimmering in the heat as the day warmed up.

The tower cleared him to enter the runway and take off. As he turned down the strip, he pushed the throttle into the panel and the engine roared into life. The Cessna quickly gathered speed as it got lighter and lighter on its wheels then soared up and levelled out.

Nairobi game park spread out beneath him, then the Athi Plains with the Ngong hills to his right.

His flight would take around two and a half hours which would get him to Mombasa in time for lunch. He flew over the town of Voi with Mount Kilimanjaro clear on his right with glimpses of the old railway line snaking its silver way from Nairobi to Mombasa. Tsavo was laid out beneath him, miles and miles of nothing with the occasional glimpse of great herds of elephant ponderously making their way through the hot bush in search of water, the plains dotted with the majestic baobab trees for which it was famous and the rocky outcrops amidst the undulating hills.

Soon he glimpsed the Mombasa creek with its swamps of mango trees and the sands and palm trees of the coastline. He flipped open his side window and breathed in the smell of the sea, feeling the warm humid air filling the cockpit.

He contacted the tower at Mombasa and prepared to land. He would re-fuel, although there was enough to get back to Nairobi, then lock the plane, before heading for the beach house.

*****

As darkness fell, David stepped out onto the generous wrap around wooden deck of the house, the beach was deserted. He walked out onto the creamy white sand still warm from the sun that day. The sea was calm with white capped crests, as white as the collar of a newly ordained priest, as it gently met the dry shore then retreated hissing and bubbling over the sand before rolling in again.

The water was warm against his calves as he walked slowly along. Memories of another sea, so many years ago when he was a boy, rose to the surface of his mind. A sea so far away in a place they now called Malaysia.

A huge silver moon was rising over the dark sea, turning it to the colour of beaten silver. The silence was soporific. He sat down on the powdery sand and put his head in his hands.

He'd played the game under dangerous circumstances. One fatal miscalculation and it was all over.

There was nowhere to run. Nowhere to hide.

He stood up, brushed the sand from his shorts and made his way back to the house.

Chapter Three

The Delamere Bar at the Norfolk Hotel was crowded; it always was. Outside an endless stream of safari vehicles pulled up waiting to collect their passengers for the short trip to Wilson Airport from where they would board their light aircraft and head out to the safari lodges the country was famous for.

The passengers congregated around the reception area of the hotel, others stood at the steps outside, clutching their maps and hand luggage, cameras and binoculars hanging from their pale necks eagerly awaiting a sighting of their promised safari vehicle sporting the tour operator's logo on its side.

Fortunately, they were not privy to the gossip and speculation rippling through the locals as they enjoyed their drinks and lunch. Waiters deftly made their way from table to table, trays held aloft as they served lunch, their faces glistening, their shirts billowing with the movement of air from the fans overhead.

Unlike the tourists, the locals were tanned by years of living under the Kenyan sun, the women dressed in light colourful dresses, the men in the standard attire of shorts and shirts.

Above the percussion clatter of cutlery and crockery, the restaurant was abuzz with the latest news.

"Does anyone know what happened? Where it happened? Who was the pilot? Any survivors? How many passengers did he have with him?"

One of the diners speared a piece of calamari off his plate. "Someone said it was a female pilot – not many of them here, so it shouldn't be difficult to find out who she was?"

"Apparently there was no Mayday call. It seems the plane crashed into a rocky outcrop in Tsavo, flipped over and burst into flames. Well, that's the conclusion everyone is coming to. It wasn't on the normal flight path for any of the lodges in the area.

"Another pilot saw the wisps of smoke the next day, but he had passengers with him, not something he wanted them to see as he flew them to their safari camp. Probably used the pilot's private radio frequency and spread the word to his fellow pilots, then radioed the tower at Wilson Airport. That's it – that's all we know."

*****

The receptionist put the phone down and whispered to the manager.

"Some bad news, I'm afraid, Len. The pilot was one of our guests. He checked in four days ago. Had some business to do here in town before he flew back to Nanyuki where he lived.

"His plane crashed into a rocky outcrop at Tsavo, then exploded. He checked out yesterday, in more ways than one. That was the British Embassy. They want to come and talk to you?"

The manager tapped at the keys on his computer. "David Cooper? Was it him?"

The receptionist nodded. "Yes. Sir David Cooper."

Len scanned the computer again. "We've logged in here that his wife called last night. Obviously, she had no idea he had checked out and taken a trip to the coast." He frowned. "Why are the Embassy so concerned with all of this, I wonder. He must have been someone important if they're involved?"

The receptionist looked at him. "Well, he was British and titled, so of course the Embassy will be involved. It's what they do."

Chapter Four

The Kenyan sun speared the glorious colours of the stain glassed windows, throwing a kaleidoscope of rippling colours over the sombre clothes of the congregation gathered there for the memorial service. Spreading an illusion of warmth within the thick cold walls of the old church. There was a sense of the others who had gone before Sir David. Some old, some young and the children of course. Africa always expected a price to be paid for the magnificent opportunities it bestowed.

Outside in the neglected graveyard, headstones with barely visible messages of love, lolled drunkenly towards each other. Their permanent residents lost in the mists of time; their names forgotten as the resolute bush reclaimed all the memories. Families returned to the countries they had come from, leaving loved ones far behind beneath the hard baked African soil. Forgotten by the generations who would follow them.

Because it was so in Africa.

Young and eager, adventure and hope pulsating through their veins, many had pulled up their roots and come to Africa, with its promise of a different life, a more exciting life than the mundane one they had been living. Here there was opportunities, laid out before them like a banquet. A banquet they were eager to partake of.

They grabbed this adventure fearlessly and never looked back.

*****

The congregation turned and watched the widow dressed in black with a veil obscuring her face. Her tall, but slight, body bent as she made her solitary way out of the church, seemingly weighed down by grief at the age-old and inevitable ceremony of saying good-bye to a loved one.

Beneath the veil with her hat pulled forward as though she were looking down, the widow's eyes scanned the crowds. She did not find what she was looking for – there were too many people.

It had been decided there would be no celebration of life party after the memorial service. The widow it was said, had been so shattered with grief she was not able to countenance any kind of social gathering, perhaps at some time in the future but not today. Definitely not today.

The young African grave digger, dry mud caking the boots gaping around his ankles, paused to wipe the sweat from his brow. His ragged shorts and stained vest a testament to his daily task. He watched the woman dressed in black as she left the church. There would be no hole dug for her lost one.

Madeleine Cooper had been insistent, via her lawyer whose eloquent eulogy would long be remembered, that she would not be receiving any visitors as she tried to piece together her world after the sudden death of her husband, Sir David Cooper.

They watched her being driven away in an Embassy car, respecting her need to grieve in her own private way, but not quite understanding why. This was a time when friends gathered together, to offer comfort and sympathy, but Madeleine Cooper had cut herself off from all of them. She clearly did not feel the same way about things.

In fact, few of the congregation had ever met her. They had known the charismatic David, of course, but his wife was an enigma. There were no dinner parties, nor did she attend any of theirs. David had entertained his friends and business associates in various clubs and restaurants in Nairobi. Few dared to ask him about his wife and what she did out there at their home. David had been quick to brush any questions aside and changed the subject with a smoothness everyone had come to accept.

*****

Reaching her home Madeleine unlocked the front door, her hands trembling. Her gardener, Juma, bowed his head in greeting then returned to his vegetable patch, the sweat glistening on his face in the heat of an African summer. She had given Blossom and Alfred, her housekeeping staff, a month's leave as she wished to be alone in the house now.

Removing the veil and discarding her hat and shoes, she closed the door behind her and made her way to her bedroom.

Madeleine moved towards the large windows, squinting at the glare of the late afternoon sun. She looked down. Juma was turning over the rich soil of his vegetable garden. He glanced up, then turned back to the task in hand.

She grasped the edges of the thick red velvet curtains and drew them together, then threw herself onto the bed in the now dark room, her whole body shaking, the tears streaming down her face.

They were not tears of grief.

They were tears of rage. Her carefully laid plans now in ruins.

Why hadn't David told her he was flying to the coast? The airport authorities in Mombasa had confirmed to the Embassy that he had landed in Mombasa, then, the next morning he had filed his flight plan back to Nairobi.

What had he been doing there? Was it business? Did he perhaps have a mistress stashed away somewhere; something she had long suspected?

"Damn you, David," she shouted to the empty room. "Why did you always have to be so bloody secretive!"

Chapter Five
2018
South Africa
Now

Jack Taylor, a journalist known for his instincts for a story, sat back in his cane chair and looked over the Franschhoek valley, the heat haze distorting and blurring the outlines of the hills and mountains surrounding it. The temperature during the day had been brutal, forty-five degrees and counting.

His furnished cottage had views he had come to love since he left London over two years ago and based himself in South Africa. Then, he had been pursuing a dream, which had not turned out the way he had hoped.

He had been a successful journalist in London, cleaving into the belly of the underworld, chasing cold cases with remarkable results. The editor of *The Telegraph*, Harry Bentley, had sent him off to South Africa to follow an intriguing story. The cold cases he had pursued all over England had put him at the top of his game, other newspapers had tried to poach him, but Jack was loyal to his editor Harry.

Harry with his navy-blue braces which he pulled when he had the sniff of yet another extraordinary story Jack would provide. Harry, who was larger than life with his silver hair brushed back from his enigmatic face. Harry who was the most respected editor of a national newspaper in the whole of England.

*****

That story had changed Jack's life. He had made the decision to leave the newspaper and relocate to the country he had quite fallen in love with.

The ever-astute Harry Bentley had not wanted to lose him. He had appointed Jack as his man in Africa. Within reason he would pay Jack's expenses and give him a retainer. In return, he expected Jack to fill column inches with unique stories – and a weekly column describing the extraordinary people who lived in South Africa and what it was like to live there as an expatriate.

*****

Jack had returned to South Africa and decided to rent a cottage in Franschhoek, the famous wine growing area of the country. He had looked at Cape Town and despite its incredible beauty, the famous mountain, the endless coastline and spectacular views from Chapman's Peak, decided he didn't want to live in a city. He could file his stories and write his weekly columns, from anywhere in South Africa.

Franschhoek had captured his heart, like the woman he had fallen in love with. His affair had not worked out but his love affair with this beautiful town in the Winelands had endured.

He ran his hand through his untidy mop of blond hair, feeling the dampness on his neck. Christ it was hot, even at six in the evening.

He padded through to the kitchen and retrieved a cold beer from the fridge. He hopped back to his chair; the heat of the tiled deck searing the soles of his feet. He moved into the shaded part of the deck and propped his swollen feet on the wooden balustrade.

This heat sapped the strength from his bones and made him feel lethargic and tired. He had been through two hot summers and here was another, a particularly brutal one.

He checked the time on his phone. He would call his parents in Somerset and tell them he was coming home for Christmas. The thought of bitterly cold mornings and the darkening sky at three in the afternoon suddenly had a great deal of appeal.

Right now, he would give anything to throw himself down into some snow and be cool. He hadn't seen his parents for two years; he felt a little guilty but knew they had understood his thirst for chasing stories. He had a longing to walk down country lanes, bundled up against the bitter cold and feel the crunchy fields of frozen shards of grass beneath his boots. No blistering hot sun burning down on him.

Jack was Harry's man in Africa. Providing him with columns and stories which had his readers pausing over their porridge in the mornings, as they read Jack's tantalising tales.

Many readers had their own stories of life abroad, but they were gradually dissipating in the mists of time. Jack brought all the senses of Africa back to them. The smell of the dry dusty rural roads, the irreplaceable smell of the first rains hitting the hard baked earth and tarred roads, the thunder of rain on the corrugated roofs, the distinctive smell of the bush and the animals. The laughter and exquisite singing of the African people who needed no orchestra or song sheets to sing from. The sound of their clear voices as they celebrated or mourned, or sang when the mood took them, their bodies swaying. Even when they were angry and striking about something or other, they still managed to bring song and dance to the occasion.

The almighty thunder of the gum boot dance which shook the earth beneath the male dancers' feet, their beads and animal skins vibrating as they slapped their boots in unison. This was the dance of the underground mine workers, who communicated down the mines with the slaps on their boots.

Jack had a knack of evoking the senses with his writing and awakening long forgotten memories and feelings with his words and observations of the country.

He took a long pull at his ice-cold beer then rolled the can around his throat and the back of his neck. He closed his eyes briefly until he felt the can warming from the heat of his skin. He slapped at a mosquito which had landed on his bare leg, leaving a trail of blood as thin as a strand of hair.

Yes, he thought, it was time to go and see his parents, time to see Harry again, go down to his father's local pub, have one of their famous steak and kidney pies washed down with a pint, and huddle around a roaring fire.

The air was still and humid, not a single leaf or frond from a palm tree moved. Suddenly he felt a coolness in the air where seconds before it had been stifling hot. Lost in thought he had been unaware of the heavy build-up of bloated purple clouds as the evening drew in.

There was a faint sound, like the creak of a floorboard, then silence again. He looked around his modest garden, a slight movement here and there otherwise only silence, no birdsong either, as if they too had had enough of the heat. Then he saw the intermittent heavy drops of rain darkening the tiled decking.

He screwed up his eyes as a vivid flash of lightening ripped through the now brooding sky, followed by a deafening clap of thunder. In seconds the heavy drops of rain came thundering down in a streaming waterfall, bouncing on the deck like frozen peas, blotting out his view of the garden.

Grinning he pulled his cane chair from under the canvas awning then swung his feet and long legs over the wooden balustrade. He sighed with relief as the cool rain washed over them.

He sat for half an hour watching nature at its absolute best. The dust sliding off the bushes and trees which were now becoming visible, leaving their brown dusty leaves shiny and green. The thin slivers of rain making snake like rivers in the garden. The thunder rumbled off into the distance, the rain now a steady downpour, the air comfortably cool. From the canvas canopy, over the deck, the rain formed long dripping lines.

Jack had a huge desire to tear off what little he was wearing and run out into the rain, but hesitated. He never could work out just how dangerous lightening could be here in Africa.

Perhaps a cold shower would be safer, if not as exhilarating.

Then, as so often happened, the lights went out. He sighed. Now this was something he thought he would never get used to. But Eskom, the country's power supplier, would strike when least expected and the entire country would be plunged into darkness for an indeterminate time. There would be sounds of generators kicking in for the fortunate few, but for the rest of them it was back to candles, hurricane lamps and torches.

Jack smiled. He could certainly afford to get some fancy light which would snap to attention as soon as the power failed, but he rather liked what he called the 'old Africa experience'. He liked the way his hurricane lamp attracted moths and bugs, but not necessarily the mosquitoes. He knew they would be out in their droves tonight with the hot humid day and the damp warm night to come.

He prepared his portable *braai*, then sat next to it until the coals had burned down. He dropped a rack of spare ribs on it, basted them generously, then dropped a tin foil wrapped potato into the coals and balanced a loaf of garlic bread on the hot grill.

Jack was a happy man, content with his lot in life. He finished his dinner, wiped the plate clean with the last of the garlic bread and sat back with a sigh of utter contentment.

Two hours later the lights sprang back to life and Jack went inside. He would call his parent's, and Harry, once he had booked his flight. He knew tickets would be at a premium, flights would be full. People flocked to South Africa to escape the grey winter, whilst friends and relatives here, relished the thought of a possible white Christmas in England, a country they loved to visit – but not live in.

Then he would call his friend and sometimes fellow story chaser, ex-police detective inspector, Piet Joubert, who was now living in Hazyview, a town close to the world-famous Kruger National Park.

Piet and Jack had worked on two cases together, one in the Eastern Cape where he had first met the disillusioned ex- police detective and the second in Hazyview. Harry had been more than pleased with the stunning results and the stories they provided for his newspaper.

Piet Joubert had served with the South African police. Then when Mandela became the first black president of the Republic of South Africa, there had been a stealthy, but inevitable shift within the police departments. White officers who had served their country with uncompromising loyalty for years, were offered early retirement or found promotions slow to come their way as black South African policemen were promoted above them.

The bulk of the previous police force had been tough, but mostly fair. Afrikaners had their roots deeply embedded in the country they called exclusively their own. They had served it with pride. Now the changes were upon them.

Many stayed on, accepting the new South Africa and their change in status. Accepting this was how it was going to be whether they liked it or not. Many left and became bodyguards, or formed their own security companies offering a plethora of services as the crime rates all over the country slowly escalated. Some looked to other lands far away and left.

Piet had taken early retirement in the rural town where he lived called Willow Drift. He too started his own security company in the sleepy town where there was little crime, only domestic abuse and petty theft. He obtained his private investigator licence but there was very little to investigate.

It was in Willow Drift where Piet had met Jack who had then been chasing a twenty-year-old cold case for his newspaper.

Initially Piet was antagonistic. This was his patch after all, and the case Jack was chasing happened to be the one the police detective had handled all those years before and been unable to solve.

Piet also had, like a lot of Afrikaners, a deep-seated dislike of all things English, including Jack. Stories of the Boer war had been handed down through the generations and many blamed the English for everything that had happened during that particular war and the stories of the concentration camps which held their women and children in unbearable conditions under the smouldering African sun. Hundreds of their *vlok* had perished in those British camps – the Afrikaners had a long and bitter memory of what had happened to their land, their people, their children and their womenfolk.

But Jack, being the astute journalist he was, knew Piet had a policeman's blood running through his veins. He knew Piet wouldn't be able to resist finding out what had happened to the child who had gone missing all those years ago – it was his old case.

Jack coaxed and cajoled Piet into joining up with him to search for the truth. Piet had information about his old case which Jack needed. Piet was curious to find out what Jack had discovered. So, the pair reluctantly joined forces and became unlikely friends.

When Jack returned to South Africa and made it his home another curious story came to his attention. This case took him to Hazyview, a small town close to the Kruger Park.

Although Jack had a habit of bringing stories to their conclusion in England, where he had a vast network of contacts - South Africa was something else altogether.

Once again, in Hazyview, Jack came up against the frustration of the Afrikaans language. The local police in the town were unhelpful, to say the least. Jack didn't know if it was because he was a journalist, or because he was so obviously English and didn't speak their language.

Frustrated, he had contacted Piet Joubert and persuaded him to leave Willow Drift for a week or two to help him out with the case he was following in Hazyview. He sweetened the offer with a generous offer of payment for his services as a private investigator.

They pursued all their leads and the result had led to an incredible story. Piet was offered a job as the security officer in the small but comfortable hotel, they had stayed at, which included his lodgings and meals from the hotel kitchen.

Piet didn't hesitate. He took the job, moved to Hazyview and left his bad-tempered cat to find his angry way in the world of Willow Drift, without him. Jack remembered sitting in Piet's office on what had to be the hardest and most uncomfortable chair in all of South Africa. Piet's cat didn't seem to mind the hardness of the seat. Piet had thrown a newspaper at the cat. "*Voetsak,* get out of here, you hear me." The cat had spat at Jack and hissed at Piet before walking away his tail lashing with anger.

Jack had been curious about how many dogs and cats in the little town had the same name.

Piet had explained, suppressing his laughter. "*Ag*, Jack. *Voetsak,* means *fok off.* Dogs and cats know what it means."

Piet had unexpectedly fallen in love. His fate was sealed. Hazyview was now his home.

*****

Jack printed out his ticket, called his parents and went to retrieve another ice-cold beer from the fridge. He picked up his phone and punched in the familiar number. He smiled as he waited.

"What do you want Jack?" Piet growled down the phone. "*Bleddy* tourists crawling all over the place. Can't a man eat his dinner in peace?"

"Ah, Piet. Sounding as sunny as ever. It's high season, my friend, the whole of South Africa is buzzing with tourists, what did you expect? How's the job going?"

He heard the clatter of cutlery. "Good enough. Not exciting, no murders so far, but I live in hope. Plenty bad behaviour from some of the guests, all pissed off because they didn't see the big five on their first ten minutes of a game drive in the Kruger. *Jeez,* Jack, what's wrong with these people? Complaints, complaints, complaints. It's too hot, the pool's too cold, the monkeys are nicking things from their room, they don't like eating kudu or crocodile, they want eggs and *bleddy* chips instead. They want chips with everything. "Hysterical if there's a spider in their room or a gecko."

Jack stifled a laugh as Piet continued. "*Jeez,* man, don't know why they bother to come to Africa. Should stay home in their grey misty houses, peering out into the damp night."

Jack laughed out loud. "English people, right?"

Piet grunted. "A tour operator brought a busload of them for a three-night stay with trips to the Kruger every day. They came straight here from off of their flight in Joburg. One couple asked me if there would be elephants walking through town!"

"What did you tell them Piet?"

"I told them, 'Hey, it depends on how much you've been drinking.' They looked at me, Jack, just looked at me. *Ag*, you English – no sense of humour. Then on the first night here there was a hysterical call from room eight. I went to see what was going on and there was this aunty with a sheet over her head, standing in the bath. Asked her what was wrong and she said there was a killer bee in the bedroom.

"Went to check it out Jack, *Jeez* the smallest wasp you've ever seen in your life. I told her 'Listen here ma'am, this is no killer bee, it's a wasp. I've put it outside.' She comes creeping through from the bathroom and asked me if there were killer bees in South Africa. I told her no, but for her I would make a plan and obtain some immediately. Glad she didn't see the big hairy rain spider lurking in the corner, size of a *bleddy* saucer, I'm telling you, hey."

Despite himself Jack roared with laughter.

"Then after midnight they all fall out of the bar, pissed as rats, can't remember their room numbers, can't remember their *friggin* names, can't remember what their husband is called, or what he looks like. I'm telling you Jack it's not funny. Why do English people complain so much Jack? What is it about you peoples?"

"Come on Piet, we're not all like that. Your guests are on holiday having fun, enjoying themselves, having a big adventure in Africa. They'll be gone day after tomorrow and maybe you'll get some excitable Italians or French people who are more to your taste."

Piet grunted. "Hmm, if those English are enjoying themselves, I hate to think what they're like when they're not. What do you want, my friend, why are you calling me? Another story to chase maybe?"

Jack could hear the hope in his voice.

"Afraid not. I've just booked my flight back to the UK. I'm going to spend Christmas with my folks and check in with Harry. Wanted to know if you wanted me to bring anything back for you?"

"Like what, my friend? What would I need from there I can't get here in my own country, hey? Certainly, don't want your *bleddy* weather. *Yous* English up to your necks in the grey stuff for nine months of the year. Nah, give me a decent thunderstorm, with proper rain when you can't see your hand in front of your face. We don't do baby stuff, my friend, we like a bit of drama here."

"I thought maybe I would bring you a spotted dick, Piet. Thought you might enjoy the experience."

The silence was long and intense. "What you saying here Jack? Don't play funny with me, man, I'm in a bad mood. I'm thinking, so long, and I don't like what I'm hearing. So, bugger off, Jack, I don't want any kind of dick, spotted or otherwise, you hear me? *Jeez*, you people eat some funny stuff, hey?"

"Piet, you're losing your sense of humour, not that you ever had much of one. A spotted dick is an English pudding, I thought you might like to try it with your recently obtained sophisticated palate?"

Another silence. "You been drinking, my friend?"

Jack stifled his laughter. "No, a couple of beers maybe. Okay. I'll bring you a box of Harrods's finest biscuits, will that suit?"

Piet sighed. "I don't eat biscuits, only Ouma's rusks when I'm out in the bush. Nice with a cup of South African coffee, crouched under the stars in the bush with a fire and my sleeping bag. Bugger off, Jack. If I need anything fancy, I'll go to Woolies in town and buy good South African stuff. Glad you're going back to where you come from. Sun has gone to your head, my friend.

"I'm going now. Found a place in town, all my Afrikaner mates go there. We can speak in our own language, listen to our own music, understand our own jokes, chew the fat, complain about State Capture, politics, crime and all the rest of the stuff. Won't be taking you there though, with or without your spotted dick. Go well my friend." He growled down the phone and cut the call.

Jack frowned. Piet was grumpier than ever, sounded a bit down actually and no mention of his love life. He wondered if all was well in the world of Piet Joubert and the lovely Kenyan woman he had fallen in love with.

Chapter Six

Jack boarded the British Airways flight bound for Cape Town and shuffled along behind the other passengers as he made his way to his assigned seat in premier class. He stowed his hand luggage in the overhead locker and sank into his seat. The two seats next to him were empty and he hoped they would stay that way, although he knew it was a faint hope. The aircraft was packed to capacity.

He looked out through the oval window at the flickering lights of the luggage carts, catering vans and buses transporting passengers from and to the waiting aircraft. He loved the hustle and bustle of the airport; it evoked a sense of adventure in him.

He thought back over the past two weeks. Christmas with his parents in Somerset was everything he remembered. The decorations, the roaring fire in the sitting room and kitchen, the magnificent festive dinner his mother had produced. A golden-brown turkey, traditional stuffing, chipolatas, roast potatoes and vegetables. The dogs happily dozing in front of the fire, their paws twitching with long ago memories of rabbits to be chased.

They had been delighted to have him home and his mother had even hung up his boyhood Christmas stocking at the end of his bed.

They went for brisk walks with the three family Spaniels in and around the village before scuttling back to the house, the dogs running ahead eager to get back to the warm fireplace. He and his father had many an enjoyable hour at the local pub, catching up on news and enjoying each other's company. All in all, he had loved every minute of it.

In London, Harry had been delighted to see him again. They had arranged to meet at the press club. Once a gentleman's club, it was now far more raucous with its mix of male and female journalists from all over the globe. The walls were lined with photographs of journalists killed in action whilst covering international stories. A sombre reminder of a dangerous career.

"Welcome back, Jack. If I'd known you were so keen to see me, I would have flown to Cape Town for a meeting. Saved you the ordeal of an English winter, at your expense of course. Good Christmas with the folks?"

Harry leaned back in his chair and stretched his navy-blue braces without waiting for an answer. "So, Jack, when can I expect my next big story? Your columns are extremely popular, but I need another big story which will hopefully turn into a book. Anything on the horizon?"

Jack shook his head, unwinding his thick scarf from his neck. "I have a few leads from people who have been in touch with me after reading about the last couple of cases. But, so far, they haven't led to anything particularly interesting. It's the height of the season over there and with all the Christmas and New Year festivities all sorts of things go on. People disappear or turn up where they're not supposed to be. Good time for divorce lawyers though, but mostly South Africa grinds to a halt for six weeks or so, nothing much happens. But if anything does, you can be sure I'll hear about it."

Harry looked disappointed.

"Cheer up Harry, something interesting will turn up. You'll get another story; I'll find one for you."

"Well watch your expense account, my boy, no more fancy trips to game lodges for you and your mate, Joubert."

Jack grinned. "Piet Joubert. He's also hungry to get stuck into another case. I think he's a bit bored with his new job. Not enough sleuthing for him to do. I'll see what I can do to keep you both happy. No pressure, then?"

"Yes, lots of pressure! Get me another story Jack, I'm serious."

Jack sighed. "Look Harry, there's a huge amount going on in South Africa at the moment, apart from the constant power cuts. The State Capture investigation is massive, you couldn't make up some of the stuff which is coming out of the Zondo Commission. Mind you listening to the directors of the national airline, they probably did. All eyes are on the culprits who brought major companies to the edge of bankruptcy, if not bankruptcy itself. We're talking about billions and billions of Rands which have mysteriously disappeared into private bank accounts in Dubai and other places."

He took a sip of his beer. "Crime is on the rampage, murders, hijackings, farm attacks, kidnappings, cash in transit heists, you name it, it's all going on there. It's not only the elephants, rhinos and pangolin who are in desperate trouble through poaching. Young children disappear and turn up dead missing bits and pieces, they call them muti-murders. There's a market for this as well. Ignorant witchdoctors who think human parts cure anything and everything."

Harry stretched his braces and shuddered. "Sounds like a dangerous place to me. Don't understand why you want to stay there, especially now the love interest has blown out of the window."

Jack smiled at him. "Because I love it there, love everything about it despite all the crime and the power cuts. I'll get you your story Harry, give me a bit of time, will you."

"Listen Jack, I don't care about the politics, the crime, the lack of electricity or the bloody weather. I want the human-interest stuff. You hear me? That is what our readers want as they plough through their porridge and muesli, peering through their frosted-up windows."

Now Jack watched the passengers shuffling through the aircraft looking for their seats and heaving their hand luggage into the overhead lockers.

A young woman checked her boarding card and gave him a nervous smile as she slid into the seat next to him.

Jack smiled back at least he would have someone attractive sitting next to him on the long journey to Cape Town.

Chapter Seven
2018 - London

Lara stood on the pavement battling with her umbrella and the sweeping rain. It was four in the afternoon and already dark. Pedestrians hurried along their umbrellas up looking like colourful mushrooms. She squinted as she tried to find a taxi with a light on, one swept past her throwing up a wave of an icy cold puddle. She looked down at her boots in despair. A vicious swipe of wind turned her umbrella inside out. She looked around for a rubbish bin and angrily plunged what was left of it into its depths.

She ran for the nearest bus stop and heaved a sigh of relief when the bright red bus indicated it was going to stop. One way or another she was going to get home, out of this rain, out of the darkness, to the safety and warmth of her little flat.

The bus made its ponderous way through the traffic, the windows steaming up with the other passengers as they looked out of the windows, or stared at their phones, tap, tap, tapping, not looking up.

Lara watched the brightly lit shops. The restaurants had optimistically put chairs and table outside under dripping awnings, bedraggled pigeons pecked half-heartedly for crumbs under the empty tables. Waiters, sporting long white aprons, looking hopeful but bored, stood in the doorways watching the pedestrians hurry past clutching their Christmas shopping.

Lara looked around at her fellow passengers. Bright young things with their shiny shopping bags, middle aged women with their not so shiny bags, filled only with food to feed the family, already exhausted with a full day working and only the prospect of having to prepare a meal for their ever-hungry family. Then tomorrow would be another day of the same old routine. Lara could see the despair and disappointment on their faces. Hope had given way to reality.

Young students, oblivious to anything except what was happening on their phones, their music or games plugged into their ears. Having no idea that at some point they would be sucked into the brutal reality of the world. A world where they would become part of the other passengers. A long day at work, the shopping, the routine. But for now, they were unburdened by all the years to come as time marched on with its relentless tread. Sparing no-one.

The routine, Lara knew, killed all hopes and dreams people might have had when they ventured out into the real world. The meeting of someone, the stomach churning of hope for a phone call, the anticipation, and the despair when it came to nothing. Then came marriage, babies, and suddenly they were the same as these people on the bus.

The nothingness of human contact as their daily lives swept them along. Train doors slamming, impatient commuters shoving and pushing their way to the exit, staring at their phones, avoiding eye contact, no laughter, no smiles, no courtesy, no manners, no offers of help with luggage. Those days had gone, and she was so tired of it all. Longed for a different life, any life but here in London. Christmas was around the corner, a time of the year which always depressed her with its false sense of jollity, windows packed with plastic trees and tinsel, the insane level of shopping for gifts and Christmas fare. The eye-watering cost of everything. The panic when the bills arrived at the end of January.

But sometimes she saw a glimmer of hope, a gesture of help. An elderly lady or gentleman, trying to pull their suitcase from the train as impatient passengers behind them rolled their eyes. Sometimes someone kind would reach out to help, but it was rare.

Oh yes, but one day, she knew, the ones who rolled their eyes would find themselves not able to move so fast, not able to lift heavy things. Time would catch up with them. But she doubted they would remember when they were young and impatient and the world was full of endless possibilities and potential.

Lara pressed the bell. This was her stop. The rain swept across her face; her wet feet were freezing but she still had a bit of a walk before she could get to her flat.

She trudged down the pavement, seeing the cosy lights in other people's windows. She turned right, then left, then right again. The pavements were wet, black and shiny with the endless rain and spotted with grey blobs of chewing gum and soggy cigarette ends. A dog

24

howled, followed by another one. A car swept past throwing up a mist of wetness from the road.

An ambulance, with its blaring sirens going, swept past her and she put her hands to her ears with annoyance.

Lara pulled off her gloves with her teeth and inserted her key. Home. Shrugging off her coat, her boots and her scarf, she turned on the lights, lit the gas fire and stood there shivering, waiting for the heat to take the chill out of her bones.

Unpacking her shopping she placed a ready-made meal into the microwave, before going to the bedroom to change into her warm pyjamas, dressing gown and sheepskin slippers.

The room had warmed up, she was warm and her dinner was in front of her. Lara turned on the television.

She watched the news, despairing at the state of the world. Flooding and gale force winds sweeping across the UK. Hysteria at the crisis of plastic polluting oceans and rivers, sexual assault charges made against famous people, wars, refugees, famine and drought, mass shootings in the States, wildfires in Australia and Europe. She closed her eyes briefly, nothing but bad depressing news.

As the ads came on, she was about to turn the setting to mute, but there was something about this one which captured her attention. It had been filmed in black and white. A girl's pale face looking out from within a taxi, the rain slithering down the windows, the taxi ploughing through the dense traffic with its lights on, the windscreen wipers defiantly clearing the driver's windows, giving a brief glimpse of the vehicle ahead with its brake lights winking on and off.

Suddenly the screen exploded into colour to a place, a vast place, with endless skies, the sun, and the most gorgeous landscapes complete with a flat-topped mountain. South Africa.

She put her fork down, her food forgotten. Now there were lions, elephant, buffalo, majestic mountains, sweeping valleys of vineyards, endless beaches, the people looked so happy? Was it the light in their skies, the light in their eyes?

It looked such a vibrant place, a place full of colour whether it was the clothes, the almost blindingly white sand, the swaying palm trees, the ever changing blue and turquoise shades of the sea. Where was the place where all the little historic houses were painted in so many different colours? The scene in front of her changed to the dry and dusty bush, she had never seen so many gloriously coloured birds of turquoise, pink, yellow and red. Even the animals, created to blend in with the colours of the bush, wore their colours bravely, the comical zebra, the giraffe with their mottled coats, the antelope with their majestic antlers, the lions with their tawny pelts and sumptuous manes.

Acres and acres of soft coloured flowers; orange, white, purple and yellow, one day an arid landscape of brown and green, the next a glorious expanse of unimaginable colour.

It looked glorious. A country she knew, despite its turbulent history, had found its way back into the international market place. It hadn't been an easy road for the people of the country, but now it seemed they were quite determined to show the world that all races and religions could happily rub shoulders, knowing the world would be buying their exotic fruits, first class wines and other produce. Some shoulders perhaps a little chafed in the beginning – but now all looked promising for the rainbow nation of South Africa. Lara pushed her plate of cold food to one side and reached for her laptop, wanting to know more about the country. Over the years she had seen brief news clips on television, mostly scenes of violence and unrest, the ugly side of the country, the desperate side.

President Mandela has been loved and admired by people all over the world. He had been a man of peace, determined to pull his country together. Determined his people should forgive and forget.

Even the tough and determined Afrikaners who had fought him to the bitter end, grudgingly had to admit the peacemaker had made a point of trying to win them over, using the Afrikaners passion for rugby as his trump card when he appeared on the pitch, wearing a Springbok jersey at the World Cup in 1995, before the game started. His appointed personal secretary was a white Afrikaans girl.

Even the most embittered Afrikaner started to take the first tentative steps of hope towards President Mandela and his fledgling government. Some tears for the past now gone were shed, but through the brightness of the tears they saw a promise of a future. A future the President wanted them to be very much part of.

Two hours later Lara had researched as much as she could on the history of South Africa. Pushing aside the tumultuous history of its politics, she had dug even deeper.

Now here was a place she could find some interesting pieces of antique silverware. A place full of stories and history, of families long gone, handing down their precious belongings to the future generations. She might find old pieces of silver with family crests; with a little research she would be able to give each piece the provenance required and perhaps a story of how such pieces had ended up in Africa.

Lara specialised in historical pieces of silver wear. Her work had taken her all over Europe, to opulent, though sometimes distressed homes, of the aristocracy. As an intern she had trained and worked for Sotheby's and Christie's before she branched out on her own. This experience opened the doors to many estates of families who now struggled to maintain their ancestral homes. She had unearthed many a fascinating piece which had sold well on eBay, and to her tight circle of antique dealers.

Lara travelled up and down the UK attending every Antiques Roadshow event, (a hugely popular television series) fascinated with the history and the personal pieces brought to the experts by ordinary people. Things bought for a few pounds at a car boot sale could sometimes turn out to be worth thousands of pounds.

She had contacts, antique dealers, and collectors all over the country who were interested in anything she discovered and willing to pay the prices she asked, once the provenance had been verified.

She sat back absently; her meal forgotten. She knew what she was going to do next. No pets to worry about, all she had to do was pack a bag, lock up her flat and book a ticket.

Her parents lived in the country, in Cornwall. She had no siblings. Lara was independent and free to make her own decisions.

She would go to South Africa.

Lara stared at the darkness outside her window, her ghostly reflection looking back at her. She would start in Cape Town and work her way up through the country, looking for auctions, antique shops and deceased estates.

A treasure trove to be discovered under the hot African sun.

Lara turned back to her computer and studied the geography of the country. It seemed one almighty road linked the most southern tip of the country in Cape Town all the way to the border with Zimbabwe. Maybe she should consider a visit there as well?

Tomorrow she would buy a map, tack it to her wall and plot her course around the country.

She had a friend in Cape Town, a lawyer who specialised in property law and estates, whom she had had a brief affair with some years ago when he was visiting London. He would know through the Master of the Supreme Court, which estates were being wound up and where.

December and January, she discovered was high season in South Africa, the tickets were expensive, but she didn't hesitate. She booked her ticket already anticipating the warm January sun on her skin.

Chapter Eight
1997
Kenya
Then

Madeleine sat at David's desk. His study was normally off-limits to her.

A member of staff from the Embassy had arrived the day after David died and accessed the study. He had left with a box under his arm carrying away, she had supposed, sensitive government documents which the Embassy clearly considered to be the property of Her Majesty's Government.

The heat was lifting as the sun turned its back on another day, reducing the sky to a creamy gold which blurred the hard outlines of the trees and bushes in the grounds of the house. A light breeze caressed the leaves on the trees changing them to a softer feathery green, etched with shadows now. Old bougainvillea bushes clung tenaciously to the arched walls of the estate, their red, purple, white and magenta flowers changing from the dry dusty cloak of the day to a softer palette of colours. The golden showers of flowers cascading over the sun-bleached walls seemed immune to all weathers, glorious no matter what the weather threw at them.

Against the now bruised and threatening sky, birds made their way home to roost. Their wings a startling white against the gathering storm as they dipped and swooped.

Madeleine ran her fingers around the silver frame of David's photograph and stared at the face looking back at her. He had been a tall strong man, with compelling dark blue eyes and black curly hair that brushed his shirt collar. His teeth white and even against his sun flushed face. He had, she always thought, a bit of an Irish look about him. Sexy and passionate, fearless. Yes, fearless – a pre-requisite for the job which he had been good at – working for the Foreign Office.

For twenty years she had accompanied him on his trips to Europe, the Far East, India and Africa, and what turned out to be his final posting here in Kenya. Geographically it had been a good place to base himself for his work across Africa.

A gilded life in a gilded country which they had both come to love and made their home, temporary or otherwise.

Madelaine had been happy to join her husband as he visited surrounding countries. Tanzania, Zanzibar, Ethiopia, Somalia, Uganda and Nigeria, delighted to discover new places and enjoy the cultural collisions, as David went about his business.

Yes, it was true she had tired of the required cocktail parties, the endless business dinners and lunches; the luxury hotel rooms in countries around the world. Sometimes when she awoke in the mornings she couldn't remember where she was. But it was her job as his wife and assistant to support him. As long as she kept taking her medication she could keep going.

She unclipped his photograph from the frame. Tearing it into small pieces she threw them into the fireplace.

David had been as British as they come, having been born and brought up there. She had met him in Cape Town, and it was there she had come up with her plan for a future with him.

Oddly enough she had met him at a funeral. Afterwards there had been a reception at the Embassy, held in their sumptuous grounds. It had been a sweltering hot summer's day; Madeleine remembered it well. The Embassy was in the southern suburb called Bishops Court, nestling in the Constantia Valley. Palatial properties surrounded by vast gardens with extremely high levels of security. A prestigious address and home to international and local celebrities, embassies and a sprinkling of lesser royals from other countries. Surrounded by world class vineyards and restaurants and some of the most expensive private schools in the country, Bishops Court was a much sought-after address.

Madeleine had been sitting beneath the boughs of an ancient oak tree, fanning her face with her hat as she watched the squirrels scampering across the lawns, unaware she was being observed with great interest by the tall man with dark curly hair. He made his way towards her, held out his hand and introduced himself.

"Sir David Cooper. May I join you?" He gestured towards the white cane chair next to hers. "You seem to have found a decent spot, away from the crowds and under the biggest oak tree I've ever seen.

Plus," he grinned, "I'm sure the squirrels are better company than the other guests here. Well, quieter anyway, sober, and more simply dressed."

Madeleine looked up and was ambushed by the bluest eyes she had ever encountered. She smiled at him. "Madeleine." she gestured to the vacant chair. "Lovely service wasn't it. I love all those old hymns; I thought it was very dignified."

David had looked at her and raised an eyebrow. "Did you know Lawrence well, then?"

She shrugged. "Not really, but my boss did. Unfortunately, he was unwell and asked me to represent him."

Madeleine looked back at the crowds on the lawns, the ladies wearing beautiful hats and designer outfits, the men looking hot and bothered in their jackets and ties, the waiters moving smoothly between them, trays held aloft with champagne and canapes, their shirts clinging to their backs in wet patches.

Madeleine turned back to David. "With your accent, you must be English. What are you doing here in Cape Town? Are you on holiday?"

David twirled his glass in his hand. "No, I'm passing through. I had a bit of business to attend to. Lawrence was one of my contacts here, that's how I met him. Nice guy, well connected. Even had a title to boot. Came from some ancient French family, but preferred the weather here. Can't say I blame him...a title offers an instant *entrée* in this country. South Africans love a title. He used it ruthlessly, as I use mine."

Madeleine nodded in agreement. "Yes, they do love titles here. But where are you actually based David?"

He paused, eyeing her over his glass, his eyes traversing her face with its high cheekbones, wide brown eyes and full mouth. He looked away from her watching the guests.

"Here, there and everywhere. Nowhere in particular. I guess the answer would be in the UK where my family have lived for generations. I work for the British government, the Foreign Office. And you? You obviously live here?"

"Yes, I was born in Bloemfontein. Both our parents died when I was young. I was sent to a private boarding school here in Cape Town. My sister stayed in Bloemfontein with my aunt and uncle, we grew apart. She was happy with her life there.

"But I wanted so much more. I wanted to see that world, see what else was out there. In the end I became a secretary, not any old secretary though. But I can't tell you any more – Government business."

He looked amused. "The old guard, eh. Must be interesting with things as they are in the country at the moment. Won't be like this for much longer. Nelson Mandela has a strong voice and a massive following around the world. What's going on in the townships and around the country will change the political landscape forever. It will never be the same, but maybe it's a good thing.

"Still, I didn't invite myself to sit with you to discuss politics. In this beautiful city we should talk about other things."

They chatted easily together for the next hour, exchanging potted histories of their lives.

"So, David, are you married?"

He shook his head. "Unfortunately, not. It would take a very special person to adapt to my lifestyle. She would have to be my personal assistant, as well as my wife. I need someone who knows their way around the diplomatic world, someone who can mix with politicians, top businessmen etc., someone who likes to travel the world. She would need to be able to mix with all sorts of people and entertain them, host dinner parties, all that sort of thing. It's a big ask of anyone."

Madeleine ran her fingers around the brim of her hat and grinned at him. "In return for all of this high living, what would a wife get in return?"

David smiled. "A very nice life. First class travel, stay at some of the finest hotels in the world, meet interesting people, all that sort of thing. Oh, and she would become Lady Cooper of course and be entitled to a British passport if she didn't already have one."

Then David had glanced at his heavy watch and stood up. "I'm afraid I have to go. Um, would you like to join me for dinner tomorrow? I'm staying at the Waterfront, plenty of good restaurants there, or perhaps you have a favourite you can introduce me to?"

Madeleine looked at him thoughtfully, then lowered her eyelashes shyly. She gave him a wide smile. "I'd love to…"

She was still smiling as she watched him walk away.

*****

32

A taxi took David back to his hotel at the Waterfront. He changed out of his suit and into something cooler and more comfortable. Long khaki trousers and a cream shirt. Barefoot he walked out onto his balcony, propping his hot feet on the railing he looked out over the busy working harbour.

Yachts, fishing boats and tourist boats bobbed on the water, sleek seals diving between and under them, their shiny black pelts and comical whiskered faces glimpsed briefly before they disappeared again beneath the oily iridescent sea.

He thought about Madeleine. She was a beautiful woman, intelligent as well. Yes, she would do very nicely indeed. The Foreign Office had checked her out and approved her.

He already knew she worked for the Minister of Defence as his personal assistant. She was well placed, had impressive contacts, and would be invaluable to his government when sanctions against South Africa were lifted.

She had all the qualities he was looking for with the additional bonus that Madeleine was the sort of woman he could never fall in love with.

*****

Madeleine watched the clouds tumbling over Table Mountain from the window in her flat. David Cooper was an extremely attractive man.

She had had great hopes for her future but ended up becoming a personal assistant to the Minister of Defence. Maybe, if she was clever, and she knew she was, something could come of a relationship with Sir David Cooper.

If things worked out, she would be able to travel the world as she had always planned to. David clearly had money and an impressive career.

Madeleine was attracted to him and all he could offer; she had all the qualities he was looking for in a wife. He was her only option to change her mundane life, a life she was desperate to escape from. When the new government came into power, as it surely would, she was certain there would be no place in it for her. She was tired of the unrest, the politics, the uncertainty.

Here was the opportunity she had been waiting for, an opportunity to secure a safe future for herself with a British passport and a title thrown in. Plus, she would have the pleasure of sharing his bed with him.

Chapter Nine

They had honeymooned at a game lodge in the Timbavati. A private reserve west of the Kruger Park boundary, famous for its white lions. A place David had never had the leisure time to enjoy before.

They spent their days together on game drives where David saw the magic of it all. The magnificence of the rolling bush. The tall giraffe with their disdainful look at the world and all who inhabited it. The mighty elephants who trod their ancestral paths. The leopards, lions and cheetahs who came out at night to hunt, taking only as much as they needed to feed, before sauntering away and leaving what was left to the skulking hyenas and the vultures, who goose-stepped high up in the trees beadily watching; their dark wings like shrouds around their bodies and pink scrawny necks.

In the evenings, after a dinner under the stars, the tables set amidst lanterns, the snowy white cloths, the silver and the candles flickering in the slight breeze, they would make their way back, hand in hand, to their tented suite and sit outside, listening to the sounds of the bush at night.

A fine mist spread across the trees, that night, then a sudden thundering downpour of rain sweeping across their deck. The vivid lighting followed by the deep drum rolling rumble of thunder, then another deluge of rain.

Then there was silence except for the monotonous plop of raindrops on the bush surrounding their suite and the rising discordant harmony of croaking frogs.

The moon made its presence known, a sliver of silver against a navy sky. A spider's web draped itself between the two trees in front of the deck. A cartwheel of perfection, glistening with drops of water, like diamonds.

David waited until Madeleine fell asleep then slid out of the bed, fumbling with the skirts of the voluminous mosquito net, he padded softly out to the deck. The camp was quiet, the staff and guests had long since retired. Their thatched rooms like dark mushrooms under the moonlight.

The leaves of the tree sheltering their suite rustled and whispered in the cool air.

David lowered himself into one of the cream armchairs and stared out into the night, alone with his tumbling thoughts.

Marriage had been something he had always avoided. He liked Madeleine well enough, was fond of her in some ways, they were good together in bed, but he didn't love her. She could be a little unpredictable sometimes, seemingly wanting to be on her own, but this he understood. He liked to be alone himself.

Marriage was an acquired taste and took a little getting used to. He wasn't finding it easy. Nor, he suspected, was Madeleine.

The Foreign Office had given him the all clear to proceed with the marriage.

A marriage of convenience. A man of his status should have a wife, leaving no room for rumours and speculation or possible opportunities for blackmail.

He tried to block his mind from the thoughts threatening to sabotage the sense of peace he was feeling, the aloneness out here in the bush. This is why, he now understood, people hungered to go on a safari. Out there in the vast African wilderness a person felt more alive, found a sense of themselves again. The pantomime of real life peeled away like layers of an onion. Senses they had forgotten, feelings and thoughts of themselves which had been lost over the years, rose silently to the surface of their being.

It was a world he knew well. A world where wealthy people thought of their sumptuous houses whether in America, Europe or the Far East, their heaving bank accounts, the cost as they fought their way up the corporate ladders or presided over board meetings in luxurious conference rooms where billions of dollars were discussed and deals were made. The endless dinners and entertaining, the business trips where they hoped to make even more money. Their hidden bank accounts in shell companies around the world protecting their wealth.

Their friends from childhood and university faded away into the past as they forged strong bonds with people they didn't even like, in order to increase their personal wealth. All this was forgotten, though fleetingly thought of, as they found the elusive forgotten child they once had been out here in the wilderness of the bush.

*****

Madeleine had chosen not go on another game drive on their final evening in the reserve, so with a great deal of relief David went alone.

With a cream Panama hat shielding his face and neck from the still hot sun, he had gazed out over the stillness of the bush. He shut his mind off from the other four guests in the tiered safari vehicle as it made its way along the rutted narrow track of the reserve.

The scent of the wild sage as the vehicle brushed against the bush, awoke a memory of Christmas dinners many years ago. A memory he swiftly squashed. Christmas was the time for a family to get together. He had no happy memories of that.

He watched the elephant herd ponderously making their way to a water hole, their babies hidden between their giant bodies and legs. The ancient matriarch of the herd guiding them on, communicating with each other through the rumblings in their cavernous stomachs.

The elephants were free to go wherever they wanted to, David thought. They didn't need to leave hundreds of years of history for the very sake of it and all who would inherit such a heavy load. But they were, without doubt, a family who looked after each other. Unlike his own.

The ranger pointed out a family of Meerkats. David smiled to himself. They stood to attention, heads turning, eyes watching, always watching, looking out for each other.

Someone was always watching in the world he inhabited.

As the fiery sun set over the bush, the ranger found the lions. The male stood sentinel, silent and watchful, on a rocky outcrop, watching his lionesses as they formed a perfect ambush for the terrified victim, a young, fawn coloured impala. Lying low on their bellies, only their tawny ears twitching in anticipation they readied themselves before rising up and perfecting their unique formation skills. Like a well-disciplined army manoeuvre they moved in for the kill. The thundering sound of hooves of the terrified impala shivered the leaves on the bushes and shook the earth beneath. The young buck zig-zagged back and forth, desperately leaping into the air then down again as the lionesses moved in for the kill.

The other impala in the group stiffened, their golden heads held high and still before they too bolted and danced away.

David had watched the predators move in on their hapless prey. They brought it down in minutes. A lioness sank her teeth into the throat of the impala. The impala kicked its legs then lay still, its large dark eyes finally closing in defeat.

After the game drive David walked along the dusty parched path and unzipped their tent.

There was no sign of Madeleine, no doubt she was sipping a glass of ice-cold wine out on the wooden deck of the lodge which overlooked the mud rimmed water hole rutted by hoof and paw prints, where thirsty animals drank thankfully after the brutal heat of the afternoon.

The room was modest, exactly as he liked it. He could have booked into one of the luxury lodges in any of the other private reserves in the area. He knew luxury well, but this time he had wanted something more.

He wanted the essence of Africa. He did not care for the silver and the crystal or a private butler. So many lodges and hotels he knew, turned their places into little English stately homes – absolutely the last thing he wanted to remember even today. He wanted to feel what had always been denied him. A sense of place, a sense of belonging and being loved.

He showered and changed then went out to the deck. He poured himself a glass of wine and looked out over the shadowing bush.

He closed his eyes and wished it all away – the other life.

But it all came tumbling back.

He was eight years old when his family had abandoned him.

Chapter Ten
Malaya 1957

When David looked back at his life, he realised he had done everything that was expected of him. His father, Sir Thomas Cooper, had inherited his title and had a distinguished career as a military advisor for the British government where he and his wife, David's mother, had travelled and enjoyed foreign postings.

David's friends were fleeting, one term at school they were there, the next term they were gone; their fathers posted to some other far-flung place determined to fly the British flag. Then, as they watched the flag being lowered and another perhaps more colourful one raised on the staff pole, they knew they would be leaving the place they had hoped would become their home.

David thought everyone lived like this. What else could he compare his life with? Babies and young children became attached to one amah, then they would be taken away from her. One moment they were employed to look after the babies and children of foreigners, caring and nurturing and becoming attached to their little charges. Then with the swipe of a pen, or the lowering of the flag, their world also changed. The children were taken from their arms, never to be seen again.

David thought about it often. All the promises to keep in touch, well, they came to nothing. The parents moved on and the child was loved and cared for by another nanny or amah.

He liked to think those patient women loved the children they were responsible for. But, at some point they too must have wondered about the lives of these foreigners living in their country, they would never turn the care and love they had for their own child over to a complete stranger, a foreigner. They had extended families, grandparents, aunts and cousins who would care for their children if needed.

As predictable as the sun rising, the time came when David's parents sent him away. It wasn't a choice. It's what they did. In the circles they moved in, and the circles their parents and grandparents had moved in – it was a given. The child had no say in the matter.

When David was eight years old, he was sent to boarding school to the promised land of a good education, a place which would make a man of him. England.

They had been living in the Far East at the time, Malaya. His amah had packed his tin trunk. Ah Lan, had spent two days sewing his name tapes on everything. He could see her exquisite stitching, even today.

Ah Lan accompanied his mother and father to the railway station in Kuala Lumpur. David's trunk was unloaded by his father's driver; his name stencilled on the side, his destination and future written in stone. There was no return address.

He remembered the railway station with its dome capped pavilions of Indian origin along the roof line, and the soaring archways designed by British Colonial architects. The porters running up and down the platforms loading luggage, their bare chests shiny with sweat, wearing only sarongs in the stifling heat. Vendors and hawkers moving alongside the carriages with trays of food balanced on their heads, giving off the rich aroma of curry, garlic, noodles, rice and cooked meat.

Passengers were a mix of British military personnel and families, sombre Chinese, chattering Indians in colourful saris and turbans and a handful of little English boys. David watched as his tin trunk disappeared into the baggage section of the train.

His mother bent forward and patted his arm. "Mrs Wright will be along any minute now. She will accompany you to England. You will be quite safe with her; she'll take you to your new school. We'll come and see you there. Oh, here she comes now."

David remembered turning to his mother, trying to hold back his tears. Displays of public emotion were not acceptable. "Will it be at the weekends then, Mummy? When you come and see me?"

His mother had frowned at him.

"England is quite far away. We'll come and see you every year. You can write to us, and we'll write to you. Every week, darling. Now come along, pull yourself together, this will be a lovely adventure for you."

His father shook his hand, and his mother gave him a brief kiss on the cheek.

*****

Ah Lan stood rigid, knowing any show of affection for this little boy she had known from a baby would be strongly disapproved of. She took his hand as though to shake it and whispered to him. "I have put something in your school box for you to remember me by, David, ah. You must be brave and strong. I will always be here. I will not forget you."

As the train pulled away from the station his parents waved, dry eyed, then turned and hurried away. No doubt, he thought, his mother planning what she would wear to the Embassy party that evening and once there telling everyone with great pride their son was on his way to Eton. One of the most prestigious schools in the world. He imagined her basking in the admiration of the other parents, congratulating herself on a job well done.

Ah Lan had waited. A forlorn figure, the tears streaming down her face, her arm held high as she watched his little hand waving frantically from the carriage window, his small face white and pinched with bewilderment. Unlike his parents she had waited for the final last glimpse of him before the train turned and was gone.

David remembered her clearly, the spicy creamy scent of frangipani and coconut oil which she used on her long black hair, as she held him. She was the one who had loved him the most.

Her simple clothes, the black wide trousers, the white blouse with the Mandarin collar, her conical hat. He had loved her more than his parents. She was the one he would go to when he was frightened, when he was hurt, when he needed love. She was always there for him. His parents didn't have the time, nor would they tolerate any sign of emotion – it was a weakness his father declared. Something one didn't do.

So many years ago, now. Had Ah Lan forgotten him?

*****

Mrs Wright was a cold but efficient chaperone, who spent her days with her nose in a book on the deck of the ship which was cleaving its way through the ocean to England.

Dutifully she made sure her young charge had three meals a day in the dining room, before marching him back after dinner to their cabin to get him ready for bed.

Sometimes he found the courage to ask her a few tentative questions about where he was going and who would look after him. Where would he be staying in the holidays – would he be going home to his parents and Ah Lan?

She had looked at him in the hard way she had. "You'll find out when you get there. My job is to deliver you safely. What happens afterwards is no concern of mine. Now read your book and we'll have no more silly questions."

He had rarely experienced tears as he grew from baby to boy in Malaya. If he hurt himself, Ah Lan would attend to him, murmuring softly as she washed yet another grazed knee, or dabbed Tiger Balm on his insect bites.

It was the smells of that place that evoked emotion in him. Sometimes, if his parents were away overnight, Ah Lan would take him into the town of Seremban. They would take a trishaw to the open markets where he inhaled all things Malay. The charred smoky smell of meat being cooked on open fires, the noisy chatter between the vendors as they cooked their noodles and rice, the rich smell of garlic and spices, the food served in banana leaves.

Her world was more familiar to him than any other.

Holding his hand she would take him into another area of the market with its rich fabrics of gold, red, turquoise, pink and green, the smell of the warm material, the glittering displays of glass bangles, hair clips and jewellery and wind chimes. Which, she told him, if you hang in the garden would attract good spirits.

On the way home Ah Lan would point out the temples with their fragrant joss sticks burning outside, lit up with gold and red and the faint sound of cymbals.

If he ever felt miserable for some reason, she would carry him on her hip and walk him around their large garden, pointing out the flowers, the frangipani, the blood-coloured hibiscus, the insects and the colourful butterflies.

She would tell him stories of her own childhood and his misery would soon be forgotten as she let him into her secret world of paper tigers, friendly dragons and colourful lamps as they floated down the river, and the many Gods her people worshipped. The friendly ghosts of the departed who were never forgotten and each year received gifts of food and paper money, to ensure their life in the next world they would never be hungry.

Ah Lan had been a wonderful story-teller and the little boy had lost himself in all of them. Going into a different world when he was with her, a place where he felt safe and loved.

He never saw her again.

Chapter Eleven

So began the next phase of David's life in a hostile land, full of strangers, where the sun rarely shone. The boarding school was an ancient, elegant building under dark brooding skies.

Mrs Wright handed him over like a parcel to the house Master who was standing at the top of the cold grey stairs, waiting to greet the new boys.

Then she too turned her back on him and walked away.

*****

Boarding at the prep school was something he had not been prepared for. He was homesick, he was lonely and he was bewildered. Had his parents not wanted him? Had they given him away so they could get on with their own lives?

The environment crippled him for life. Hundreds of boys, shouting and pushing each other as they greeted their friends from last term. The confused new boys, some younger than him, fighting back the tears as their parents drove off.

He didn't want to think about it anymore...he didn't want to remember. But the memories were indelible and refused to leave him.

To survive in such an establishment the little ones learned very quickly. If you didn't fit in and obey the rules, if you showed any emotion at all, if you didn't run around after the seniors making their beds, running their errands you were a target. Subject to bullying and taunting from the more confident boys.

He would say, today, his parents made a terrible mistake in trying to make him a 'little English gentleman' when he was eight years old.

David became old before his time. They had given him wings he would concede later in his life, but had left him rootless. Without a place he could call home.

But he was smart enough to know he had to fit in. His voice didn't have the polish of the older ones. When he shyly tried to tell them about his home, his amah, the gardens and the people, they looked at him with complete disinterest. They had no idea what he was talking about and laughed at the little boy who had lived in the jungle in a place they had never even heard of.

He had two choices. He either had to excel at sport – and the bullying would stop. Or he had to have some other kind of distinction. His father was a knight, a title passed down for his family's distinguished service to monarch and country, but it wasn't going to help young David now.

As a little boy, unknown to his parents, when Ah Lan used to tell him her wonderful tales of dragons and butterflies and ghost people, he knew he wanted to learn to speak her language, then all her stories would have more resonance.

It was their secret. His father would not have approved of him learning any kind of native language. David was a quick learner. He learned the language of the Malay people and Ah Lan's own language, Chinese.

She had given him, he realised later, the gift of languages. Latin, of course, was compulsory at school, the basis of most European languages but to him it didn't have the richness or resonance of the languages he had already learned.

This gift saved his unhappy life at school. There were Chinese and Malay students at Eton, who gravitated towards him. It didn't go unnoticed by his fellow students or the Masters. These young students were also far away from their homes, too far for them to return, like him. They formed a tight knit group and kept each other company during those long holidays when the school was almost deserted and the other boys had gone home to their families.

From then on, he was held in some esteem by his classmates who had never travelled further than London, or their family's country estate. They were suitably impressed with the kid who was brought up in the jungle and could speak exotic languages.

David saw his mother once in two years. Dutifully, as the rules of the school required, he wrote to her once a month. Her letters back to him were short and erratic.

His mother was a stranger, someone easy to forget. He erased her from his life. At ten years old he forgot the smell of her perfume; he couldn't remember her voice. He let her go.

During the holidays at prep school, the cars would pull up on the crunchy drive and excited children would swarm out to greet their parents. Laughing and chattering, shouting across as they bid farewell to their friends. He would watch from the shadowy arched pillars of the outside of the school, numb with hope and longing. Would anyone come for him?

David saw a big shiny car with what looked like an angel with spreading wings on the bonnet pull up. A chauffeur opened the rear door and an elderly woman stepped out and made her way to the front of the building. The headmaster was seemingly waiting for her. She disappeared into the shadows of the school building, as he sat and watched the children collected and taken away, back to their families, back to their homes.

One of the kindlier Masters was making his way towards him. He touched David's shoulder.

"Cooper. Your grandmother is here to take you home for the Christmas holidays. Come with me. Remove your cap, boy!"

He stared at the formidable woman in front of him, twisting his cap in his hands. Once more he saw there was no emotion, she didn't smile at the sight of her grandson.

He ran back to his dormitory and packed his bag. Scarcely breathing with excitement, he returned to the waiting car. The chauffeur opened the door and he was bundled in with his bag.

His grandmother stared straight ahead – she didn't utter a word to him. He watched the English countryside roll past, it was winter, Christmas was coming.

His grandmother's house loomed up in front of him through grey fog. He thought it was the ugliest house he had ever seen. Not like the sloping roofs of the homes he had known, with their wide wrap around balconies built on sturdy stilts, the gardens full of glorious flowering plants.

The large gardens here were submerged below the rolling fog, the trees and bushes gnarled and grey with the cold. Darkened windows peered out from beneath heavy fringes of ivy which covered and clung to the front of the house.

This then was Mellow Woods, where his father had grown up, the place he would eventually inherit himself.

His grandmother swept up the uneven wide curved steps, past two stone lions who stared into the distance from their lofty perches, their grey chipped mouths open in a soundless roar. He stumbled after her then stood at the open doors of the great house, his mouth open as his eyes took in the faded tapestries lining the walls, and the dark brooding portraits of long-gone relatives. Their dead eyes following his every move.

David stared at them in horror, a shiver of fear running down his already frozen back. He tightened his school scarf around his neck and meekly followed the chauffeur who was carrying his bag up the cold marble stairs to the room which had been allocated to him.

The room was bitterly cold and gloomy. A single bed and a chest of drawers sat side by side. Near the window a faded green sagging chair.

The chauffeur placed David's bag on the bed and turned to him, speaking softly.

"You'll be alright, lad. Speak when you're spoken to and don't ask any questions. I'll come and collect you on Sunday and take you back to school. Your grandmother doesn't like conversation, it makes her tired... and she has a right old temper on her as well. You'll have to eat in the kitchen with me and the housekeeper. Nice and warm in there."

"I thought I would be here for the Christmas holidays," David whispered, his voice breaking.

The chauffer shook his head sadly. "Sorry, lad, they should have told you. Your grandmother is going to visit her sister for Christmas. You have to go back to school."

David sat carefully on the edge of the bed and stared out of the window; tears rolled down his pinched face. Tears he had withheld for two years for fear of being teased and taunted by the other boys at school.

Chapter Twelve
1972

David left Cambridge at the age of twenty-three, clutching his impressive Master's degree in foreign languages. He applied for a job, amongst others, with the United Nations as a translator.

He rented a furnished flat in Earl's Court, London and spent his days exploring this great capital as he waited for a response from the organisations he had approached.

His parents long tour of duty in the Far East had come to an end and they were returning to Devon to take up residence on the family estate, at Mellow Woods.

David knew exactly what he was going to do once he had carved out a good career. He was going to travel as much as possible and get as far away from England, his parents and the ancestral home as he possibly could, and sever all ties with his fractured family.

This time it would be on his own terms.

Chapter Thirteen

It was a bright spring day and David was browsing through the books at Hatchards in Piccadilly, the most famous and oldest book shop in the city. During the winter months he had spent many hours there, keen to discover more languages and learn about the history, politics and geography of different countries.

Lost in other worlds he was unaware of a man in his late thirties who had been watching him and was now standing next to him.

"Planning on travelling the world, eh? You'll get no finer education if that's what you have in mind? Might need to speak a language or two. But this shouldn't be a problem for you, should it?"

David turned and looked at him, his white cricket jersey draped around his shoulders. "Yes, that's my plan," he narrowed his eyes and frowned. "How do you know I speak other languages?"

The man ran his hand through his already greying hair. "Eton and then Cambridge, eh? You excelled in languages. Impressive. United Nations would be a waste of your considerable talents."

David frowned. "How do you know so much about me? Were you teaching at Cambridge? I don't recall seeing you?"

The man with the greying hair shrugged. "No, I didn't meet you there. But I, of course, have heard about you. We've been following your impressive years at Eton and Cambridge. My name's Smith, John Smith.

"Tell you what, why don't we nip down to Rules for a spot of lunch? It's the oldest restaurant in London, bit like this book shop. They make the best Shepherd's Pie in the world. England may not be known for its gastronomic delights, we're not up there with the French for instance, but for traditional English grub there is no finer restaurant. Shall we go? I've booked a table for us."

And so began his life with the Foreign Office. A position which gave him all the freedom, travel and the use of his languages he could possibly have wished for.

The interviews were long and exhaustive, the paperwork never-ending. They scrutinised his life, did background checks on his parents, the schools he had attended, his friends, his sexual preferences, the girls he had dated, his political views not only in England but in other countries as well. They tested his knowledge on which countries traded what, their politics, their leaders and their history.

He was questioned meticulously for the position they wanted him to eventually fill. Head of the Department of International Trade and Industry. His territory would include the Middle East, Europe, Africa and Asia where his language skills would be invaluable.

He would work with the British Embassy in each country he was sent to and would assist in any Embassy led initiatives, events and activities, plus give any other assistance when called upon.

Finally, he was summoned to the office of the Director of the Department for International Trade and Industry. Sitting behind an enormous desk bereft of any paperwork was John Smith, who had approached him in the book shop so many months ago.

"Take a seat, David." He laced his fingers together and leaned back, a broad smile on his face. "Well, you've jumped through all our hoops with dexterity. We are suitably impressed. A position within the department is ready and waiting for you. You'll have to start at the bottom and work your way up, but I have no doubt in my mind you will get there quicker than most?"

David smiled back at him, feeling the excitement rise in him but forced it down, showing no emotion at all, something he had honed to perfection during all his years at boarding school.

"Now, Cooper. Our current Head of UK Trade and Industry is Sir Giles Montague. He will be retiring at the end of the year after working for us for thirty-five impressive years. You'll be travelling with him for the rest of the year. Sir Giles will introduce you to his contacts around the world and show you the ropes.

"Sir Giles has had the same secretary for the past fifteen years; you will inherit him. His name is Harold. Understood?"

David reached across the desk and shook John's hand. "It will be an honour to work for the Government, sir. Thank you for the opportunity."

50

John leaned forward and put his elbows on his desk. "Right. Now, Sir Giles is expecting you to join him for dinner at The Savoy this evening. Make a good impression. May I suggest you wear black tie?"

Smith glanced at his watch and stood up. "My secretary, will have all the required paperwork for you to sign, plus the Official Secrets Act. You have a golden career ahead of you, don't screw it up. Personal relationships are not encouraged. Be discreet."

David knew he wouldn't have any problem with personal relationships, he avoided them.

"Follow me and I'll introduce you to Harold. He might not look too impressive, but he is invaluable. Knows how everything works. Don't want you spending your time and talent shuffling the endless paperwork around the place. Harold will take care of all of that."

Harold stood up as the two men entered what would one day become David's office. He was of average height and thin as a rail. His grey hair was receding although he was probably only in his late thirties. His thick glasses did little to hide his dark obsequious, but intelligent eyes. To David he epitomised so many of the 'grey men' who hurried through the corridors of the Foreign Office.

From that day David never looked back and left his old life behind – exactly as he had planned.

*****

John Smith watched from his window as David Cooper left the building and jogged through the crowds below. He was a cold hard bastard of this there was no doubt. The product of the establishment; the product of one of the best educational facilities in the country, if not the world. He doubted the man had one emotional bone left in his body.

Chapter Fourteen

David's parents never adapted back to life in the UK, the cost of keeping the ancestral home going, the never-ending bills, the staff they needed to keep the house and grounds going – it had aged them both. Their carefree privileged lives abroad, with everything paid for was now far behind them. The memories of those halcyon days faded with each bitter winter and the weight of their now crippling debts.

Now, eight years later, David was sitting with them both, the table in front of them covered with paperwork for the estate. "Father, we can't keep this place going any longer, there isn't the money any more. Your pension, though generous, simply doesn't cover it."

He looked at the stranger who had once been his mother. He felt no filial emotion. This had been lost when she had abandoned him to pursue her heady social life abroad.

His father rubbed his face wearily, looking old and grey now, not tall, strong and suntanned as David had always remembered him. His shoulders were stooped, his hair grey and thinning, like his body.

"Well son, I'm sorry the old heap won't go on for you to inherit," he turned to his wife and put a comforting hand on her bony shoulder.

"We must do what has to be done. I have made a new Will. You will inherit the proceeds of the house, David, and the contents. My only request is you look after your mother once I'm gone. You may wish to select a few things for yourself. Now, if you'll excuse me, I think I'll take a nap. Feeling rather tired with all these figures…"

He looked out over the grey fields already smouldering with mist, the sky darkening. "Damn weather…"

He left the room and David looked at his mother. "I know what you're going through. The loss of your home, the isolation, the abandonment, the utter desolation of it all. I doubt whether you have thought much about it, but it has made me what I am today, what I feel today. It's what you did to me, you see, when I was eight years old."

She looked at him, a puzzled look on her face. "Pour me another gin and tonic, darling. Now, what on earth did you mean by your last remark?"

He put her refilled glass on the table next to her. "Did you ever think how badly being sent away so young affected me?"

She looked at him sharply. "That was how it was, David. The tropics was not a place to bring up children, all the mosquitoes, the disease, the climate, the lack of good schools. The natives getting above their station. It simply wouldn't do."

"But did you miss me?"

His mother sipped her drink and sighed. "Like I said, that's how it was, darling. I really can't remember. We wanted the best for you. I missed you, of course, but after a few days' life was normal. The usual cocktail parties, dinner parties, the races, surely, darling, you must remember. We were out every evening attending some social function. But Ah Lan looked after you."

"What happened to Ah Lan?"

She looked at him in astonishment. "Goodness, how would I know, David! I had to give her notice, of course. With no child to look after there was no work for her. Anyway, she was promised in marriage by her parents to someone she had never met so I suppose this is what she did – got married. I have no idea what happened to her. I can't even remember what she looked like, we had so many servants over the years."

Shaking his head, he stood and walked to the drinks tray to pour her another drink.

*****

His father died in his sleep that night. The funeral was impressive, lots of military presence, dressed in their finery, medals glinting in the watery sun. Some old chums from his father's London club and many other people whom he didn't know or care to.

He was thirty-one years old when he became Sir David Cooper, and had been with the Foreign Office for seven years. The title meant little to him as a man, but he knew it was impressive in the circles, both private and business, which he now moved in.

Overnight his mother had shrivelled before him. Now she sat in her faded worn chair and looked at him. "So, what happens now, David?"

He looked at her coldly. "The house will be sold with most of the contents. There's an excellent care home not far from here, they'll take good care of you. The money from the estate will more than cover the expenses. I'll take you there next Friday – it's all arranged."

"But I'd like to be with you, David."

"You never wanted to be with me," he said bitterly.

She plucked at her skirt. "I could arrange your social life. It's what I do. What I'm good at."

"I'm sorry mother. It won't be possible. I don't need looking after as you put it. I travel extensively and I don't plan on buying a home here in England. I think you'll be happy with the care home, lots of interesting people who have travelled the world, like-minded people, the sort of people you like. People like you."

*****

He drove his mother to the front of the care home. The grounds were beautiful, the building impressive – another stately home which had had to be sold to pay mounting debts.

"I'm going to say goodbye now mother. I know you'll find new friends here; you'll be well looked after."

She looked up at him. "Will you come and visit, darling? You will come and see me, won't you? Perhaps at the weekends?"

"You will come and see me, won't you? At the weekends?" He heard his own eight-year-old voice.

He briefly kissed her cheek then turned and walked away. Just as she had so many years ago.

Chapter Fifteen

Sir David Cooper was well satisfied with his extraordinary career. He had no intention of buying a property anywhere in the world, he had no need of a place to entertain his business contacts or handful of friends.

When he returned to London to report to the Prime Minister and the Foreign Office, he used one of the company's fully furnished flats in Eaton Square.

He didn't need a car. A car and chauffer were at his disposal. Harold, his secretary, effortlessly handled all the government contracts, documents and other paperwork. David couldn't stand the man.

His own personal life suited him well. In many of the countries he visited on business, he was a welcome guest at many a hostess' dinner table. With his dark curly hair, sapphire blue eyes, his wit and gift for telling stories and the fact he had a title, had been to the right public schools and had the right accent, all worked in his favour. He had girlfriends in many cities, including London. He saw them, wined and dined them, slept with most of them, before he once more said goodbye. If he felt any of these relationships was becoming serious, he simply walked away.

He had no wish to marry nor did he want children.

But the Foreign Office had other plans to enhance his already superb career.

They included a woman called Madeleine Hunter.

*****

When his mother died. He attended her funeral and watched whilst they buried her next to her husband.

There were no tears, no regrets. Once more he walked away from the last of his fleeting memories of them both.

He now accepted they had done what was expected of them. But he had paid the price – not them.

Tomorrow he would be on his way to Africa for more meetings and negotiations on behalf of the British Government.

He was looking forward to it. It was there he would meet Madeleine Hunter, as arranged.

Chapter Sixteen
Kenya
Then…

Madeleine had been an efficient wife. She organised David's life, both business and social. His secretary, Harold, organised all their flights, hotels and restaurant bookings and David's business meeting and conferences around the world.

Madeleine, in her personal capacity booked flights and hotels for him when he made certain trips of a more private nature. She bought an expensive notebook with a soft dark blue calf skin cover, the imprint of a phoenix on the front and kept meticulous accounts of where he went, and when, who he met and where. Occasionally she accompanied him on these private business trips when she was more of a personal assistant than a wife.

Madeleine observed the people, listened to their conversations as they were entertaining and drew her own conclusions. Keeping scrupulous notes of everything and everyone, paying all the expenses from David's personal accounts, she knew where all of them were and which country, and dealing with the necessary correspondence.

She had never told David about her dark blue book or what she wrote in it. He would have been very alarmed indeed.

Now, with a sigh she turned back to the task in front of her. So many letters and cards from friends across the world, expressing their condolences. Carefully she read each one and put them to one side. She wouldn't be replying to any.

Madeleine took a sip of wine from her crystal glass and with a steady hand placed it back on the silver tray on David's desk.

She wondered what David would have made of it all. She had always thought it rather sad when somebody died and all the condolences poured in. How marvellous it would be if one could see all those messages before one passed on? She wondered what they would say about her…when the truth finally came out. If it ever did.

Madeleine smiled to herself. Not one message saying what a tough bastard he was, how his cutting remarks could slice a person in half. How secretive he could be. She knew he had only told her what he thought she needed to know about his private life.

Once they had settled in Nairobi, he had gone along with her wishes not to be part of the social scene which she had tired of. He understood her desire to spend time on her own. Over the years she had been the perfect wife, always by his side when he was entertaining his business contacts, whether she wanted to be or not.

Once a month she would go with Juma and do the monthly shop, collect her pills from the pharmacy, and have her hair done at the Norfolk Hotel, then sit quietly and enjoy her lunch on the hotel terrace. Watching and listening to the conversations going on around her.

A flash of lightening now lit up the dark room where she was sitting, thunder growled in the distance making the wine in her glass shudder. Large drops of rain slid down the picture windows, gathering momentum until it looked as though someone had turned a hosepipe at the glass, reaching over she turned on the Tiffany lamp and soft light filled the room.

Madelaine stood up and stretched before reaching for her glass of wine and wandering over to look out over the garden. The rain was torrential now, the wind strong as it bent the branches of the trees and plants. Leaves in the normally immaculate garden swirled and danced briefly before being flattened by the rain. Small ripples blew across the impressive swimming pool.

A loud crack of thunder made her jump. It had been a stressful day. The church had been packed. Had anyone been watching her? She smiled, yes, of course they had. They had all been watching her, wondering who she was – apart from being David's widow – and what she looked like.

She drew the heavy curtains and went back to his desk.

Sliding the top drawer of David's desk open she reached for the thick brown envelope and spread the contents in front of her.

Everything was there.

The Embassy had assured her they would take care of David's personal things and ship them back to England to his lawyer, and respect her own wishes of what would happen to her own few possessions.

The house didn't belong to the Coopers, it had been provided for them, like all the others had been. She had hesitated for a few seconds over the dark blue notebook. It should be destroyed.

Madeleine reached for her journal with the phoenix on the front. What harm could come of it? Just a few notes of how she felt, how yesterday had felt. Her own feelings for what she now knew was inevitable. Her own little bit of insurance should things go wrong.

No-one knew it existed. She reached for the tall malachite bowl, filled with pens and pencils, then bent her head and brought everything up to date.

Madeleine sat back, satisfied. She would be one step ahead of them all. They had used her – all of them.

Her task complete she sat back in David's chair. Her hand hovered over the small bottle of pills. Had she already taken two? She shrugged. Another two wouldn't hurt if she had. She emptied the pills into her hand and washed them down with a mouthful of wine.

Over the past three years David had changed. Little things at first. She had suspected a mistress or two. Kenya was a hot bed of extra-marital affairs. She hadn't quite worked out if it was the way of life here, the history of the old white mischief she had read about. Perhaps it was the heady air, the sense of freedom, the way sun kissed skin was more attractive than pale white skin. It seemed acceptable here to have affairs, almost a way of life, even after all those years of so-called white mischief.

People here seemed to live life to the full – despite the consequences, there seemed to be no price tag on their freedom to do what they wanted to do.

Of course, she knew this was not so with everyone who lived in the country. But if you had the money and the connections, youth and beauty, adventure in your soul – then this was the place to be. Oh, yes, this was the place to be.

Her final conversation with David had not been pleasant. They had dined in silence, on what turned out to be his last night with her, until she could bear it no longer.

"Look David, I don't know what's going on, but something is. You hardly talk to me anymore; you always seem to be angry and preoccupied. I know I can be difficult to live with sometimes, but I do try to keep things under control with the medication. Is there someone else in your life, someone perhaps you have actually fallen in love with? I know you've never loved me. I was perfect for the role you wanted a wife to play that's all."

"We had a deal Madeleine, a deal which we both fully understood. It brought you a title, a British passport and a very nice life-style."

She had looked at him. "Yes, I agree we did have a deal and I have enjoyed the life-style. But, you see, I wanted more, I wanted children, a home of our own, but most of all I wanted you to love me, which you never have."

He had pushed back his chair, carefully placing his napkin on the table. He gestured around their elegant dining room. "I don't want to be here. I've had enough of it all."

Madeleine had narrowed her eyes and stood up, carefully pushing back her chair. "I don't know you anymore, David. Perhaps I never did.

"If you want a divorce then I shall give you one. This relationship died a long time ago. I'm expecting you to be more than generous David. I won't go quietly; of that I can assure you."

He had turned his back on her and retreated to his study, locking the door behind him.

The housekeeper, Alfred, who from the shadowy depths of the kitchen had listened to the exchange, shrank back further before silently returning to the kitchen.

*****

Madeleine now tapped her fingers on the side of her glass. What on earth had David been doing in Mombasa? What did he mean when he said he'd had enough of it all? If he wanted a divorce, then so be it. She had more than enough information on him to ensure a comfortable financial future, and although she would lose her title, she had her British passport. She could go anywhere on that.

A disconcerting thought surfaced, but she pushed it down immediately.

It had been a tragic accident that's all, and he had cheated her out of the financial future she had anticipated. No doubt there would be some kind of pension, but not anything like the amount of money she would have received with the divorce settlement.

She felt the combination of the pills and wine kick in. "So, what am I now?" she said to the silent room.

"A widow that's all!"
All her plans had shrivelled and died with Sir David Cooper.

Chapter Seventeen
2018
South Africa

The flight was ready for take-off. It roared down the runway before rattling and lifting shakily into the dark night. The lights of London receded as the aircraft flew into the clouds blotting out any final views of the city.

The lights came on once the flight had levelled out and reached cruising altitude. Jack loosened his seat belt and glanced at his fellow passenger. She was leaning back against her headrest her knuckles white on the armrests.

"You can open your eyes now; it should be smooth all the way to Cape Town. Nothing to worry about."

The woman opened her eyes and turned to him giving him a tight smile. "I have to say flying is not my best thing. I've never quite got the hang of it."

Jack smiled at her. "There are only a few people who actually like flying – most passengers are nervous flyers. Putting your life in the hands of strangers is not something one normally does. Fortunately, I'm one of the few who actually enjoy it. It's a big adventure flying off to a different place. Have you been to Cape Town before?"

She shook her head and took a deep calming breath. "No. I've flown before but only around Europe; this is something else altogether." She looked around at the other passengers all busy rummaging around in their hand luggage for their laptops or headphones. "This plane, it's a big bugger, isn't it?"

"Yes, indeed it is and absolutely packed. Ah, here's the drinks trolley looks as though you may need something to calm your nerves."

They ordered their drinks. A beer for him and a double scotch for her.

"I'm Jack, by the way."

She held out a slim, slightly shaking, hand. "Lara Summers."

Jack knew from experience, getting nervous passengers to talk soon took their minds of other frightening thoughts they might be having.

"So, Lara, are you off on holiday, visiting friends, business?"

Lara removed the clip from her hair, and it tumbled around her shoulders like a straight dark curtain. She rubbed the back of her head. Jack guessed the big toothed clip had dug into her scalp as she pressed her head back during take-off.

She was a nice-looking woman, around thirty-five he guessed, big grey eyes, hardly any make-up, even features and wide full lips. A fairly husky voice, a slight gap in her even upper teeth which he found attractive, it gave her face an open trusting look.

"I'm on a treasure hunt actually." She explained to him what she did, her line of work, what she was looking for. "I look for unique pieces from the 1800's, silver ware, that's what my buyers want. You know, goblets, tongs, snuff boxes, trays, table ware, tea sets."

Lara took a sip of her drink. "And you, Jack, holiday? Business?"

Jack briefly told her what he did for a living and that he lived in a place called Franschhoek. She looked suitably impressed, although she admitted she had never heard of him, or the place he lived in.

She reached down and hauled a map out of her bag. He brightened up immediately. He loved maps, even though he could never quite get them back to their original shape once opened.

Lara spread it out over the tray in front of her. "I plan on driving through the country in search of treasure, as I said."

Jack frowned, following the red line where she had plotted her course around the country. "I hope you're not going to be travelling alone, Lara. Not quite the safest thing to do in South Africa. There's a lot of crime there and if you're driving alone, you'll need to keep your wits about you. I wouldn't advise it. Flying would be far safer."

Lara stared at the map. "I don't like flying as you now know. Besides how will I ever find mysterious houses, deceased estates and such like if I'm flying? No, I need to drive. I can assure you I'm much braver on the ground than in the air. I can look after myself."

Jack finished his beer. "Well, hire a good solid car. Keep it locked whilst you're driving. Get off the roads before it gets dark and don't under any circumstances stop for anything or anyone – unless it's the police of course. Even then ask to see their ID."

Early the next morning the aircraft started its graceful descent into Cape Town International Airport. Jack suggested to Lara they swap seats so she could get her first breath-taking view of what he considered the most beautiful city in the world.

Lara sat in stunned silence, craning her neck trying to take in the glimpses of sparkling blue sea, the famous flat-topped mountain, the sweeping beaches, the traffic streaming along the wide motorways, the bright blue swimming pools in people's gardens.

"Wow!" she whispered. "Oh wow!"

She turned to Jack a wide grin across her face, forgetting her fear of flying as the wheels came down and the aircraft danced lightly, left and right, then settled down and roared down the runway, before turning and slowly making its sedate way to the arrivals building.

Waiting for their luggage to come through the flapping skirts of the rubber carousel they swapped business cards.

Jack hauled her suitcase off and put it down next to her before finding his own. "There are a few mobile phone companies in the arrival's hall. I suggest you get a local SIM card before you pick up your hire car. Once you have it give me a buzz with your new number.

"I've put another contact on my card. His name is Piet Joubert, he was with the police for years. If you get into any kind of trouble, give him a call, okay?"

Impulsively Lara gave him a hug. "Thank you, Jack, that's very sweet of you. Lovely to meet you. I'll let you know if I find any creepy haunted houses with sinister histories and dead bodies hidden under the floorboards."

Jack lifted his hand in farewell and was soon swallowed up in the crowd of other passengers pushing their loaded trolleys.

Who knows, he thought to himself, she might find something interesting on her travels which could be worth following up.

Chapter Eighteen

Lara checked into her hotel in Sea Point, unpacked and set off to drive around. After an hour driving in the heavy traffic, she decided it would take too much time. The next day she hopped onto one of the open topped red tourists' buses and let them do the hard work as she gazed at all the famous landmarks.

Around every corner she needed to catch her breath. Camp's Bay with its palm trees and white beaches, Chapman's Peak and the working Waterfront, crammed with designer shops, wine bars, restaurants and plush hotels.

The old castle and Signal Hill, where the traditional noon day cannon, one of the oldest in the world, boomed across the city, causing the pigeons, who never seemed to get used to it, to scatter in all directions and gave a good many tourists a moment of pure terror before things were explained to them. It was, indeed, a stunning place with breath-taking views wherever she looked. It felt more like Europe in Africa than an African city.

Then it was time to get down to work.

She trawled through the antique shops in town but didn't find any gems of interest. Then she went to the old suburb of Diep River, well known for its second-hand shops. In one, which specialised in old silver, she found items she knew would sell well. An Edwardian jewel box, a silver belt buckle, a snuff box and a gorgeous set of intricately engraved silver candlesticks. She knew she would get double for what she paid for them, even factoring in the excess baggage fee she would have to pay for the items and anything else she discovered on her travels. Lara spent hours rooting around amongst years of memorabilia, lost in a world of other people lives.

Soon it would be time to move out of the city and hit the smaller, more rural places. Her ex-lover whom she had hoped would give her a list of deceased estates and places up for auction, had got married and taken off for New Zealand. So, no help there. She would have to go it alone.

Leaving Cape Town after a week, she left the main highway, and took secondary roads. Visiting rural towns, each one with some kind of antique shop where she sometimes found something collectable. Staying in small guest houses, she always picked up the local newspaper – a mine of information for what was going on, and a mirror into the lives of the people who lived there. They listed any auction which would be taking place.

Lara went to the local auction houses and visited deceased estates, collecting items which caught her eye.

The next day Lara pulled up outside a guest house in a place called Wolmaransstad, a small town between Johannesburg and Kimberley. Buying the local newspaper, she saw the contents of what had once been a modest game lodge, not far out of town, were up for sale. Her instincts told her this would be interesting. Many years ago, it had originally been a farm, before being turned into a game lodge called Cloud's End.

That evening she chatted to the barman as she consumed a glass of ice-cold wine, the bar was empty. She asked him about the game lodge and its contents which would be on public display the next day.

The barman had lived in the area all his life. Seventy-five years he told her. His name was Gift.

"Oh, I love your name! So, tell me, Gift, what do you know about the place selling off everything tomorrow?"

Gift scratched his grey grizzled hair and wiped down the bar.

"There is much history there, *mama*, one of the first places to bring people here to see what the town has to offer. The original family were well known hereabouts, before it became the town you are seeing now. This area is famous for its diamonds, you have heard of the big hole in Kimberley where all the diamonds were found?"

Lara nodded, recalling her research before she left London.

"The home was out in the bush, not so far from here. When the old people died the children of this family decided to build more rooms and make a place for visitors. Not many at first. They are saying diamonds were found there. The guests could scratch the earth and look for them. If they found them, they were allowed to keep them. It was a clever idea. But there was much tragedy there… *eish.*"

Lara took a sip of her wine and smiled at him. "So, no chance of staying there anymore then, if the family are selling everything off?"

"No, *mama*, no chance. Soon the children left there and moved to the cities or overseas. The lodge it is closing. Then, one day, when the place had been empty for some years, a woman came there. No-one knew who she was. This place she made her home – no more game lodge, no more visitors. No visitors at all."

Lara pushed her hair back behind her ears. "What was her name Gift?"

"This I do not know, *mama*. My cousin, Eunice, was working there once, she called her *mama,* the same as I am calling you. This is the name we give to an older woman; it is a mark of respect."

Lara smiled to herself. She didn't look that old, did she?

Gift wiped down the bar again then reached for one of the glasses and started to polish it vigorously. Lara watched him, she had an idea he was going to tell her more, so she didn't push him.

"*Eish,* this woman with no name had something wrong in her head. I saw her sometimes in town, walking alone, talking to herself. On her hands she is wearing short white gloves. When she came here to this bar, when she paid for her drink she took the money from small bags, the ones the banks keep their silver money in. She is not liking to touch things. In another plastic bag she had a *lappi*, a small cloth, it was smelling of bleach and this she used before she sat down and then once more when she finished her drink, wiping the glass also."

He shrugged his shoulders and shook his head, looking puzzled. "Not one word she said to me, only two perhaps – '*white wine.*' Nothing more. I was feeling sad for this lady. She would come here to my bar, drink the same thing, say nothing, wipe with her cloth, pay and then leave."

Lara twirled her glass. "So, what happened to her?"

"Ah, *mama*, this was most sad. Some say the loneliness came to her. Made her do what she did."

Lara shivered. "What did she do, Gift?" she asked softly.

"It is said one day, she went to a place on the farm, a place where people used to come and watch the game, but the game could not see them, because they were hidden. Then one day this hidden place with the chairs and table for watching, did not face the water hole, it faced in a different direction, as though this woman was always looking watching something else, waiting perhaps?"

Gift carefully put the polished glass back on the shelf behind him. "One day this woman put a small camp bed out in the open, near the hidden place and there she is shooting herself. The bush can be a cruel place, *mama*, the vultures are always looking, always looking. This place where she lived," he shrugged. "It is a well-known nesting site for the Cape vultures...they would have seen her there."

Lara pulled her shawl around her shoulders as a cold shiver ran down her spine. "She lived there alone, then? No children?"

Gift shrugged his shoulders. "There was no-one there for her. She died alone as she wished to do – or perhaps not. No one wishes to die alone. My cousin, Eunice, who worked for this lady was not there at this time. She had gone to work in another place."

"Was she old then, this woman, or perhaps she was sick?"

"*Eish, mama*, it is hard to say the age of white people. I'm thinking she was not old like me, but she was not like you. Maybe more like me perhaps."

"How long ago did she die, Gift?"

The old man screwed up his eyes in thought. "This would be perhaps a year now when she did this thing."

*****

Lara dined alone. Even this old, dilapidated hotel felt spooky to her. Later as she lay in her bed, she thought about her conversation with Gift.

Who was this mysterious woman who had given up all hope and chosen to die by her own hand? Clearly, she had an issue with germs if she wore gloves all the time and didn't like to touch things, or perhaps, if she was old, it was just a quirky thing she did? Lara had met enough elderly people through her work to know some of them became obsessive with being tidy. Making sure everything was exactly as it should be, everything in its place, everything lined up. It wasn't unusual, she thought, it probably made them feel as though they were still in control of their lives even if they weren't.

Tomorrow she would go out to the farm. Surely with such a tragic tale there would be some clue as to who the woman was? She would need some information if she found anything interesting. Some kind of history as to who had owned the things now up for sale. A good story would add to the sale of anything she found of interest.

Chapter Nineteen

Lara went off road and drove down the dusty rutted road towards the place called Cloud's End, the signs advertising the sale of contents of the house were placed intermittently along the way.

The vast plains to her left and right were more reminiscent of the Serengeti, which she had seen on wildlife programmes at home. The wide, open, flat spaces of endless yellow grasses. It reminded her of some of the scenes in a film she had seen long ago and not forgotten; *Out of Africa.*

She pulled up in front of the empty homestead. There were only five cars parked there.

Wrapped around by a generous veranda was a single storey house. She stepped up to the entrance. Chairs and sofas lined the outside walls, interspersed with tall potted plants in mud spattered grey holders. Faded blinds shielded the old furniture from the sun.

Set slightly back from the main house were round thatched dwellings, three to the left of the house and three to the right. All had their curtains drawn. Dead leaves littering the flat stone dusty verandas. Guest cottages when the place had been a game lodge, she surmised.

Lara wandered from room to room, running her hands over the furniture with the price tags hanging from them. The sitting room was quintessentially English with its chintz covered furnishings, empty bookcases and a fireplace. But, she noticed, no photographs anywhere.

The kitchen was simple and basic. The bedrooms as if no-one had slept in them for years, the curtains drawn. The place had a lingering smell of bleach or some other cleaning product.

On a long trestle table on the back veranda were laid more things for sale, their price tags fluttering in the languid breeze. Lara, feeling the absence of the late owner of the house, made her way down the table.

She picked up the silverware, the cutlery and the crockery, then put them back on the table. A silver box caught her eyes. She examined it carefully. There was a crest embedded on the top, but she couldn't work out what it was. She would need her loupe for that.

Lara opened the lid, and the faint smell of tobacco escaped its confines. It was pretty and because hardly anyone smoked anymore, she knew it would be collectable. Next to it was an elegant silver bell used, she knew, to summons the staff in the old colonial days in India and Africa. She would buy that as well.

A curious box caught her attention. It stood out from everything else on display.

It was the size of a large shoe box. The wood was carved intricately. She recognised it as Chinese by the willow tree and pagoda design of the inlaid wood.

She picked it up. It didn't appear to have any openings. No lid to lift up. It was exquisite. The heavy grain of a master carver told her it was very old, the heavy red lacquer protecting the artist's craftsmanship. She knew she had to have it and knew exactly where she would put it in her flat.

*****

An older man was also looking through the things on display. He glanced at the woman who was examining the exquisite Chinese box. He waited, seemingly looking at other things on the table, whilst watching her discreetly.

Lara carried the box to the agent who was overseeing the sale. It was heavier than she thought it might be. She checked the price tag, doing a quick conversion from rand to pound, she flinched. It was expensive, over three hundred pounds. But she'd fallen in love with it and knew she had to have it. It would look perfect on the table in her hallway.

Paying with her credit card she stowed the silver bell, the cigarette box and the Chinese box in the boot of her car.

The agent had told her she was welcome to drive around the property. Not much to see he had assured her, apart from the stables.

The man's eyes followed her as she left. He had watched her put the box and other things in her car, then lock it.

He waited until she was out of sight then sauntered over to her car. To anyone watching he had simply dropped his keys. He stooped and picked them up, then walked towards his own car.

*****

Lara wandered over to the stables. Two horses looked up with interest at her approach, as did a middle-aged African who was mucking out one of the stalls. His overalls were tattered with a faint logo of the long-gone game lodge. He touched his cap as she approached.

"Good morning, missus. I am Nico, the groom. You like horses?"

She smiled at him. "Love them. I've been riding since I was a little girl. I'm an experienced rider. I haven't been on a horse for a couple of years now. Not much chance in London where I come from."

"If you have the experience, you are welcome to take a ride, missus. I try and exercise them as much as I can, but this one here," he patted the rump of a chestnut horse, "Diamond, she needs more exercise. Perhaps you will take her out?"

Lara hesitated as she glanced nervously over the landscape. "I've never ridden in Africa – is it safe out there with the game?"

He grinned at her; his perfect white teeth enhanced by his dark skin. "There is only plains game here, missus, very safe to ride. Only giraffe, zebra, buck, and warthogs. They are used to the horses. The horses are trained and obedient. They know this place well; they know where to go. You will be quite safe. Sometimes the zebra and buck, if the horse is galloping, will be running alongside. They run because they think the horse is being chased by a predator but we are not having predators here."

He glanced at what she was wearing, trousers, safari boots and a long-sleeved shirt. "I will saddle Diamond up and find you a hat to wear. When you wish to return home turn Diamond in this direction, and she will bring you back to the stables. The house can be seen from everywhere on the property."

Lara rode out. She knew what she was looking for. The place where this woman had died. The agent had been evasive, not telling her where this had occurred. But with her Chinese box and other things safely tucked in the boot of her car, she followed her instincts.

The Chinese box had a history, and without any doubt it had belonged to the woman who had killed herself. The woman who seemed to have no name and had also been the owner of a silver box with a crest on it.

The horse appeared to know its way around. Diamond had obviously galloped across these plains many times before. Lara threw back her head and laughed with the pure joy of this new experience. She pulled off her riding hat and let the warm winds permeate her hair.

The plains game completely ignored her. The giraffe only briefly stopping their foraging to watch them as they galloped past. A few ostriches attempted to join in and ran alongside her, then gave up and went back to pecking the ground. The vast open spaces and miles and miles of unspoiled nature was exhilarating.

Lara slowed Diamond, bringing her to a walk as she gazed around. The game around her, zebra, impala, kudu and other buck looked at her briefly then carried on grazing. A troop of baboons watched her pass as they perched on an outcrop of rocks. She looked up at the cloudless sky. High above large birds, their wings motionless, glided on the thermals dipping and turning.

She shuddered. Remembering how the woman had ended her days. Were these the vultures then? Were they watching her and the other animals, watching and waiting? She knew from her research they wouldn't attack anything living – even so…

She urged Diamond into a trot and tried not to look up again.

Diamond unexpectedly swerved to the right and started to slow down. Lara patted her neck and relaxed in the saddle letting the horse take her wherever she wanted to go.

Diamond stopped, lowered her head, pawed at the ground and started to graze. Lara looked around, soaking up the sound of silence, hearing only the grasses whispering across the *veld* and the soft calling of doves. The silence was intoxicating.

Her eyes were caught by the corner of what seemed to be a thatched roof. She dismounted, looped Diamond's reins around a bush and went to explore.

It was a simple structure. A short deck camouflaged by heavy trees. But the two canvas chairs and table didn't face the water hole Lara could see glinting in the noon day sun. They faced a different direction altogether with a view across the soft yellow grasses, towards the main road which joined the towns of Wolmaransstad and Kimberley. In the distance she could hear the low rumble of the traffic.

Lara shivered despite the heat. She knew exactly where Diamond had brought her, the horse had obviously been here many times before.

Lara ran her hands over the slatted table between the two dark green director's canvas chairs. The wood was dusty, smooth and worn. She looked out and wondered what the woman had thought about as she sat there alone.

Waiting and watching?

But for what? Why wasn't she watching the animals at the water hole as they came down to drink?

Shaking her head, she returned to Diamond. The place, and the silence, was spooking her out. She didn't want to explore any further.

Once mounted she turned Diamond in the direction of the old lodge, as the groom had told her. Horse and rider headed back.

Nico came out of one of the stables and smiled at her. "It was good, the ride?"

"Oh yes, it was marvellous. Diamond took me to a little thatched place. You must know it, of course?"

A shadow crossed the groom's face as he looked at his feet. "Yes, I know this place…"

Lara dismounted and handed the reins to him. "It's where the lady who owned the house died, isn't it?"

"Yes, missus. This is so. Her horse came back alone. I waited some time before I went to look for her, this is when I found her dead."

Lara handed back her hat and shook out her hair, wiping the sweat from behind her neck with her sleeve. Nico looked agitated and she decided to leave the subject there.

She held out her hand. "Well thank you so much for a wonderful ride. What will happen to you when this place is sold?"

Nico looked into the distance, then scuffed the dirt with his riding boot. "Perhaps the new owner will like horses. Perhaps they will buy them and keep me here. This is what I am hoping for. If not, then I shall return to my family in Zimbabwe. There is no work around here for looking after horses."

Lara smiled at him. "Well, Nico, I'm sure they will buy the horses and keep you on to look after them."

Lara knew there was a story here. She had been to many houses of deceased estates in her career. Most of them felt as dead as their owners. Only a few still carried a lingering essence of a once felt presence.

A pall of sadness had lain over the simple thatched structure and also the soon to be auctioned off house. So where was Nico when all this happened? He surely must have heard the shot? Or maybe he was asleep, perhaps it was dark when the woman pulled the trigger?"

She had the feeling he hadn't been telling her the entire story.

A story her flying companion, Jack Taylor, would surely be interested in?

Lara remembered him well. The tall, good-looking Englishman with his wild blond hair, intelligent dark brown eyes, tanned face and rather nice accent.

A plausible excuse to make contact with him again.

Lara didn't notice the car parked under the tree as she left the property.

The man started his car and followed her.

Chapter Twenty

Jack Taylor was planning another trip to Hazyview. The intense suffocating heat of the past month in Franschhoek had him thinking about finding somewhere a little cooler to live. The town was beautiful, the people friendly, but when the last tourist left town at the end of summer the place was too quiet for him. He had decided he needed more.

He had liked the busy town of Hazyview, where he had worked with Piet Joubert on his last case. He liked the safari feel of it. His instincts, which never failed him, told him there were more stories to be had in that neck of the woods than here.

Most of the wine farms in Franschhoek were owned by foreigners, no doubt with stories of their own. But he needed a place where there were more international people coming and going on safari in order to keep Harry and his readers happy over their cornflakes and fry-ups.

Although he had his own car, he didn't fancy the long drive to the northeast of the country. He would fly to Johannesburg, collect a hire car then make his way towards the Kruger Park. Checking out places along the way to see if he could find another place to live. Somewhere with a bit more buzz.

His phone vibrated on the table next to him he snatched it up.

"Jack Taylor."

"Hi Jack, it's me, Lara. We met on the flight from London?"

He smiled broadly into the phone. "Hello Lara. How's the treasure hunting going? Any problems?"

She laughed. "No. No problems. I'm having a marvellous time driving here there and everywhere. I've collected a few nice pieces, which I'm quite pleased with. How are you? Found any stories to get your teeth into?"

"I'm working on a couple of interesting things at the moment, as well as filling my editor's weekly columns. But nothing to get the adrenaline going. But something will turn up now things are getting back to normal after the festive season. Where are you, Lara?"

"I'm about to leave Johannesburg, heading towards the northeast of the country. I thought I might spend a couple of days somewhere and maybe go on a safari for a day or two. It would be a crime not to do so, after all I've seen and heard about the bush.

"Nowhere fancy though. I looked at the prices of some of those fabulous lodges and it made my eyes water, even with the exchange rate. I think I might try a place in the Kruger. Those rest camps look clean and well equipped. Have you ever tried one of them Jack?"

Jack could hear the thunder of traffic and the impatient hooting of vehicles, and the whoop whoop of a police car siren which convinced him even further he didn't want to live in a city.

"Not exactly. I stayed in one stunning luxury lodge, but I was on a case, so everything was paid for. Couldn't have afforded it otherwise. But you'll see all the game, whether you're in a luxury camp or a rest camp. The animals don't care how much, or how little you're paying."

Lara interrupted him. "Hey, listen Jack," he could hear the excitement in her voice. "I went to a place called Wolmaransstad; I think that's how you pronounce it. There was a sale of the contents of what used to be a game lodge. Now a deceased estate. I found a few things I liked. But better still I think there might be a story there."

Lara briefly gave him her impressions of Cloud's End.

Jack felt the old familiar sizzle down his spine. Lara's impressions of the place and the mysterious woman who had died there did indeed have the components of an intriguing story.

He looked up over the vineyards and the mountains, shimmering in the heat. "Lara, let's meet up. I was planning on making a trip to a place called Hazyview up where you're heading. I'm thinking I might like to move from Franschhoek and re-locate to somewhere a bit cooler.

"You could base yourself in Hazyview for a few days. There are a few small towns around that might hold some of the treasures you're pursuing. You can take a couple of days and go on safari, it's next door to the Kruger."

He paused, liking his impromptu plan. He wanted to see her again. "I normally stay at a place called The Inn, run by an English chap. I can recommend it. Lots of interesting people, locals and guests, hang out there. Good food as well.

"I'd like to hear more about your story, it sounds as though it might indeed have legs. What do you say?"

She gave a squeal. "Oh, my God, these taxis, they're terrifying! They drive all over the place with music booming, those poor passengers. Um, yes, sounds great – let's do that. Let's meet up. I'll let you know when I get there. Probably in the next day or two?

"Hey, another thing Jack. When I went to fill up the first time here, I climbed out of my car and headed towards the fuel pump, as you do in England. Suddenly there was a flurry of attendants around me. Washing my windscreen, taking the pump from my hand. They laughed at me. They did everything, filled the car, checked the oil and water, checked the tyre pressure – I mean, I couldn't believe it? I could get very used to this way of life Jack!"

Jack rang off feeling pleased. It would be nice to see the lovely Lara again. Even better it sounded as though she may have come across a potentially interesting story.

He booked his flight then called ex-detective Piet Joubert.

"What are you doing back so soon, my friend," he growled. "I was hoping you would decide to stay on that soggy little island you call home?"

Jack laughed. "Bad luck, Piet. I'm back. This is my home now. Even better news. I'll be staying in Hazyview for a few days. I'm heading your way tomorrow."

Piet sighed down the phone. "Just ruined my day, Jack. Had enough of you English. *Eish, bleddy* tourists. Thought we'd got rid of them all, now you pitch up again."

"I'm not a tourist, Piet, remember, I live here. Anyway, I met this woman, Lara. We were on the same flight from London. I'm meeting her in Hazyview in a day or two."

"*Ag*, Jack, why should I be interested? Last time we spoke you were going to bring me something called a spotted dick. Didn't like the sound of it, my friend. We get good food here in my country. I don't do foreign food, especially when it sounds *kak* like that."

Jack stifled his laughter. Piet was in a bad mood. "Lara has been travelling around the country, she came across something interesting. A story Piet…"

There was a short silence. "Okay. Now I'm glad you're back, Lara or no Lara. What's the story?"

Jack told him, with the little information he had. "My gut feel is we need to follow it up. But, hey, it's up to you Piet, maybe you're not in the mood. See you."

Grinning to himself he rang off before Piet could reply.

Chapter Twenty-One

Jack took the early morning flight from Cape Town to Johannesburg, collected his hire car and drove out of the airport. He saw the signs for the main highway to the north and the other to the south.

He hesitated for a few moments. This deceased estate Lara had talked about was south…without another thought he turned in that direction. The place was only a couple of hours from Johannesburg. He would check it out see if he could come up with any more leads as to whom the woman might have been.

The deceased estate, now on the market, had, by law, to be registered with the Master of the High Court in Johannesburg. There he would find the name of the owner. Unless it was in the name of a company or a trust. There would be a lawyer involved somewhere.

Two hours later he was driving through the main centre of the wide main road of the town of Wolmaransstad. A typical old Afrikaans farming town, complete with a majestic soaring, Dutch Reform Church. It's proud spires and arches reaching up into the brightness of the sun and the hope of better things to come.

The main road passed through the usual places you see in any rural South African town. A Spar supermarket, a hardware shop, a couple of pharmacies and banks, a steak house or two and a petrol station at both ends of the main road with their ATMs, rest rooms, and small shops for stocking up on cold drinks, sandwiches, hot pies and snacks.

He stopped at an estate agency, of which there were many. All seemingly huddled together to keep an eye on who was selling what.

He recognised the green and gold logo of Pam Golding Properties, found a parking place and made his way to the entrance of the agency.

A sturdy iron gate barred his entry. Inside five women and a man were manning their desks. The young man looked up, and smiled at him as the gate swung open.

"May I help you, sir?"

Jack made his way to the young man's desk and sat down. "Yes. I heard there was a property for sale. A place called Cloud's End? I'd very much like to take a look at it. I have a client who is keen to purchase something modest and remote in this area. Would you, by chance, have this property on your books?"

The young man beamed at him. "Indeed, we do sir. It's due to be auctioned off next week. If we don't sell it first. We have the sole mandate. When would you like to see it?"

Jack looked at his watch. "How about now? I need to get back to Johannesburg to meet with my client. He has a few other places he's looking at…"

The young man stood up and put out his hand. "Tinus Jacobs."

Jack reached into his shirt pocket and drew out one of his many cards which he used depending on the situation and who he was supposed to be. "Jack Taylor. Shall we go?"

Jack followed Tinus through town. He turned left onto a dirt road and within twenty minutes he had his first sighting of Cloud's End.

It was exactly as Lara had described it. He looked at the landscape around him. The rolling flat bush of golden grasses and acacia trees. Yes, very East Africa he thought. So different from the landscape of the Sabi Sands and Kruger National Park.

He parked next to Tinus's vehicle and joined him at the entrance of the house whilst he fumbled with a bunch of keys. Tinus opened the door and gestured for Jack to enter. Then followed him, as eager as a puppy.

Jack paused. "Tinus, would you mind if I wandered around on my own and take a look?"

Tinus hesitated briefly. "No, of course not. Take your time. I'll meet you in the dining room when you've finished your tour of the place. What used to be the six guest cottages are now empty. Completely stripped of everything. But I can show you them afterwards, so long?"

Jack walked through each room, the sitting room, the dining room, the kitchen, a library, then through to the four bedrooms and two bathrooms. It felt as though the owner had just stepped out. All the usual ornaments, cutlery, crockery and other pieces were still scattered across a trestle table now in the kitchen of the house. Throughout the house there was a faint smell of something like bleach.

Lara had been right. There was an air of great sadness about the place. But there were no personal traces of the woman who had once lived here. Who had got rid of those?

Jack wandered back to the dining room where Tinus was sitting with an expectant smile on his face.

"Hey, Tinus, I've had a good look around. There seem to be no pictures, no paintings, no books anywhere. Nothing personal only a pile of magazines. Were they all sold when you had the open house here?"

Tinus looked a little puzzled. "I don't recall any paintings or pictures, books or photographs. A lot of people came to rummage through the things for sale. Maybe she didn't have any."

Jack sat down opposite him. "The woman who lived here seems to have been a bit of an enigma. An odd way to live with no mementoes left behind?"

Tinus shrugged. "Maybe a relative came and took her personal stuff."

Jack thought he looked a bit uncomfortable.

"Look, Tinus, I know how this woman died. We did our research. We know she died about a year ago. My client will want to know her name. He will insist. He won't consider buying the place, and I think he would like it very much, unless he knows the paperwork behind it. The name of the woman for a start. Did she have a husband at some point? Children? No buyer wants to inherit something where an unexpected relative might come out of the woodwork somewhere down the line and cause a problem."

Jack crossed his arms across his chest. "Now, who was she? Was she South African or maybe English?"

Tinus shrugged his shoulders. "I honestly don't know. I'm sorry. The property is in a trust."

Jack gave him a tight smile. "Then find out for me, Tinus. This Estate must have been registered with the Master of the High Court when the woman died. A death certificate would have been required. They will know the people who administer the trust and the name of the woman. She must have had an identity number, like everyone else in this country. I need to know, okay? I want to know how long the woman lived here as well. I need to go back to my buyer with all the names involved, otherwise he won't be remotely interested."

Jack walked back outside and looked around. "I'll take a quick look at the stables, Tinus. Give me a few minutes, will you?"

The horses looked up with interest as he approached. He went from stall to stall greeting them both. He loved horses.

There was no sign of any groom. Presumably he was somewhere else on the property, or maybe in town collecting hay and supplies.

Jack made his way back to the house and he and Tinus walked to their parked cars. "You have my details, Tinus. My client will love this place, it's exactly what he's looking for. Come up with the names and I think we might, just might, have a deal. The price is right. It won't be a problem. He'll like the horses as well. Who looks after them? I didn't see anyone there?"

Tinus shrugged. "Maybe the groom went to town for something. Obviously, someone looks after them."

Tinus was desperate for his first sale. He wanted to prove himself to his fellow agents at the agency. This property sale would put him where he wanted to be.

Tinus kicked at the dust beside his car. His mind made up.

"The property, as I told you, is held in a trust. I don't know the name of it, I'm sorry. But the woman who lived here? Her name was Marlene Hartley. I don't know how long she lived here though. Some years I would imagine."

Chapter Twenty-Two

Jack was making good progress on his journey to Hazyview. Despite his detour to Cloud's End, he would still make it to his destination in time for dinner.

As he drove, he worked out his next moves. Firstly, he had to find out who the mysterious Marlene Hartley was and where she came from. The road could lead to nowhere but, again, his instincts told him there was a compelling story here somewhere.

He drove through Hazyview, then pulled up in front of The Inn, there were a lot of cars parked there. He hoped one of them might belong to the lovely Lara.

Grabbing his bag, he locked the car and made his way to reception, checked in and found his room. After a brisk shower and change of clothes he made his way to the bar for a pre-dinner drink. The day had given him an appetite for more than food.

Piet Joubert was nowhere to be seen. But he knew where his cottage was and knowing the wily Joubert, he would know soon enough Jack had checked in.

The bar was as busy as ever. Hugo, the owner, stood behind the bar enveloped in a wildly coloured shirt he looked up when he saw Jack, lifted his arm in greeting, a wide grin of pleasure on his tanned face.

Jack found an empty bar stool and felt himself relax.

"Hello Jack! Good to see you again."

Jack leaned across the bar and shook Hugo's hand. "Nice to be back I must say." He looked around the crowded bar. "I see you're busy as ever. How was the season for you?"

Hugo beamed. "Excellent. Kept our Head of Security on his toes. Does Piet always look so gloomy, Jack?"

Jack smiled. "Well, yes. He has that kind of face. It's how he comes across to people. He doesn't care what anyone thinks of him."

He felt something nudge his knee and looked down at a young golden Labrador with big brown sad eyes.

Jack stroked his head. "Hello, who are you then? Didn't see you around the last time I was here."

Hugo laughed. "That's Piet's dog, Hope. She's supposed to be out on patrol guarding the place, looking fierce. I have to say she's pretty useless, but quite loveable! Hangs around the bar all the time making friends with everyone when she should be out working. Ah, here comes your friend, no doubt looking for his ever-alert patrol dog. Hope might be lacking on the security skills, but she's added a dimension to the hotel. Everyone falls in love with her, good public relations, Jack. Not one of Piet's greatest attributes, but he does a damn fine job around the hotel. Best move I ever made, bringing him on board."

Jack swivelled around on his stool as Piet Joubert came ambling through the door. His eyes scanned the crowd in the bar, his eyes missing nothing. Spotting Jack and his dog he headed towards them.

He scowled at the Labrador. "*Bleddy* useless security dog she is. Come, Hopeless. Heel!"

Hope looked up surprised to hear her master's voice. She ran towards him, rolled over on her back and waved her legs around, her long pink tongue hanging from the side of her grinning mouth.

"Need to get a proper African dog, like a *Boerboel*," Piet grunted. "Ugly as all hell but they know how to get the job done. Bite anything it doesn't like the look of. *Jeez,* look at this thing." He gestured towards the grinning dog, still lying on its back, tail wagging furiously. "Waste of time, that dog."

He placed his battered cap on the bar. "Thought of getting a German Shepherd. Nice looking breed but the Germans can be as difficult as the Brits. Don't want a grumpy dog, Jack, one with a bad attitude."

Jack laughed. "Maybe you should get a German Shepherd, you'd make a good pair. Anyway, maybe she ignores your commands because you call her Hopeless. Labradors are sensitive, you're making her feel inadequate. It's good to see you again. Pleased to see me?"

Piet ran his hand through his short dark hair, greying at the edges. He looked at Jack with his piercing blue eyes, fringed with long dark lashes and tried to suppress a smile.

"*Ja,* I suppose so." He shrugged. "You're here now. What can I do?"

Piet shook Jack's hand with gusto making him wince. Then gave him a friendly pat on the back almost knocking Jack of his bar stool. His beer slopped over the side of his glass.

Piet perched on an adjoining barstool. Hope came and sat down next to him, putting her head on his knee, gazing at him with adoring eyes. Jack noticed he immediately started to fondle the dog's ears.

"So, Piet, where's that woman of yours? Thought she might at least have put a smile on your face. Not an easy thing to do I know."

"My woman, as you call her, has gone to visit her daughter in your country. Won't be back 'til end of March. Speaking of women where's this Lara person with the big story you were telling me about?"

Hugo edged his way past his bar staff. "Hey, Jack there's a woman at reception asking for you. I think she may be a bit daunted by my somewhat rowdy bar…she's already checked in."

Jack slid from his seat. "I'll go and fetch her. Don't go anywhere Piet. I want you to meet her. It must be Lara."

Lara was standing outside reception admiring the lawns lit by discreet lights placed strategically behind bushes and trees.

"Lara?"

She spun around, a smile lighting up her face. "Jack!"

Jack manoeuvred his way back towards Piet, through the crowds, his hand on Lara's elbow.

"Piet? This is Lara. He does have some charm Lara, depending on his mood."

Piet ignored his remark and turned to Lara with a smile. "Good to meet you, my girl," he looked at his watch. "Have to go now, so long. Come on you useless dog, time to do the rounds."

Lara turned to him with a nervous smile. "Not too friendly is he, your Piet? But I love his dog. She's gorgeous."

Jack ordered her a drink and turned back to her. "He comes across like that, but I can tell you he sussed you out in seconds. He's one of the sharpest people I've ever met. We work well together.

"I don't know about you, but I'm starving. Let's finish our drinks and then have dinner together. I want to hear all your news."

*****

Piet Joubert stopped at reception on his way out. Blessing, the Zimbabwean receptionist, gave him a broad grin and swung his computer screen around for Piet to check.

Piet did this every evening. Noting names, room numbers, identity documents. He saw Lara Summers name, and a final guest who had arrived twenty minutes after her. Daniel Van Heerden. Piet looked at his identity number.

South African identity numbers held a wealth of information; date of birth, gender and whether you were a Permanent Resident or a citizen. Van Heerden was in his late sixties and a citizen of the country.

He turned the screen back to the receptionist. "See you tomorrow, Blessing. Looks like we're almost full tonight. That should please the boss." He rolled his eyes as Hope's grinning head and paws appeared over the reception desk in front of him, before disappearing again as she padded around to his side and walked with him out into the grounds of the hotel.

Hugo was the well-liked host and owner of the hotel. He spent more time with his guests in the popular bar than he did anywhere else. Before Piet had arrived on the scene the security at the hotel had been sadly lacking. But now Piet had streamlined everything. Putting in security systems, a guard house at the entrance where guests had to show their identity before entering the property. Hugo had baulked at the suggestion of changing all the locks to the guests' rooms, he liked the old-fashioned keys they handed to the guest after they had checked in and didn't want a card key.

Piet installed a large safe in the main building where guests could leave their valuables. The generator, often in demand due to the erratic power cuts, was impossible to get to without the right security key and code to enter its enclosure. Piet knew that black-outs presented golden opportunities for criminals.

When guests checked in, they had to record their names, car registration and proof of identity, be it a foreign passport or, for South Africans, their ID number.

Hugo has been rather lax, to say the least, about the check in formalities. But not anymore. Piet liked to know exactly who was entering the property and all about them, he didn't want any dodgy people hanging around his patch. The locals who regularly came to the bar had a small sticker with the hotel logo on their windscreen so they didn't have to go through all the formalities.

With Hope at his heels, he wandered past the parked cars, checking the registration numbers, he put his hand on the bonnet of an expensive looking BMW 4x4. This was the vehicle belonging to the last guest who had checked in, Van Heerden. The engine was still hot. He had spotted the guest, at the bar.

Probably had been tall at some stage before age had rounded his spine, his white hair and goatee beard were trimmed and tidy. His eyes framed by tinted glasses. Ordinary looking bloke.

Piet made a circuit of all the guest cottages, ensuring the security lights were working, nodding his head at the guests as he passed.

Some guests sitting out on their patios enjoying the sunset lifted their glasses to him in recognition. With all they had heard about crime in South Africa, Piet was a comforting sight as he made his uniformed way around the grounds.

Hope, eager to make as many friends as possible in the shortest space of time, left his side and greeted all the guests with a grin and wagging tail and a hopeful look in her eyes as she innocently eyed the snacks, especially the biltong, which the hotel provided every evening along with other nibbles for their guests.

Piet had given up months ago trying to keep the dog to heel. But the guests loved seeing the Labrador. Everyone made a big fuss of Hope, making sure there was always a shaving of biltong kept for her.

Although Piet despaired of his dog doing anything like a proper job, he was astute enough to know as far as public relations was concerned, Hope won hands down. Everyone loved the happy dog with a smile like a dolphin.

Although he would never admit it to anyone, he loved her too. He recognised her definite shortcomings as a working dog, he knew she was a lost cause, but he liked having her around him as he went about his duties.

Guests felt secure knowing they had an ex-police detective watching over them with his dog next to him.

Chapter Twenty-Three

Jack and Lara found a corner table in the busy restaurant. The tables were well spaced with their cheerful red tablecloths and white napkins, a candle in a small glass box lent a romantic atmosphere to the place, but it was actually more for the unexpected power cuts.

Lara and Jack chatted easily. She told him all about her travels, what she had seen, who she had met on the way, what she had collected. Her overview of the country.

He sliced through his fillet steak, covered with creamed mushrooms, crispy golden roast potatoes and a green salad on the side.

Lara, with a healthy appetite he liked to see, had chosen the Kingklip, a fat firm fish glazed with garlic butter, with golden chips and a Greek salad.

She mopped up the garlic butter on her plate with a wedge of bread then sat back and sighed. "Heavenly. I know why you live here Jack, it's fabulous, everything. The country, stunning views, the weather, the roads, the food, the wine, the people. It's like living on another planet. I don't think I ever want to go back to London, I really don't.

"It's so different here in Africa. Like I'm living and not merely existing. It sounds stupid, I know, but I feel as if all my senses are on high alert, senses I had forgotten I had. I feel lighter somehow!"

She took a sip of her wine. "My routine life of getting up every morning, doing what I have to do, then returning to my dark little flat, the long dark evenings stretching ahead. Every day with a predictable ending. I might find something which makes my head spin, during the day, some gem of an antique, but I still go home to my dark flat."

She gestured around. "Here I know, every day won't be the same, it's heady stuff, Jack – addictive."

Jack pushed his plate aside; a swooping waiter removed it immediately.

He nodded in agreement. "I understand what you're saying. To me it's the most glorious place in the world. But there are huge problems here, crime, corruption and all the rest of the stuff. But if you can hold your nerve, ignore all the things you can't change, then, yes, heaven on earth."

He leaned back in his chair. "By the way Lara, if you have found some items of value on your travels, might I suggest you keep them in the hotel safe? Security, thanks to Piet and not his dog, is good here, but crooks are more than wily, if someone wants to nick something they'll find a way. You mentioned a couple of other things you bought from the clearance sale. What were they?"

"Oh, a little silver bell, a square silver cigarette box and a beautiful Chinese box."

Jack nodded. "Blessing, our cheerful Zimbabwean receptionist, will keep them safe for you."

Lara stifled a yawn. "I think I'll take your advice there, Jack, then I'll turn in for the night. I'm feeling a bit weary after all the driving today and my terrifying drive through Johannesburg with all those mad taxi drivers flying around in every direction, with their booming music."

She reached for her handbag and stood up. "I know I've completely hogged the conversation tonight, and I still have to tell you all about the rest of my visit to Cloud's End, and my gallop across the property and what I saw there.

"I don't eat breakfast, but how about we have coffee around ten, if you're not doing anything else, and I'll tell you all about it? I want to show you my Chinese box."

Jack nodded. "Good idea, I'll see if I can get Piet to join us. He'll want to hear your story as well."

*****

Jack made his way to his room. He still had work to do for Harry, his editor. His weekly column was due tomorrow and he had to get it done tonight, no matter how long it took.

He had been happy to let Lara chatter away about her long trip. He hadn't told her about his own trip to Cloud's End and how he had found out the name of the owner. He wanted to hear her story after she'd had a good night's sleep. Her mind would be clear in the morning. He wanted her first impressions of the house then he would give her his.

Chapter Twenty-Four

The following day promised to be a hot one. Lara sat in one of the comfortable green striped chairs under the shade of a large tree, its skirt of leaves brushing the ground, her box stood on the table, the odd shaft of sunlight glinting on its lacquered sides.

Jack, Piet and the dog made their way towards her. Hope flopped down under the table. The waiter busied himself with their coffee tray, putting a bowl of water down for the dog, before heading back to the kitchen.

Piet put his battered baseball cap down on the table then helped himself to the coffee before settling back. "So, my girl, I've heard from Jack about your trip around the country. Now I want to hear about this house called Cloud's End."

Lara relayed her story, her conversation with the barman at a hotel in the town, before she had made her way to the house. What he had said about the woman, how she had died, her rather odd habit of wearing short white gloves, not wishing to touch anything, her obsession with wiping things down with a damp cloth.

"Gift, that's the barman's name," she grinned, "I just love his name. He thought she might be a bit bonkers, he felt sorry for her because she seemed to be so alone. That aloneness some people emanate. Mind you, Piet, when I got to the house myself, I could understand anyone going bonkers out there, it must have been awfully lonely. But apparently, she did go into town sometimes, not sure if she drove herself or the groom took her. She would go and have a glass of wine at Gift's bar."

Lara leaned forward and ran her fingers lightly over the lid of the Chinese box. "She had some help around the house, Gift said his cousin, Eunice, had worked there at some point. But I didn't see anyone, only the groom down at the stables."

Then she told them about the thatched place with the hidden deck, way out in the bush on the property. "According to Gift, this was where she dragged a camp bed out into the open, lay down on it and shot herself. Apparently, the area is quite famous for its nesting vultures."

She shuddered. "I don't even want to think about it."

Piet was listening carefully, then he looked up and frowned. "It's unusual, almost unheard of, for a woman to commit suicide by shooting herself. Women are more inclined to overdose on tablets or gas themselves in a car, they don't use a violent method to end their lives. It's men who choose guns, hangings and suchlike.

"I've seen many violent deaths and suicides in my career with the police, but I never had one where a woman commits suicide by shooting herself. Something not right there. But, who knows what her mind was like living out there on her own, I suppose it's possible. But carry on, my girl, let's hear the rest of your story."

Putting his now empty coffee cup down on the table, Jack leaned back in his chair, happy to look at the lovely, animated Lara as she finished her story.

Jack re-filled his coffee cup. "When you went into the house, Lara, what was the first thing you noticed?"

Lara screwed up her eyes for a moment then opened them. "Well apart from the trestle table with what was left of the things which hadn't been sold, the place was obviously furnished. There were no pictures on the walls, no photographs, no books anywhere. The furniture was nice enough, very English in style. I didn't get to look into any of what would have been the guest cottages. They looked as though they had been closed up for years, paint peeling of the verandas, no-one had swept up any of the leaves and branches around them, spider's webs all over the place. Couldn't miss those."

Lara took a sip of her coffee and continued. "Oh, the other thing was the faint smell of some kind of cleaning agent, bleach maybe. But hearing about how this woman wore gloves and wiped everything around her, I presumed she was like that at home as well. Maybe not wearing the white gloves but definitely a bit over the top with the cleaning, or her house help was. I don't know. But the smell was in all the rooms, there were three other bedrooms, but it didn't look to me as though they had been used either. All a bit odd actually. It's why I thought you might be interested in the place, Jack."

Her voice trailed off. "Oh yes, in the main bedroom which the woman obviously slept in, there was a sort of pot full of pencils and pens on a rather nice writing bureau. Nothing in the drawers though, I thought this was strange as well. No notepads or paper, not even a paper clip.

"The agent who was supervising things told me everything had been left exactly as it was when this woman died. Then the place was locked up until the estate was wound up and the agency opened the place up again to sell off what was left inside."

Piet interjected. "What about the horses and the groom? Were they going to be auctioned off as well?" He smiled. "Well, not the groom, he was kept there to look after the horses, of course. But where did the groom live, I wonder? Did you see any vehicle anywhere near the stables?"

Lara thought hard, trying to recapture the stables in her mind. "Yes, there was a sort of little truck, with an open back. I guess Nico, that was his name, must have used it to bring in hay for the horses and other supplies. He must have needed food himself, so I guess the estate paid him to stay on until everything was wrapped up legally."

She took another sip of her coffee. "I didn't see any accommodation for him, but there were three stables and two horses, so perhaps one of the stables had been converted into some sort of room for him. Grooms always like to stay close to their horses," she said knowledgably.

Jack nodded. She was a clear thinker and, because of her profession, obviously had an acute eye for detail. She hadn't missed much.

He briefly told her about his own trip to Cloud's End and finding out from the agent that the property was in a trust and the woman who had lived there was called Marlene Hartley.

Piet leaned forward and picked up the box turning it over in his hands studying it. "This box came from the house? It's quite heavy, hey?"

Lara nodded. "Yes, it stood out from the rest of the things on the trestle table, it's Chinese. It caught my eye immediately. I fell in love with it and bought it. It was jolly expensive, but I couldn't resist it. Chinese artefacts are not my area of expertise, so I know little about that world. But I'm quite sure I can find an expert in that field who will tell me more about it when I get back to London. I googled it but came up with nothing. I didn't really know what I was looking for. So, the owner of the Chinese box was called Marlene Hartley was she, Jack?"

Jack nodded. Lara reached into her bag and brought out the silver bell and cigarette box. "These belonged to Marlene as well then?"

Jack picked up the bell, examined it and put it on the table. He ran his finger over the small crest on top of the cigarette box.

"This looks English to me. The crest is too small to work out what it might be though. Any ideas Lara?"

She shook her head. "I used my loupe but still couldn't figure it out. I also think it's English, and the bell, which has no markings on it at all."

Piet frowned at the wooden box. "*Ag man*, never did understand the Chinese." He stole a look at Jack from beneath his thick lashes. "Bit like the British, never understood them either, always talking about the weather and they eat funny things as well."

Jack laughed. "Don't take any notice of Piet, Lara. He likes to take a poke at me about being English. The remark was aimed at me not you."

Piet ignored him, then turned and smiled at Lara. "So, tell me, my girl, why would some Chinese person make a box like this with no way to open it. See here, no lines anywhere, no lid to be opened. The wood is not thick enough to make this box so heavy, must be something in it."

Lara shrugged her slim, now lightly tanned shoulders, watching as Jack took the box from Piet and studied it himself. He shook it, if there was anything inside it didn't move.

Jack whistled softly and they both looked at him. "I think I know what this is…even though there are no lines or openings anywhere, I think it's a Chinese puzzle box."

Piet rolled his eyes. "Well, my friend, you got that right. Of course it's a *bleddy* puzzle box, it's why we can't open it. *Jeez,* Jack, can't you come up with something better than that?"

Jack frowned at him and Lara suppressed a giggle. "Hear me out, Piet, okay? A Chinese puzzle box, from what I can remember, looks as though it's solid with no openings, that's why it's a puzzle, see? But there is a way of opening it if you know how. Might be something of interest inside, you never know. A bit more info about this Hartley woman."

Piet looked hopeful. "Go on then, Jack, open it up."

Regretfully Jack put the box carefully back on the table. "I would if I knew how, but I don't. It takes a certain kind of brain to know how to do it. It's like a Rubik's Cube, you have to know the sequence of movements to get all the right colours lined up – never cracked it myself."

Piet stood up and picked up his scruffy cap. "Right then. I can't wait for you to find an expert in London, so long. We need to see what's inside this box, if anything."

He rammed his hat on his head. Hope scrambled clumsily to her feet and stood next to him.

"Where are you off to in such a hurry then, Piet?" Jack called to his retreating back.

"Going to find me a Chinaman, so long. See you just now," and he sauntered off.

Lara looked at Jack. "Where on earth is Piet going to find a Chinese person out here in the bush?"

"Trust me, Lara. If there is a Chinese to be found – Piet will find him, or her. He has a massive network of contacts all over the country. He'll find someone – the trick will be to see if the person he comes up with knows how to open a Chinese puzzle box. He'll probably go somewhere this evening and have a Chinese dinner in town, there's always a Chinese restaurant in every town. That's where he'll start."

She looked puzzled. "He said he would see us just now, so I guess we should wait and see what he suggests."

Jack snorted with laughter. "Ah, Lara, it's a common expression here. Just now can mean precisely that, but it can also mean this afternoon, tonight, tomorrow or next week!"

*****

The man, sitting at another table in the garden appeared to be reading his newspaper and drinking a coffee.

He had watched the security man, in his dark uniform with the epaulettes, the woman with the box and the tall man with the wild blond hair.

He glanced over the top of the newspaper again. The security man had walked off with his dog and the other two continued to talk together, the tantalising box sitting on the table between them.

The security man would be the one to watch. He recognised the type, mid-fifties, average height, well built, ex-police, no doubt. He had watched him walk into the bar the night before, his eyes raking the faces in the room, missing nothing.

Yes, he would definitely have to watch him.

The tall blond man was now standing, he reached for the box and tucked it under his arm. The woman headed for reception. He watched the blond man as he walked past.

He folded his newspaper carefully, finished his coffee and went back to his room.

Chapter Twenty-Five

L ara left her precious box with Jack. He told her he would keep it in his room, he was going to be working all day and it would be quite safe under his watchful eye.

"Go speak to Blessing at Reception, Lara. You said you wanted to go on safari for a couple of days? He'll arrange it for you. You don't need to go to any of the safari operators in town, he'll fix everything for you and make recommendations, it's what he does."

Jack smiled at her. "Take a drive around town, you'll enjoy it, very safari, lots of good-looking rangers walking around. It'll give you a feel for the bush and the people who live around the Kruger. There's a real buzz to the town, lots of quirky shops selling all things safari, but no rare silver pieces I'm afraid. There are a couple of antique dealers in town, so go and take a look, who knows what you might find amongst the old dusty steamer trunks, boxes of books and what have you."

*****

Jack had finished feeding Harry, with the latest goings on in South Africa, trying to keep it light, more of social events, horse racing, polo matches, gallery openings, surfing competitions, restaurant openings, wine award events, keeping well away from politics. The wonderful work of the charity organisation called Gift of the Givers. There was always something good to write about them. He knew Harry's UK readers enjoyed a bit of glamour with their porridge every Sunday morning.

He was reading through what he had written when there was a tap on his door.

Piet poked his head around the door. "Hey, Jack. Thought I would spend a bit of time with you and chew the fat. All quiet around the hotel at the moment."

He sat himself down and frowned. "Not writing bad stuff about my country are you, my friend?"

Jack closed down his laptop and smiled. "No, Piet, not at all, only the good stuff. Did you find your Chinaman?"

Piet rolled his eyes. "You can't just go out into a town like Hazyview and find a Chinese person who knows how to unlock a secret puzzle box, Jack. But a Chinese restaurant will be the place to start…"

Jack sat down next to his ex-detective friend. "So, tell me Piet, how's it all going here? Apart from the tourists and the guests, who are the life blood of this place, whom you dislike so much, is everything else to your liking?"

Piet gave him one of his rare smiles. "*Ja*, Jack. This is a good place to work. I like Hugo, even though he is English, but fortunately after living here for over twenty years he is more like us than the English. The Englishness is rubbing off him, unlike you, but I have hope for you, my friend."

Jack looked up as the door was nudged open and in came the ever-smiling face of Piet's dog, Hope. She greeted Piet as though he had been gone for weeks.

Piet sighed. "Useless *bleddy* dog. Anyways, as I was telling you, at first it was difficult to up the *kak* security when I started here.

"Hugo didn't want the property fenced with barbed wire, electric gates and fences, cameras, and so on. He agreed to a few things, but wanted this hotel to be like one of those country places you have back where you come from, where nothing much happens, except for a fox or two slinking past, raiding a dustbin. I don't think he realised the high level of crime might one day pitch up at his place, so long."

Piet stroked his dog's head. "Anyways, when he said no to my recommendations, I thought about it and made a plan. I contacted one of my old buddies in the police and told him what I was looking for. Then, one day this Zulu warrior pitched up in Reception, wearing his traditional stuff, leopard skin headband, feathers, shield and not much else I can tell you."

He ran his hand through his short hair and grinned. "Some of the guests freaked out thinking the Zulus had finally arrived to take back what was theirs. I took him to my office. He's a splendid looking fellow, as you English would say. When he was young living in a *kraal,* the village where he was born in what is now Kwa Zulu Natal, he wanted to be a warrior like his forefathers before him. But unfortunately, there were no more wars to be fought, although you can never be quite sure of anything in this country.

"The Zulus also have a long and bitter memory of the past, as we have. They can wait a very long time before they strike again, they wait and watch as they have always done... behind the bushes. Then when they're ready they rise up as one, rattling their spears against their skin shields – scaring the hell out of everyone. Hey, they even beat you Brits at one point. I mean what were your soldiers thinking of, my friend, wearing bright red uniforms? Sitting ducks, they were.

"*Eish*, I have to say, they put up a good fight. Although, after they had slaughtered the entire regiment, the Zulu's raised their assegais and shields in salute to their bravery. But, hey, Jack the Brits still didn't win did they – didn't see the salute, the gesture of respect. Shame, hey?"

Jack wasn't going to let him get away with that remark. "That maybe so Piet, but may I remind you we British won the two great wars – just saying'."

Piet leaned back. "Whatever," he muttered, and continued.

"Anyways, this Zulu left his village and joined the police. The Murder and Robbery squad is where he ended up. The Zulu people are no strangers to blood and violence, Jack, but like you with your cold cases and the things you saw, he eventually decided he didn't have the guts for it anymore. Enough was enough already.

"That's where I found him and offered him the job of watching over the hotel at night. Hugo, being the public relations man he is, saw some potential in him, as I did."

Piet ran his hand down his dog's back and grinned. *"Jeez,* that Zulu was scary to look at, my friend. He was over six foot tall, very black, never smiled. But, of course, you can't have a Zulu warrior walking around a place dressed like that, terrifying the guests and showing his bare bum?"

Jack snorted with laughed as Piet continued.

"He took the job. Had to have a uniform of course, can't have someone like him covering everything in front, and not much behind. But we allowed him to wear his leopard skin headband with a few feathers and his leopard skin cape. Of course, we assured the guests the leopard skin cape was not real leopard skin, guests are funny about real fur and stuff these days, Jack. But, of course, it was real. The man had his pride after all, wasn't going to toss a fake fur cape over his big black shoulders.

"Anyways, this proud Zulu warrior, his name is Shaka, yeah, yeah, I know. He works here now, for me. Scary bugger, silent as a ghost, never smiles – ever."

Jack frowned. "I haven't seen him around, Piet."

"Nah, you wouldn't see him around. He does the night shift, gives me a much-needed break. You can only see the whites of his eyes as he moves silently through the grounds at night. He even makes me nervous, so long. But he's good. Shows no emotion, just gets on with the job."

Piet sat back in his chair. "Hugo loves having him around. The guests, when they catch a glimpse of him, know they are safe with a real taste of South African history on their doorstep. Sometimes Hugo has a *braai* outside for his guests. Then out of the darkness comes this Zulu warrior, wearing his feathers and skins, brandishing his spears and shield, scaring the hell out of everyone, then he sits with the guests and tells them stories of his people's past. They love it, Jack, South Africa and its history, right here in the hotel grounds."

Jack smiled at his animated friend. "So, what are you going to tell me next Piet?"

Piet nudged the dog with his foot. "The puzzle box will be quite safe with you. Tomorrow I'm hoping someone will come and be able to discover its secrets, if it has any."

There was another tentative knock at the door. Jack went to see who it was and was surprised to see Lara standing there.

"Hey, come on in. Piet and I were just talking about your box."

Lara took the only other available chair in Jack's room. Piet had taken over the other one. Jack sat at the desk where he did his writing.

Lara sat and looked around. "Nice room, mine is nicer. So much space compared to hotel rooms in the UK. Unless you are wealthy enough to pay for a suite in a swanky hotel. A suite which you could safely accommodate my entire flat in."

Jack bent forward and put his elbows on his knees. "So, tell me Lara, what have you decided about your safari. What did Blessing suggest?"

Lara frowned. "Blessing, just love his name too, told me there were four other people booked to go on a two-day safari to the Kruger tomorrow morning, and there was room for me... two from France and two from Italy."

She looked slightly embarrassed. "The thing is, and I don't want to sound pretentious, but I don't fancy sitting with a bunch of other people I don't know. I've always been a bit of a loner and I don't want to have to sit and make idle chatter. I don't speak Italian, although my French is passable. I just want to soak up the atmosphere of the bush, see the animals…" she finished lamely.

"I know what you mean," Piet muttered. "Can't think of anything worse than a bunch of people jabbering away in a foreign language. Nah, the bush can only be enjoyed in silence, so long, with a fire crackling, throwing up embers into the night, a nice *braai* going, the smell of chops spitting and cooking and *boerewors*. The sound of the animals going about their business, the insects humming and chirping away in the background, the dark skies drowning in stars."

He looked slyly at Jack. He had set the stage, now all he needed was the participants.

"Hey, Jack?" His face was a picture of pure innocence. "Now here's an idea, my friend. Why don't you take Lara on safari for a couple of days? I'll clear it with Hugo, you can take one of the hotel vehicles, without any other guests. You've been on a safari or two, you can spot an elephant from a kudu, well, I hope you can. One has big ears the other big horns.

"Whilst you're away I can do a bit of checking on this Marlene Hartley and wait for my Chinese code breaker. I'll put the box in the hotel safe, so long".

He turned to Lara. "Don't worry, my girl, once I find this Chinese person, I'll wait until you both get back, so we can see together, what's inside – if anything? Good plan, hey, what do you think?"

Jack narrowed his eyes. Piet was a wily old fox; he knew exactly what he was up to. Those eyes, which missed nothing, had seen the attraction between himself and Lara.

Lara swept back her long dark hair and looped it behind her ears, her big grey eyes wide with excitement. "Oh, I would love to! It sounds perfect. What do you think Jack? Can you take a couple of days off? Your readers might like to take a trip to the Kruger with us. I think it's a great idea."

Jack tried to look non-committal. He had met all his deadlines with Harry. He could easily take a couple of days off and Lara was right, his readers would love an account of a self-drive safari in the Kruger National Park.

Oh yes. There was nothing Jack would like more than to have Lara to himself for a couple of days and get to know her. He could almost smell those chops spitting and cooking as he sat there alone with the lovely Lara. He wondered what her hair would feel like sifting through his fingers, he thought it might smell of freshly picked apples.

No music, no screaming sirens, no hooting of cars, no noisy motor bikes. Only him and Lara alone in the bush.

Piet grinned at him. "*Ag*, Jack, don't pretend you don't want to do it, or you don't have enough time. This is what Africa is all about, a moment in time. A moment to be seized before it's gone."

Jack shrugged resignedly. "Could be good for my next column, I suppose," he said casually. "What do you think Lara? Would it work for you?"

Lara smiled at him. Oh yes, her smiling face said it all; this would certainly work for her.

Piet hauled himself out of his chair. "Come on Hopeless, time to do some work, if you're up for it, which I doubt."

Hope rolled over and stood up, then followed Piet out into the grounds of the hotel.

Chapter Twenty-Six

Hugo had made all the arrangements necessary for Lara and Jack's self-drive safari. A large hamper with enough food to keep them going for days, was already stowed in the vehicle in a cooler box.

In another box one of the waiters had packed plates, cutlery, cups, saucers, glasses and napkins.

The vehicle was waiting at the front of the hotel when Lara and Jack appeared from their rooms with their overnight bags.

Piet was leaning next to the vehicle waiting for them.

Jack got behind the wheel, Lara hopped into the passenger seat. Jack started the engine, trying to ignore her long legs exposed by a short khaki skirt. He failed.

Piet leaned into the driver's window. "Only ten kilometres to the entrance of the park, Jack. Here's your accommodation voucher which you need to show at the gate and your permit to drive around. Keep to the main public roads at all times, no going off road, you hear, and keep to the speed limit. Do not get out of the vehicle under any circumstances. Strictly forbidden.

"The directions to your rest camp are on the back of the voucher. The kitchen staff have prepared a hamper for you, you'll find everything you need stowed in the back. There's a couple of *braai* bags there as well. All you have to do, my friend, is sling one on the *braai* and set it alight. Even an Englishman wouldn't be able to screw it up. No messing around with kindling, wood and *braai* bricks, hey, and don't burn the chops…"

He slapped the side of the vehicle. "See you in a couple of days, I should have found my Chinese puzzle cracker by then. Enjoy yourselves, so long."

He raised his arm in farewell. Jack put the vehicle into gear and set off down the drive.

They went through the formalities at the entrance to the Kruger then set off, keeping well within the speed limit to see what they might find. The bush was green and lush, the vegetation thick in places, then wide open spaces where Lara would be able to see zebra, giraffe, kudu, springbok and other buck as they grazed.

There were plenty of other vehicles on the tarred and gravel roads, including tiered safari vehicles, like the one they were driving, packed with eager tourists.

The day was heating up. They came across six or eight vehicles all parked in a huddle watching something. Jack pulled up alongside them.

"Oh, Jack! Look lions and their babies, and so close to the road." A female lioness looked up at the vehicles, flicked her golden ears then flopped down in the grass. Lara could hear the playful cubs squeaking and mewing as they chased each other around their elders, climbing over their sleeping mothers, biting and batting at their flicking tails.

They watched them for a while before driving slowly off again. A large herd of elephant were crossing the road ahead of them. Jack braked and kept well back so as not to impede their progress.

"Gosh, they're massive when you get close up, quite scary. Don't let's get any closer Jack, I can see everything quite well enough from here."

Jack smiled. She was nervous, he didn't blame her, they were big buggers up close. "Okay, let's wait until they've all crossed then we'll find a rest spot and have a bit of lunch. We can stretch our legs and watch some humans."

Lara looked at him nervously. "Piet said not to get out of the vehicle, will it be safe then?"

Jack squeezed her hand reassuringly. "As long as it's a designated picnic spot and we stick to the Park rules we'll be perfectly safe."

Jack found a rest spot half an hour later. There was a round table and half-moon shaped seats, all made of cement, sheltering under a heavily leaved tree, offering a skirt of shade.

They lunched on cold chicken, potato salad and a fresh baguette, as they listened to the sounds of the bush around them. In the trees small vervet monkeys, their black faces fringed with white fur, peeped down at them through the leaves, hoping to grab a spot of lunch themselves. Jack made sure the lunch hamper was securely closed.

They washed their lunch down with a cold beer, before loading everything back into the vehicle and setting off again.

Jack glanced at the clock on the dashboard. It was almost three o'clock. He turned to Lara who was still looking a little nervous.

"Tell you what, why don't we head for our rest camp, settle in, have a shower and then sit outside and have an ice-cold glass of wine, as we watch the sun go down? Apparently, there's a water hole close to our rooms, might be a bit more comfortable, and cooler, to watch the game come down to drink. They can come to us for a change."

Lara smiled at him. "Sounds wonderful. Let's do that. It's so hot at the moment. I could do with a cold shower and a glass of icy wine sounds perfect. I can relax and watch you slave over your barbecue. Sounds good to me."

*****

Lara looked around her thatched *rondavel* it was compact but absolutely spotless. Two single beds taut with snowy white sheets and a light cream blanket draped over the ends. There was a squat white box between the beds with a lamp. A simple shower, basin and toilet, and best of all, an air conditioner which she immediately switched on, full blast.

Outside on the dark green cement patio was a square wooden table with two wicker chairs, two long sun chairs with yellow striped cushions and a fridge in the corner, humming quietly with life. A few steps down, a permanent barbecue structure, scrupulously clean with its tongs and a long fork, placed on the grid and a fire ready to light. Her room looked out over the bush; she could see the water hole glinting in the distance.

She sank into one of the chairs and sighed. This was perfect, absolutely perfect.

Jack's *rondavel*, identical to hers she presumed, was within shouting distance. She could see him sitting on his patio looking over the same scene as she was.

Lara had wondered what the sleeping arrangements might be. But now knowing Jack as she did, she knew he wouldn't pull any surprises and have them sharing a room. Apart from being a hard-nosed international journalist, he was a gentleman through and through.

She went back inside, shrugged off her clothes and took her longed-for shower. Then she changed into a loose, pale blue dress and drifted back outside. The patio was still hot under her feet from the day's heat. She sat in a chair, put her feet up on the low wall and let her wet hair dry in the warm air.

"Hey, Lara?" Jack called across. "How about the promised glass of wine? I have an enormous hamper here from the hotel, shall we see what delights it might hold?"

She gave him the thumbs up sign and within minutes he was heaving the hamper over. "I'll leave you to see what's inside. There's another couple of boxes in the vehicle which I need to retrieve."

He came back and dumped another box on the low table near the fridge, then went back once again to see what else the staff at the hotel had provided.

Lara opened the box and gasped. A snowy white tablecloth with the hotel logo, crystal glasses, silver cutlery, napkins, silver candlestick holders and a posy of frangipani flowers wrapped in ice and plastic, complete with a cut glass flower holder.

She set to work. By the time Jack finished unpacking the vehicle she had the cloth draped over the wooden table and the table set; complete with the wine glasses, the flowers in their exquisite bowl and the candles in their holders ready to be lit.

Lara stood back and admired her table. Romantic didn't even begin to describe it. Fine dining in the bush; the table looked as though it belonged in a five-star restaurant in London.

She opened the hamper holding the cooler box and peeped inside. She stacked the contents into her fridge, lifted out the platter with the steak, chops and sausages, already marinated, and set it down near the barbecue on the shelf provided.

The wine was ice cold, she lifted a bottle out and placed it into a silver bucket, surrounding it with ice cubes from the modest freezer.

Jack brought the paper bag Piet had insisted he would need for his *braai*. He dumped it on the ground and turned around. "Wow! This looks fantastic. You've made it all look great, Lara."

"Okay, I'm going to take a quick shower and change, then I'll be back. In your bathroom there should be a can of something called Peaceful Sleep, you might want to give yourself a quick spray. It was hot and humid today and I think there might be a bit of a storm tonight, the mozzies will be out in their droves," he hesitated. "You are taking your anti-malaria pills, aren't you?"

She waved her hand at him. "Off you go Jack, don't be long, let's watch the sun go down and have the glass of wine you promised me. It's chilling as we speak. The sky looks fantastic, all gold and cream tinged with pink…"

*****

The impala tip-toed towards the water hole, their ears twitching as they watched warily for predators, making soft sneezing noises before bending their necks and lapping at the water, sending ripples of gold and pink across the still surface.

Lara watched as Jack ignited the barbecue. He was a good-looking guy, and looked particularly good in his khaki shorts and shirt, but more than this, there was a gentleness about him, as though he had seen enough of what human beings could do to each other. There was a humility about him which she found endearing.

As she watched the animals, the redness of the sky as the sun sank behind the achingly hot bush, and the concert of sounds as evening fell, she knew life after this would be a poor second. She didn't want to go home. She wanted this more than any piece of antique silver she might discover. No, she didn't want to go back to the life she had known.

Jack presented her with his efforts. Sizzling chops, perfectly cooked steaks and bronzed sausages. Garlic bread warmed in the coals, sending a heady aroma around the prepared salad. Potatoes wrapped in tin foil had nestled in the hot embers, once opened, squeezed and slathered in butter, adding to the feast in front of them. They sat together eating contentedly, listening and watching, saying nothing.

Darkness descends suddenly in the bush. Jack lit the candles, refilled their glasses, and they sat back looking up at the majesty of the canopy of stars above them, completely satiated.

Lara pulled a shawl over her shoulders, against the slight chill in the air. She turned to him.

"So, Jack, tell me more about you. You know all about me, now it's your turn."

He shrugged, and took a sip of his wine. "Born in the UK. Went to the right schools, Eton as a weekly boarder, then Cambridge. My parents had high hopes for me; lawyer, doctor, whatever. But I excelled in English. Even when I was twelve, I could write a compelling story. I knew I wanted to be a journalist.

"I was an avid watcher of the news. I liked to work things out, why people did such diabolical things to each other. How people got away with what they did. How people disappeared without a trace. How the ones left behind coped with such terrible losses. I became fixated on knowing there was an answer out there. Someone knew something about something? It's been my mantra for years.

"I used to drive my parents nuts with all my questions. I wanted the answers – badly, but they didn't have them. So that's how I ended up doing what I do now. Trying to find answers to questions. What actually happened? Why? I like to think I brought some comfort to the ones left behind with some of the answers to what had happened to their loved ones, but I doubt very much if I did. Losing someone you love is a deep hole to fill – if that's possible. I don't think it is."

Lara took a sip of her wine. A bat flew swiftly past, she ducked her head. "What about your love life, Jack, if you don't mind me asking?"

"I've fallen in and out of love. Haven't we all? But my line of work then, in London, didn't make for pleasant conversation. I was obsessed with finding the truth about cases which would turn most people's stomachs. Didn't make for pleasant romantic dinner dates. A bit like asking an undertaker about his day at the office, or parlour."

"So how did you end up here then?"

"It was another case. A child missing for twenty years, here in South Africa. I chased the story and fell in love with one of the people involved. But it didn't work out."

Lara felt the atmosphere change slightly, sensing by his body language he had been hurt badly. She quickly changed the subject.

"Do you think you'll be able to find out exactly who Marlene Hartley was?"

He smiled at her. "Oh, yes. With Piet and all his contacts across the country, we'll find out she was. Why she ended up as she did. It's what we do. Pursue the story."

Lara took a deep breath, looking up at the dazzling stars above them. She sighed. "I don't want to go home, Jack, I want to stay here…"

"You're on a business trip, with a holiday slotted in between. Thousands of people who come here feel the same way, Lara. Visiting here and living here are two different things entirely."

Lara stood up. She went behind Jack and draped her arms around his neck. "I like you, Jack, very much. I want to remember tonight…I'm not asking for happy ever after. I loved today but I have to tell you although it was wonderful to see all the animals, they scared me. I preferred my gallop at Cloud's End, I wasn't afraid there.

"I'd be happy not to go and look for any more game tomorrow, just sit here and watch the day, see what happens. I guess I'm one of the rare few who find the whole thing about wild animals truly terrifying."

He clasped her wrists between his hands and looked up at her. "I can't promise you anything. Only what we have now."

"It's okay, Jack. All we ever have is now."

Lightening slashed across the dark sky, followed by a huge deep rumbling of thunder. The temperature had dropped and the stars had disappeared. The rain scattered across the stone floor of the patio, then within minutes it was a sheet of thundering rain.

Lara disentangled herself from Jack and stepped lightly down the steps. Throwing her arms up in the air she lifted her face to the rain. Swooping and turning, she laughed. "Come on, Jack, this is fabulous. Come and dance in the rain with me. It's glorious!"

There was no music, only the roaring of the wind and rain. He held her in his arms, and they danced to nature's fury, their clothes clinging to their bodies, her hair wet against his cheek.

Then he took her hand and led her up the steps and through to the bedroom.

Chapter Twenty-Seven

Piet Joubert, rubbed his hands together, cracked his knuckles and got down to work. He spent some time studying his private list of contacts, or 'connections' as he liked to call them, which he had built up over the past decade or two.

Finally, he found what he was looking for. A contact in Home Affairs, the government department who monitored all entries to and departures from South Africa, and who had a database containing the identity number of every person who was a permanent resident or citizen of the country, or a visitor. Personal and private information available to only a few – one of them being Piet's contact – Bertie Erasmus.

Bertie had once been a part of the bigger scheme of things before the country moved into the new phase of its history. Although not on the front line anymore, working for Home Affairs, he was still valued as a computer expert, second to none. He worked for the Government in a private capacity now, as a valued consultant with years of experience.

Piet tapped his number into the phone.

"*Yebo*, Piet, *howzit*? You never call me unless you want something, so what is it?"

They spent a few brief moments exchanging pleasantries, then Piet moved smoothly in.

"Listen Bertie, my man. I need some help with something here. A buddy of mine is trying to find something out about an old friend of his who died out on a farm near Wolmaransstad. Her name was Marlene Hartley, she died a year ago. I don't have the exact date for you. But her death must have been registered somewhere in order for the lawyers to wind up the estate. She must be in your database somewhere?"

He heard Bertie cough and then let out a long sigh. "Hey, listen, I'm good, very good, but I need more information. Any identity number, address, was she married, husband's name? Passport number, maybe? Children? Mobile phone number? Her age would be useful?"

"Bugger all on that side, Bertie. Maybe in her sixties? But you'll find a way, you always come up with the goodies. The farm was called Cloud's End, it's all I can give you."

"*Jeez*, Piet, can you at least tell me where she came from? English, South African, Australian, give me a clue?"

"That's it, my friend, it's all I have. I need the info now?"

A heavy sigh came down the phone. "Okay I'll do my best. I owe you for sorting out the little business with my wife, or ex-wife as she is now. Give me a day or so, okay?"

"Wait a minute, before you go, can you check on some number plates for me, also a name? Daniel Van Heerden?" He gave him the number plate.

Bertie sighed. "Christ, Piet - Van Heerden! There will be thousands of them with that name here. Have you got an ID number for me?"

Piet rattled it off and waited, hearing Bertie pecking away at his computer.

"Okay, the plates match the name and the ID number of said Professor Daniel Van Heerden. But I have no address for him. Pays his television licence, files his tax returns, not even a parking fine. Can I go now please?"

Piet rang off. Sounded like a dead end then. Daniel Van Heerden was legit.

Piet put the phone down on the table and scratched Hope's golden head. "Okay, let's give you some dinner. Then I have to chase a Chinese code cracker. "You can hang out in the bar whilst I go and enjoy a Chinese dinner in town. We're on our way to another story, Hope, I can feel it in these bones of mine."

Hope wolfed down her dinner in minutes, skidding the bowl around the floor, lapping up every last bit. Piet took her through to the bar, telling Hugo he was going out for a couple of hours.

"Hey, almost forgot to mention something, Hugo. Jack is thinking of re-locating from Franschhoek, can't take the heat of summer down there. He's thinking of moving to this area. Put the word out, will you? Something simple and furnished he said. Not some great *larney* place with a garden the size of a rugby field."

Hugo glanced around the busy room. "Sure thing, Piet. Someone will know someone who is looking for a tenant." He clicked his fingers at Hope. "Come on girl, I've got some biltong for you behind the bar."

"Hey, Hugo, I know you're busy, but tell me something. The guy sitting at the end of the bar, with the white hair? Has he been in here before? Is he a regular?"

Hugo looked around quickly. "Daniel, you mean? No, he's not a regular, he's one of my guests. Nice chap, Afrikaans, lives out on a farm, not far from here. Writes books, historical novels apparently. Look I have to go Piet…"

*****

Lara and Jack spent the following day sitting on the wooden deck down at the water-hole, shaded from the heat by the generous thatch covering it, watching the game and the brightly coloured birds swooping down to drink.

The hours passed in idle chatter, both of them dozing as the day became hotter. At lunch time they retreated back to Lara's room and raided the hamper.

That afternoon they retreated even further into her air-conditioned bedroom, emerging some hours later to find that evening had stealthily approached.

They finished the contents of the cooler box with another *braai* before walking back to the jetty, hand in hand, to watch the hippos playing in the water, grunting and belly laughing, splashing the water around them and blowing up plumes of spray and twitching their ears before sinking down again into the cool water, sending hardly a ripple across the fast-darkening water reflecting the blood red of the sky.

Jack glanced at Lara, her long straight hair lifting slightly in the breeze as she took a sip of her wine. He liked everything about her, especially her laughter.

She pointed to a tree to the left of the water hole. "I was watching some yellow birds this morning, diving in and out of what looked like miniature haystacks in the tree over there. They seemed so busy, building nests, I think. Their nests looked like Christmas decorations, so neat and round."

Jack looked to where she was pointing. "Ah, yes, they're weaver birds, the architects of the bush. The male spends hours and hours building what he thinks is a perfectly engineered and very acceptable

112

nest for his lady love, then she comes to inspect all his hard work as he waits anxiously by to see if it passes muster.

"She checks everything out and if she doesn't like it much, she lets him know, pecking angrily away at his delicate weaving skills, making holes all over the place. Then the poor bugger has to start all over again and build something more to her liking, desperately hoping she'll like his next masterpiece."

Lara threw back her head and laughed. "If they were a newly married human couple, I doubt the marriage would last very long. Maybe after the third or fourth attempt he goes down to the pub to find someone less bad-tempered and more accepting!"

Jack laughed and reached for her hand. "You have a vivid imagination, Ms Summers."

For the first time in almost three years, he felt truly happy. The two days in the Kruger were ones he would remember for a long time. Lara was easy to be with, as curious about life as he was and she made him laugh with her questions about life in South Africa. She would find it hard to leave behind when she returned to London next week.

He also knew a tenuous love affair where the two people involved lived on different continents had only a slight chance of longevity. He had been down that road before and ended up alone.

Jack knew he would never return to England permanently; this was his home now. As for Lara, he knew she would come back in a heartbeat if she thought their relationship could become permanent.

But he was not ready for that kind of commitment. Lara had a plane to catch and he had a story to investigate.

All they had, as Lara had said the night before, was now. They would be returning to Hazyview at first light tomorrow.

Chapter Twenty-Seven

The next day, a voice over the phone told Piet, in perfect English, that perhaps his son would be able to help with the puzzle of the box.

"He is, and always has been, good with computers. He has a curious mind. He is top of his class with all these things."

They arranged a time for Mr Chan to bring his son, William, to the hotel. Piet knew Lara and Jack would be back sometime during the day.

At around six in the evening, Piet, Jack and Lara sat together, the box in front of them, waiting for Mr Chan and his son.

A dark shadow appeared at the window of Piet's cottage. He stood up and opened the door. "Ah, good evening, Shaka, you have brought my guests?"

Shaka nodded, unsmiling. "I have brought two people from a land far away. The people who steal our ivory, our rhino and pangolin. Their eyes are different to ours, *sah*. They speak like they are singing in this their language."

Piet smiled at him. "They are not all bad people, Shaka, only some of them. Bring them in please."

William was a tall gangly teenager. His face pock marked with the traces of acne, wisps of downy hair grew along his jawline, his eyes framed by thick glasses. He looked around nervously, pushing his glasses back on his nose with his forefinger.

His father pushed him forward then stood in the corner of Piet's cottage with his hands laced in front of him. His son would be well paid if he could open the box in front of the three people sitting in front of him.

Nervously young Willian picked up the box and examined it closely.

"Hah! This beautiful box, very valuable, made by master craftsman in China!" He turned it back and forth, looking underneath.

114

Then he stretched out his arms, cracked his knuckles and felt around the box.

Lara, Jack and Piet watched him closely. Suddenly a piece of the box, no bigger than half a wooden ruler they had all used at school, moved slightly to the right. Lara reached for Jack's hand and squeezed it with excitement.

They all looked at each other, then back at the box, as the young boy's fingers moved around. Slowly at first, then as he worked out the puzzle of it, more deftly.

The box was a master of secret panels, each one moving in symphony with the other. Pieces moved back and forward and down as William manipulated the puzzle of the box.

There was a light 'ping' and William sat back, grinning. "Hah! This box now open…"

The box looked completely different, with pieces sticking out at all angles. Jack leaned forward. A tiny key with a few wisps of silk beckoned.

William turned it and pulled. A drawer slid out. Within its depths it revealed a thick dark blue book with the faded outline of a phoenix branded on its cover.

William fiddled some more. "Hah! Here two more drawers hidden. Hard to find, different way to open."

Using two thumbs William pulled at another red tassel and the drawer opened with another 'ping.' This drawer was empty. Finally, William located the last drawer and applied the same technique, inside was one faded photograph.

Lara reached forward and lifted out the blue book, then pulled out the photograph. She stared at it. Then she laid everything out on the table so Jack and Piet could see.

William gave the box a final shake. "Box empty now."

William's father coughed discreetly, his son stood up and hooked his rucksack over his shoulder. "When you want to close box, put pieces back, quite simple. Hah! Excellent box by master of puzzles in China."

Piet stood up, passing the young man an envelope. "Well done, my boy, thank you."

A dark shadow loomed up at the window again, then opened the door. "It is I, Shaka, who will see these visitors to the gate, *sah*."

Piet thanked him then returned to his chair, he fumbled in his pocket for his glasses and reached for the book. Lara picked up the photograph again.

A couple, the man wearing a Panama hat and dark glasses, the woman also wearing a hat and sunglasses, somewhere hot she guessed. Both of them sitting astride horses.

"I wonder if this is Marlene and maybe her husband?" she murmured to herself.

Piet flicked through the pages of the book and dislodged three more photographs. He stared at them. Then placed them next to the couple on horseback.

Two young men near a river somewhere, lying beneath the shade of a tree, possibly the UK.

A little boy holding the hand of a young Chinese woman, with long dark straight hair beneath a conical hat, who looked shyly at the camera, her hand over her mouth as if to hide a smile.

The fourth, and final photograph, caught her attention immediately. It was her puzzle box. She checked the back of it, no date, but the words written there sent a shiver down her spine.

So, you have found your way into my box, discovered my past perhaps? Now what will you do... apart from being extremely careful? There's a digit missing somewhere. You'll never find it.'

Wordlessly, she handed it to Jack. Piet looked up. "You're doing the thing with your foot again, Jack. Let's see what you've got there?"

Piet stared at the writing on the back of the photograph. "Well, well, well, what do we have here then?"

He looked at Piet to see him scowling as he turned the pages of the blue book. "What have you got Piet, anything interesting?"

"Nah, looks like a hysterical child was let loose with a pencil. Just a bunch of squiggles and dots and some numbers now and again." He handed Jack the book. Lara leaned over to take a look.

Lara sighed. "I was so hoping it would be a diary or something, but it does look like a scribble book of some sort. What an odd thing to hide away in a box, Jack."

Jack went quickly through the pages, then closed it softly with a grin.

Piet narrowed his eyes. "You've got that look, Jack, makes me nervous. Does the book remind you of your childhood, before you learned to write properly?"

They both looked at Jack. "Oh no, Piet. This is not a book full of childish scribble. This, my friend, is a language all of its own. It's called Pitman's shorthand; no-one uses it much anymore. Technology has taken over in almost every area where it was once used."

Jack picked up the book again and opened it at a random page. "See here, every one of these dots and squiggles, as you call them, means a word. Shorthand is phonetic, in other words it's the sound of the word which is used instead of the word itself.

"After shorthand came a dictation machine, then computers, then programs that convert speech to text. You talk into your telephone or computer, or whatever, and the programme instantly translates it into a text document. Shorthand started to lose its popularity in the late seventies."

He stared at random pages with their dots and dashes. "Journalists used it all the time, until technology replaced it. Although some journalists use a form of it even today, in case the battery runs out on their device. But not much, I have to say. I've certainly never used it, being the bright, tech savvy, young journalist I am…"

Piet scratched his head then ran his hands through his hair, determined not to let his friend out flank him. "*Ag*, yes, of course. It was used in courts, I remember now. Never understood it then, don't understand it now. How come you never learned it Jack, in the old days when you were starting out as a journalist?"

Jack laughed. "Looked too difficult to learn so I made up my own sort of shorthand. Now, as I said, it's mostly been replaced by technology. Depends what suits you, what you feel comfortable with."

Lara looked blank. "I've heard of it, but never actually seen it until now. So, guys, where will we find someone who can decipher all this for us? It looks like quite a tome."

Jack thought about it for a moment. "My editor, Harry, might be able to help us there. I need scanned copies of a few of the pages. I can send through to him. He'll find some retired secretary amongst his massive network who should be able to help. Taking pics of a few pages with my phone won't work with said elderly secretary, she, or he, will want proper pages, sent as an attachment."

Piet looked at his watch. "Need to go check around the hotel. Come on Hopeless, er, I mean Hope, let's get to work. See you guys later."

Jack also checked his watch. "I need to make a quick call to Harry, get him purring happily with my latest news."

He reached for the blue book. "Let me get Blessing to scan a few of the pages, then I'll send them on to Harry."

Lara looked at her box with its pieces of wood sticking out. "Okay, then I think we should put the book back in its secret drawer and try to put it back together again. I think it'll be safe there where it's obviously been hiding for years and years. Do you think you'll be able to open it again Jack, having watched William?"

"Yes, I think so, I'll give it a go anyway."

"I'll keep the photographs, Jack. I want to study them later with my loupe, see if I can come up with anything. I'll take the box back to my room."

"Okay. I'll come back in an hour. By the way you do like steak don't you?"

"Love it, but hugely expensive in restaurants at home…"

"Right then, I'll take you to the steakhouse in town, where you get the best steaks in the country. Their spare ribs are pretty good as well. I need to get my teeth into one of their rump steaks with crispy onions, golden chips and a Roquefort salad. I'm drooling just thinking about it!"

*****

Jack drummed his fingers on the table in his room, waiting for Harry to pick up.

"Where the hell have you been, Jack, tried to call you last night but no luck. Where were you? Not in a fancy game lodge, I hope. Budget won't stretch to that, not unless someone else is paying! Where's my goddam story?"

"Good evening to you too, Harry. I was, as a matter of fact, out in the bush. With a lovely woman…"

Harry groaned. "Now listen to me Jack, I need something more than your weekly column. I need a bloody story; my readers have come to expect it from you?"

"No pressure then, Harry? As a matter of fact, I do have something which I think will have you stretching those navy-blue braces of yours."

He quickly gave Harry an overview of the story he was now after. The deceased estate in the middle of nowhere, the mystery woman with a phobia about germs, who had shot herself. The Chinese box and all it had revealed so far and the silver box with the crest. How he had met Lara and what she had told him which had led him to this point.

"By the way Harry, the mysterious Chinese box has revealed a few things I need a bit of help with. I'm sending through a few pages of what I think is some kind of diary, thing is, it's all in Pitman's shorthand. Need you to find someone who can translate for Piet and I. But we need to be careful. The fact that the book was hidden in the first place means it's important to someone. So, whoever you choose to help needs to be completely trustworthy and have the ability to keep whatever is in this book confidential?"

Harry's voice brightened. "Right. Got it, and you're right to be cautious. Back with Piet on this one then, good news! Where are you exactly?"

"I'm back in Hazyview. Phew, the heat Harry. Franschhoek is too hot for me and a bit dull to tell the truth. The action is all up here in Hazyview. I can work from anywhere, so I'm going to look for a place to rent in this area. Not necessarily Hazyview, there are a few other places I like. White River might be a possibility…definitely not going to a place called Hot As Hell, or somewhere called Dullstroom, the names speak for themselves."

"I don't care what colour the bloody river is, whether it's hot as hell, or dull as buggery Jack," he boomed down the phone. "Just get after the story, will you?"

"It smells like an interesting one to me Harry. I'm on it. I'll send through the scans later this evening."

*****

An hour later, as promised, he went to Lara's room. "Here's your book back."

They both sat down on the patio, the open box now in front of them. Lara pulled open the drawer and carefully placed the book back in its hiding place. She struggled for a few minutes trying to get the smooth pieces of wood back into their original places, then gave up.

"You have a go, Jack, otherwise we'll be here for hours. I put the silver box and bell back in the safe."

Jack had watched William pushing and pulling the panels, he had seen immediately there was a knack to it. He rubbed his hands together and blew on his fingers.

"William pulled one panel out halfway before moving to the next one, once that one was halfway out the other panel moved all the way out, or up. So, let's see if I can apply the same technique to getting it all back together again to its original shape, using his method in reverse."

Fifteen minutes later he slid the last panel smoothly into place and turned to Lara with a triumphant smile. "There we go! I should be able to open it again as well. The drawers could be a challenge though, William used a different method to open those. Always loved puzzles as a kid, the more complicated the better."

Lara looked impressed. "So, everything is in the side panels, the lid doesn't open at all."

"Yup, it's a real beauty. A good find. Now, how about we go into town and get stuck into a steak?"

*****

Just before midnight, Jack and Lara returned to the hotel. The grounds were quiet, the guest rooms in darkness.

Lara unlocked the door to her room and turned on the lights. Jack followed her in.

Suddenly she stopped. "Oh, no Jack!"

Surprised he looked at her. "What?"

"My box! It's gone!

120

Chapter Twenty-Eight

Within five minutes of Jack's call, Piet was at the door of Lara's room. Still tucking his shirt into his trousers.

"*Jeez,* Jack what's the problem here?"

"It's the box Piet. Lara's box – it's gone. It was right there on her dressing table when we left for dinner. I put it there myself. We put the book back inside and I closed it up again, it wasn't easy but I managed."

Piet looked swiftly around the room, checking the windows. "You locked the door when you left?"

Lara nodded, looking pale. "Yes, absolutely. I had the key with me in my bag." She frowned. "Actually, no, I can't be one hundred percent I locked it, but I think I did. I always lock doors behind me, it's a habit living in London."

Within minutes the tall dark shape of Shaka appeared at the door. "There is trouble here, *sah*? I saw the lights of this room and your place, when all was supposed to be dark."

"Yes, there's trouble here, Shaka. Someone has entered the lady's room and stolen something of value from her."

Shaka shook his head. "This is not possible, *sah*. No-one has come through the gates, only these two people," he nodded to Jack and Lara. "They came a few minutes ago. I saw them enter the property and walk to this room."

Piet bent down and examined the lock on the door. "Go check with Blessing, see if all the spare keys to all the rooms are still locked in his cupboard in the office behind reception."

Shaka loped off as instructed.

Piet shook his head, looking worried and puzzled. Lara looked frightened and tearful.

Jack had other things on his mind. Piet's security of the hotel and grounds was faultless. As far as Jack knew there had never been a break-in at Hugo's hotel.

Until now.

Whoever had broken into Lara's room had been after one thing, and one thing only.

The Chinese puzzle box and what it contained.

Chapter Twenty-Nine

At dawn the next morning Piet went through to reception. "Morning Blessing. Let me check the computer for yesterday please?"

Blessing, looking concerned, turned the screen around for him to see. Piet scanned the screen. As was normal guests had checked out at ten, the day before. New guests had checked in after midday. There were no single bookings in or out.

The single male who had stayed there, Daniel van Heerden, had checked out the day before.

"Blessing, when the housekeeping staff arrive, please tell them to gather in the kitchen, I want to speak to them all. I'll be back in fifteen minutes. They should all have arrived by then.

"All the duplicate guest room keys were safely locked away, Shaka told me last night. Was there any guest who needed a duplicate key to get into their rooms, for whatever reason?"

Blessing shook his head. "No-one, Mr Piet. If a guest requires a duplicate key, a member of staff will always accompany the guest, open the room and return the key to me, where it is once again locked away."

Piet nodded thoughtfully. "I'm going to check with the guards at the gate before the day shift comes in. Make sure the housekeeping staff, the gardeners and kitchen staff are assembled."

*****

Piet addressed the worried looking staff in the kitchen. "An intruder broke into one of the guest rooms last night and stole an item of value.

"Housekeeping I want you to not only clean every room as you normally do, but keep your eyes open for anything unusual. The missing item is a decorated box, about the size of a shoe box. I want you to check everywhere, under the beds, behind the toilets – everywhere." He looked down. "If suitcases are open, or not so open, I want you to press the contents and feel for something solid and hard, not what we ever do, but this situation is different."

He turned to the gardeners. "Check all the grounds thoroughly. Behind the bushes, in the bushes, up in the trees, everywhere, in case the box was thrown away."

Then he turned to the kitchen staff. "I want you to go through the trash bags, before they are collected this morning, and see if you find anything."

He took a deep breath. "No-one is accusing anyone of anything. All of you have been with the Boss for many years. We need your eyes to see if we can find this box. Right, let's get to it."

Piet, with a subdued Hope at his heels, strode across the lawns to Lara's room. "We'll find the bastard who stole the box, Hope. Pity you're not a retriever, that's what we need now." He patted her head. "You know somethings going on, don't you, something different in the air?"

Jack, he recalled with a smile, hadn't put up any resistance to his suggestion he spend the night with Lara in her room. The woman had been understandably unnerved by the intrusion.

He tapped on Lara's door. It was almost seven thirty. "Hey, Jack," he called. "It's not room service with your coffee, it's me."

Jack opened the door; he was dressed but clearly hadn't got around to brushing his hair. "Lara's still asleep. Coffee sounds good, let me order some. It was a long night."

Piet gave him an innocent smile. "Yes, I'm sure it was. Mine was equally long but probably not as pleasurable."

Piet sat on a chair on the patio whilst Jack ordered the coffee. Then he came out and sat next to him. "So, what do you think, Piet?"

"Our intruder wanted one thing, and one thing only. The box. I don't think we're talking about your average *oke,* here. Nothing else in the room was disturbed, nothing else taken. The lock on the door had been tampered with, which makes me think we're dealing with a pro. Someone picked the lock, Jack, unless Lara did forget to lock her door. I don't want to think this, but I think it might have been another guest."

Jack tried to hide a yawn. "But how the hell did they know which room Lara was staying in?"

124

"They were watching, Jack. Most guests set off for the day around ten in the morning, or check out. Then the housekeeping staff move in and start the cleaning. Anyone could have walked into any of the rooms when the maids were busy tidying. They would have no idea if it was one of the guests who was staying in the room, they were cleaning. A quick look around a few rooms and the thief would have located Lara's room and the box."

A worried looking waiter delivered a coffee tray and placed it on the table, then hastily retreated.

Piet continued as he poured himself a large cup of coffee. "I have a meeting with Hugo in half an hour. He's not a happy bunny I can tell you. But I see no reason for any of the guests to get wind of what happened. We'll keep the matter quiet, so long."

Jack blew on his coffee. "Will you report it to the local police?"

"If Hugo agrees, then I think it better we don't, hey. Don't want a police vehicle rolling up the drive and asking the guests questions. Bad for business, my friend, very bad. No, I'll handle this. It's what I do. No dead bodies have been found, so, nah, nothing the police would be interested in."

Jack looked out over the grounds noticing more than the usual activity from the gardeners as they scoured the grounds for the missing box.

"What is it about the box, Piet? There's a story here and it all leads back to the lodge, Cloud's End, and the woman who died there."

"But maybe, Jack, it wasn't the box the thief was after but the contents…one thing for sure he knew the box."

Piet picked at one of the warm muffins which had arrived with the coffee, he chewed it suspiciously before he gave the rest to Hope, who had been eyeing it with a look of complete indifference. She gulped it down in one bite.

"*Eish*, don't they have any decent rusks in this place, my friend? Something you can dunk in your coffee to start the day? Not this cake with fancy bits stuck in it?"

Jack laughed. "I tried a rusk once, almost broke my teeth on it. Tasted stale as all hell. I prefer the muffins myself.

"Anyway, I'm planning on going back to Wolmaransstad. I need to find the hotel Lara stayed in there, she'll remember the name, then find the barman; shouldn't be difficult. He said his cousin, Eunice, had worked for this Marlene Hartley at some point. We need to talk to Eunice. Find out who came and went to the lodge once it closed down as a commercial venture? How often she went out, apart from her monthly visit to the bar where Gift works, and if she had any visitors."

Piet nodded. "*Ja*, good plan Jack." He stood up and brushed the crumbs off his uniform. "Time for my meeting with Hugo. I'll see you later. Come Hope."

Jack went back to bed, and Lara.

Chapter Thirty

Shaka made his way slowly around the outside of the perimeter fence of the hotel, checking for recent signs of activity. His sharp eyes soon spotted the thief's entry point into the hotel grounds. The bent grasses, the disturbed dirt, stones turned over.

He tracked the thief's boot prints away from the gap in the fence into the thick tangle of bush.

The box was lying on its side partially hidden in the long grass. Shaka reached for it, wrapping it awkwardly in his cape. He found the track marks of a vehicle, but nothing else. No footprints leading into the hotel grounds.

He jogged back to the hotel.

*****

Piet's meeting in Hugo's office had been tense, to say the least. Hugo had listened gloomily to the events of the night before.

"This is the first robbery we've ever had here, Piet, in the twenty years I've owned it. How the hell did someone get into the grounds with no-one seeing them, access a guest room, and steal something?"

Piet felt this would not be the right moment to remind Hugo he had suggested he get rid of the old-fashioned keys and replace them with something more modern and secure. He had also mentioned security cameras, which Hugo dismissed as intrusive in a hotel like his.

"Shaka, the guards and myself, are doing a full investigation, Hugo. The entire staff of the hotel are on the lookout for the box. Something will turn up. The only way someone could have entered the premises is through the perimeter fence. I know it's an expensive exercise, one you've dismissed before, but we need to put in electric fencing. Crime is on the rise in this country. People are hungry, they steal things. They're desperate, Hugo."

Hugo had looked even gloomier. "You're probably right, Piet. I don't like the idea of electric fencing, but this sort of thing must never happen again. I want my guests to feel safe and comfortable, sleeping securely in their beds at night. Let's get a couple of quotes and get the job done. Let's also look at upgrading the keys to the guest rooms, as you suggested when you first started here."

Hugo fiddled with the pens on his desk. "I should have gone along with your recommendation and not been so stubborn. I don't want security cameras around the place. People come here to relax, not to be bloody spied on. Also, they might not be with whom they are supposed to be with. So, it's a definite no to the cameras, Piet."

There was a tap on the door. They both looked up. "Come on in." Hugo shouted.

Shaka's body filled the office door. "I have found this missing box, *sah*."

He carefully unwrapped it and placed it on Hugo's desk. "It was hidden in the bush some way from the hotel, outside the fence. The thief came through the fence like a snake on its belly."

Hugo frowned. "Strange looking box, if you ask me. What are all those bits sticking out the sides?"

Piet smiled. "It's a Chinese puzzle box, Hugo. Extremely difficult to open unless you know how."

Hugo picked it up and examined it. "So, this was no ordinary theft. Is this what you're saying, Piet?"

"It's exactly what I'm saying. Whoever stole this from your guest's room knew exactly what they were looking for and where it was. They also knew how to open it, so long. It's possible it could have been another guest; it's a possibility we need to consider.

"Unfortunately, the contents have been removed. There was some sort of book in there, written in shorthand. It's gone. It's what the thief was after – the book."

Hugo stared at him. "How do you know what was inside the box Piet?"

Piet sighed and rubbed the back of his neck. "The box belongs to your guest called Lara Summers."

Hugo grinned. "Ah yes, the lovely Lara. I hope they enjoyed their safari…"

Piet smiled. "I'm sure they did, hey. Lara showed it to me and Jack. Jack recognised it as a Chinese puzzle box. None of us could figure out how to open it. I found a young Chinese kid in town; he came to the hotel last night and worked out how to open it. That's how I know what was in it."

Shaka nodded. "I was there when this happened, *sah*. I saw this Chinese person." He looked down at his dusty, cracked, bare feet. "Chinese take everything," he muttered. "Our tusks and pangolin, these are not good people. They come to Africa to take away things. Maybe this skinny China boy came back later and stole this box."

Piet frowned at him. "Come on, Shaka, I told you they're not all bad people, only some of them. I've already checked with the father of the boy; he was working in the restaurant until four yesterday afternoon. Then his father took him back to university in Nelspruit, where he's studying. Checked it out and it is so."

He turned to Shaka. "Show me where you found the gap in the fence and the box. Well done, my friend, good work."

Hugo stalled him. "If someone came in through the fence, Piet. Then this someone could not have been another guest, right?"

Piet looked back at him. "It's what I intend to find out Hugo. There were no footprints into the property. The whole thing was made to look like something else."

Chapter Thirty-One

Piet spent most of the day getting quotes for the electric fencing, new guest room key cards and organising for the hole in the fence to be secured.

Then he had called Bertie Erasmus to see if he had made any progress with finding out more about Marlene Hartley and Cloud's End.

"So, Bertie, my man, what have you got for me, hey?"

Bertie had sighed down the phone. "I'm on its Piet, but it's not easy with the little information I have. I've run Marlene Hartley through the system but came up with zip. There are eleven Marlene Hartleys in South Africa, but not in the age range you gave me and not in the Wolmaransstad area. I checked out the name of the lodge. I found it but it used to have a different name. Originally it was called Hunter's Moon. The property is owned by a trust called Bay Water, registered in somewhere called the Isle of Man. I still have to dig about there and try to come up with the names of the trustees. It will be like looking for a *bleddy* black hair down a coal mine, my friend.

"Anyways it got me thinking, hey? Why change the name of a lodge and call it something else? I'm thinking this woman was maybe not South African. So now I'm applying algorithms to see what I can come up with."

"What's a *bleddy* algae rhythm, Bertie, something green and slimy that sticks to the side of your swimming pool? I'm a policeman not a *friggin* computer scientist."

Bertie roared with laughter. "Get with the programme, my man, move with the times. See, let me explain. With English names the second letter of a Christian name is invariably a vowel, sometimes the first letter is a vowel, then you get variations of some other names like Sinclair sounds like St. Clair, so...."

Piet interrupted him. "Bertie, Bertie, you lost me in the first five seconds here. I don't know what the *fok* you're talking about, hey. Just keep on digging, will you? Call me if you come up with anything with your *bleddy* algae rhythms. I'm out of here. Got better things to do than listen to you speaking a foreign language."

Getting no response to his knock at Jack's door, Piet wandered around to his patio and found him pounding away on his laptop, a glass of beer next to him.

"Hey, Jack. Sorry to interrupt but I have some news."

Jack slumped back in his chair and reached for his beer. "Come and sit Piet. I need a break anyway. What news have you got?"

"Shaka found the box out in the bush behind the perimeter fence of the property – it was open. I returned it to Lara." Piet told him what had happened. Then filled him in on what Bertie had told him.

Jack felt the familiar shiver of excitement along his spine. "So, someone else knew how to open the box, someone who badly wanted the blue book…"

His phone vibrated on the table. Harry. "Have to take this Piet, could be important. I'll put it on loudspeaker."

"Afternoon Jack. Nice weather there in sunny South Africa? Bloody awful here. There's a storm coming in with a wind strong enough to blow my dogs off their feet."

Harry cleared his throat. "I thought of using one of our interns to see if she could translate, she's into cryptology, but what you mentioned about who we can trust made me think. You're right, we have to be careful, however I have solved the problem.

"There's an elderly lady who lives in a care home just outside of London. She worked at Bletchley Park when she was a young teenager, a code cracker of note by all accounts and knows her shorthand, of course. She's a distant relative of mine. So distant I couldn't remember her name, but, more importantly, she remembered mine. Quite a gal, that aunt of mine, must be nearly a hundred but still sparking with energy. She was delighted to have something to do and use some of her old talents. I printed out what you sent through to me, then couriered it to her. But unfortunately, the pages foxed her as well."

Piet rolled his eyes wondering why the English always talked about the weather before anything else, and what did a fox have to do with anything?

Harry continued. "It's definitely Pitman's shorthand, but although an expert shorthand writer herself, she couldn't understand a word of it. Another thing she noted, which she thought was rather odd.

There were no dates, times, names or indication of where the diary, or book, might have been written, but there were lots of numbers and letters. So, a bit of a mystery, which I shall leave you and your side-kick Piet to work out for us. Must dash and catch my train before this storm hits. Cheerio."

Jack cut the call and put the phone back on the table. "Tell you what Piet, you're off duty now, how about I order a couple of beers and we sit and pool all our information and see where we are and what we should do next."

Piet grinned at him. "Good idea, bit of a rough day, one way or another. Order some snacks, will you? Haven't had time for lunch today."

The waiter arrived twenty minutes later; his tray laden. Cold shelled prawns with garlic butter, calamari rings with a seafood sauce, some slices of French bread, a smoked salmon dip with biscuits, and a whole brie cheese oozing its golden creamy contents on a plate with more rounds of French bread. The waiter placed everything carefully on the table, including two ice cold beers, two plates, two napkins and a bowl which he whipped off the tray.

"This, Mister Piet, is for giving to Hope. The Boss said is not for humans. It's for Hopeful dog."

Hope gave him a loving look and cleared the biltong in less time than it took for Jack and Piet to reach for their beers.

They both filled their plates from the feast laid before them. "Where's Lara then, my friend?"

Jack dunked his biscuit into the dip and popped it into his mouth, his eyes closing briefly as he savoured the creamy salmon mix.

"She went to take a nap, then she'll start her packing. She'll want me to close the puzzle box you returned to her this morning. Easier to pack I would imagine. I've been flat out all day writing my weekly column on a self-drive to the Kruger."

He glanced at his watch. "She'll be along soon. I'm taking her back to Joburg tomorrow for her flight back to London, then I'm planning to make another visit to the lodge. Find the woman who worked for Marlene Hartley. Eunice."

"You like this Lara, my friend?" he said softly.

Jack nodded. "Yes, I like her a lot, but it won't work Piet, as you well know. Too like my other affair. You can't have a romance when you live continents away from each other. It doesn't work. I have no intention of ever going back to live in the UK."

Piet frowned at him. "*Jeez,* Jack, I was hoping you'd leave me alone at some point, after we solve this little mystery. Wasn't planning on you hanging around here forever, when I'm trying to do my job, so long.

"*Ag,* well I suppose I'll have to get used to it. By the way Hugo put the word out for me, about finding you a place to live. There's a couple of places you should look at. I've already checked them out, see if they're secure. One is, one not so secure. Go take a look at them anyways, when you get back. If you find one you like, I'll take care of the security for you. Can't have you being murdered in your bed if we're practically going to be neighbours, hey?"

Jack smiled at him. "Thanks Piet. Now, let's see where we are with this story."

He fished his notepad, which he religiously carried everywhere, out of top pocket of his shirt and flipped through the pages.

"Okay. We have a possible suicide, or an accidental death on a farm. A deceased estate where a Marlene Hartley lived, but owned by a trust called Bay Water, registered on the Isle of Man. Nothing odd about that…except the name was changed from Hunter's Moon to Cloud's End – why? I think there's an English connection here, and not just with the silver box with the crest. I took a shot of it and then tried to enlarge it but I can't make out the crest at all."

Jack pursed his lips. "I mean why not change the name of the farm to something more fitting. An Afrikaans name? Or something more suited to the history of Kimberley and its legendary diamonds?"

Piet shrugged, busy with the prawns and calamari.

He continued. "Then we have the Chinese puzzle box and within its depths there are four photographs, one with a bit of a threatening sentence on the back and a blue book, written in shorthand with no names, no dates and no indication of where or when it was written, and a load of numbers. Even more interesting, an expert, ex-Bletchley Park…" he paused. "You know all about this place I presume, Piet?"

Piet looked at him from beneath his thick eyelashes. "Listen, my friend, you might think we Afrikaners are a bit wild and woolly and live out in the bush, surrounded by wild animals and not much else. But let me tell you something. Afrikaners, South Africans, have made their names all over the world in the fields of science, medicine, technology, space travel etc. Don't forget it wasn't an Englishman or an American who performed the first open heart transplant surgery.

No, my friend, it was us. Professor Chris Barnard, an Afrikaner through and through, he did this.

"The CAT scans? Invented by us. Q10 lubricant? Us again, most used lubricant used worldwide. PayPal? Yup, invented by a South African. Pratley's putty, the stuff they took to the moon to fix things if needed? Us again. The list goes on. Our doctors and scientists are sought after by companies all over the world. Nothing shabby about us Afrikaners, my friend."

He snorted. "Course I know about Bletchley Park! We Afrikaners always admire courage and faith, it's in our blood. Those uncles and aunties at Bletchley Park probably saved your country, not so?"

Jack smiled. He liked Piet and his fiery personality, his passion for his country and the great pride he still had in it.

Piet grinned at him. "Bet there were a few Afrikaners working at Bletchley Park, to sort out the hard stuff to decipher, stuff you lot couldn't figure out, hey?"

Jack chose to let that one go and continued. "Okay, okay. The Bletchley Park lady thinks the shorthand is written in a foreign language, possibly European. The key to all of this is the woman called Marlene Hartley. The puzzle box, the diary, the silver box. All roads lead to her. Who exactly was she? Did she have a husband? At some point she must have had family connections, mother, father, sisters, brothers maybe. Where are they all now? Who does the crest on the box belong to – which family? Maybe your friend Bertie will have some answers, will come up with something?

"Who wanted this box and what it contained so badly? And why?"

Piet stared into the distance, watching the sun sinking between the trees. "The person who wanted the box and what it contained, knew her, I'm sure of it. Marlene may not be with us anymore, but, sure as hell someone is. We have to find this someone Jack."

Jack rubbed his neck. "Yup, you're right. The connection is Marlene Hartley. Someone knew her. Possibly a relative, maybe. A brother? A sister? A cousin?"

"This person is a pro, Jack. I think he, or she, followed Lara here, must have been there when she was going through the things on the trestle table, she took the box they wanted. Why else would they be there? Probably popped a GPS bug on her car when she was off horse riding. Easy to do. Drop your car keys, or something, near her

134

car, it takes seconds to attach the tracking device. They knew where to find her, Jack. They followed her right back here to the hotel.

"Only one other guest checked in after Lara. A Daniel Van Heerden. I need to find out more about him."

"You think this person is a man then?"

Pict fondled Hope's ears. "Yes...See the thing is Jack. If this Bletchley Park auntie can't read this shorthand, then it's in a different language, not so? Same squiggles and dots but another language?"

Jack took a sip of his beer. "Yes, it has to be the answer. The book was found here in South Africa. The shorthand is possibly in Afrikaans? It's what you're saying, right?"

Piet nodded. "Makes sense to me. Send me the scans and I'll print them out and take them to the local court here. They must have someone who can decipher the pages."

He looked despondent. "Thing is Jack; we only have a few pages. The rest has gone. The book is gone."

Jack turned to him, trying not to look too smug. "Surely, Piet, you didn't think I only scanned a few pages? No. Blessing spent a lot of time and scanned the entire book. Nothing is lost. We have it all. Now we need to find someone who can make some sense of it? We are still ahead of the game here. Whoever stole the book thinks their secrets are safe – but we have a copy of the entire book. No hiding place for them, Piet."

"Good one, Jack. Good thinking. Oh, I spoke to an old buddy of mine, an ex-police detective, like me. He's given us a contact at the Wolmaransstad police station. Might be able to get some info about the suicide, or whatever, from her. Her name is Precious Khumalo. Been there forever, not working as a police officer but working for the police as a secretary. She should be able to pull a file or two. Here's her number. Maybe invite her for a coffee and persuade her to bring the file on Marlene Hartley. Everyone is short of money, Jack. Perhaps make the invitation a little more exciting, hey?"

*****

Between the shadows of the trees Lara headed for Jack's cottage, carrying the opened box. They both stood as she approached them.

"Lara, come and sit. Would you like a glass of wine. Something to eat maybe?"

She shook her head. "Nothing to eat, thank you. But I would like a glass of wine." She sank into a chair. "Could you close up the box again, Jack?

"Of course, it'll be easier to pack that's for sure."

"Remember I told you about the other things I found at the auction at the lodge? Well, I've spent some time this afternoon, in between packing my clothes and my silver treasures. Using my loupe, I think I might have found something interesting."

Piet looked puzzled. "A loupe? What is that exactly?"

Lara reached for the glass of wine Jack had poured. "It's what we use in the trade. A single lens magnifying glass, held close to the eye, which greatly magnifies whatever you're looking at. I was looking at the old mark on the cigarette box I found at Cloud's End."

She reached into her bag and pulled out the tarnished cigarette box and placed it on the table. "It definitely looks like an old crest, there are some initials."

She leaned forward to Jack, her hair a dark silky curtain on one side of her face, caressing the top of his hand.

"See here, it's definitely a crest, with two lions, mouths agape, rearing up to some kind of shield. I can try and find out more about the coat of arms and the initials. I know experts in that field. I wanted to show it to you both, in case it was important. Google came up with nothing…"

Piet and Jack glanced at each other – was this the possible English connection?

Lara continued. "Another thing I've been thinking about. If you both need the Chinese box to follow your story, I'm happy to leave it with you."

She touched Jack's hand and grinned at him. "But there's a proviso. Either you return it to me personally, or I'll collect from you here?"

Piet sensing the moment, stood up. "Have to get back, check the perimeter fence. "Go well, my girl, come back soon, hey?"

Lara stood up and wrapped her arms around Piet. "I hope I'll see you again someday. I don't want to leave your beautiful country, but I have to go home."

Piet smiled at her, looking slightly embarrassed. He was unused to impulsive shows of affection from women. He normally scared the hell out of them.

"You will come back, my girl," he said gruffly. "Once you've tasted Africa, you will look at the world differently. Africa is a harsh mistress, but she is forgiving. Think of us here when you return to your home. We'll take good care of your box."

With Hope at his heels, he left them both together.

Chapter Thirty-Two

The next morning Jack and Lara checked out of the hotel. Hugo would arrange for the hire company to collect her vehicle from the car park.

Jack left the puzzle box in the care of Piet. Also, a full print out of the blue book. The photographs and a shot of the crest on top of the silver cigarette box he stored on his phone.

Lara had found the name of the hotel in Wolmaransstad where Gift, the barman, worked. Jack booked a room ahead of his visit. He wanted to mingle with the locals and see if he could find anything more about Marlene Hartley.

Lara had been unusually quiet on the drive to the airport, and Jack knew why. He would miss her as well; in the short time they had had together, he had become used to having her around.

He pulled up outside the departures building, helping her with her suitcase and one heavy box containing the silver she had acquired.

"I hate saying goodbye, always have." She took a deep breath and put her arms around him, holding him close. He let her. Then he pulled back and looked down into her rapidly filling eyes.

"Hey, no tears, okay? We'll keep in touch. I'll let you know what we find. I'm hoping you'll find out who the crest on the cigarette box belonged to. Plenty to keep you busy, and all that fine silver you need to clean and sell. Don't forget we have the deal with your box – I'll bring it to you, or you'll come and fetch it from us. This isn't over, Lara. We've got something going here. It would be really easy to get swept away by bold declarations, but circumstances being what they are, I don't want to rush into anything. I told you a little about my last relationship. I don't want to get hurt like that again and I really don't want to hurt you. We just need to take a step back, and figure it all out…"

His words didn't help. The tears spilled down her cheeks. He held her close again before she pulled away and pushed her luggage trolley through the glass doors to the check in desks. She looked back briefly and lifted her hand in farewell. Then she was gone.

Jack watched her being swallowed up with the hundreds of other passengers, then turned slowly and got back into his car and drove off in the direction of Wolmaransstad, already feeling the emptiness without her next to him.

*****

Jack checked into the hotel in the middle of the old town. It had seen better days and was probably one of the oldest buildings in town, only three storeys, the outside walls bleached over the years by the African sun. Dusty sprays of what might have been magenta and red bougainvillea, draped over the entrance gates, their colours as faded as the building.

He took a shower then made his way to the bar.

There, as he had been for so many years, was the old barman called Gift.

Jack perched on the bar stool in the empty bar. "Hello Gift, a friend of mine told me about you and how long you've been here. Bit of a legend, she said. I checked into your hotel so I could meet you."

Gift gave him a beaming smile. "Welcome sir. What may I get you?"

"An ice-cold beer would go down well, Gift. Call me Jack."

Gift carefully poured his beer and slid it across the bar on a coaster. "It would not be proper to call you Yak. I shall call you Mr Yak until we are further acquainted. Your friend, Mr Yak, she was the white lady with the straight dark hair? Coming to look at things to be sold out at the old farm called Cloud's End?"

Jack was impressed. He smiled. For some reason no-one in this country could get his name right. He had been called Mr Yak by all the locals he had ever met here.

"How did you work that out, Gift? Yes, she was my friend. Lara."

Gift looked at him carefully. "It is unusual for two white people with the voice of the English to be here so soon after each other. You are both from the same country I think?"

Jack laughed. "Indeed, we are. My friend, Lara, thinks the woman who lived at Cloud's End was from the same country too, from England. We would like to know a little more about her. I heard she died alone on the farm. It's possible there are relatives, family, in England who would wish to know of her passing. I was hoping you might be able to help me?"

Gift looked at him, his wise old eyes penetrating. "I think it is more you are looking for Mr Yak. You are looking for my cousin, Eunice, who worked in the house belonging to the white lady who died, not so?"

The game was up. Jack smiled at him sheepishly. Busted. "Yes, Gift, it is your cousin I wish to meet. Eunice. Would you be able to help me?"

Gift wiped down his already spotless bar counter. "This is possible, Mr Yak. But times are difficult for all of us here…many problems in the country. Food is expensive now."

Jack took a sip of his beer. "I am sure I'll be able help Eunice in these difficult times, Gift. It won't be a problem."

*****

The breakfast room was empty the next morning. Jack ordered his breakfast. A tiny woman, her face as creased and brown as a walnut, put his breakfast down in front of him. "I am Eunice," she whispered. "You are Mr Yak? My cousin is telling me about you?"

Jack had been thinking about Lara, her lonely flight home, her hands gripping the sides of her seat, her tears. She would be back in London now making her way back to the dark flat she had told him about.

Eunice's voice brought him back to the present. "Hello, Eunice. Yes, I would like to talk to you."

She nodded at him. "I will be finished with the serving here at nine, Mr Yak. Perhaps we could meet outside in the garden then?"

*****

Jack drummed his fingers on the table outside in the garden. Another blisteringly hot day lay ahead. The iron chairs were already retaining the heat despite being under a rather faded umbrella advertising something called Fanta.

Eunice made her way towards him and sat down. "What is it you are wanting to know, Mr Yak?"

He put his elbows on the table. "The woman, her name was Marlene Hartley, you worked for her, yes?"

Eunice nodded. "This is so, Mr Yak."

"Tell me, Eunice, how long did you work for her?"

"Perhaps five years, Mr Yak."

"During this time did Mrs Hartley have visitors, friends for dinner, people staying with her?"

Eunice shook her head emphatically. "No-one came, Mr Yak. She was all alone there, always watching and waiting. She would ride out to this place in the bush she liked. But it was not to watch the animals who came to drink, like before. She was watching the road, far away in the distance. You could not see this road, but you could hear the sound of traffic if there was no high wind or storm.

"Before this time the groom, Nico, from Zimbabwe, he is telling me the missus would ride maybe three times each week, down to watch the animals at the water. It was afterwards she turned to watch the road and not the animals. Lexi, her dog, stayed behind with me in case he was attacked by baboons."

"Your cousin, Eunice, he told my friend Mrs Hartley wore white gloves and wiped everything she touched with a cloth? Why did she do this. Did you have to do this too?"

Eunice nodded. "It is so, Mr Yak. I have not seen this before...but this only happened after I had been working for her for some years. Before this it was normal washing and cleaning.

"Then, one day, someone came. I think the person she had been waiting for."

Jack straightened up in his seat. "Who?"

Eunice squeezed her apron around in her hands. "I do not know who this person was. It was a man. A white man. Someone I am thinking she is knowing. For the first time I saw this woman happy. The person she was waiting for had finally come to this place called Cloud's End."

"How long did he stay then Eunice?"

"Not long, Mr Yak, a few days perhaps."

Jack looked at her and decided not to beat about the bush. "Did this man share her bed then? You would have noticed this?"

Eunice shook her head. "He did not share her bed, but perhaps they met there in the night? Or perhaps he was a relative of hers, a brother maybe, or an uncle. Then I am thinking he would not have come to her bed."

"They knew each other well then, from some time ago perhaps, Eunice?"

She nodded. "Yes, they knew each other. They were, how you say? Easy together? Yes, easy together. The missus was very happy. The day after he arrived, she went out to ride. But this time, no hat, just her hair blowing behind the horse.

"This man, I was watching from the kitchen, he was looking for something. He looked in all places. Searching for something he could not find. He did not see me watching from the kitchen and following him from room to room. I am a small person, Mr Yak, I move quietly like a mouse. I saw all of this."

Jack sat back in his chair. "What did this man look like, Eunice?"

She looked puzzled. "He looked like you, Mr Yak, you all look the same to us. Same size, like you, maybe not so tall."

Eunice looked out across the garden. "Then, maybe some days later, this man left again. It was at this time the missus started to wear the gloves and wiping, wiping, wiping."

Jack ran his hands through his damp hair. God, it was hot today. Would he ever get used to it?

Eunice was wringing her apron through her hands looking agitated.

"When this man arrived at the farm, the missus was very happy. But late that same night, she came to where I was living, a *rondavel* a little way from the big house. She was carrying a box. She asked me to keep it safe for her. To hide it.

"I did this for her. It was a beautiful box, very shiny with pictures on it. I hid it under my bed. Also, there was a silver box, which I cleaned many times, this she wished for me to hide also."

Jack felt the familiar tingle along his spine. "Did this man go to your place?"

"Yes. He was looking for this shiny box, this I knew. But he did not find it. I had taken it from under the bed and hidden it in the straw down at the stables. This box was important for the missus. I liked her, she was kind and good to me. But sometimes she would be very angry for no reason."

Jack opened his phone. "Is this the box, Eunice?"

Eunice squinted at the enlarged picture on the phone. She nodded lifting her eyebrows in surprise. "Yes, this is the hidden box. But how did you get this picture if this was a hidden box?"

Jack explained how his friend had found it when the contents of the house were being sold.

Jack leaned forward. "Did you ever hear her say his name, when they were having breakfast or dinner? Did they speak to each other in English?"

Eunice shook her head, looking puzzled. "No, they are speaking together in our language, Afrikaans. But he did not call her Marlene, I cannot remember what he called her, but it was not Marlene. Perhaps a name from childhood?"

Jack moved his chair more into the shaded skirts of the tree. "Did you ever see her with the box open? Did you ever see her writing at her desk?"

Eunice gave a toothless smile. "Oh, yes, many times. She wrote in a blue book, when she did this, the box was looking different. When she finished writing she would put her book inside and make it to look like a box again.

"Also, the missus she liked to write in the newspaper and her magazines. The small square boxes where she would write words. Each month she would drive to town, with the groom Nico, and come back with the newspapers and the magazines, for writing these words in the square boxes."

Jack frowned. More boxes and words?

Eunice started to fidget with the gold chain around her neck and Jack realised she was not feeling comfortable with his questions. But he had gleaned more information for his story. He now knew the author of the book was Marlene Hartley and she must have written the cryptic message on the back of the photograph of the box.

"When did you stop working for this woman, Eunice?"

Eunice frowned. "Maybe three months after this man came. Mrs Hartley said she would find me another job and this she did. I never saw her again, but my cousin, Gift, said she came to the hotel each month for her magazines and papers. Then she died."

He stood up and felt in his shirt pocket for the envelope containing five hundred rand. "Thank you, Eunice. Here is something for you, for the help you have given me. I hope it will help you."

Eunice stood up, taking the envelope, she gave a little bob, a sort of curtsey, and left.

Jack sat back in his chair. Was Eunice getting her boxes and words muddled up? Then he smiled to himself. Boxes for words.

Newspapers and magazines. Of course! They all had them. Crossword puzzles!

Jack glanced at his watch. He had another meeting with the secretary who worked at the police station in town. Precious Khumalo.

*****

Precious, as arranged, met him at a pavement café in the centre of town.

She was rather a large African lady, carrying a huge shoulder bag. Thankfully she lowered herself into the seat next to Jack, fanning herself with a large red handkerchief.

He ordered coffee for himself and a coke for her. "My friend, Piet Joubert, is a friend of one of your retired detectives, as you know, Precious. He thought perhaps you might be able to help me. I'm trying to find out a little more about Marlene Hartley. I think her family might like to know she has passed?"

Precious took a long gulp of her cold drink. "Yes, Mr Yak, I know all this. There is little I can tell you. It was an open and shut case as far as we were concerned. Nothing suspicious about it."

She gave him a wide smile enhanced by dazzling white teeth.

Then she frowned. "Mrs Hartley took her own life, out on her farm. It was very straight forward. She was a woman in her sixties who decided she did not want to be here anymore, finish and *klaar*."

Jack presumed this meant something like done and dusted.

Precious continued. "The groom found her body; the gun was on the ground next to her. It was a terrible thing for him to discover. I went to her memorial service. One of us always does this in case there are any relatives who might be of interest and of course to pay our respects as a member of the local community police department. But there was no-one there at her funeral service, only the pastor and me and the groom who worked on the farm, the one who found her."

Precious shook her head. "Very sad, no family members at all. When we Africans have a funeral, it is a big occasion, many people come even if they are not family – all are welcome. We wear our finest clothes for this."

She heaved her huge shoulders. "She must have had some relatives, Mr Yak. But where were they?" Precious glanced at her watch. "I have to go now. There is nothing more to say about this case and I must return to the office."

144

Jack hesitated for a moment. Piet had suggested a gift of money might be appropriate, but he felt she might be offended if he offered her money.

He stood as she heaved her huge bag over her shoulder. "Thank you, Precious. You've been most helpful."

He watched her trudge down the dusty pavement, fanning her face with the red handkerchief. Marlene Hartley's life had come to a sad and lonely ending, with only Nico the groom, the police secretary and the pastor to see her off on her final journey.

He had gathered a little more information and didn't think hanging around Wolmaransstad any longer would reveal much more.

But he was puzzled. If Marlene and her visitor were Afrikaans, this was the language they were speaking to each other, and Eunice couldn't be wrong about this. Where was the English connection?

If Piet's speculations about this Daniel Van Heerden, and his earlier suspicions that he might possibly have been the thief, and knew what he was looking for, were right, then he had to have been the one and only visitor to Cloud's End. It made sense. What didn't make sense was if he was a close friend of Marlene's or possibly her brother, why had he not attended the funeral?

But the Daniel Van Heerden trail had led nowhere. He was simply a guest at the hotel. All his papers were in order. He was legal. He and Piet both agreed on this. But Jack still had his doubts.

Jack went back to the hotel, packed his overnight bag and checked out.

The previous afternoon he had glanced at the properties in the window of Pam Golding Estate Agents, the farm had a red sticker crossing it, announcing it was sold.

Going back out there now, to try and speak to the groom called Nico, might not be such a good idea after all.

But, good idea or not, he was going to take a chance.

He parked his car. There was no-one around, the place was locked up. He walked over to the stables, the horses looked at him with interest. He could hear someone moving around inside one of the stalls.

"Hello, Nico, is that you?"

Nico appeared a look of surprise on his face. "I am Nico – what is it that you are wanting here? This house is sold now. No-one here anymore."

Jack held out his hand. "My name's Jack. A friend of mine came to look at things for sale here and you kindly let her ride one of your horses?"

Nico frowned. "This is so. But why are you here now? What is it you are wanting?"

Jack knew how to play the game. He reached into his pocket and withdrew some notes from his wallet. Nico stared at them and then at Jack.

"I write for an English newspaper Nico. We are trying to find the relatives of Mrs Hartley. We would like to inform them of her passing?"

Nico gave him a startled look. "But the missus died some time ago, why are you only looking now? If she had family they would have come for the funeral of the missus. But no-one came."

Jack gave him what he hoped was a warm and friendly smile. "We have found some of her family in England and they wish to know what happened to her, for which they are willing to pay."

He handed a handful of notes to Nico, who took them reluctantly.

"So, Nico will you tell me what happened? We know she didn't die in the house but somewhere out on the farm. How long had she been out there before you found her? You must have heard the shot surely?"

Nico leaned his rake against the stable door. "I went to the town and only returned in the evening; her horse was here at the stables when I arrived back. The house was dark, with the security light on, I am thinking she was sleeping inside. This she would do often, go to sleep early. The missus did not ride every day. I was busy the next day and did not see her. This was not unusual."

Jack wiped the back of his neck. "Well, how long did you wait before you went to find her Nico?"

Nico's brow creased with concentration. "Two days maybe."

Jack thought carefully about his next question. "She used a gun to kill herself, Nico. Where did she shoot herself?"

Nico started to look angry. "I told you, she did it at the bush place."

"No, Nico, that's not what I'm asking you. Did she shoot herself in the head, in her heart? Where?"

Nico picked up his rake, and Jack took a step back.

"It was not easy to know – there are many vultures here…I am thinking it was an accident."

Jack felt his stomach contract. He knew he would get no more information from Nico.

But he knew Nico was holding something back, he hadn't told him the whole story about what really happened down there at the water hole.

An accident? Not what the police had concluded.

Chapter Thirty-Three

Jack pulled up in the hotel car park late in the afternoon. Dumping his bag in his room, he took a quick shower and made his way to the bar.

Hugo was busy with his customers. Jack ordered a beer from one of the staff and mulled through the events of the day. He was pleased with what they had so far. There was definitely a story well worth pursuing.

Hugo moved towards him from behind the bar. "Hey, Jack. Good to see you back again. Piet should be here in half an hour or so. He's doing the rounds with the hotel guard dog. This is when Hope is truly at her best, showing her noble lineage. Late afternoon is snack time, the guests have all sorts of interesting nibbles delivered with their sundowners. She will be investigating all the dishes to ensure they are safe to consume. Hope shows a keen interest in everything going on, but mostly what's in the bowls on their outside tables. How was your trip to the land of diamonds?"

Jack smiled at him. "Good, Hugo. There's a story here worth my undivided attention. I'm going to need some of Piet's input and time. Is that okay with you?"

Hugo wiped down his bar. "Sure. I knew Harry years ago when I was a tour operator flogging safaris to South Africa, from London where I was based, when no-one wanted to come here. Harry gave us a good bit of exposure in his columns, in exchange for a good bit of expensive advertising I have to say.

"Harry knows you always stay here at my hotel, and, of course, he knows about Piet. We have a sort of gentleman's agreement. I let you have Piet when you need him, you mention my hotel in your articles, I give you a damn good rate to stay here – and everyone's happy, a splendid arrangement! Ah, here's Piet now, I'll leave you both to it."

Piet made a beeline for Jack, sitting at the bar. He threw his tattered baseball cap down on the counter and climbed up on the bar stool.

"So, Jack, how did it go?"

Jack filled him in on the information he had put together on his trip to Wolmaransstad and his conversation with Gift, Eunice, and the groom Nico. "Nothing more to pursue there, Piet. Suicide or accidental death." He shrugged his shoulders. "We'll probably never know after all this time. Now we must cast the net further. Let's see if Lara comes back with anything from the crest on the silver box. What's the progress on the diary?"

"*Jeez,* Jack, it took me a long to find an old auntie who knew what this shorthand language was. But I found someone. Retired from the courts now, of course. It will take her some days to translate the dots and squiggles into something we can read. But, yes, the language is Afrikaans, this she confirmed. We shall have to wait. You can't hurry these legal aunties along. You, of course, will have to pay her for the many hours it will take to translate these squiggles into a known tongue. Sorry, my friend, but there it is. She'll be expensive, that I can tell you."

He signalled for a beer from the barman. "Also think about this Jack. The book is written in shorthand. The message on the back of the photo is not. There will be no way to compare any handwriting..."

Jack shrugged. "No problem with the budget. Harry's happy, he knows we're on to a cracking story, well I hope we are. I'm going to call him later, bring him up to date. Then I'll call Lara. See if she's come up with anything on the crest on the silver box. You're right about the message on the photo and the shorthand. But, maybe, just maybe the entire book won't be in shorthand. I only need a couple of words to make the comparison."

Jack rubbed his tired eyes. "I'm going to have room service tonight. Feeling a bit knackered to tell the truth." He slid of his bar stool. "See you tomorrow, Piet."

Hope's grinning face loomed up over the bar. Piet shook his head in despair. "Hopeless, that dog, absolutely *bleddy,* hopeless."

He rammed his hat on his head and stomped out of the bar, the devoted dog at his heels.

He thought about his conversation with Jack. Suicide, accidental death or murder – there was a big difference.

Chapter Thirty-Four

Jack finished his room service dinner, then sat at his desk. Putting the light on, he studied the photographs on his phone.

Whoever the little boy was, it was obvious, judging by the low looking colonial house, the lush gardens and the arch of large white flowers they were standing under, it could be India or the Far East, even Africa. The woman holding the boy's hand, was clearly Malay or Chinese, which possibly, to Jack's mind, put the place somewhere out in the Far East. That would be a match with the puzzle box.

He studied the writing on the back of the photograph of the box, no clues to anything there. The photograph with the couple both wearing hats against the sun and sunglasses, could have been taken anywhere. They could have been anyone. He studied the flat landscape, the few trees. Africa perhaps. Whoever they were he knew they were also connected to the story of the box.

Finally, he turned to the shot of two young men lounging next to a river, their faces in the shade. A weeping willow draping itself along the edge of the water.

Jack had no doubts whatsoever this was England. Something stirred in his memory. He enlarged the photograph.

Now he could clearly see the straw boaters and the uniforms of the university students. Long trousers, white shirts and blazers. He sat back in his chair and smiled. It was his old university – Cambridge. He recognised the college badge stitched to the blazer pockets. Here then was the possible English connection. But who were the young men lounging around on a late sunny afternoon?

His phone purred on the desk; he snatched it up: the lovely Lara.

"Hey, Lara, how are you? How was the flight?"

"Extremely long with no-one interesting to talk to and it was jam packed as well. Horrible. Didn't enjoy it one bit. But I do have good news for you. About the silver cigarette box."

Jack sat up straight. "I sent some pics to a friend of mine who specialises in family crests. He called me a few minutes ago. The family who owned the crest were called Cooper. It's not old by the usual standards, maybe a couple of hundred years. Probably a trinket box originally, then a place to store cigarettes.

"The last of the line was Sir David Cooper. He was an only child and he had no children himself, so the line died with him, no more Cooper Knights of the Garter. The interesting thing is, he was killed in a plane crash in Kenya, twenty odd years ago.".

Jack, who had been holding his breath, let it out slowly. "Brilliant. Anything else?"

"Not much. The family estate, called Mellow Woods, in Devon, was sold off after David's father, Sir Thomas Cooper, died. It's now rather a swish hotel and Spa."

Jack drummed his fingers on the top of his desk. "So, the son, David, inherited it and then sold it off? Probably up to its collapsing roof in dry rot. Costs an absolute fortune to maintain those old family heaps. Sounds like he sold it alright, but where did he go after that – Kenya? Well, I guess, if he died there, it's a possibility. But he may have gone somewhere else before there."

Lara sighed; Jack heard the almighty clap of thunder seven thousand miles away. "Oh, this weather, Jack. It's so cold and dark outside. It's taking a bit of getting used to again."

"Yes, I'm sure it is. I remember it well, those long winter days. But cheer up. Spring is around the corner, daffodils will be showing their bright sunny yellow faces, blue bells sprouting up in the woods. Lovely time of the year in England."

"Then why don't you still live here, Jack," she said dryly, "if it's so fabulous. I'm afraid I'm thinking about hot days, stormy nights, the smell of rain on dusty roads – and you. I miss it all. I miss you, Jack. Miss dancing in the rain with you."

He could hear the longing in her voice. "Hang in there, Lara, you're doing a great job. I miss you too. As for dancing, we'll do it again, I promise. But I do warm rain not cold." He laughed. "If we did that in the UK someone would probably throw a net over us and cart us away.

"Now let me bring you up to date on what's happening this end.

"So," he finished up, "thanks to your detective work we now have one more piece of the puzzle. I was looking at the photograph of the young men under the tree. I'm pretty sure it's my old alma mater -

Cambridge. Now you've given me the name of the family who owned the crest, I should be able to find out a bit more.

"I'll put my money on the fact the young men lounging under the tree next to the river, went to Cambridge. As an old boy myself, I would say one of the boys was probably Sir David Cooper. Couldn't have been his father, the photograph would have been in black and white if that was the case.

"The photograph of the couple on horseback could then be Sir David and a lady friend. We don't know if he was married or not. She could be anyone. I thought the landscape looked African. Now I'm thinking it is definitely Kenya. That's the connection I think."

"You'll keep me in the loop won't you Jack? I'm going to be busy with a ton of other stuff for the next week, so I won't be able to give you any more help. But I need to hear your voice now and again."

"Of course. I'll call you every couple of days. You've done a great job – wonderful!"

After they said goodnight, Jack called Piet and brought him up to speed on the latest news.

Piet sighed down the phone. "So, you're saying there is now almost certainly a British connection and perhaps a Kenyan one also?"

"Yup. The question is how the hell did the Cooper family silver and a Chinese puzzle box end up out on a farm near the sleepy town of Wolmaransstad? Anyway, that's where we are with the story. Have you ever been to Kenya, Piet?"

Piet grunted down the phone. "Nah, why would I? I like it here. Same sun, same animals. Why would I go and sit somewhere else and stare at the same things, my friend? I know Kenya, read all about it. All that white mischief stuff, you Brits behaving badly. Drinking, parties, wife swapping and such like, sniffing the white stuff. Oh yes, I know all about this, the place called Clouds, up in the Highlands of the country somewhere where it all happened."

He sighed dramatically. "While *yous* white folk, you Brits, were having a good time, we Afrikaners were pulling our wagons across the *veld* long after the *bleddy* oxen had dropped dead from exhaustion, just looking for a peaceful place to live with our people."

Jack chuckled. "It's history, Piet, you have to let it go. Not all Brits behaved badly. There were decent folk in Kenya who worked the land, lead quiet lives, hardworking folk."

Piet sniffed. "Well, whatever…"

Jack sat back in his chair. Piet had mentioned a place called Clouds, Jack had heard of it from the books he had read…not much of a stretch to call a place Cloud's End.

Another Kenya connection perhaps?

Chapter Thirty-Five

Twenty-five minutes after leaving Hazyview, Jack found the short dirt road which led to the single storey stone cottage. The agent Piet had spoken to, had given him the keys to what he hoped might be his new home.

He parked his car under a large oak tree and looked around. There was no garden, as such, just lawn. Two oak trees bent and bowed over the green tin roof of the cottage which was surrounded by a white wraparound patio. He could hear the gurgle of a stream which ran along the bottom of the garden. Frangipani bushes bordered both sides of the property, their heady fragrance hanging in the humid air, a lush green lawn led down to the stream.

The interior of the cottage was cool, the thick stone walls keeping out the heat. It was simply furnished, cream couches and chairs, a knobbly cream and tan carpet covered the sitting room floor, a large flat screen television and a square glass table in the centre.

Through an arched doorway was a dining area, a round table with four chairs and a sideboard. The kitchen was small but functional with a microwave, fridge, freezer and oven.

Jack poked around in the cupboards, absolutely everything he needed was here. Pots and pans, cutlery, crockery. In the main bedroom, a linen cupboard, a large double bed covered in a cream bedspread with pale yellow cushions. Pale yellow curtains brushed the floor. The bathroom was a delight. A power shower and everything else which should be in a bathroom.

He stepped out onto the stone patio and sighed. It was absolutely perfect. Another square table, four comfortable looking chairs with red striped cushions and a cream hammock swayed in the corner. Two sun loungers basked in the shade under the oak trees.

All he needed to do was pack his suitcase in Franschhoek and move in. There was air conditioning and fans in every room. Perfect for what he knew could be extremely high temperatures in the lowveld. But not much good if Eskom decided to turn off the power on a regular basis. But with all this he knew he could hack it and the monthly rent was more than affordable for him.

He rummaged in his pocket for his phone. "I'll take it." He told the agent.

Piet had already checked out the security with the agent. The alarm systems, linked to the local security company, were more than adequate and security lights which would light up with the slightest movement around the garden, be it a two legged or four-legged interloper.

Jack drove back to the hotel, happily imagining himself living there, entertaining Piet and his woman when she eventually returned, with their dog and Lara. Yes, he hoped Lara would come back. He could imagine them living there together, having sundowners, lying back on the sun chairs, listening to the stream gurgling past. Maybe, when the evenings were warm, they could lie amongst the pebbles and rocks of the stream and enjoy a glass of ice-cold wine, perching their glasses on a rock half submerged in the cool water.

He suddenly had a longing to put some roots down, maybe get a couple of dogs. He wanted somewhere he could call home.

Lara. Maybe she was in the future he hoped for. Meanwhile he had a story to chase. He would call her later and tell her he had found a new home, but not yet share his hopes for them both living in it. Lara had to make her own decisions.

He would return the keys to the agent and hopefully unlock his dreams of a future in the little stone cottage by the gurgling stream.

Chapter Thirty-Six

Jack and Piet were sitting in Hugo's noisy bar planning their next move.

"I think I should go to Kenya and see what I can find out there about this David Cooper," Jack said. "I've scoured the internet and only found one reference to his death in the obituary columns in my newspaper. There was apparently a big turn-out for his funeral but strangely no photograph of him."

Jack continued. "He was born in 1949 in the Far East, graduated from Cambridge in 1972 with a Master's degree in foreign languages, then worked for the Foreign Office, as head of their International Trade and Industry section. Did a fine job as far as I can gather. Highly thought of. Even got a gong from her Majesty for services to British industry. He *was* married but his wife died shortly after he did. No mention of her name and there's nothing about any children. So presumably they didn't have any, which matches with what Lara found out. He died in a plane crash, he was the pilot, no passengers. He was forty-eight. There's nothing more about him I can find. All a bit odd really considering who he was. There should have been a lot more information about him, a lot more, but I couldn't find anything at all."

Piet smiled at him. "Well, what did you think you would find, Jack, the man is dead and dead men don't continue to talk after they're, well, dead. There was nothing more to say was there?"

Jack drummed his fingers on the bar counter. "I know, but there is a connection somewhere with the silver cigarette box with the crest and initials and the Chinese box. Don't forget he was born in the Far East. It could have been his and the photographs Lara found; and what about the message scribbled on the back, in English? Did he write that, or his wife?"

He turned the image over and read aloud. '*So, you have found your way into my box, discovered my past perhaps? Now what will*

156

you do... apart from being extremely careful? There's a digit missing somewhere. You'll never find it.'

"Nope, I don't agree Piet, there is more to this. Why the threat to be extremely careful? David Cooper may be dead but I have a feeling his story may live on. I have to find out more about him. You mentioned this place called Clouds, where all, as far as you are concerned, the rich Brits came out to play in Kenya. Marlene's place became known as Cloud's End – there's a connection there. I know there is. Hey, are you listening Piet?"

"Well, well, well," Piet said quietly. "Look who's just walked into the bar?"

Jack glanced around the busy bar. "Who?"

"Daniel Van Heerden is who. Now what's he doing back here, I wonder?"

Jack looked casually around. "The guy in the corner with the white hair, beard and glasses?"

Piet nodded. "Yup. That's him."

Hugo sidled up to them, the smile gone from his normally cheerful face. "Now listen, guys, don't go upsetting my guest, okay? I know this Daniel chap was of interest to you. But he is, at the end of the day, my guest. Why would he come back if he had something sinister to hide? So, leave him alone, okay? The word is already out something happened here, I don't need any more bad publicity."

Daniel Van Heerden stood up and made his way towards Jack and Piet. "Howzit guys? I've noticed you around the place." He held his hand out. "Daniel Van Heerden. Great little hotel this. Wish I'd discovered it sooner."

He was speaking English with a heavy guttural Afrikaans accent. Piet greeted him in his own language. "Come join us, Daniel. This here is my friend Jack. He's a journalist from England, but living here now.

"I'm Piet. Head of Security here, noticed you checked in for a couple of days last week. Always good to see a guest return."

Daniel shook both of their hands and once again reverted to English out of deference to Jack.

"*Ja*, I live on a farm some ways from here, moved here from Joburg a few months ago. Had enough of the traffic, the crowds and everything else. Rented a small cottage there. Thought I would take a couple of days in the Kruger, then a day or two here, before going home. Good to meet you both. Can I get you a beer or something?"

Jack and Piet looked at each other. The guy seemed legit, friendly even. They both nodded to the offer of a beer.

Daniel turned to Jack. "So, you're a journalist. Who do you work for?"

Jack took a sip of his beer. "*The Telegraph*."

Daniel nodded his head, his little finger tapping the glass as he spoke. "Ah, yes. It was my favourite newspaper when I visited the UK in my youth. So, what are you doing here, apart from following all the stories of corruption and greed in our country? I can't afford to have the international newspapers sent here. There's one UK one that comes out once a week, but it's boring as all hell and *bleddy* expensive."

Jack took a sip of his beer. "This and that. Nothing in particular. I live here now."

Piet was watching Daniel closely. He seemed genuine enough, sounded like he had good Afrikaans blood running through his veins. He wanted to know more about the man, apart from an irritating habit he had of tapping his glass with his fingernail.

"*Ja*, so Daniel, where you from?"

Daniel shrugged his shoulders. "Born in Bloemfontein, my parents were teachers in the local school there. Went to Rhodes University in Grahamstown. Got my Master's in history, then went on to teach. Now I sit out in the bush and write historical novels. Not a great deal of demand for them in the new South Africa, but things should be recorded for future generations, not so?"

Piet and Jack stole a look at each other. They had definitely got something wrong. This guy, Daniel, seemed genuine enough. His accent was cultured whether in English or Afrikaans.

Jack reached for his beer. "So, when you went to England, what were you doing there?"

"*Ag*, Jack, all young South Africans wanted to go to England and Europe. Wanted to get out from under the heavy yolk of their history. I did what they all did, explored the hundreds of years of European history. We folk were not welcomed there, but we went there anyways. South Africans were the pariahs of the earth then, but we handled it all. But, hey, look at us now. Part of the international community, welcomed everywhere as hard workers, black or white.

"Then I came back here to my homeland. It was where I wanted to be."

Piet looked into his beer. "You ever been married Daniel? Children?"

Daniel paused slightly. "Nah, never been married. I met someone, but she wanted to stay in England, I wanted to return here. So, no it didn't work out."

Tap, tap, tap. It was starting to irritate Jack. But he knew he jiggled his foot when he was excited, it probably irritated people too.

Jack checked his watch. "Good to meet you, Daniel. How long are you here for?"

"Going back to my place tomorrow. Leaving early, so long."

Piet also stood. "Time to check the grounds and so on. Where's my dog? Ah, there you are."

Hope bounded up to him and then stopped. Her tail straightened and she gave a low growl. "Come on Hope, I thought you loved guests. What's the matter with you?"

Daniel grinned. "Probably because I'm the only person who won't share my biltong with her."

Piet shrugged. "Sorry about that. She must be hungry. See you around."

Piet and Jack left together; he walked Jack back to his room. "*Jeez,* Jack, we slipped up there, hey. A highly educated Afrikaans professor living out in the bush! Maybe we're losing our touch?"

Jack grinned at him. "Like hell we are. Just got him a bit wrong that's all."

Piet clipped the leash on Hope. "Not worth spending any more time on Jack. Go chase the story in Kenya. I'll give you a lift to the airport in the morning."

Jack checked his watch. It was four in the afternoon in the UK. Still time to make a call.

"Where are we Jack?" Harry boomed down the telephone.

Jack told him. "Listen, Harry, I know a little more about Sir David Cooper, but I need someone to dig a little deeper, see if I've missed anything small but significant. Bit of scandal maybe?

"I'm off to Kenya tomorrow, as you know. I have a plateful of questions and things to follow up. I need a bit of help?"

"Of course, my boy. I'll put someone on it right now. I've hinted to our readers you're following up something rather interesting, as no doubt you have seen online. What else do you need help with?"

Jack smiled into the phone. "Maybe one of your young bright reporters, could contact Cambridge for me. See if anyone remembers

David? Might add a bit of an angle to the story. He left there in 1972. Maybe there's a lecturer or a friend, buried in the past, we can dig up and interview?"

"Travel down the back of the plane, Jack, the bean counters are starting to mutter. There's a new British Ambassador in Nairobi, a woman called the Right Honourable Edith Cummings. Don't bother trying to flirt with her, apparently, she's a right old dragon. Seen service in Ghana, Nigeria, Abidjan and a few other tricky places. Obviously knows Africa well.

"Anyway, she's receiving guests at the Embassy residence on Thursday evening. Use your Press Card, get in there and give me a couple of columns on her. She's a spinster with, obviously, no children. But you never know these days…

"Good luck in Kenya, and for Christ's sake keep the expenses down…"

Jack rang off.

Chapter Thirty-Seven

Jack took a taxi from Nairobi Airport into town. It hadn't changed much since he was last there a couple of years ago. Still the chaotic traffic in town; buses belching black smoke, taxi's zig zagging through the traffic. Pedestrians dodging through the cars to get to the other side of the road. Women with babies tied to their backs carried firewood, or containers of food on their heads. Men either carrying briefcases, or the tools of their trade, pushing loaded trolleys through the traffic. Another was going to and from idling cars, trying to sell a handful of feather dusters.

Eventually the taxi pulled up at the Norfolk Hotel. Jack got out and stretched before leaning in and picking up his leather bag and his computer. He paid the taxi and headed for reception.

Jack loved the buzz of the Norfolk and its history. Walls were lined with black and white photographs of famous people who over the years had stayed at the hotel before going off on safari. The Delamere Terrace and bar was to his right as he mounted the steps, buzzing with locals and tourists alike.

He would check in, take a shower, change his clothes then join the throng on the terrace.

*****

Jack found an empty table on the crowded Delamere Terrace and ordered lunch. No gloomy faces here, everyone looked relaxed and happy. Now he had to find someone who could get him into the Aero Club out at the domestic airport, where he would begin his research into the crashed flight of Sir David Cooper over twenty or so years ago.

*****

Jack arrived at the Aero Club at around three in the afternoon. He watched the pilots coming and going and tried to look bewildered. This always worked. A young, tanned man noticed him. "Can I help you at all? You're looking a bit lost."

Jack thrust out his hand. "Hi, I'm Jack Taylor. I was hoping to look around the club, but I'm not a pilot or a member. I'm a journalist with *The Telegraph* in London. Impeccable credentials I can assure you. I'm doing a piece on one of your pilots who died over twenty years or so ago now. Sir David Cooper?"

The young man frowned. "Way before my time, I'm afraid. Although I have heard of him, I think. Look, I can get you in, as my guest. I'm Phillip, by the way."

Phillip led him through the doors of the club. The place was heaving with memorabilia of a past long gone. Jack felt as though he had taken a step back in time. The walls were crowded with photographs of names he recognised from books he had read about East Africa.

There was a panelled restaurant, a terrace overlooking the airfield and a garden with a small swimming pool. The bar was thatched, in East African style, with an old Spitfire engine perched in one corner and an ancient Pratt & Whitney engine in another. The walls were plastered with memorabilia from the golden age: faces of the magnificent aviators at that time in Kenya's history. Finch-Hatton, Hemingway, Carberry and Beryl Markham amongst them.

Philip went to the bar and bought them two beers. "So, tell me Jack, what's the story here? What are you looking for?"

Jack looked out over the busy little air strip, the planes merely dots in the sky before coming or going, loaded with tourists.

"I have a column with the newspaper. The readers like to know about interesting people who lived in Africa, whether it's now or over eighty years ago. Kenya seems to have a magic and a history of interesting people. Sir David was quite a name here, from what I can gather...to tell the truth I don't know what he looked like. His obituary was brief, with no photograph."

Jack gestured around the walls at all the photographs. "I don't know what it is about this country and the people who lived here, but it still fascinates to this day."

He took a sip of his beer. "Sir David Cooper was a well-respected man, worked for the Foreign Office, Trade and Industry. He came here to Kenya, a posting I presume. Or maybe he had retired, or was thinking about it? Anyway, one day he flew to Mombasa, then on the return journey the plane he was piloting crashed in Tsavo. I wanted to follow up and see, if there was any more to add to the story? Interesting chap by all accounts."

Phillip shook his head. "As I told you, years before my time. But Stanley, the barman, has been here for over forty years. Maybe he can remember what happened. Let's go and ask him, shall we?"

Jack felt the familiar shiver. Now here was someone who would remember Sir David, if he was a member of the Aero Club, which he most definitely would have been.

The smiling barman adjusted the turban on his head. Yes, indeed, he did remember Sir David Cooper. Not well. But Stanley remembered all his pilots over the years. Sir David was not a frequent visitor to the bar. But when he did drop by, he normally sat alone, had one beer then was gone.

"He was a loner, sir. Didn't invite company. On one or two occasions he had someone with him, some business thing, I am thinking. There is nothing much I can tell you about him. He wasn't one of the characters of the club," he nodded in the direction of four other pilots who were laughing uproariously at the end of the bar, "like those guys. The last time I saw him was before his plane crashed in Tsavo. A long time ago now."

Jack thanked Phillip for his help and made his way back, by taxi, to the Norfolk hotel.

*****

That night Jack dined alone in the restaurant and had the best lobster thermidor he'd ever had in his life. The terrace was busy. He signed his bill and made his way outside for a final night cap.

A woman in what he thought might be her late sixties was weaving her way through the crowds, looking, he presumed for somewhere to sit. There were no seats at the bar and the tables were all full of tourists and locals.

She was wearing a pale pink, calf-length dress, diamonds glinted around her neck, a light shawl thrown across one shoulder. On her right wrist she wore what looked like a dozen or so gold bangles. Her hair piled high on her head, her face carefully made up, her dark blue eyes magnified behind stylish glasses. She nodded and wiggled her fingers at people she obviously knew as she neared his table.

Jack took his chance and stood up. "You're welcome to join me at the only table with a spare seat, ma'am." He pulled out the chair.

The woman looked at him briefly. "Well, how can I resist an invitation from such an attractive young man?"

With a smile she sank gracefully into the seat he was offering, then held out her hand, her bangles jingled softly, like wind chimes. "Daphne Forsythe-Phillips. How do you do."

Jack bent slightly over her hand. "Jack Taylor. May I order you something to drink perhaps?"

He recognised her as a lady of breeding, with a cut glass English accent. Definitely old school.

"How lovely, yes. I should like a double gin and tonic with ice and lime, in a tall glass. Thank you."

Jack gave the order to a hovering waiter and ordered a beer for himself.

"So, hello Jack. I most certainly would have recognised you if you had been a local. So perhaps you are here on business, or going on safari?"

Without waiting for an answer, she continued. "Marvellous movie, *Out of Africa*. Did more for tourism here than any politician ever could. I met Robert Redford, you know. After filming for the day, out in the bush, he would return to Nairobi, to this very hotel in fact. He preferred it to staying out there in the bush. Meryl Streep, absolutely charming, a wonderful actress, she preferred to stay out in the bush, mix with the locals, see their schools and such like.

"She brought her children out to Kenya for the making of the film and insisted the children mix and attend one of the local bush schools where they were filming."

Jack smiled at her. "Yes, it was a wonderful movie. I think when anyone in the world thinks of a safari, they think of that movie and Kenya. This country still attracts so many international tourists, because of it. Even today."

Daphne took a large mouthful of her drink. Then reached into her handbag and drew out a packet of cigarettes, a gold lighter and a long dark cigarette holder.

Jack looked around for any signs of a cigarette with a red bar through it. Not finding one, he leaned forward, took her lighter and lit her cigarette for her.

Daphne blew out a film of smoke and used her hand to deflect it from Jack's face. "We're inclined to ignore signs here banning this and that. I wouldn't smoke inside, but out here on the terrace, well, no-one minds. Plenty of smokers here. So, tell me Jack, you haven't answered my question. What are you doing in Nairobi?"

Jack sipped his beer. "You have a new British Ambassador here, The Right Honourable Edith Cummings. My newspaper, *The Telegraph,* asked me to write something up about her. She's having a cocktail party on Thursday, to meet the British here and other important dignitaries."

Daphne flapped her hand. "Yes, I know all about it. I shall be attending myself." She narrowed her eyes. "But you didn't come all the way to Kenya from England to write about that. We have stringers here who could easily cover such a small event. So, what are you really here for? Digging for more information on the old white mischief crowd?"

She raised an elegant eyebrow. "I honestly don't think there is anything more anyone can write about that time in our history here, Jack. It's been done to death. All the major players have gone and, no doubt, causing chaos somewhere else, if there is somewhere else that is. There are a few of their children and grandchildren sprinkled around here and there though."

Jack took a handful of peanuts from the wooden bowl in front of them, careful not to toss them back and have salt and peanut shells cascading down his shirt. "You've lived here a long time then Daphne?"

She smiled. "Goodness me, yes. I was born here! I couldn't imagine living anywhere else. I visit relatives in England every couple of years, but I wouldn't even think about living there. I love England, love the seasons and, of course, the social life there. But this is my home and always has been. Everyone knows everyone else. I belong here. So, what are you looking for then, Jack? There has to be something else you're interested in?"

Jack ordered another double gin and tonic for Daphne. He was only halfway through his beer and wanted to remain clear-headed. "There is, Daphne. I'm living in South Africa now, but I'm still with the newspaper, on a free-lance basis. I'm following something with a definite connection to Kenya and the UK."

He looked at Daphne's rapidly diminishing level of liquid in her glass. He would have to get to the point quickly.

"There was a plane crash here many years ago…"

Daphne interrupted him. "There have been so many crashes here, Jack. They say you shouldn't drink and drive, and by the way I have my driver, Bashir, waiting outside, so no need to be concerned about me. But flying and drinking definitely do not go together. Which one of the many plane crashes are you referring to? Finch-Hatton, maybe?"

Jack brushed back his hair and waved a mosquito away from his face. "His name was Sir David Cooper."

Daphne put down her glass carefully. "David." she said softly.

"You knew him then?"

She sighed. "Yes, I knew him – but then so did everyone else. But it was a long time ago, Jack. Why would anyone be interested in him now? He's been dead for over twenty years."

Jack nodded. "A friend of mine who deals in old silver collectables came across a silver box in South Africa. It was a deceased estate. The executor was selling off the contents of the house before it was auctioned off. The house belonged to a woman called Marlene Hartley.

"It turns out the crest on the box belonged to the Cooper family. I followed the story, but it came to an abrupt end when I researched Sir David's past and found out he had died here in Kenya. But there's almost nothing known about him. His obituary in our newspaper was short and not terribly informative. I know he was with the Foreign Office, highly respected, was honoured by the Queen for his services to the country. He had a wife who died shortly after he did. That's it."

Jack brushed a peanut shell from the table. "But I think there's more I need to know about him, don't ask me why, but there is a bigger story here. How did the silver box end up in South Africa? Plus, there was something else. A Chinese wooden puzzle box. I think it belonged to him."

Daphne fingered the diamonds at her throat and glanced around the terrace. "I don't think this is the time or place to talk about David."

Jack tried to stop jiggling his foot. "How well did you know him then?"

Daphne stood up shakily, abandoning her drink. She reached for her shawl lying over the back of the chair.

"Quite well. But I can't talk about this now. Why not come and call on me, perhaps luncheon tomorrow? My driver will collect you at twelve if this is acceptable. I will tell you what I know about Sir David."

166

Chapter Thirty-Eight

Jack was waiting outside the hotel as Daphne's driver pulled up in a sleek Mercedes with tinted windows.

Daphne lived in the suburb of Muthaiga, one of the most prestigious residential arcas in Nairobi. Jack, of course, had heard of it because of the famous Muthaiga Country Club and its long history of legendary members who had gone down in history books with their penchant for wild parties and even wilder behaviour.

The car made its way through the lush landscape with glimpses of old houses hidden behind grounds with well-established gardens and trees. The car made a turning to the left down through an archway of thick jacaranda trees, not yet in bloom, but magnificent, nevertheless. Through the thick branches and leaves, spikes of sunlight glinted off the car's highly polished paintwork, before it pulled up outside of a one storey, old colonial style homestead. Its walls were cluttered with well-established bougainvillaea bushes, clinging to teetering trellises, their colourful leaves of red, white, magenta and purple embracing the white arches surrounding the veranda. Pale blue muslin curtains fluttered lazily on the terrace, drawn to keep the hot sun away from the interior and giving the place an almost Bedouin feel.

Waiting on the steps to the entrance of the house was Daphne.

She wore a cream kaftan with a gold belt, her hair held back in a ponytail, her feet bare. She raised her arm in greeting her gold bracelets glinting in the harsh sunlight.

Jack stepped out of the car and lifted her hand to his lips, in a French style greeting.

"Hello Jack. Lovely to see you again. Do come in out of the hot sun. Have a seat. What may I get you to drink?"

She gestured to the wicker chairs, plump with pale blue cushions, tall white planters held bushy green ferns, the cover of a magazine on the square white table lifted its covers encouraged by the rattan fan paddling the air above and around them.

Jack looked around. It was a veritable calm and cool oasis from the heat. He sank into one of the more than comfortable chairs and smiled at her.

"A beer would be wonderful. Thank you."

Daphne settled herself into the chair opposite him and picked up a dainty silver bell which she shook gently. Like a genie, a tall elderly African appeared from the shadows of the house.

"Ah, Bashir. A glass of beer for my guest and I should like a gin and tonic. You may serve lunch at twelve thirty. Thank you."

Bashir melted back into the shadows. Jack watched him disappear. Then turned back to Daphne.

"Bashir doesn't say much, does he? I tried to talk to him on the journey here, but he just nodded his head."

Daphne smiled at him. "It's the way he is, Jack. A man of few words."

"You have a wonderful home, like an oasis. Is it very old?"

Daphne waited whilst Bashir returned with a prepared silver tray and their drinks. Then he padded away again.

Daphne picked up her drink. "Yes, it's one of the oldest houses in Muthaiga. Over a hundred years old as you can see by the gardens and the trees. It belonged to my parents. I've lived here all my life."

An elegant Siamese cat strolled out of the shadows of the house and stared at Jack with its big blue eyes before curling up on a chair and falling asleep. Daphne smiled. "That's Yum Yum. Not terribly sociable. I have six cats, all Siamese. Love the breed, so elegant, so aristocratic, but rather noisy if you're not used to them. They talk, you see, well not actually talk obviously, but they demand your attention with their distinctive call. They'll all be out before long to check you out and see if you're acceptable. I think you'll do…"

Five more cats wandered through, all identical. Jack smiled at them. "They are certainly beautiful creatures, aren't they? How do you tell them apart?"

"I can't actually. They are all from the same litter - absolutely identical."

"But obviously they all have names, Daphne?"

She smiled. "No. They're all called Yum-Yum. That way I don't hurt their feelings by trying to work out which one is which and calling them by the wrong name. So much easier."

168

Jack laughed at the logic. He took a grateful sip of his ice-cold beer. He was a hardened journalist but he knew diving straight in with his questions about David would be a serious breach of etiquette with a woman like Daphne.

He chose safer ground. "Tell me about you, Daphne, and your life here?"

She raised her eyebrow. "One thing I wish to make quite clear with you, Jack. Our conversation here at my home is strictly between you and I. I do not wish to see my name in any of your columns. I have done a little research on you, you see. I remember your name now. I have your newspaper couriered to me every week from London and have read your columns. I know about the stories you have covered. Your cold cases, I think they call them?

"Yes, I do have the internet and obviously a computer. I'm fascinated with everything going on in the world, most of it truly depressing. The news in particular. But technology has been the most wonderful thing ever introduced. Of course, it has been abused with social media but for information about anyone and everything, well, it's a glorious place to explore."

Jack nodded in agreement. "Indeed, it is. Although it can be frustrating when you're looking for something and can't find it."

Daphne looked at him quickly then continued. "The world we knew in Kenya, fifty years ago, has gone. We still have our dinner parties, cocktail parties, the races, of course, weekends on safari, days down at the beach in Mombasa at our holiday homes. It's all still here. Unlike a lot of the older people, I don't wallow in the past. It's gone and time is something you can never bring back. It marches on oblivious to one's personal feelings. I accept that. What else can one do, Jack? Wishing for things which have gone is not going to bring anything back. Not going to bring back someone you loved?"

Jack shook his head in agreement but said nothing, letting her talk. Was she talking about life in general, or a particular person?

"I have had three husbands, but no children. My life was full here. I didn't feel the need to have them, well, not with any of my husbands. They would have made terrible fathers. That's the type of men I married…adventurers, big game hunter. Men who didn't want to be tied down by the minutiae of life. I call them my lovers of life, rather than husbands. All dead now I'm afraid."

Jack smiled at her and took a sip of his beer, then leaned back in his chair and let her continue.

"Never regret life, Jack, take it with both hands and enjoy the pure adventure of it – it's what I have done. Ah, here comes lunch. Let's eat and then I will tell you about Sir David. But, again, I must insist anything I tell you does not appear in your newspaper. Are we clear on this?"

Jack held his palms up in front of him. "Of course."

He recognised an adversary when he met one. He would learn nothing from her unless he played by her rules.

"Quite clear, Daphne. You have my word nothing will appear with your name, or anything you may wish to share with me about David Cooper."

"Sir David Cooper, Jack…not just David Cooper. Titles are important even today," she said tartly.

Bashir laid a snow-white tablecloth on the table. The silver, Jack thought, would make Lara's mouth water. Bashir brought through a green salad and a quiche, then once again melted into the shadows of what Jack thought, was a house full of memories. Daphne was quite something. He was impressed.

Daphne encouraged Jack to help himself. "Bashir has been with me for over thirty years now. He's a Somali. I trust him with my life. I'm extremely fond of him. His brother, Saul, looks after my beach house in Watamu."

Whilst they lunched, they talked about things going on in the world, the politics in Kenya, his life, her life. Jack felt himself relax. This woman had something about her, something which made him feel easy and comfortable. A rare thing he had found in women he had met over the years.

Bashir came to clear the table. "Shall we move inside Jack? It's getting quite warm out here."

Jack thanked Bashir, then followed her through the alcove into the sitting room. There was an enormous fireplace, generous cream couches with fat cream cushions and two huge turquoise candle holders either side of the fireplace.

The floors were old wood, shiny with care over the years. Boxes with brass studs, a complete wall lined with book shelves and packed with books. The simplicity and style of the room was faultless. With the white outside arches, the soft blue curtains and her sitting room it reminded him of homes he had seen in coffee table books. Bedouin styled homes reminiscent of Mombasa and Lamu.

Daphne smiled at him. "As you can see, I don't have much, but what I have here is of great value to me, like my friends. I never wanted huge pieces of furniture which swamp a room. I like simple things, valuable yes, as you can see, but simple. I have never wanted the debris of someone else's life. Someone else's value of old things. It means nothing to me. I want my own things. David was like that…"

Jack nodded; Lara would see things differently. This is what he had been waiting for. Daphne had reached this point in her own time. He leaned forward and let her talk.

"I met David many times at the endless cocktail parties we have here. He was hosting yet another function, it was his job. I was bored with the whole thing. Yes, it was nice to see some of my old friends there, but these people were young, more international, all the talk was of business. I went outside to have a cigarette. No smoking at those embassy do's, let me tell you, even then.

"I was sitting outside looking at the stars, watching all the bodies moving around inside and outside in the grounds, when he walked up to me.

"The place where I was sitting was in the shadows of the grounds of the embassy. But he found me there and sank down into the chair next to me. It was a black-tie event, obviously. He wrenched open his top button and looked at me with what I can only describe as a look of utter despair. I remember his words clearly. Even now. It was a few months before he died.

'Daphne?' he said, 'I need a place where I can get away from all of this…'

"I saw something in him then, Jack. A man who had had enough of everything. Tired of being in the spotlight. It seemed to me he was just plain exhausted.

"I had watched David over the years at countless social events. The confident, successful man from the foreign office was tired. He looked haunted. Something was wrong."

Jack didn't say anything and let her talk.

"I didn't hesitate. 'Come and stay with me,' I said, 'you can be yourself. Away from it all. No-one will know where you are unless you tell them. Tell them you're going off on some mission. No-one will find you; I promise. I hope you like cats though…'

Daphne smiled at the memory and took a sip of her coffee. "He came here of course. Bashir picked him up outside a restaurant in town after one of his business dinners. No-one questioned where he was. He was always off somewhere. He could be himself here. That's how I came to know the real David Cooper, the man behind the mask, if you like.

"I think he was the loneliest person I had ever met in my life, Jack. He seemed to view the world and his job as a sort of outsider, an observer not really part of it – it's difficult to explain."

Chapter Thirty-Nine

Shadows started to seep across the lush lawns as Daphne talked, frogs, large ones Jack thought, began to burp in harmony somewhere near a trickling fountain, or a pond, in her garden.

"David had a life of privilege. All the right schools, his father was a knight, as you probably know, having done your research. David inherited the title and went on to become the shining star of the Foreign Office. He was Britain's Head of International Trade and Industry. A diplomat of some note, recognised by the Queen and so on.

"He travelled the world flying the British flag. He talked about his Chinese amah, when he was a child. He was born there you know, not many people knew this about him. Then packed off to boarding school in England when he was eight, I think. He loved his amah very much, far more than he ever loved his parents and, I would presume to say, far more than he loved his wife. He hardly mentioned his wife or if he did, I don't remember. Being ripped away from everything he had known and loved, the emptiness that left in him. Well, I think it damaged him quite considerably.

"I let him talk, Jack. I was suddenly seeing a completely different man from the one who had been presented to me at various social occasions over the years. He felt comfortable with me, he trusted me, as he knew he could. An instinctive thing, I think."

Jack took a sip of his cooling coffee. He could easily understand how someone like Daphne could become a safe haven, a keeper of secrets if necessary. Someone who David had so obviously trusted with his private life.

"Did he stay with you often?"

Daphne blew a plume of smoke into the air. "No. It wasn't often. Then he died."

Bashir appeared out of the shadows of the house. "How about a drink, Jack?"

Jack shook his head. "But you go right ahead Daphne."

Daphne smiled at him. "Of course, I will."

Jack flipped open his phone and scrolled to the photo of the two young men relaxing next to the river. He enlarged it as much as he could before it became distorted.

"I know it's a long shot Daphne, but would you be able to recognise if David was one of these young men?"

Daphne studied the photograph wistfully. "So young and attractive their whole lives stretching ahead of them, full of promise, full of hopes and dreams. Where did you find this?"

Jack decided if David Cooper could trust her, then so could he. "There were some photographs in the puzzle box I mentioned to you, this was one of them."

She pointed a manicured finger at one of the young men. "This could possibly be him, but I couldn't swear to it, especially as they're all in shadow under the tree."

"And this one?" He scrolled through to the couple with their protective hats and sunglasses, on the backs of horses.

"Oh, honestly Jack, they could be anyone! A hot place, for certain, but, no, I have no idea who they are. It's possible it could be David if the photograph was found in the box. But, as I said, they could have been anyone."

Jack scrolled to his final photograph and enlarged it. The one with the little boy and the woman with a conical hat and her hand over her mouth.

Daphne sucked in her breath. "Oh yes. This must be David as a little boy in Malaya, as it was then. The young girl can only be Ah Lan, his amah."

She stared at the picture for a long time and Jack imagined she was recalling her conversations with David as they sat here, as he was now.

"Oh, David," she whispered, her voice breaking. "Your life was perfect then, wasn't it? You had no idea what it had in store for you, did you? I hope you have found some peace now."

She stood up abruptly, handed the phone back to him, and disappeared into the shadows of the house. A few minutes later, having composed herself, she re-appeared.

Bashir delivered her drink on a silver tray. Daphne took a sip and leaned back in her chair. Two Siamese cats appeared from nowhere and settled on her lap. She stroked their heads gently, lost in thought.

Jack waited and thought about his next question. But Daphne pre-empted him.

"You're wondering if I had an affair with David. No, I didn't. He was looking for something he seemed to have lost years ago. I think I gave him comfort by being here, listening to him, asking nothing. A bit like the amah he had as a child."

Jack looked out across the darkening gardens. "Did you ever meet his wife? I mean they lived here for some years from what I found?"

"Yes, they did. South Africa was opening up, the British government thought David would be best placed in Kenya, where he could travel to other African countries. South Africa was not an option at the time. He would have been regarded with great suspicion with all that country's political past. He knew certain products were being made in South Africa and then shipped to Swaziland, where they would slap a '*Made in Swaziland*' label on them and sell them on to other African countries. Breaking sanctions was the name of the game, and it was a win-win situation for governments in the region. David knew things were changing and he wanted to be there when the world finally dropped their sanctions against South Africa.

"But his wife? No. I don't know anything about his wife, what she did, where she went."

Daphne looked at the golden orb of the sun as it made its way down behind the trees. "She was never at any of the social functions, although from what I can gather, she did attend business dinners and such like, but rarely in Nairobi. You have to remember, Jack, he was busy with all sorts of things in Africa and around the world. He had an apartment in Nairobi, provided by the Foreign Office, of course, but he also had a modest house in a place called Nanyuki. It was his private place, where he lived with his wife, no doubt paid for by his government as well. Sometimes he stayed at The Norfolk if he was entertaining."

She tapped her nail on her glass looking thoughtful. "He had a pet name for her – he called her Lulu. I don't know what her real name was, he never told me. He mentioned once she was difficult to live with, had days of deep depression. They probably have some specific medical name for it today.

"So, David spent time here. I let him wander around the place, I was here if he wanted to talk, but mostly I let him be. Be who he so desperately seemed to want to be. Who this was, I have no idea," she said vaguely.

Jack swatted a mosquito away from his face as the lights in the garden sprang into life.

Daphne continued. "I went to his memorial service. I rarely show any emotion, Jack, but I became fond of David and the trust he had in me. The time he spent with me was special. A time I shall never forget. To die so young was difficult to accept."

She looked down at her hands. "It was the only time I saw his wife. Appropriately dressed in black, she stood alone at the front of the church. I never saw her face; she was wearing a black veil which was rather strange. Widows rarely wore them even twenty years ago, especially in a hot climate."

Jack pulled at his earlobe. "Alone? Didn't anyone from the Embassy came to the memorial service – that was a bit odd wasn't it, considering who he was?"

"The Ambassador at the time was Sir Ian Douglas. Lovely man, an absolute gentleman. He was away on extended leave at the time, but I'm quite sure someone was at the service to represent him, maybe someone from London. I don't know. I was too upset at the time to notice."

Jack made a few notes in the book he always carried in his shirt pocket. "Where is Sir Ian now then? It would be useful to have a word with him."

Daphne toyed with her gold bangles. "He was in his mid-sixties then; he retired and went to live with his son in New Zealand. I doubt if he's still around. He'd be quite elderly now if he is."

Jack made another note. "David's wife died shortly after him, right? Was she sick? Is this why she never accompanied him to any social events here in Nairobi?"

Daphne gestured to the lawns with her glass. "I have no idea if she was sick or otherwise. I only know she suffered from depression quite badly. David said it made it difficult to live with her. He married her in South Africa somewhere. Perhaps after she died, her personal effects were returned to her family there. This could possibly be the connection with the silver box and other things your friend found. The

176

Chinese puzzle box may well have belonged to David, considering where he grew up."

Daphne frowned. "I would say his wife *must* have had a relative there. In fact, it can be the only explanation, given what you have told me about the auction of this woman Marlene's effects and the house? Actually, now I think about it, David mentioned that his wife had an estranged sister. So, it must have been this Marlene. It has to have been, Jack?"

Jack watched her as she talked, he could see Daphne was distressed about something. "Did you attend David's wife's funeral, Daphne?"

She frowned. "No. There wasn't one, well not here anyway. The Embassy apparently took care of any arrangements his wife might have wished for, which I presume included the repatriation of her body."

"Is there anything else you can remember about him?"

She put her drink down carefully on the table. "Yes. You see, Jack, I think David had had enough of his life, despite how successful it had been. There was an emptiness in him.

"I don't believe it was an accident. David simply didn't want to be here anymore."

She stood up and adjusted her gold belt. "Bashir will take you back to the hotel now. I will see you at the Embassy reception tomorrow."

*****

Daphne withdrew to her bedroom. Turning her bracelets around on her slim arm she watched the car disappear through the tangle of trees down the driveway.

Then she reached over and picked up the phone.

On the way back to the hotel Jack mulled over the intimate insight Daphne had given him into David Cooper. He hadn't considered the fact that David might have committed suicide.

It was a distinct possibility, then, Marlene was Lulu's sister. That would make a lot of sense as to how the puzzle box, the silver box and the photographs had ended up in South Africa.

What didn't stack up and what he had not told Daphne, was the book hidden in the drawer of the box. Eunice had told him she had seen Marlene writing in it. But he didn't dismiss one possibility altogether. Perhaps the sisters, Marlene and Lulu, had forged a bond again, after all the years apart. Maybe Marlene picked up where her deceased sister had left off with whatever was written in the book.

But who then had written the message on the back of the photograph in English?

So, you have found your way into my box, discovered my past perhaps? Now what will you do... apart from being extremely careful? There's a digit missing somewhere. You'll never find it.

Sister to sister it could be a warm and loving message, to be careful with a past her sister had clearly not known about.

But if Marlene had written it then it had a different connotation altogether.

But one thing Jack was absolutely sure about now.

Whoever had stolen the book had known both sisters.

He smiled to himself. Daphne had neatly avoided his question about how often Sir David Cooper had visited her.

Chapter Forty

At six the following evening, Jack joined the queue of people waiting to be introduced to The Right Honourable Edith Cummings, at the Embassy residence.

He spotted Daphne way ahead of him in the long line of people, she chatted briefly to the new Ambassador before moving on and out into the gardens where waiters were filling glasses with champagne and passing around *hors d'oeuvres*. Jack smiled to himself, Daphne was right, there was a tight social circle here today in Kenya, as there had always been.

Then, there she was, in front of him. A tall thin woman, her hair scraped back in an unflattering grey bun. Her cold eyes the colour of washed pebbles. He introduced himself.

"I know exactly who you are Mr Taylor," she said testily. "I can't imagine what you are doing here this evening. I understand you work for *The Telegraph,* not a newspaper I personally subscribe to, but I read them all – whether I like them or not. You live in South Africa now, I understand?"

Jack nodded, a little taken aback she knew about him. "So, what brings you here to Kenya to cover this rather unimportant story of my new appointment. I'm sure it could have been covered by any of the British reporters who actually live here in Kenya?"

Jack's hackles went up. Edith Cummings clearly did not want him at her party this evening.

"I was passing through, ma'am. Following another story which originated here in Nairobi. It made sense for my newspaper to send me to meet the new Ambassador, whilst I was here. I think you will find my credentials impeccable."

She narrowed her eyes and spoke to him softly. "I happen to know what *other* story you are trying to follow. Nairobi is a small place and people who move in certain circles are inclined to speculate and gossip. If you wish to write something about me, my secretary will send you a Press Release – you're staying at The Norfolk I believe. You're wasting your time here Mr Taylor."

"That may be so, ma'am. But it's what I do and I'm doing it with the blessing of my editor, the renowned Harry Bentley. Both he and I shall decide whether there is another story or not. I don't think it comes under the jurisdiction of your new position as Ambassador."

With that he turned on his heel and made his way out to the gardens. He turned back briefly to look at her – she was watching him, her face impassive. Then she turned to her next guest with a practiced, thin lipped, smile.

*****

Jack wrenched his tie from his neck and bundled it into his jacket pocket. Part of him was fuming at the lack of manners shown to him by Edith Cummings. But another part of him fizzed with possibilities. Edith had clearly been warning him off pursuing his story about Sir David Cooper. Either the gossip had filtered down from the Aero Club. Or from Daphne.

He doubted it could possibly have been Daphne, given her relationship with David all those years ago.

"Not done to remove one's tie until the party is over, Jack, darling. I have to say you're looking rather cross?"

Jack turned and smiled at Daphne. "Not really. However, one could say the new Ambassador should hone her diplomatic skills with representatives of the British Press. You would have thought I'd presented her with a dead rat along with my credentials."

Daphne snorted with laughter. "Yes, she comes across as a bit of a dragon, I have to admit. Reminds me of my old headmistress, she had the same sour expression on her face. Never mind, suffice to say I shall try to avoid any social events where she may be present in the future.

"Come on, Jack, have a glass of this ghastly warm champagne, actually it's sparkling wine. We can go and sit on the bench over there, where no-one will see you have no tie and have breached the high code of etiquette here in these hallowed grounds."

Jack beckoned one of the waiters over with his tray laden with champagne filled glasses. "Any chance of a cold beer?"

The waiter beamed at him. "Of course, sir. I will bring you one immediately."

Daphne reached for a glass of champagne before the waiter moved away, then sat on the bench and eased her shoes off, wriggling her toes in the soft cool grass. Jack sat down next to her.

"Now Jack, I've been thinking about your story and about David. People don't like mysteries; they want the truth. A story with a conclusive and satisfying ending.

"Perhaps some things should be securely locked away, but it's the need to know the truth which drives someone isn't it, Jack? I have a few questions of my own about David, always have had. I'd like to know what really happened."

The waiter returned and presented Jack with his cold beer; Daphne helped herself to another glass of champagne.

"What are you planning to do next?"

Jack looked out over the crowds of people who were clearly enjoying themselves at Her Majesty's expense. "I'd like to take a look at the house where David lived with his wife. Maybe whoever lives there now might have taken over some of the staff. They must have had them."

"Well of course they had staff, Jack. Everyone has help around the house and garden. But one can't simply drive up, introduce oneself and ask to speak to the servants. It just won't do at all. Anyway, it's highly unlikely they are still around after all this time."

Jack looked slightly defeated at this news. Daphne patted his hand. "I'll tell you what we can do, but you'll have to buy me dinner when we leave here. I know a lovely restaurant in town, it's been there forever. It used to be owned by a South African but I'm not sure if it still is. Bashir can take us then drop you at the Norfolk later."

Jack's face brightened considerably. "What's your plan then, Daphne. How do I get into the house and talk to the staff?"

Daphne grinned at him. "I'm no slouch when it comes to a bit of sleuthing. I thought your next move would be to find the house. I asked Bashir to ask around, see what he could find out."

She looked at him smugly. "The house has been rented to three different families over the past twenty or so years. As you know it's in Nanyuki.

"A lot of ex-pat families who come to Kenya to work or start a business keep the staff of a house on. It makes sense as the staff member knows how everything works, where the shops are, where to get the best meat or vegetables and so on.

"Bashir tells me there is only one member of staff left who has been working at the house for over thirty years. His name is Juma, he's the gardener and driver. It would appear every Friday he drives the memsahib into Nairobi where she likes to do her shopping. Tomorrow is Friday, Jack."

Jack perked up immediately as Daphne continued. "The lady of the house does her shopping then meets her friends at the Norfolk for lunch. Juma waits outside for her. Now, all you have to do is hang around the hotel entrance and wait for him."

Jack shook his head and kissed her on the cheek. "You are quite something, Daphne. But how will I know what Juma looks like, what car he drives, what the lady of the house is called?"

Daphne put her glass down on the lawn where it toppled over. "Her name is Penelope Cartwright. The car is a dark blue Volvo. Juma will obviously be driving it. Bashir has told him you wish to speak to him so he will be expecting you.

"It's who you know, Jack, and I know everyone who counts - and some who don't.

"Shall we go? I'll leave first, if you don't mind. If Edith sees me leave with you, I shall be struck off her list of guests for any future functions here. Bashir is parked in the VIP car park at the front. You know the car. Don't be long now. I'm absolutely famished."

Jack watched her leave as he put his tie back on. Dinner with Daphne would require it. He shook his head. She certainly was quite a character. He was looking forward to an entertaining and most enjoyable dinner with her.

Chapter Forty-One

Jack was waiting outside the hotel when the dark blue Volvo pulled up. A rather frumpy looking woman wearing a long dark skirt and blouse and large sunglasses, got out. Juma pulled away from the curb and parked under a tree, out of sight from the people lunching on the hotel terrace. He climbed out of the car and leaned against it.

Jack approached the driver, his hand extended. "Hello Juma. I'm Jack. Thank you for agreeing to speak to me."

Juma inclined his head. "It is Mr David you wished to speak to me about, or his wife perhaps, for your English newspaper?"

Jack smiled at him. "Yes, that's right. My newspaper would like me to give you this envelope," he pulled it from his inside pocket. "We are happy to pay you for your memories of Sir David and Lady Cooper."

Juma slid the envelope into his own pocket. "It is good things you are writing about them? They were good people, Mr Jack. I wish them no harm even if these people are now dead people."

Jack nodded. "Only good things, Juma. Mr Cooper was an important man in Britain. We would like to remember him and his wife with a story about their life here in your country."

Juma frowned. "There were three people working for them. Blossom worked in the house, but she has gone to do more important work with our Lord. Arthur also worked in the house. He went to his brother in Mombasa many years ago. It is possible he has also gone to be with our Lord as he was old those many years ago. I worked in the garden; the memsahib loved her garden and spent many hours there working with me. I drove the memsahib to Nairobi when she wished to shop and change the colour of her hair and make it shorter."

Jack hid a smile. "Did they have many visitors to the house, Juma?"

He shook his head. "No visitors, Mr Jack. Many times the memsahib was alone, but working in her garden, when her husband was busy with his work. Then he would fly his small plane to town and leave her there. But not lonely – I am thinking she liked to be alone. Many times she seemed angry, speaking no words. Then loud music, sometimes in the house at night. Sometimes things were broken, she would be throwing things. Alfred told me this. It was our thinking she was *kali,*" he touched his temple with his finger.

Jack tried again. "Did no-one come and see Mrs Cooper, not even friends from Nanyuki?"

"No, no friends, Mr Jack. She had no friends, no family, no children." He hesitated. "Alfred, who worked in the house, said many times they are sometimes shouting at each other. More so before Mr Cooper died in this plane, he was liking to fly in."

Jack frowned. "What happened after Mr Cooper died, Juma. How was his wife then?"

Juma scuffed his toe at the dust next to the car. "I remember this day well. I did not take the memsahib to the funeral they were making in Nairobi. Someone else took her and brought her back with the black cloth over her head, so no-one could see the tears on her face."

"Had you seen this car before?"

He nodded. "Yes, when the white man came to help the memsahib collect the things belonging to Mr Cooper. Important papers, I think. Only a small box for carrying them."

"How was the memsahib afterwards, Juma?"

"The memsahib told Arthur and Blossom they must take holidays, she wished to be alone in the house with only herself. I myself stayed to look after the garden."

Jack swatted a fly away from his nose and put on his sunglasses. "I hear the memsahib died soon after Mr Cooper. Was she sick do you think?"

"It's possible the memsahib was sick. Perhaps it was a sickness which hides inside and only comes out when there is much trouble and sorrow with a person? Or perhaps a sickness inside the head. This was possible with the memsahib. She could be angry for no reason. Sometimes it was difficult for me to understand."

Juma shook his head sadly. "One day the same car came again. This time with an African woman wearing a white coat and shoes like a doctor. This person was here only a few days and then the memsahib, they are telling me, died in her sleep.

"An ambulance came the next morning and took the woman with the white coat and the memsahib away. The other car came back again the next day with a van. Some boxes went into this van, they were the things belonging to the memsahib.

"Then the white man with the car locked the house. He told me I must stay there and take care of the garden and make sure the house was safe."

Jack scratched his chin thoughtfully. "This man with the car was he from Kenya do you think?"

Juma frowned at him. "All white people in Kenya sound the same to me, Mr Jack. The man sounded like you, like the British."

"How long was the house empty? Where did you get your money for looking after the house and garden?"

Juma rubbed his sleeve on the door of the car. "This man paid me my wages for two months. He was giving me this money before he drove away. Then another person came with many keys, then people came to look inside and outside the house.

"The person with the many keys told me new people would live in the house and wished for me to stay on and work in the garden. This I did and I am still working there as you know, Mr Jack."

"There's nothing else you remember for our newspaper, Juma?"

He shook his head. "It was many years ago, Mr Jack, some things I am forgetting. But if I am remembering something it is to Bashir I will tell."

Jack thanked him for his time and walked thoughtfully back to the hotel. He planned to spend the afternoon in his room, writing up his notes before packing and taking a taxi back to the airport for his evening flight to Johannesburg.

After dinner with Daphne the previous evening he had said goodbye to her, promising to keep in touch.

"So lovely to have met you Jack, you have brightened up my days whilst were here. Next time you come to Kenya you must come and stay with me. I do enjoy your company."

Jack had kissed her on both cheeks. "I think I should persuade Harry to take you on as a freelance writer. I'm sure there are many Kenyans around the world who would enjoy a bit of gossip and society news out of Kenya. You could write under a different name."

Daphne had given him a big smile. "Oh yes, I think I could do that, it would be fun, especially if I could remain anonymous. I know Spain has become a refuge for dodgy characters, but they still come here you know. The well-heeled, the titled, the aristocrats, and the rogues, of course, with perfect accents. Kenya still seems to attract the British elite. Quite extraordinary actually. I, of course, have met them all – yes, what a fun proposition, to write under a different name!"

*****

Daphne, surrounded by her Siamese cats, lay back on her pillows in her bedroom, the fan turning slowly above her head.

She thought back to the time she had spent with David, the things he had told her and what, she knew, he hadn't.

Her diary, recording her thoughts at the time, lay next to her, the pages lifting with the lazy flow of air from the fan above.

She wondered how long you should keep the secrets of someone's life. At what time should the truth be told? Should it even be told?

Daphne opened the drawer next to her bed and pulled out the silver chain and Maltese cross. It was the final wish of a man about to die that the cross and chain be given to his daughter. She ran the chain through her fingers.

David had left Daphne with a story which could never be told to anyone.

Jack, she knew, had the bit between his teeth. He was looking for the truth about David and he wouldn't give up until he found out what it was.

186

Chapter Forty-Two

The flight back to Johannesburg had been a bumpy one. Once there Jack checked in for the domestic flight which would take him back to Hazyview.

Piet was there, waiting for him. Hope was busy engaging with all the new arrivals, hoping there might have been some little packets of biltong on the flight which might be shared.

Piet clipped her leash on and smiled when Jack finally came through the arrival's hall.

"Hey, Jack. Good to have you back. How was Kenya?"

Jack followed Piet out to the car. "Great country, Kenya. So unlike South Africa, more rough and tumble, more African somehow. It has a different feel altogether than here. It's almost like the white folk there are caught in a time warp. I met this amazing woman called Daphne."

Piet rolled his eyes as he opened the back of his car so Hope could climb in. "*Ag*, please Jack, not another woman. What is it with you? Is it the scruffy hair you have, or what? Anyways, I have the keys to your new home, put some food in there for you. Your belongings from the cottage in Franschhoek have been delivered there also.

"So, what say you, we go out there now, have a *braai*, and you tell me all about your trip. Your car is already there. I organised it for you. Cold beers in the fridge."

Jack grinned. What a welcome! He was spending his first night in his new home. Piet had taken care of everything. He could think of nothing better than a *braai*, a few beers under the stars and bringing Piet up to date on what he had found out so far from his trip to Kenya – and Daphne.

*****

Piet sucked at the crispy fat on his lamb chop as he listened to Jack. At night Jack's new home looked even more seductive than in the sunlight. Lamps had been discreetly set in the reeds down near the stream which gurgled and whispered on its way, frogs performing a harmonious ping-pong burping symphony. Piet quietly joined in as he put his chop on his plate and pushed it away, trying to ignore his dog's hopeful eyes. He took a sip of his beer and wiped his hand across his mouth.

"So, Jack. You're thinking David Cooper perhaps took his own life? Then his wife Lulu," he sighed and rolled his eyes. "*Jeez* Jack what kind of a name is that, must be English…anyways, she dies and the Embassy repatriate her body to wherever it was she wanted it to go. You think South Africa? Also, she had a sister here?

"Then you meet the dragon lady who tells you to *fok* off and leave the story alone. The old gardener, Juma, pretty much confirms the fact that perhaps the Cooper's didn't have much of a marriage. Also, this wife sounds as though she was a bit off her head at times – unpredictable."

Piet helped himself to another chop. "They sound like an odd couple to me. David Cooper was a loner except when he was on business of course. His wife had no friends or any visitors, only when she was dying and a nurse came to look after her. Then the ambulance pitched up and took her away. I know when folks have been married forever and one dies, it's not uncommon for the other to die shortly after. But these guys were only in their forties?"

Jack nodded. "That's about it, Piet. Not an altogether wasted trip though. Daphne was a mine of information. She was fond of David, knew him well, and seemed to be intrigued with the puzzle box, the photographs and the silver box. I'm pretty sure she'll have her ear to the ground and be asking a few discreet questions herself.

"But Edith Cummings was definitely giving me a warning."

Piet stroked his chin as he digested all the new information. "You think this Daphne woman had an affair with Cooper?"

"Nah, sounded like good mates to me. But then again, who knows? Not the sort of question you ask a lady such as Daphne."

Jack's phone vibrated on the table, *unknown caller*, he glanced at it then picked it up quickly. "Jack Taylor. Oh, hello Harry, where are you calling from? I didn't recognise the number." He put the phone on speaker.

Piet gathered up the plates and cleared the table, packing everything, rather messily, into the dishwasher. He put down a bowl of dog biscuits for Hope, who looked at them with disgust and gave him a reproachful and disappointed look.

Through the open door he could clearly hear the conversation Jack was having with Harry.

"Harry, it's good to hear from you. I've just got back from Kenya. I'm sitting here at my new place bringing Piet up to date on what happened."

He pretty much repeated the conversation he had just had with Piet. "That's all I have so far, Harry. You might want to think about taking Daphne on as a stringer. She has a fine pedigree, lived in Nairobi all her life and knows everyone worth knowing."

Piet came and sat back down, rubbing at a grease mark on his safari boot from his lamb chop.

"There are still plenty of things going on in Kenya, Harry, she could write a social column which would appeal to Kenyans who have left the country and gone to live elsewhere. Our readers would love it. Then we'll have South and East Africa covered. What do you think? Hey, are you still there Harry, you're not saying anything?"

Harry cleared his throat. "Jack, I have some unfortunate news for you I'm afraid. The shareholders of the newspaper have made a decision. I had to go along with it."

Harry continued; his voice devoid of emotion. "I'm afraid there won't be any stories, or your weekly column coming out of South Africa anymore. We'll give you a severance package, of course, and pay your repatriation expenses if you wish to return to the UK. But there will be no more story about Sir David Cooper. Is this clearly understood, Jack?

"You won't be able to write anything further for *The Telegraph,* under our banner and we will require your press card to be returned to us. You have a signed legal contract with us which doesn't allow you to write for another newspaper or magazine anywhere in the world for twelve months as per the confidentiality and non-compete clause, in your contract with us. You will be compensated for this.

"I'm sorry, Jack. But there it is."

Jack felt the colour drain from his face. The shock he was feeling came through his rising voice. "Is this some kind of a joke Harry? I've worked for you for over twenty years? You're kidding right? Mad at me for my expenses? I've been more than careful with this on my trip to Kenya. There's a great story here I can feel it."

There was a long silence. Piet watched his friend closely what Harry was telling him had shocked him to the very core of his being.

"As I said, Jack, I'm sorry. The matter has been taken out of my hands. As of now you don't work for the newspaper anymore. I know it is shocking news for you and I'm glad your friend is there with you. I have his number somewhere. I'll give him a call sometime and thank him for his hard work on the last two stories. He's also not on the expenses pay roll anymore."

Harry rang off without saying another word.

Jack sat back in his chair shocked. His hand shook as he put the phone down on the table, his face ashen. "I don't believe this. It's simply not possible!"

Chapter Forty-Three

Piet left Jack sitting in his chair looking stunned. He brought him a beer from the fridge. He put it down on the table and waited, as he had done with the hundreds of people accused of one thing or another, over the many years of his career as a police detective. His face was creased with concern for his friend.

Jack ran his hands through his hair and downed his beer in two heaving gulps. "I've been fired, Piet. The newspaper has let me go. I don't work for them anymore. Jesus, Piet, the newspaper has been my life for over twenty years. I can't believe it! I just can't believe it!" He shook his head and stared straight ahead.

"Harry sounded like a stranger, cold and uncaring after all we've been through together. He once said I was like the son he never had, and now he's kicked me out of a life I loved, without a backward glance. I have to hand in my badge of honour, my press card. Can't write for them anymore. Can't write for anyone for twelve months, as per my contract. It also means you're no longer on the expense account Piet."

Piet leaned forward and spoke softly, gripping Jack's wrist in his hand. "Jack, Jack. Calm down a bit, okay. Forget about me. This is about you. Think the whole thing through. This, according to Harry, was not his choice. Not what he wanted. The shareholders put the pressure on him, he had to go along with it. Whether he wanted to or not.

"He called you from a phone, a number you didn't recognise. Why? I know you're in a state of shock and you're not thinking clearly. But I am. Also, he didn't mention me by name, only referred to me as 'your friend'. Right?"

Jack nodded miserably.

"Harry did something he had to do – but it doesn't mean it's what he wanted to do. Something big is coming down, my friend. Get a grip on yourself, okay?"

Piet stared at his own phone, willing it to ring – it did. *Caller unknown.* "I think this call might be for you, my friend. I'll put it on speaker – we're in this together again, working as a team as we've always done. I think it's Harry – in fact, I'm sure it is, so long."

Jack, his hands still shaking pressed answer. He held his breath and prayed this call might make the nightmare go away.

"Jack Taylor."

Harry sounded completely different. "That side kick of yours Piet, is one smart guy Jack. The last call I made to you was the hardest thing I've ever had to do in my life. Worse than telling someone their loved one has died, or even worse, having to put down one of the dogs."

"Jesus, Harry," he said gulping angrily. "You almost gave me a bloody heart attack. What the hell is going on?"

"It came from right at the top, Jack. Number 10. I was told to kill your story, get rid of you. Bury it. The shareholders don't know you as I do. They all remember what happened to that rag *The News of The World.* Been going for a hundred years, one mistake and it was tomorrow's news. Dead in the marketplace. Closed down. Our shareholders took this order from the government mouthpiece and didn't want to take the risk.

"Now, I might be the editor of our newspaper, Jack, but I'm a newshound just like you. Something is going on here. Something big. Something they want to stay buried."

Jack ran his hand distractedly through his hair. "I hear you, Harry, but it doesn't make my position any more tenable, does it? I'm out. That's the bottom line. Thrown out with the baby and the bathwater. If your hands are tied, well, it doesn't change my position now does it," he said bitterly.

"Thing is, Jack, I am not going to throw the baby out with the bathwater. I want this story more than any other this newspaper has ever tracked. Something is going on here. Something so important the government has come down on our collective heads."

Jack heard Harry take a deep breath.

"So, this is what is going to happen - if you agree. I want you to stay on this story. Let's go along with what the government want, no actually what they have instructed us to do. Well, we don't really have a choice there, we have to go along with it. I'll get another phone with which I will communicate with you. A number no-one else has.

Likewise, you will do the same. Obviously, you won't be able to email or get in touch with the newspaper, but I'm not letting you go, Jack."

"Whose phone are you using at the moment Harry?"

"My brother's landline. He's gone down to his shed to have a fag, no-one else here to listen to this conversation, only his dog, don't think we have a problem there. It's a French bulldog, doubt it understands English."

Harry continued. "I personally will pay all your expenses and not bitch about them anymore. I will pay your retainer and your expenses into your South African account. You might want to open another one. The spooks are out looking at this one, Jack. We can't make any mistakes, or leave a trail. Maybe Piet can help, pay everything into his account. Yes, that could work. You trust him, I trust him.

"Everything must be watertight, Jack. The spooks in the UK are not stupid, super-smart in fact. I think this Sir David Cooper was someone of great interest to them, and you, my boy, are going to dig deep and find out exactly what happened to him and what he did to spark such an outrage in the bowels of government twenty years ago – okay?"

Jack's foot began to jiggle again, Piet smiled. They were back on track again. Although the spooks from the British Government, might be a cause for concern.

Harry continued. "There are politicians here I admire for their honestly and openness, but there are other politicians with their own agendas, their snouts in the trough, cutting deals all over the place. Contracts being awarded where they shouldn't have been, back handers, and so it goes on."

Harry took a deep breath. "The Russian oligarchs, owning some of the most prestigious properties in the country, half of bloody London in fact, we don't like it, don't like it at all. Putin's Pawns as I call them.

"So, Jack. What do you say?"

Jack looked across at a smiling, nodding Piet. "We'll follow this story. But what will you tell my readers, the ones who love their weekly columns, their stories out of Africa? I can't suddenly disappear, despite the British Governments wishes and your shareholders?"

"I've already worked it out Jack. You'll be taking a sabbatical to India, taking a year out. Leave it with me."

"But, Harry, what about all my colleagues at the paper? What will you tell them?"

"Same thing. The savvier ones won't believe it for a minute, but they'll recognise the reasons why. Trust me."

Jack frowned as he thought things through, quickly discarding some thoughts and focussing on the immediate. "Okay. I've only just told you about Daphne in Nairobi. No-one knows about her yet, or her connection to Sir David Cooper. Only me, you and Piet. I'll let her know this story has been squashed. Tell her to watch out for Edith Cummings."

Jack stood up and paced around. "I get the feeling Daphne will be more than happy to oblige and help in any subversive way she can. I very much doubt the spooks know how well she knew David. He went there to her house to disappear for a while. He trusted her. She will protect that trust, I know. I'll use Piet's phone. I'll tell her not to get in touch with me in any way. No calls, no emails. Cummings might well have seen me with her though."

He took a deep breath and continued. "The fact the book from the puzzle box has disappeared makes me think the British Government may well have had something to do with it, suspecting it may reveal things they wish to slam a heavy lid on. Does anyone know about your Aunt Clair's attempt to decipher the shorthand?"

"No, Jack, no-one knows about it. It wasn't important at the time, but clearly it is now. Should Clair be approached by anyone, which is highly unlikely, I'll tell her to be prepared. Those Bletchley Park gals know how to look innocent and confused when necessary."

Jack looked up at the stars. "This whole thing, Harry, started with the girl called Lara Summers. She was the one who seems to have opened this can of worms with the puzzle box, the crest on the silver box and the photographs. I need to protect her. I think she will be safer here with Piet and I in Hazyview."

"I agree Jack. Send through Piet's bank account details. Let him book Lara's flight back to South Africa. The spooks are all over this thing. Use Piet's phone to call her. They have no record of Piet's number. I have a feeling there will be little resistance to Lara agreeing to come back to South Africa."

Jack smiled into the phone. The evening had started off well in the first night in his new home. Then Harry had dropped the bombshell on him. But now, it seemed he had a seriously good story to chase with Piet. Everything paid for and the added bonus of the lovely

Lara, if she agreed, and he had no doubt she would, on the first available flight back to South Africa.

But, unlike his other stories out of Africa he knew this one had sinister undertones. Lara had unleashed a pit of vipers in her search for collecting old silver.

Jack had no idea where his story was going, but he knew there would be many other eyes watching this particular one.

Harry interrupted his train of thought. "What's the progress on the translation of the book Jack?"

"The Afrikaans lady is ploughing her way through it but not finding it easy apparently. Some of the things seem to be written in some kind of code which is making it difficult. Unfortunately, she didn't do time at Bletchley Park. Piet tells me she should be finished in a week or so. But then we have another problem, Harry.

"We need to get it back to your aunt. If there are codes in the content. How are we going to do this? You can't be involved now."

There was a short silence from Harry at the end of the phone. "There is a way. Lara could help us out there if she's willing. Piet could send it through to her. There's no connection there – should be safe enough."

Harry was right, he thought, no connection between Lara and his editor's aunt. He and Piet could go through the translation see what they could come up with and Harry's aunt Clair could have a go at any codes she might find.

"There are a few other issues which need to be addressed, Harry. My parents for a start. What am I supposed to say to them? If this is as serious as I think it is their phone will probably be tapped. I guess we could apply the same technique though. I could use Piet's phone, tell the folks I'm going undercover for a while. They're used to that with the cases I was investigating in the UK.

"It will be a bit trickier here in Hazyview though. Take Hugo who owns the hotel I always stay in for instance. I'll have to come up with something creative. He knows I've only just moved into my own place, so going off to India for a year is not going to wash. He won't believe it for a second."

"You forget Jack, I've known Hugo for years, when he lived and worked in London, we would often have a beer together. He's old school. You can trust him. Tell him you have to lie low for a bit. Tell him to keep his ears and eyes open for anything he may hear in the bar. Now what else?"

Jack rubbed his eyes. "So, basically, I'll have to lie low here at my new place. Not a problem, I'll miss the buzz of Hugo's bar though. Piet can feed back any information to me, get me a couple of phones. We can meet here and start digging a bit deeper to find out exactly what David Cooper must have got heavily involved in, in order for the British Government to come down so swiftly on my head and slam and lock the doors on the whole thing."

He paused as he thought. "Daphne's comment about him possibly committing suicide could be closer to the truth than we originally thought."

Harry interrupted him. "Another thing Jack. Get rid of your car. Piet will be able to help you get another one which we'll put in his name. Keep well away from this Hazyview place for a few weeks, until all this fuss has died down. Cheerio, must dash, train to catch."

Piet closed his phone and rubbed his hands together gleefully.

"Plenty of things to do, hey. We'll get you another car tomorrow. I'll fix everything, get the garage to follow me out here then swap it for yours. I'll organise the insurance.

"Also, I'll bring you a couple of phones. You have internet access here; you have your laptop; it's time to get to work."

He checked his watch. "Tomorrow you can call Daphne, Lara and your folks on your new phone. I'll handle Hugo. There's enough food in the fridge for the time being. Once you get your new car you can go shopping, so long, and stock up. Go to Nelspruit, no-one knows you there, safe enough."

Piet stood up. "*Jeez,* only came out here to have a *braai,* next thing I know I've got a load of British spooks on my back, hey!"

He clapped Jack on the back, though not as heartily as he normally did. "Get some sleep, my friend, plenty to do tomorrow, not so? Come on, Hope."

Jack nodded feeling a headache coming on. Dinner last night with Daphne in Nairobi seemed a lifetime ago. The Chinese puzzle box was sitting on a side table next to the bookcase. He ran his fingers across its glossy top.

So, you have found your way into my box, discovered my past perhaps? Now what will you do... apart from being extremely careful? There's a digit missing somewhere. You'll never find it.

196

"Oh yes, we have found our way into your box and, as advised, we are being very very careful. You can be sure of that," Jack murmured.

He pulled the security bars across the doors and locked them before switching off the lights. He lay down on his bed, his head spinning. Within minutes he was asleep.

Chapter Forty-Four

Jack woke refreshed early the next morning, showered, dressed, and unpacked his luggage, hooked up his laptop, put it in incognito mode, and registered another new email account, then made himself bacon and eggs for breakfast.

He sat out on the veranda watching the birds swooping over the bubbling stream. It was quiet, no sounds of any traffic, only the faint whisper of the wind in the trees and the doves calling softly to each other. Three large hadada birds made an ungainly landing on his lawn, tucking their wings untidily in place they proceeded to use their long beaks to dig around looking for insects and worms.

Jack narrowed his eyes. *"Voetsak"* he yelled at them. Indignantly they took off, with their screeching raucous call. He thought not only were they quite ugly, they were unbelievably noisy and clearly didn't like flying. He assumed it's why they made one hell of a noise when they took off.

He pushed his plate aside and brought out his notebook. There was a lot to put in place today, but he couldn't do anything until Piet arrived with his new car and the phones.

He needed to speak to Lara – he wanted to speak to Lara. She had involved them in something none of them understood.

He took a long drink of fresh orange juice – yes, he could see her here with him. If he was going to be isolated for a few weeks he couldn't think of anyone he would prefer to be isolated with.

Perhaps, after all, fate had taken a hand in everything.

*****

Piet pulled up at three that afternoon. Jack's new car following his.

"Hope you like the colour, Jack. White, like thousands, if not millions, in this country. Keeps the heat out."

198

Paperwork was signed for, keys exchanged hands, the driver drove away in Jack's old car.

"Brought you some pies from the hotel, my friend, for dinner."

Piet placed a square box on the kitchen table. "Here are your new phones. Registered to me, let me know when you want them topped up, okay? I need to get back to the hotel. I'll leave you to make your phone calls to Lara, Daphne, your parents – and Harry. I'll have a word with Hugo. Tanks full in the car. Let's get on with this, Jack. I've waited a long time to confront the Brits again. See you around."

*****

Jack called his parents on his new phone and explained the situation which they accepted, as they had done so many times over the years when Jack had to go undercover for his job. Then he called Lara.

"Oh, it's you Jack! Hello! Have you changed your phone number?"

"Hi Lara, yes, I have. You must only use this number from now on. Something has come up." He explained the situation.

"Surely, Jack, I'm not in any sort of danger, am I? The British Government aren't planning on knocking me off simply because I found a couple of old things connected to Sir David Cooper?"

Just hearing her voice cheered Jack up enormously. "Highly unlikely. But because of your connection to me they might show a bit of interest in you. They would have worked out by now that you were the one who found the silver box.

"Harry thinks it would be a good idea if you came over here for a few weeks until things have blown over, plus we need your help. In a few days we should have the translation of your blue book. We need to get it to Harry's elderly aunt who is in a care home in London. Obviously, Harry can't do that now."

Lara laughed. "So, you'll go to ground in your new place, which sounds fabulous, and I'll be happy to go and visit Harry's elderly aunt. I've always wanted to meet someone who worked at Bletchley Park. I'll get another burner phone to communicate with you and Harry. You've given me the number of the phone I have to use for him. Gosh, this is sounding quite exciting!"

Jack took a deep breath. "I'd like you to come over here, Lara. If I am going to be isolated, then I'd like it to be with you."

"That's what I wanted to hear," she purred down the phone happily. "Not because Harry and Piet suggested it, I hope? You honestly want me to come?"

"Yes, Lara. I do want you to come. I miss you."

She hesitated. "I have two auctions I must attend in London, Jack, and when I finally get the translation of the book it will take Harry's aunt a few days or longer to go through it. So, it looks likely I won't be able to fly over for a couple of weeks. I'd fly over tonight if I could!"

She laughed happily. "Have you got good internet connections over there in your new place? I can work from there quite easily. I have little stock left, it's all here in my flat. There's a young student upstairs who could pack and post off anything I sell. He's always keen to make a bit of pocket money and I trust him.

"Then I shall look forward, at the end of the day, to sitting in your babbling brook with a bottle of wine nestling in the water to keep it cool. Keeping a wary look out for British spooks, lurking in the bushes…"

Jack laughed. "Yup, superb internet access, the sun's shining, the wine is in the fridge already."

"By the way, Jack, where is my Chinese puzzle box and what's left of the contents?"

"It's right in front of me, Piet brought it back. It looks nice in the afternoon sun here on the table."

Chapter Forty-Five

Jack was settling into his new life, enjoying it even. The silence and lack of interruptions helped him clear his thoughts and look at the whole situation with the Chinese puzzle box more clearly.

He had called Daphne in Nairobi and explained the situation giving away as little as possible.

"Well, Jack, this story of yours is taking an interesting turn, isn't it? I'll keep my eyes and ears open but as with anything with the British Government, well, they don't give much away. But my dear friend David, if he is eliciting such an interest, well, I want to know why.

"That ghastly woman Edith, whom I swore I would avoid like the plague," Daphne paused. "Well, it seems to me I should try and get closer to her, invite her over for dinner or something, after all she virtually lives next door to me here in Muthaiga. The cats will dislike her. But perhaps after a drink or two, she might let her guard down a little, soften up. But don't put your money on it."

Jack reacted immediately. "Be careful, Daphne, she might well have seen us together at the Embassy do. Most certainly, with her contacts and with her trying to threaten me about the story, she will likely know we dined together. Her security detail at the Residence will have seen me get into your car."

Daphne had laughed. "Well, Jack, anyone who has lived here in Nairobi and moved in the right circles, will know most of us would have met Sir David Cooper at some point. Should the subject come up, I shall tell her I found you as tedious as any other journalist looking for a story. Sorry, darling, I actually loved meeting you. I shall pretend I thought you were too ghastly for words. Trust me, I can do this. I want to help in any way I can. This is so exciting, isn't it, also a bit worrying. Why such a high interest in David now?"

Then Jack called Harry giving him the new number. "We've battened down the hatches here Harry. Everything is in place. Lara, Piet, Hugo and Daphne are all on board. I have a new car, new email address. We're good to go. Lara will contact you with her new number."

*****

Piet arrived late in the afternoon the following day. Jack had shopped in Nelspruit for everything he needed. He had stacked his trolley with enough for a few weeks. Out of habit, when he got to the check-out, he piled everything in front of the till point, then moved his bags along ready to pack it all away. A laughing African girl gently pushed his hand away and took over the packing of the bags. Jack smiled at her and thanked her. Yup, what was not to love about this country he now called home?

Knowing Piet was going to arrive in the late afternoon he had prepared for a *braai,* he didn't think Piet would appreciate a ready-made dinner from Woolworths.

The fire was glowing, the pork ribs and sausages marinating in the fridge. Potatoes were wrapped in tin foil waiting to be delivered into the hot embers of the fire. Jack had prepared a salad of butter lettuce, feta cheese, baby tomatoes and avocados, and, of course, a highly pungent loaf of garlic bread, which he had prepared himself.

Piet got out of the car, Hope following at his heels in great anticipation of some decent food. The rounds of the guests with their sundowners had been sorely disappointing…

Jack stood up to greet his friend, surprised at the speed at which he was crossing the lawn. "Here it is, Jack. This is what we've been waiting for! The translation of the book. My legal auntie has done a fine job, although she was puzzled by some of the content.

"So, hey, my friend, how about a beer before we go through it. I had the auntie make two copies, one for you one for me. Haven't sent it through to Lara. I wanted you and I to go through it first."

Jack felt the excitement fizzing down his spine. "Take a seat, I've filled Hope's bowl with water and, um, dog biscuits, but I think she's slightly hopeful for something from the *braai.* Alright if I put some *boerewors* on for her? I'm thinking we might have something to celebrate."

Jack brought out two cold beers and the platter of meat. Piet stacked the mound of paper into two neat piles. The meat hissed and spat as Jack dropped it on the hot grill of the fire. He nestled the potatoes into the embers and perched the garlic bread on one side.

They reached for their beers and the papers in front of them.

So lost were they in the words written so long ago, they didn't notice the sausages had caught fire, until Hope barked a warning. Jack stood up swiftly and threw his beer over the charred meat, a haze of grey mist hissed and rose into the air. Then he went back to the copied pages of the blue book.

Piet had not said a word, only a puzzled frown on his face, as he sipped his beer and read through the pages. He had looked up when Hope barked.

"*Ag*, Jack, I thought I had taught you how to make a *braai*? No-one can screw up a *braai*, well it's what I was thinking. Hey, let me take over here, looks like we'll be eating the *boerewors* and Hope will have to make do with the burnt offerings."

Hope licked her lips staring at the meat.

Jack continued to read, completely absorbed.

Finally, he looked up. Piet had brought out the salad, the plates and cutlery, the meat was rescued, as well as the potatoes. They heaped the food on their plates. Jack tore open the bread and they ate hungrily without saying anything. Both of them absorbed in their own thoughts and the words in front of them.

Jack pushed his plate aside. "So, what do you make of all this Piet?"

Piet tossed a piece of meat to Hope. "Ramblings mostly. Day to day stuff, but then there are numbers and letters, sprinkled throughout the ramblings. This I don't understand. It makes no sense to me at all. There are some Afrikaans words the auntie in Bletchley Park won't understand but I can translate these words for her, so long, pencil them in for her. *Jeez,* this woman might have travelled but I'm thinking, judging by her ramblings, she lived a dull and boring life most of the time. However, having said that, I think there is a story this woman is telling. A story beneath a story, if you like?"

Jack stretched his legs out and took a sip of his beer. "Basically, Piet, its David's wife talking about her trips around the various countries with her husband. She mentions some names of people she met, only used their initials though and the restaurants they went to. But then it becomes muddled, to me anyway, with these numbers and letters – quite a few of them. But there are no dates or actual places, only which continent they were on at the time. Africa, Asia, the Middle East, Europe. But there's no mention of her parents, any siblings, and we think she had a sister who lived in South Africa. Why nothing about her, Piet, or even where she lived? How come she never mentions any friends? He frowned. "But I agree with you, there is a story beneath a story here, something hidden."

Piet shrugged. "Maybe she didn't have any friends. Maybe she wasn't a nice and lovable person, like me, hey?"

Jack looked up at him and frowned. "Why no mention, no personal anecdotes, of her and her husband? Why no thoughts, why no comments, no loving memories of anything? I know she suffered from depression, but it seems she suffered more than most. Even so..."

Piet ran Hope's silky ear between his fingers. "Perhaps there were no loving memories, Jack. We have no idea of the time span of this book. When she started to write it, or what her last words were before she died. Apart from the mention of the funeral of her husband it's the only time, as far as I can see, she seemed to write with any passion and not much of it. In fact, she seemed more angry than sad, if you ask me?"

Jack tapped his glass on the side of his chair. "She doesn't mention anywhere she was ill, apart from the odd reference to a touch of malaria. Except for this bit."

'I know everything is coming to an end now, my life is over. But I'm not afraid. I'm angry, yes, very angry. But I'm not afraid.'

Piet nodded. "*Ja*, still no mention of any sister. The last part of this diary was written by someone else maybe, it has to be her sister, right? *Shoo*, she was one angry woman as far as I'm concerned.

"Thing is, Jack, it would be impossible to see if the handwriting had changed because of the shorthand. But the tone of the entries in this diary stays the same, how can this be? Still the same writing style. Life out in Wolmaransstad, riding out most days, the odd trips into town, but no more.

"It sounds like the same woman, but there are no numbers or letters in this final part of the diary, how so?"

Jack rubbed the back of his neck. "Sisters can be close. With twins even closer. But even sisters who are not twins can think and feel alike. Know what the other one is thinking, know if something is wrong, whether they live next door to each other or in different countries. Sisters have an uncanny knack, not all of them of course, some sisters hate each other. Which begs the question of why Lady Cooper never mentioned her sister's name?"

Piet looked out over the gardens, now lit with lights. "This is what I'm thinking, my friend. We need proof. A death certificate."

Jack nodded his head slowly. "I'm thinking you might be right. There was no funeral for Mrs Cooper. The Embassy in Nairobi sent a nurse, it's true, according to Juma. Then the ambulance arrived and took her away. Pure theatre?"

Piet leaned forward, rubbing his hands together. "This David Cooper was up to something so sensitive with the Foreign Office and when he died, maybe they had no alternative but to knock off his wife and there the trail would have gone cold. Sir David and Lady Cooper now dead."

Jack rubbed his cheek. "Pretty dramatic assumption Piet."

Piet shrugged. "I need to get in touch with my old pal, Bertie. And run a few more things through that fine brain of his. He will be able to find out about Mrs Cooper."

Chapter Forty-Six

Jack waited for Harry to pick up, when he finally did, he sounded out of breath. "Sorry, Jack, had to run down the stairs and out into the street to take your call – for obvious reasons. What have you got for me? Bugger, it's cold out here and chucking it down with rain. Make it short, will you?"

"We have the diary back, Harry, translated. Piet had to put a few notes in where some of the Afrikaans expressions would not make sense to your aunt Clair. It's rather boring day to day ramblings of business dinners, horse riding, thoughts, you know the sort of thing women write in their diaries. But we think there's a story buried under the mundane ramblings."

Harry sounded offended. "Not something I do, Jack. Read other people's diaries. If I do, it's in the line of duty, shall we say?"

"I've destroyed both hard copies, Harry. Safer that way, given the circumstances. We have the files on the computer for reference."

Jack could hear the roaring traffic passing Harry, who was, no doubt, huddled in a doorway looking highly suspicious to anyone who might be watching.

Jack continued. "There are many numbers and letters scattered through the book, which makes no sense to either Piet or to me."

Harry waited and let a screaming police car siren pass before he answered. "What happens next Jack?"

"Lara will be calling you at six this evening, on this number, to get the directions to the care home."

"I'll arrange for a car to collect Lara. I'll wait for her call."

"One more thing, Harry. I would imagine if we checked for death certificates of David and his wife, we would find them, but they might not be what they're supposed to be."

"Jesus, Jack, the water is getting even more muddier here. I can't get involved or help you in any way, as you know. Whoever they are, they're watching to see what you and I do next. We have to leave it to

Piet to see what he comes up with. You're being watched, Jack, keep this in mind."

Jack had always depended on his instincts, and one was kicking in fast. "Listen, Harry, I think it's a bad idea for Lara to print out this book and deliver it to your aunt. It's too dangerous."

"How so, Jack?"

"Given your aunt's past, I'm banking on the fact she will have a computer, or access to one in the care home. It would be safer for everyone if Piet's legal lady here would send through the book by email, password protected, to Lara when she gets to Clair's place."

Jack was thinking aloud. "Lara can download it to her laptop, find a print shop nearby and have it done there then deliver the hard copy back to your Aunt Clair. Lara can then delete the entire file – no trace of it to anyone. Yes, that's what we'll do, much safer for all concerned. I'll get Piet to set it up. All Lara will need to do is wait for the email to come though from Piet's legal lady with the password."

Chapter Forty-Seven

Piet drummed his fingers on the side of his desk waiting for Bertie to pick up.

"*Jeez*, Piet, now what? It has to be something, right?"

"Yup, Bertie. Do you have any news for me?"

"Piet, my friend, I have tried every which way to find some information on this woman called Marlene Hartley and have come up with bugger all. Zip."

"Okay, Bertie. Here's the thing. Can you find death certificates for people?"

Bertie sighed down the phone. "Piet, can you call me on this other number?"

Piet called the number he'd been given. "Why are you being so mysterious Bertie. It's me you're talking to?"

"Listen, Piet. There's a club we geeks have. No-one knows anything about it. I'm not even going to tell you what it's called. See here, all of us are loaded down with trying to find information about people. It's what we do, except the governments don't know we exist, our club, I mean."

Bertie paused. "I know you guys think we're all a bit odd with our computers and such like. But some years ago, we decided to form this club to help each other. It's quicker. Trying to get marriage, birth and death certificates for people who live in different countries, is extremely difficult. It's not like some old uncle who died a hundred years ago. Those *okes* you can find easily enough by joining a genealogy company and for a fee they will help you find whatever you want and then, for an additional fee, will get a copy of whatever certificate you're looking for. But it can take weeks.

"We have members in countries all over the world. We help each other out. You hear what I'm saying Piet?"

Piet grunted. "*Ja,* as long as you speak in a known language, we lesser mortals can understand."

Bertie snorted. "This club, well, let's say we work together. So, if someone is looking for official records, or something else, we lean on each other, easier that way. We have access to all sorts of information on a lot of other government data bases.

"We're a tight group, and only give out information to people we trust completely. People like you Piet, you hear me?

"I have to guarantee to other club members that whoever I'm giving information to is completely trustworthy. Someone I've known for years."

Piet straightened his back a little. "So, what you're saying is you and your club members can tap into other data bases and come up with information about other people in other countries? Are you hackers then?"

Bertie sounded most offended. "*Jeez,* Piet, we're not hackers as you call us. We're professionals! We know our game. We should be up there with celebrities, but without the money the paparazzi and all the glamour. We're the brains. Making things happen without going through all the crap legal red tape stuff."

Piet tried to sound humble and chastised. "Course you are, my friend. The unsung heroes of today."

"Yup, this is what I'm saying. If you have someone you're looking for, foreigners, well, we work together as club members, and can come up with the information instead of going through the normal government channels. We're a brotherhood, my man, we trust each other. We trust who we give the information to. It has to be agreed by all club members, who we share the information with.

"My buddies have agreed to help you…"

Piet rubbed his hands together. "Good stuff, Bertie. Now here's the thing. A man called Sir David Cooper died in a plane crash in Kenya in 1998, he was British and he was the pilot. Some few days later his wife died.

"Here's what I'm thinking, Bertie. This Marlene Hartley in Wolmaransstad, the woman you and I are chasing? Well, we seem to have hit a dead end with her, right? I need the full name of Sir David Cooper's late wife. Her legal name?"

Piet could hear Bertie tapping away on his computer. "So, what was the name of the wife of this Sir David Cooper, Piet?"

Piet sighed. "All we have is a pet name, Lulu."

Bertie snorted. "Lulu? That's not a name, my man. It's what you call your dog or a sheep, or even a cow. Did she not have a proper name?"

"This Bertie is the question, so long. This is what we need you to find out. We need a death certificate for David Cooper and this Lulu Cooper person. They both died in Kenya."

Bertie cleared his throat. "That might be a bit of a problem, no club member in Kenya. But you say he had a title, he was British? Was his wife British perhaps? I'll check, hey. Lady Lulu, Piet?" He snorted with laughter again, and cut the call.

Chapter Forty-Eight

The car pulled up at the care home just outside of London. Lara stepped into the reception and asked for Clair Davenport, explaining she was expected.

"Yes, of course, Clair is looking forward to your visit. She doesn't have many visitors these days, most of her friends have passed on. We all love her here, for her age she's quite remarkable. Gives lessons to our other residents here on how to use the computer to keep in touch with their families and so on. I'll take you to her suite."

Lara followed the receptionist. She had heard about care homes, but this one was on a different scale altogether. Once a stately home it had been divided up into individual suites.

The receptionist knocked gently on the door of number 56; Clair's full name slotted into a brass card holder on the door.

The door was swept open and there was Clair.

The receptionist introduced them and then left. Clair gestured to Lara to come in. The suite was filled with light, large windows looked down on immaculate grounds.

"My dear, do take a seat, don't worry about my little dog, Joe. He's a bit grumpy but he doesn't bite."

Lara bent and stroked the head of the King Charles spaniel, with his sad eyes. "Hello, Joe…"

Lara looked around. The suite was like a luxury room in a five-star hotel. Books crowded alongside each other on tables and bookcases, a huge vase of purple irises' graced a round table in the centre of the room, large comfortable chairs looked out over the manicured gardens of the ancient house.

In the corner, by one of the windows were two computers. A laptop, two tablets, three phones, a landline, and an enormous flat screen television with wires trailing everywhere.

Lara looked at Clair. Her eyes were bright with intelligence and interest. Her white hair held back with a wooden brown clip at the nape of her neck. She was dressed in a loose cream dress, with dark brown beads around her neck. Her arms and hands bare of any jewellery, her nails manicured with a pale blush of pink.

Lara smiled at her. "Well, I always thought care homes were rather dreary and scary places, smelling of cabbage and antiseptic. But this place, your place, it's beautiful."

"Yes, I was lucky. I married a wonderful man, darling Tom, who made sure I would be well looked after."

She looked at Lara and grinned. "Did you know, my dear, there were thousands of us who worked at Bletchley Park? Years after, when it was all over and we went our different ways, many of us married, but we never talked about what we did during the war. That part of our lives was so secret. Never to be discussed, ever. A lot of couples didn't disclose that part of their lives. Never actually knew they had both worked at Bletchley Park. Can you imagine? That's how important it was."

Lara listened, fascinated to this world of code crackers and spies. "How did you get involved Clair? Maybe you can't tell me, but I would love to know. So many stories have been written about the people who worked at Bletchley Park?"

Clair looked out of the window over the grounds. "When I was a young girl, fourteen perhaps, I loved puzzles, especially crossword puzzles. I would compete with my father to see who could finish it first – I always won," she said gleefully.

Clair touched the beads around her neck. "There were other puzzles in the newspapers and magazines. There was another puzzle I loved it consisted of a set of letters which you had to make so many words out of. First prize was working out the final word of all the letters put together. Well, I just looked at all the letters and within less than a second, I had the complete word. It used to annoy my father considerably. I suppose word got around the neighbourhood. All the kids wanted to take me on, but no-one ever beat me. I didn't have many friends, they all thought I was a bit of a freak. My father was approached and I ended up working at Bletchley Park."

Clair sat down. "Now let's have tea, and then I want to look at what you've brought me? Harry has filled me in on the story so far…"

Lara stood up. "May I make some tea, or coffee?"

Clair smiled. "No need, my dear. It will be delivered, all arranged, as it was during the war. Ah, here comes Hamish. Thank you, my dear."

212

The elderly man placed the tray carefully on the table and then retreated.

Clair poured the coffee and handed it to Lara. "Hamish, what a man. Hugely attractive to all of us gals, a code cracker of note. Speaks at least five languages. Despite his name, he's Polish. I think we were all half in love with him. He likes to be here with us now."

Clair stirred her tea. "Proud of his country, proud of what he did. There are quite a few of us ex Bletchley Park residents here. Of course, we never discuss anything. But we like it that way, Lara. Bletchley Park, us, we are still a tight knit community. Of course, soon we will all be gone. Names lost in history."

Clair put her cup down. "Now, my dear, what do you have for me? Darling Harry, who I know didn't remember me until this came up. Well, I'm glad he remembered me at all! What do you want me to do?"

Lara explained the change of plan. "I need to send an email to the legal lady in South Africa, who is standing by. She will send the translated book through with a password. Then I can go into town, print it out and bring it back to you.

"This is probably going to be difficult for you. There are Afrikaans word here, numbers and letters. Piet, who works with Jack on his cases, is an ex-police detective, he's Afrikaans. He has translated some of the words you may not be familiar with."

Lara took a sip of her coffee. "So, shall we get the email through? Then I can get it printed out somewhere…" her voice trailed off as she looked at Clair's incredulous face.

"Difficult? I don't think so my dear. We won the war, after all, didn't we? Because of us at Bletchley Park, we cracked all the codes. Enigma it was called. Let me have a look at this diary? No need to go anywhere to have it printed out. I shall study it on the computer. I have firewalls which would make your eyes water. No-one can hack any of the information I have. Trust me."

Lara went through to the legal lady in South Africa and obtained the file with the unique password, giving her Clair's email address.

Clair reached for her glasses and was soon lost in her own long-ago world of, dots, dashes, numbers and codes.

Quietly Lara let herself out of the suite and made her way back to the waiting car.

Chapter Forty-Nine

Jack paced up and down his garden, the novelty of being alone with his thoughts and trying to work out who exactly Sir David Cooper had been, was wearing thin.

He had searched the internet for some kind of clue as what Cooper might have been involved in during those turbulent and momentous years of the 1980's when terrorism and wars topped the headlines. There were deals going down between governments, individuals making fortunes buying and selling on the black market. Nothing the media would ever know about.

But it seemed to Jack the media, and the paparazzi, were not only chasing celebrities, they were digging up facts and stories about other things going on.

War offered immense opportunities for making money, swapping secrets, awarding contracts. The dark side of the internet with all its offers, good and bad, mostly bad.

But Sir David Cooper? Of him, there was nothing. Like many a diplomat, Jack had to assume, his work would have been done quietly, behind closed doors.

Jack sat outside and watched the shadows of yet another evening beginning to shade the garden. He looked up at the car headlights making their way towards his drive, leaving a cloud of dust in its wake, and his melancholy lifted.

Piet.

Hope bounded towards him followed by Piet who was carrying a plastic bag. "I brought you some food from the Italian place, Jack, good stuff. Pasta and such like. Lots of cream and herbs. Not my kind of food but I thought you might like something different. Didn't fancy another burnt *braai…*"

Jack took the bag through to the kitchen, then turned to Piet who had followed him, with the ever-hopeful dog.

Jack put both hands flat on the kitchen table and sighed heavily. "Piet, I'm going crazy out here, with no human contact, without the buzz of what I do. I'm working, researching, but finding nothing. Can't even risk calling Cambridge to ask a few questions about Sir David Cooper's time there. No doubt the spooks have got that covered as well. Not sure how long I can do this. I need the stimulation of people around me; I need to chase my story."

Piet turned to him and nodded. "I know it must be hard, but be patient, my friend. Lara, the Bletchley auntie, and my man Bertie are all on the case. Just now we'll start getting some feedback. Then we can to do more digging."

They went back to the veranda and settled into the chairs. Hope took off for the stream.

Jack and Piet watched her charging through the water, grabbing sticks and stones and bringing them back to them, before dashing off again, hoping, the men assumed, her generous gifts of wet sticks and stones might elicit some decent food somewhere along the line.

Jack took a sip of his beer, as he watched Hope splashing in the river. "Must be nice to be a dog in a good home," he mused. "Hope doesn't know if she's beautiful, hasn't a clue how old she is, doesn't care much, doesn't give a bugger about politics and what's going on in the world. Doesn't give a toss if she has a doggy partner, her owner is the only thing she cares about and with Hope, food comes a close second in her affections. Never gets depressed about anything, has no fear of illness or death, doesn't care if she has two siblings or twenty, doesn't give a damn if they ever visit her. Yup, whoever coined the phrase 'it's a dog's life' got it dead right."

Piet laughed. "*Ag*, come on Jack, you're just feeling a bit down, I was going to suggest you take another trip to Wolmaransstad and have another poke around the old farm. But I'm thinking if this story has spooks crawling all over it, it might not be such a good idea – the place is probably being watched. It's definitely connected to our man Sir David Cooper, or at least his dead wife."

Jack smiled. Piet's company had always cheered him up, even though he never missed an opportunity to have a swipe at the British.

"How are things at the hotel? Still busy?" he asked.

Piet shrugged. "Not so much now, mostly locals. The bar is always busy though. Our Daniel Van Heerden comes in quite regularly now, at least twice a week.

"Often comes over to say hello. Seems like a nice guy, always asks after you. I told him you were in India doing a piece on tourism there for a magazine. I didn't mention you were no longer with the newspaper."

Piet's phone shivered on the table. *Bertie.* He hesitated but didn't put it on speaker. He had a feeling Bertie would know if he did.

"Hey Bertie, don't call me unless you have some good news. What have you got?"

Bertie dived straight in. "Sir David Cooper died in a plane crash in Kenya. No doubt about it. Death certificate issued by the Kenya authorities. No body left to repatriate to the UK. Burnt to a crisp. But identified by his plane. He was definitely the pilot, wearing what was a watch worth probably thousands of pounds – shame about that, all bent and broken but definitely his, complete with a family crest."

Piet grunted. "What else, my friend, what else have you got for me?"

Bertie continued. "He checked in with the air traffic control in Mombasa, then, boom, he was gone. Not much left at the crash site. But there were bits of a passport, issued to UK government officials and diplomats. No doubt about it. It was Sir David Cooper and his mangled watch.

"However, his wife was something else altogether. Her name was not Lulu, Piet." He laughed. "Her name was Madeleine. Obviously, this was this Cooper guy's pet name for her. Lulu.

"She died a few days later. This, of course, put the flags up for our guys. It's not unusual for a couple who have been married for fifty years to follow each other after the death of one of them. But this couple were only in their forties."

He continued. "There was no death certificate issued for Madeleine Cooper in Kenya. But there is a certificate of her death issued in the UK. So, *ja* it's a bit of a puzzle."

Bertie cleared his throat noisily. "Yeah, yeah, yeah, Piet. I know you don't like our algorithms. But they work. We use them.

"Madeleine Cooper came back to South Africa, where she was born, we have her identity number now. Her name before she married was Madeleine Hunt. She worked for the South African government for some years before she married David Cooper."

Piet interrupted him. "Okay she worked for the South African government, but in what position? Secretary to someone or perhaps she had access to sensitive information?"

216

"She was the personal assistant to the Minister of Defence, so yes, she would have had access to sensitive information during that time. The thing is, Piet, she didn't come back here in a body bag – she came back travelling first class from London with British Airways. After that we have no trace of her at all."

Chapter Fifty

Piet let out a slow whistle as he put the phone back down on the table.

"Well, well, well, my friend, you're going to love this. Mrs Cooper, this Lulu person, was really called Madeleine. Was formerly Madeleine Hunt, before she married David Cooper. She was South African and returned to South Africa after all."

Jack frowned at him. "Nothing odd about it. Perhaps it's what she requested in her Will. Back to the land of her birth. Sometimes it's important to someone. Dust to dust, ashes to ashes."

Piet shook his head, an inscrutable look on his face. "That may be so. The thing is Madeleine Cooper did indeed return to the land of her birth, only she wasn't in a coffin for the duration of the flight. She was sitting up front, no doubt enjoying a glass or two of champagne in First Class, on a flight from London to Cape Town."

Jack stared at him as he digested this information. The old familiar sizzle of excitement cascading down his spine. "Did she now…"

His foot began to jiggle. "So, let's say the UK Embassy in Kenya pretty much smuggled her out of her home in Nanyuki, in an ambulance, hid her for a day or two, maybe in the grounds of the Embassy. Flew her to London, provided her with a new identity, then put her on a flight to South Africa, where, we presume, she was never heard from again?"

Piet took a long drink from his glass of beer. "*Ja*, looks like it…" he said thoughtfully. "A quick memorial service for her husband, then she apparently dies. Hmmm."

Jack shook his head vehemently. "No, Piet, she did appear again. Marlene Hartley – Madeleine Hunt, as she was before she married. Same initials. It was Madeleine Cooper who lived on the farm called Cloud's End. The farm was previously called Hunter's Moon – it's a fit with her maiden name. But why change her name?" he wondered aloud. "She was the widow of a diplomat who seemed to have had no contact with her husband's diplomatic life towards the end, because she was depressed and unpredictable. What possible reason would she have for the name change?"

Piet frowned and considered the point. "The only reason I can come up with, was because she was being protected from something. Something she knew. Or possibly something her husband knew.

"Witness Protection Programme, Jack. That's what this is all about. Giving Madeleine Hunt the same initials as Marlene Hartley was carefully thought out. It's quite common in this kind of situation. It makes it easier for the person hiding out to remember their new name when they have to sign for anything. But there is a big price to pay for this protection."

Piet leaned forward and put his glass on the table. Then continued.

"Someone in the programme has to give up everything from their previous life – everything! No contact with anyone they have ever known. They have to cut every single tie with anyone they have ever met, friends, family, children, partners or husbands, wives, lovers, even their *bleddy* pets. It's a tough call, but it protects the person in the programme. To all intents and purposes, they're dead."

Jack nodded. "Yes. You have to become a completely different person, shrug off your old life, like a snake shedding its skin, and emerge as someone else. The government offering this programme pay all the living expenses of the so-called new person. It's an expensive programme. If that is what happened, then Madeleine Cooper must have been extremely important to the British government. But why?"

Piet frowned. "Not sure, Jack. Not sure if the important person was Sir David or his wife Madeleine. I'll put my paltry police pension, and rather attractive salary and benefits from Hugo, on Madeleine Cooper being the person of great interest. After all her husband was dead, not so? Madeleine must have known a great deal about him. They had to hide her away. What better place than the land of her birth? On a remote farm outside of Wolmaransstad."

Jack smacked a mosquito on his leg and winced. "Here's a question for you, Piet. Who or what managed to persuade Madeleine to go into such a programme, if she did? Who would they be protecting? Madeleine or themselves?"

"I'm thinking themselves, Jack. Leaving her in the UK would not be enough. They wanted her as far away from the country as they possibly could. She was a South African with all the right paperwork. Maybe tweaked a bit. Makes sense to me. The place in Wolmaransstad would have been bought by Bay Water. In other words, a safe house owned by the British government. They might have owned it for years before Madeleine came along, who knows?"

Piet stared into the distance. "She would have had to leave Kenya after the death of her husband. No more permanent resident status. No more wife of a diplomat. Probably took one look at the British weather and decided going back to South Africa was far more attractive, especially if the British government were going to foot the bill for the rest of her life. They probably threatened her with taking her British passport away and stopping any pension she might receive from her husband. This would have left her destitute. Sounds to me like she had no choice but to go along with what they proposed."

He grinned at Jack. "Maybe she had some old granny who was put in a concentration camp during the Boer War – I told you we Afrikaners have a long and bitter memory about that particular period in our history. Maybe Madeleine thought this was poetic justice and jumped at the chance – sweet revenge. A new life, all paid for by the Brits!"

The sun was going down throwing long shadows across the lawn. Hope made one final dash for the stream returning with a long stick. Dropping it she shook herself, showering both men in a fine spray of water.

Piet stood up hastily, wiping his arms and face. "Let me feed her and put the pasta in the oven, then we can go through this whole thing again and make sure we haven't missed anything."

Jack sat listening to the sounds coming from the kitchen, it was nice to have someone around, even better he was the smartest detective Jack had ever met in all his long years chasing the bad guys in the UK.

Piet came and sat down again; they both could hear Hope chasing her now empty dish around the kitchen floor.

"Okay, Piet. Madeleine was banished to a farm, owned by Bay Water. No doubt registered as a trust and owned by the British Government.

"According to Gift, the barman, and Eunice the housekeeper, Madeleine had no visitors in all those years. Then something changed, according to Eunice. A man came to the farm, she seemed to know

220

him – unlikely in a witness protection programme, unless he was a spook from the British government."

Piet looked at him. "You think this guy maybe was her so called handler, her only link with the outside world she had known?"

"Yup, that's what I think. However, why was he looking around for the puzzle box? They must have suspected she had brought it with her. But how? How did she do it? What was in it that was so important?"

"The diary…" They both said in unison.

Piet shrugged. "Maybe they didn't know she had brought it with her, although it's hard to believe. They would have checked her for anything she was carrying, making sure no one would know who she was. They would have wiped out her identity, taken everything away from her that she possessed."

Jack stared at the lights suddenly springing to life, and then, quickly doused as the power went off again. He lit the lamps on the table.

"Dinner might be a while, Piet. But let's carry on with our thoughts. Madeleine must have known she was going to be smuggled out of the country and returned to South Africa. She would have had time to package up the puzzle box and send it somewhere where she could reclaim it at a later stage? I think she probably sent the silver box as well. The spooks wouldn't have let her take that, not with the Cooper family crest displayed on it."

Piet nodded. "It's true, hey?"

Jack ran his hand through his hair. "I need to get hold of Daphne, in Nairobi, Bashir, her major domo, could get in touch with Juma, who worked for Madeleine and David. Perhaps he posted off both boxes for her. In fact, he's likely the only one who could have done it."

Jack looked at his watch. "Unless she's out and about, wining and dining, this could be a good time to call her."

He punched in her number. "Daphne? Don't mention my name. This story has taken a rather peculiar twist."

"Well, hello, my dear, how are you?" Daphne said in greeting. "I'm just on my way out, some social do in town. What sort of peculiar twist are you talking about – oh, right, can't talk about it. What can I do for you?"

Jack cleared his throat. "I need Bashir to get in touch with Juma, to find out if he posted off a parcel for David's wife, shortly before she died. If he did, and I think he is the only one who could have done so, would he remember where the box was posted to? By the way her name was Madeleine, although he called her Lulu."

"Of course, darling, I'll ask him on the way to this tedious dinner I am expected to attend. I'll call you back when I can. Madeleine, you say. Goodness me."

Jack tried to keep his voice light. "By the way, Daphne, just a thought. Did David have any distinguishing marks, apart from his brilliant career?"

There was a slight pause. "What an odd thought and an odd question in fact. Why are you asking?"

Jack paused trying to keep his questions sounding merely curious. "You were both fond of each other, trusted each other. I'm just trying to tie up a few loose ends here."

"Look, I shall have to think about this. I have to go. I do so hate being late for a social gathering. Darling, there is nothing further to chase with David, whether he died in a ghastly accident, or perhaps committed suicide. He didn't have any distinguishing marks. Nothing I can recall anyway."

Daphne hung up. Jack sat back surprised at how she had ended their conversation. Something told him Daphne had definitely not told him the full story of David Cooper.

But to be fair to her. He hadn't told her everything either.

*****

The lights were back on, Jack and Piet finished their pasta, both deep in thought.

Jack's phone sprang to life on the table outside. *Daphne.*

"Darling, it's me. Yes, Juma did post off a parcel to South Africa. A few days before this Lulu or Madeleine died."

Jack's heart skipped a beat. "Did he remember the address?"

Daphne laughed. "For goodness' sake, we're talking about twenty years ago! But, yes, actually, he did remember the address. It was the one and only time David's wife asked him to do anything unusual. The parcel was posted from Nairobi to South Africa to a post office in a place called something like Woolly Rams Hat. Sounds rather odd, doesn't it? Anyway, this is where the parcel went, to await collection by someone called Hartley. Maybe that was her sister? That's all he can remember."

Jack thanked her profusely, asked after the cats and Edith Cummings. Laughing he switched off the phone.

"Okay Piet. We now have the connection. Indeed, it was Madeleine Cooper who was spirited away and ended up in Wolmaransstad. Which begs the question who was the man who came to visit the farm and why was he looking for the puzzle box?

"Also, the message written on the photograph: *So, you have found your way into my box, discovered my past perhaps? Now what will you do... apart from being extremely careful? There's a digit missing somewhere. You will never find it.'*

Piet nodded, "*Ja,* that message has been laid right outside our door. It's a warning for sure. The thing is whoever came to visit Madeleine on the farm wasn't a British spook. Eunice said they spoke Afrikaans to each other. He was a South African, Jack, and I think perhaps he made more than one visit to the farm."

*****

Daphne Forsyth Phillips lay back on the pillows on her bed, the fan rippling the mosquito net around her and ruffling the fur on the Siamese cats spread around her.

Jack Taylor was not your average journalist. He had a keen and inquisitive mind, and he wasn't going to let this story go away. She had to do something and quickly. Making up her mind she reached for her phone, finding it under one of the cats.

Feeling agitated, and now needing a drink, she lifted the mosquito net, careful not to disturb her sleeping cats and threw a shawl around her shoulders. She poured herself a brandy. Swirling it around she made her way through to the veranda and looked up.

The stars were glorious against the pitch black of the night, glittering and twinkling as they had done for millions of years bringing Daphne a sense of peace and comfort which she badly needed now.

When she was a child, she would lie down on the lawns and stare at them, overwhelmed by the mightiness of the canopy of the stars above her. Her mother had told her each sparkling star represented someone who had died and gone to heaven where they could look down on their loved ones, watch over them, comfort them with their ever glittering presence.

Even now Daphne liked to think this was true. "Where are you, David? Are you finally happy now?" she whispered to him.

She had, of course, been utterly and completely in love with him.

But Jack Taylor was a real and serious threat. She knew, from what Jack had told her with his previous phone call, that he had been pulled off the story of Sir David Cooper. The newspaper had let him go.

She took a mouthful of her brandy. This would not stop someone like Jack Taylor pursuing the story. She had to head him off somehow.

Daphne checked the time. It was late but she would call him.

"Hello Jack, darling. Sorry to call so late but I have remembered something."

*****

The newspaper slid off Jack's lap as he stood up. "Well, hello, Daphne. Listen, let me call you back in five minutes from another phone. Your phone may be compromised."

There was a pause then he heard her laugh. "Goodness me, why on earth would my phone be compromised. Whatever do you mean?"

"Five minutes, Daphne, I'll call you back alright?"

Daphne leaned back in her chair and took a deep breath, trying to calm the rapid beat of her heart. She fumbled for her phone when it rang.

"Jack, why are you being so dramatic and mysterious? Never mind…you asked me if David had any distinguishing marks? I had a jolly good think about it. Yes, he did actually. So long ago I'd forgotten. It was a tattoo, some kind of Chinese symbol, it was at the base of his spine. Tiny little thing. As you may recall he was brought up in Malaya, as it was then, it's where his roots were. Why he had it at the base of his spine where he couldn't see it is a complete mystery I have to say?

"But what on earth has this got to do with anything, Jack? I simply don't understand."

Jack sighed. "I'm trying to build a picture of the man as he was, sounds like he was a colourful character and little bits of information, like the tattoo, add to the story."

Jack thanked Daphne and put the phone down. A tattoo on the base of his spine, eh? Now how did Daphne know about that?

He smiled; another piece of the puzzle fell into place. Only a lover would know.

224

Daphne and David had not only been good mates – they had been lovers.

He scrolled through the photographs on his phone until he found the one of the couple on horseback, with their sun hats and sunglasses. He enlarged it and studied the woman's arms.

On her right arm he could clearly see a dozen or so light-coloured bangles.

Daphne Forsyth-Phillips.

Jack frowned. Why on earth would David's wife Madeleine keep a photo of another woman hidden in the box?

He thought back to the young Chinese boy, William. William had found two drawers hidden within the opened box. One was empty, the other one held the photograph of David and Daphne together.

Jack smiled. Because, he concluded, Madeleine had no idea the photograph was there. David had hidden it in the drawer and he hadn't shown Madeleine how to open that particular hiding place.

Chapter Fifty-One

The voice at the end of the telephone was strong and very British.

"Is this Jack Taylor?"

Jack hesitated for a moment. "It might be. Who is this?"

"My name is Clair Davenport – we have a mutual friend I understand? My telephone and yours are not compromised so I think we may speak freely?"

Jack smiled. "Well, hello Clair. It is indeed a great pleasure to talk to you. As a boy I was always fascinated with all the work you people did at Bletchley Park. As a lone voice, so many years later, a different generation, I want to thank you, all of you, for what you did for the war effort. It was long before my time, the sort of stuff you read about in books now. A world I would have loved to have been involved in."

There was a slight pause before Clair continued. "Yes, it has been romanticised now, with films and books. But I can assure you at the time, it wasn't easy. But you don't want to hear about the harsh reality of it all, Jack. Best leave it alone."

He heard the sound of her keyboard. "Now, let's get down to work, shall we? I have gone through the translation of the book, with Piet's notes and yours. Without any doubt this diary was entirely written by the same person, a woman. Although written in shorthand the author has certain quirks with her writing. Even with shorthand the character of the author comes through. She was, shall we say, an angry and deeply disturbed woman.

"What puzzled me were the letters and numbers: Some numbers had letters, some not. I need to do some more work on this.

"Most of the diary is just month by month things this Madeleine attended with her husband Sir David Cooper. However, the numbers and letters mean something else altogether. There is no time frame for this diary. It could have been written over thirty years, or five or ten. But I have worked out some of the numbers and the letters."

Clair cleared her throat delicately. "They are international telephone codes for countries. Madeleine was quite clever with them, jumbling up the letters in amongst the numbers. I think there is a story under a story here."

Jack took a deep breath and let her continue.

"It's possible to follow the path of these international codes, but we don't have a time frame. Of course, over the years, countries have changed their names, some through gaining Independence or other reasons like wars, boundary changes or politics."

Clair paused. "What we need to do here, Jack, is try and streamline what the country codes were when your Sir David Cooper was flying the flag. It will give you some indication of what he was involved in and why the British Government are now trying to smother your story."

Clair paused again. "My guess would be whatever Sir David was involved in happened in the eighties. I sensed a slight change in the way Madeleine wrote in her diary. It seems to me she was more worried about something else. Her sentences were more abrupt. I also sensed her relationship with her husband had changed. Only a hunch. Also, from what I could ascertain, she was a deeply disturbed woman. It comes through in her writings. I would surmise she suffered from serious depression, which would make her erratic and unpredictable. Not a good mix when you're married to a top diplomat. But be that as it may."

Jack ran his hands through his hair, his mind working furiously. This would make sense then to use the numbers as a time frame?

He heard Clair tapping away on her keyboard. "I would go back to around then, Jack. Mobile phones were gaining widespread popularity, the internet was pretty much up and running. The world was changing rapidly, giving everyone easy access to information, good or otherwise."

She laughed lightly. "Sir David Cooper would have known all about the trouble spots in the world, Somalia, Rwanda, East Africa, Kuwait, Iraq, China, Russia and so on. They were all pretty much the areas he knew."

Jack was quiet for a few moments. "With your considerable experience, Clair, and from what you have read and surmised with the diary. Would you say Sir David Cooper was involved in some kind of anti-government activities?"

Jack could almost see her smiling down the phone. "Oh, absolutely Jack. When he was killed in the plane crash, they must have breathed a huge sigh of relief. They dropped the curtain on his life then and they're doing it again now. Madeleine would have been a huge problem with her unpredictable behaviour. That's why there is so little about him on the internet. Either it was deleted by the government, or someone else."

She was quiet for a brief moment. "He was in the perfect position to, how shall I put this…negotiate with any number of governments. Wined and dined by heads of State, meeting all the right kind of people. Perhaps doing deals with people he should not have been doing deals with. I'm not saying he was a spy, but he was in a powerful position to ensure certain deals went through. Contracts awarded; third parties involved. The Diplomatic pouch, which he would have had, would have been useful to him."

He heard her sigh. "It's disappointing, Jack, but history does repeat itself. Maybe today it's not so much secrets being passed to various governments, but where there are wars there is always money to be made. Sir David would have made a great deal of it being in the position he was in."

He heard her sigh with regret. "I don't regret one day of working at Bletchley Park, not one. But at least then we knew who the enemy was. It was cleaner then somehow. Today one doesn't know who one is dealing with. A different kind of war altogether. The faces now are grey and unknown. But I am happy to say the British Government do still have a use for my talents, even now.

"The war may be over but there are certain individuals who may think they got away with selling secrets – well, suffice to say, they are still being hunted down even today, despite their so-called respectable jobs and careers.

"Jack, I'm sorry I couldn't have been of more help. However, keep in mind many of my old colleagues had children and many of them followed in their parent's footsteps and are now in prominent and powerful positions. Do let me know if you need any other information. I am rather intrigued by this story now and would like to help in any way I can."

There was a short silence from Clair. "On the other hand, perhaps it would be better for our government and the country to let

228

sleeping dogs lie. No good will come of exposing who David was. People even today remember the unpalatable scandal of Kim Philby and his chums from Cambridge. There he was, a Russian spy, wining and dining with the elite of society and the British Government. A traitor to his country. Unforgivable in my book, I can assure you."

He heard the disappointment in her voice. "Philby deserved to die alone in Russia, which he had chosen to betray us to. Dreadful man, a terrible stain on our fine history.

"There's enough chaos going on in the world at the moment. Why add to it?"

Jack sighed loudly. "I hear what you're saying, Clair. But I can't let this one go. I'm a journalist, it's in my blood. I need to pursue this story and find out exactly what Sir David Cooper was up to and where. Perhaps Madeleine was a bigger threat than he was?"

He cleared his throat. "I would love to do a story about you sometime, Clair and your life at Bletchley Park. If we throw in Sir David Cooper to the mix, once I have his story, well, I think it will make for a fascinating piece for the newspaper."

There was a slight pause at the end of the phone. "Absolutely out of the question Jack. Under no circumstances will I talk about my career," she said sharply, "and I most certainly would not discuss Sir David Cooper, as I told Harry right from the beginning. My part in this must be strictly confidential. I do hope you understand – Harry gave me his word on this."

Jack sighed with disappointment. "Then, Clair, I shall also give you, my word. Everything we have discussed will remain between us. But I would like your permission to share our discussion with Piet Joubert who is working this story with me?"

"Of course, my dear, you go right ahead."

Jack paused. "But I hope, one day, I shall have the pleasure of meeting you."

"Well, you had better hurry up Jack – I won't last forever you know."

Thanking her profusely for all her hard work, he cut the call and wandered out onto his veranda. He wasn't quite sure where he was going to start with all this information – but he was going to start and follow the story through to its conclusion.

He had found an unexpected ally in Clair. Both he, and Harry, would find it impossible to make any further enquiries about Sir

David. But Clair, he had absolutely no doubt, would have contacts in the right places.

He would need to be patient. Give things a little more time, before he called on Clair, and any contacts she may have, to help him again.

Chapter Fifty-Two

L ara struggled with her shopping bags up the steps to her flat. She hated shopping at the best of times, and with the rain coming down she didn't have a spare hand for her umbrella and it was getting dark.

The rain trickled down her collar as she struggled for the key in her pocket. Inserting it into her front door she was surprised to find it wasn't locked.

Lara frowned, she was always careful about security and locking her front door. Always double checking before she left.

With mounting concern, she cautiously pushed it open, retrieved her shopping and took it through to the kitchen. The rain from her coat dripped on the floor as she looked at all the pots and pans, cutlery and crockery strewn and broken on the floor. The food cupboards had been tipped out, broken packets of cereal, flour and biscuits covered the floor.

Pushing open the door to the main room of the flat she stopped and stared with mounting disbelief. The place had been ransacked. The contents of her sideboard and its drawers had been tipped up on the carpet. The cushions and seat on her sofa had been slashed open, the sofa itself turned on its back. The carpet had been bundled into one corner.

The wooden chest where she stored her things for sale had been turned over, its contents of silver and collectables strewn across the wooden boards of the floor. She dropped to her knees searching for the silver cigarette box with the Cooper crest already sensing it would not be there.

Breathlessly she went through to her bedroom and saw someone had been through it. The bedding thrown in the corner, the mattress slit down the middle and on both sides. In the bathroom the lid on the cistern had been left in the bath.

Lara put her hand to her mouth and went back to the main living area. She perched on the side of the upturned sofa and looked around at the devastation surrounding her. The sour taste of fear flooding her mouth.

She scrabbled for the phone in her handbag and with shaking fingers stabbed in Jack's number in South Africa.

"Lara! Great to hear from you! Everything alright?"

Lara's voice broke, partly from the pure relief of hearing his voice but also because she was scared.

"Oh, Jack…"

Jack stood up anxiously, his newspaper sliding off his lap. "What's up Lara? What's happened?"

"Someone broke into my flat – the place is wrecked."

"Have you called the police?"

"No, I wanted to call you first. I'm scared Jack."

Jack ran his fingers through his hair and kept his voice steady. "Okay, now listen to me and stay calm if you can. Go through each room and see if you can see what's missing. Make a list if you can. You're sure you locked your door when you left?"

Lara sniffed and wiped her eyes. "Yes, absolutely. I'm always careful about security – the place is a wreck, Jack, the sofa, cushions, my mattress, all slashed. The kitchen is a nightmare. I won't be able to stay here tonight – as far as I can tell, there is only one thing missing and it's Sir David Cooper's silver box with his family crest."

Jack felt his stomach muscles pucker with concern. "Okay, Lara, here is what I want you to do. Pack your bags, get your student friend to keep your silver stock in his flat. Get him to carry your bag out of the flat, meet him somewhere. Do not, and I repeat, do not report this to the police."

He took a breath. "I'll get Piet to book you a flight to Johannesburg, then you will connect with a domestic flight to Hazyview. I want you to check into a hotel and stay put until you leave for the airport. Piet will be waiting for you – okay? Don't talk about this to anyone. You'll be safe here with me. Let Piet know which day you want to leave, he'll take care of the rest."

Lara wiped the tears away from her eyes. "Okay Jack, I'll do that, I want to. I don't know what this is all about or where it's leading, but I don't like it. But what do I tell my friend? He'll ask questions."

"Tell him you're going on another business trip and you'll be back in a couple of weeks. Now what about your rent for the flat?"

Lara's voice sounded stronger now Jack had taken charge of everything. "It's paid by debit order every month, so no problem there."

There was now an urgency in Jack's voice. "Your laptop with the print out of the book for Clair – where is it?"

"Right here with me, I take it everywhere."

"Okay, this is what I want you to do Lara. Wipe out everything you have on there. The translation of the book, the photographs, anything connected to the Cooper family. I want you to do it now as a matter of urgency, okay?"

"Alright Jack. All I can think of now is sitting in your babbling brook, with a glass of wine, and watching the sun go down. This is a complete nightmare. I feel so violated…"

"Come on, Lara. Get rid of the evidence, sort out your student friend and check into a nice hotel. Harry will pay for it. Have a bubble bath, use room service and I'll see you soon. Please get rid of everything on your computer – it's extremely important Lara."

"Okay Jack. I want to see you. I want to get away from here."

Jack smiled to himself. He had one up on the spooks this time – without doubt they had ripped apart Lara's flat looking for her link to David Cooper, maybe, if they knew about it, looking for the diary, and only finding the silver box.

Jack put his phone down on the table. Then picked it up again and called Piet. He felt responsible for the situation Lara now found herself in. But he also knew he was on to a spectacular story.

The spooks would fully expect Lara to report the incident to the police, where, no doubt they would open a case and the paperwork would mysteriously disappear.

But when no phone call from Lara to report the incident was made, they would soon realise she had disappeared, leaving no trace. By the time they checked flights, she would be long gone. On her way to him, hiding out at his place where no-one could find either of them.

He drummed his fingers on the side of his chair. The box in itself had not been a threat. But it had been taken anyway.

It was the diary they had been looking for.

Chapter Fifty-Three

Piet and Hope finished their inspection of the perimeter fences of the hotel. Tonight, Hugo was having his monthly *braai* on the lawns.

Flaming torches had been placed along the driveway driven into the ground, sending sparks and smoke up into the early twilight. Pillar candles had been placed in the close-cropped grass in clear glass bowls, lighting up the ground with a gentle flickering glow, setting the shadows of the trees and bushes, dancing across the lawns.

Over the smouldering red-hot coals two chefs, in tall white hats, basted and turned the steaks, chops, sausages, *boerewors*, racks of spare ribs, kudu, ostrich and springbok steaks and kebabs. Corn on the cob spat and darkened on the fire. Rows of garlic baguettes nestled on the corners of the fires, the heady aroma's enticing the guests to join the others around the fire.

On long trestle tables, salads, homemade breads, coleslaw and cheeses were spread, along with cutlery, plates and condiments. The barmen were ready for the onslaught. The trestle table groaning under the weight of hard liquor and mixers and thirty different South African wines, the reds breathing, the whites plunged into huge silver buckets bristling with ice, the condensation making rivulets down their sides.

Piet and Hope mingled with the guests. "*Jeez,* Hope, stop dribbling, will you? Not a good look in front of the guests. You're supposed to be on duty, not an invited guest." He reached into his pocket and surreptitiously wiped the drool coming from his dog's mouth. Guests, as they consumed copious amounts of wine, shared their dinner with the happy, most sociable dog. She pushed her way through all the legs heading for the meat.

Piet, knowing he had lost control of his dog for the duration of the *braai*, looked around at the forty or so guests and the regulars who frequented Hugo's noisy bar. The party was in full swing.

Plumes of delicious smelling grey smoke drifted languidly upwards. He felt a tap on his shoulder.

Daniel Van Heerden.

"Hey, Piet, how are you," he said in Afrikaans. "How lekker is this? I checked in for the night, I've heard all about Hugo's monthly *braai*. Don't want to drive home with too many *dops* inside of me. I'd forgotten what it was like to mix socially. Writing books is a solitary life. I need to get out more."

Piet shook his hand. "Good to see you, Prof. Yup, isolation is all well and good, but people need people. You must miss your university life, both as a student and then as a professor?"

Piet, for the first time, saw a shadow cross the man's face. "Yes, I do miss it. But circumstances change, life twists and turns. I sometimes think being alone is alright, but loneliness is something else altogether. But, hey, like you I have my dog out at my place. I lose myself in reading and writing. I wouldn't have it any other way."

Piet frowned. "Couldn't, or wouldn't, Prof?"

Daniel spread his hands and shrugged his shoulders. "Either or, it doesn't matter anymore does it – it's the now that counts."

"You were at Rhodes University, right?"

Daniel smiled. "*Ja*, that's right. Best years of my life. I've lost touch with so many people. That's the internet for you. No-one has any time for idle conversation - everyone is out there chasing the money, so long."

Piet smiled. "This is so, my friend. I used to know Grahamstown quite well, as you do. My favourite pub when I visited was called *The Horse and Wagon*, did you ever go there? You must have done surely?"

Daniel closed his eyes briefly. "Ah yes, *The Horse and Wagon*, I didn't go there often, but I do know it. Not sure if it's still going though. Is it?"

Piet shook his head. "Dunno. Haven't been back for years to that part of the country. Anyway, go help yourself to the *braai,* looks like the staff are ready to serve dinner. Then Shaka, my main security man will creep out of the bushes in his full Zulu warrior regalia, beating on his shield and scare the hell out of everyone."

Piet watched Daniel walk towards the crowded food tables. He had never quite felt comfortable with Daniel Van Heerden. He knew he and Jack had misjudged the man in the beginning, but he had checked out, he was who he said he was.

Chapter Fifty-Four

Whilst Piet was busy with his guests and looking forward to the *braai,* Jack was dangling his feet in the stream at the end of his garden, wishing he had some company and wondering why Lara hadn't been in touch with Piet about her flight back to South Africa.

He assumed she was sorting out her business. He didn't want to call her and put any pressure on her.

He reached into the stream and retrieved his wine glass from a cluster of stones holding it steady, then wandered bare foot back to his laptop in the dining room.

He was pleased to see an email from Clair, he clicked it and leaned forward. Although he would not admit it to anyone, he knew he would soon need to get his eyes checked for glasses.

My dear Jack. I trust this email finds you well? Using some of my contacts I have some further news about Sir David Cooper which I think you will find of great interest. Once I had worked out the codes of the various countries, I started to concentrate on the message written on the back of the photograph you found in the box, the photograph of the box itself?

It took me a while, but I eventually worked it out. It was rather a clever clue actually. However, I don't wish to say any more about this in an email. Perhaps you would care to call me after luncheon tomorrow? I am giving some computer lessons in the morning so shall be rather tied up.

Kind regards.

Clair.

Jack read it again, a huge grin spreading across his face. Much as he would have loved to have called her immediately, she had her reasons for the delay, he'd respect that. He would have to be patient, something he was not good at. As requested, he would call her after lunch, her time.

His phone vibrated on the table next to him. "Lara! Where are you? The champagne is on ice, but no sign of you. I'm going nuts here on my own.

"Did you perhaps decide to book your own ticket? Are you at the airport now?"

He heard her take a deep breath and his heart plummeted. He knew what was coming next.

"I'm sorry Jack, I haven't done anything about my flight back to you. I know you said to check into a hotel, but I'm afraid I'm so spooked out I decided to go and spend some time with my family in Cornwall. They live out in the country; I'll be safe there. I need some more time, Jack. I don't like what's going on. I want to see you, of course I do, but as I said, I need a little more time. I hope you understand?"

"Of course, I understand, Lara. You must do what you feel comfortable with. Let me know when you feel ready to fly out – I'll still be here waiting for you. Your box is waiting as well."

Jack put down the phone. He was disappointed but he did understand. Finding the box was one thing, having it stolen from her room at the hotel and all that came afterwards, including her flat being wrecked, well, it would be a world she could only have known from spy novels. She was frightened and needed to get back to a safe haven. He, clearly, was not the safe haven she had chosen.

He had had high hopes for their relationship, but he knew he lived in a world where bad things happened, his world of stories. Living out in a cottage far from town with the story of Sir David Cooper and having to lie low, was probably too much for her to handle at the moment, especially in a country she didn't know.

He would give her the time she had asked for, but mentally he was already preparing for the relationship not to work out. It was hard enough living seven thousand miles apart, but throwing in the mix of Sir David Cooper had been too much for Lara.

Despondent, but still hopeful, he filled his wine glass and sat outside.

In the distance of the black night, he saw the headlights of a car which seemed to be heading his way, a plume of dust rose up in the rear lights. There was rarely any traffic on the dirt road leading to his cottage, especially at night. He glanced at his watch, almost ten, and

237

he hadn't had dinner yet, wasn't even sure what he wanted to eat. He seemed to have lost his appetite with the last phone call.

Piet's car pulled up and his mood lifted slightly.

"Hey, Jack, brought you some *braai,* with some fancy salads and things. Thought you might be needing a bit of company. Brought some wine as well. Felt guilty about enjoying all the company and the food and thought about you out here all on your own. Also, my friend, I have some interesting news."

Jack looked behind Piet. "Where's Hope?"

Piet rolled his eyes. "*Jeez,* Jack, that *bleddy* dog pretended to be checking everyone out to making sure they were legit. But all she was doing was shaking down anyone who had more than three glasses of booze and was right for a nudge and some steaks coming her way. Shameless.

"Let me tell you, so long, I sometimes wonder if she prefers meat, or human food, more than me. *Ag, man,* when I called her, she hid under the long tablecloths. Doubt whether she has even noticed I've gone. But she'll go back to my cottage and fall asleep on my bed probably feeling sick as all hell. Females! What can I say?"

Piet glanced at Jack and paused. "Ah, the lovely Lara isn't coming back anytime soon, hey?"

Jack managed not to throw his arms around his old friend, but shook his hand vigorously. The smell wafting from the box he was carrying made Jack's mouth water.

Piet pushed past him. "Come, my friend, have something to eat and I will tell you what I'm thinking, so long? Go sit. I'll bring you food and a glass of wine."

They sat outside; Piet helped himself to one of the lamb chops off of Jack's plate. Jack ate ravenously. He finished everything on his plate then sat back.

"No, Lara's not coming back, not yet anyway. Gone to stay with her family in Cornwall."

They looked at each other, but said nothing.

Piet changed the subject. "See here, my friend, Daniel Van Heerden was at the *braai,* he came over for a chat. Nice and friendly, didn't ask about you, sorry about that.

"I asked him if he missed his old life as a prof at Rhodes University. He discussed it briefly, but pretty much dismissed it as a life long gone. We talked a bit about politics, the world today, the God called money."

238

Piet threw his battered cap on the table. "I told him I knew Grahamstown quite well, it's in the Eastern Cape, where I come from, as you know, where Van Heerden got his degree and eventually taught. Thing is, Jack. I mentioned a pub where all the students go to drink, as they do as students, before they get serious about actually studying, a place called *The Horse and Wagon*. Van Heerden said he knew it, of course he did."

Jack lifted his shoulders. "So?"

"Thing is, Jack, there has never been a pub called that, not then, not now, not ever."

Chapter Fifty-Five

Jack spent the morning writing up his notes then a few hours on the internet, determined to find something more about Madeleine and David Cooper. He came up with nothing.

He checked his watch. Time to call Clair. The phone rang for some time before a crisp voice answered his call.

"Oh, I thought this was a direct line to Clair Davenport. I must have misdialled?"

There was a slight pause. "Your name, sir?"

His heart sank. How could someone else know this number? It was set up so he could converse with Clair directly. A number unknown to anyone else. Had the spooks got hold of it somehow?

"No worries, I must have got the number wrong."

"Are you family, sir?"

"Family? I'm a friend of her nephew Harry. Why do you ask?"

The voice at the end of the private phone hesitated for a moment. "I'm sorry to tell you this, sir, but Clair passed away peacefully during the night. I'm manning all her phones in her suite so we can let her friends and family know. She will be such a great loss to us all," her voice broke. "I doubt we will see the likes of her again. Wonderful woman."

Jack felt his voice tighten with regret. "Yes, unlikely indeed. She was expecting a call from me this afternoon. But I'm too late."

"Your name, sir?"

"It doesn't matter now. But may I speak to Hamish? I wish to pass on my condolences?"

There was a slight pause. "Well clearly you knew Clair well, if you know Hamish. Please hold for a moment whilst I find him?"

Jack drummed his fingers on the table as he waited. Would Hamish know what Clair wanted to tell him about David Cooper? It was likely. Hamish and Clair had worked together at Bletchley Park.

A deeply European accent came over the phone. "Yes?"

"Hamish, I'm Jack Taylor. I'm a friend of Harry's. Clair's nephew?"

"Yes, Mr Taylor. Clair mentioned you. Your friend Lara came to see her. I know about this."

Jack heard Hamish's voice break with emotion. He gave him a few moments to compose himself. "I'm so sorry to hear of Clair's passing. It will be a huge loss to you after so many years working together."

"So many of us have gone now, Mr Taylor. So few of us left to tell a story which may never be told again, only in books and films, but not with the people who were actually there. Clair was someone so special - unique."

Jack could almost imagine him straightening his back, professional until the end.

"How may I help you, Mr Taylor?"

"Clair asked me to call her after lunch, she wanted to tell me something she thought would be important. Do you have any idea what it was she wanted me to know?"

"Yes, Mr Taylor. She found something which she considered clever and important. You had a private number for Clair. I think it would be better if I called you back on another number? In a few days perhaps. We have to arrange for her funeral. I think you will understand."

Jack breathed a sigh of relief. Clair had left him a message, from her almost grave.

"Hamish, I'm sorry to intrude on your grief but all the information on her computers. What will happen to it?"

"It has all been eliminated, Mr Taylor, as per her wishes. I was the only one she trusted with her secret life. I have destroyed everything on her computers and phones. There is nothing left for anyone to find – nothing. All gone. I shall take good care of her little dog, Joe, this she asked me to do. I shall honour her wishes."

Jack put the phone down, saddened he would never meet Clair. Women like her didn't exist anymore.

His phone rumbled on the table. *Harry.*

Jack pre-empted him. "I've already heard Harry. Clair was clearly fond and proud of you. I've just been speaking to Hamish, a close friend from their Bletchley days. He sounds truly broken,"

Jack heard a bus roar past to wherever Harry was. "I'm sorry Harry, last of the elite. Proud of her country, dedicated to making sure England didn't lose the war. We won't see the likes of her again."

He could hear Harry clearing his throat, either from a cold or the toxic fumes of the heavy traffic rumbling by, or perhaps regret.

"Yes, it's all very sad, Jack. I wish I had taken the time to get to know her, but I had no idea of her past, the part she played at Bletchley Park, until recently.

"You know Jack, there are so many stories of old people living alone with only the television for company. They died alone. Sometimes it was days before anyone discovered the bodies. Some, but not all, of the stories came out. There was a woman down in the south of England, she had lived there for thirty years. No friends, no relatives, no visitors. When she died it was a few days before social services discovered her body."

Harry cleared his throat and continued. "A journalist, appalled by the whole situation, did a bit of digging. Turned out she had worked with the Resistance. A remarkable woman, brave, courageous, awarded medals by the French Government. Social services found them in a box in the attic. But she died alone Jack, totally alone. All her glory days left behind. In the village, she ended up in a council house. No-one bothered with her, they thought she was a bit odd. Old. Not worth bothering with. But she was a heroine. A remarkable woman. Died penniless."

He cleared his throat again. "The local Vicar was almost embarrassed because he thought no-one would come to her funeral. But once this journalist got hold of her story, he unearthed her incredible past. It was front page news. The Church was packed, old soldiers, politicians, friends who had fought alongside her against the Nazi's. Pity they had not paid more attention to her when she was alive, Jack. It would have meant so much to her to know she had not been forgotten."

There was a short silence, then Jack plunged ahead. "Listen Harry, I can't do this isolation stuff anymore. I'm going back out there. As far as any interested parties are concerned, I don't work for you anymore. But there's no reason why I shouldn't go out and mingle with my buddies, after all I do live here?

"Sitting here waiting for something to happen doesn't work for me. Lara has postponed her trip out here. She's gone to stay with her mother. I need the stimulation of other people, Harry. There's

242

someone I want to spend a bit of time with, dig around a little. Something isn't stacking up with this guy called Daniel Van Heerden.

"So, that is what I'm going to do Harry, with or without your blessing," he said determinedly.

"Go for it, Jack!"

Jack sighed with relief. He thought he might have had some resistance, but he knew Harry was as keen as he was to get back to the story, not sitting by a stream counting the hours and watching the odd small fish darting by.

"Will you be going to Clair's funeral, Harry?"

"I would like to go and pay my respects, but to tell the truth I don't even know what she looked like. Also, if the spooks are out and about there's bound to be one mingling with the mourners. Too much of a risk and I know Clair would absolutely understand. I shall send flowers though."

Jack paused for a moment. "Harry, do me a favour will you. Clair played a big role in this story, deciphering the blue book and I know she had some news for me – but it was too late, although I think her buddy Hamish might have something for me, we'll see. But I would like to send some flowers. Proteas if you can find them?"

The roar of the traffic had increased on the streets of London. Harry raised his voice. "Proteas? Never heard of them, but I'll get someone on to it and do it for you. No message? Clearly you won't be able to put your name on them," he boomed down the phone. "To risky, too much of a connection."

Jack thought for a moment. "You're right. Um, I think just say a simple *thank you.* No name as you suggest."

"So much for bloody Spring, my boy. Chucking it down here, must get on. I'll deduct the cost of the flowers from your expenses. Cheerio Jack, keep in touch with any developments, you hear?

"Go get me my story."

Chapter Fifty-Six

Jack wandered through his cottage, he stared out of the window at the dull misty morning, the rain was coming down steadily, slivers of rain were forming small rivulets down to the stream. Birds, their feathers clumping, crouched in the trees sheltering from the rain.

He turned and looked around – his cottage was beginning to look like a tip. His bedroom was a tip. Clothes strewn on the back of chairs or in an untidy pile in the corner. The kitchen was no better. The dishwasher was piled with plates and cutlery, he needed to do something about it. In fact, he needed to do something about a lot of things. He called Piet.

"Listen, mate, can you find one of the house staff at the hotel to come and help me out here, Piet? I don't have any clean clothes to wear, too caught up in the story to bother about domestic issues. But, um, I need a bit of help."

Piet laughed. "No problem, my friend. We had a lady come by today looking for a job, unfortunately I don't have a job for her. Interviewed her myself. Her name is Winnie, a Zulu girl, well hardly a girl, around fifty, I would think. She has good references. I think she'll be able to sort you out. Do you want someone full time, or part time?"

Jack gave it some thought. "I think this calls for full time for two weeks, then maybe twice a week after that. I'm not used to having someone around full time. In London I dumped all the laundry and suchlike at the corner laundrette, ate out most nights, or had take-out."

"Okay Jack, Winnie is sitting in front of me right now, I'll drop her at your place, so long. She'll sort you out – a bit bossy, but, as I said, her references are excellent. You'll never have to do a full load of washing again, or iron. Not that you ever have. Wanted to mention this Jack, you're looking a bit creased – not a good look."

True to his word Piet dropped Winnie off an hour later. He introduced her then drove off.

Winnie though seemingly shy at first, took one look at Jack's cottage and then hissed with disapproval, her hands on her ample hips. "*Eish,* Mr Yak. Your momma never taught you to look after yourself? Much work to be done here. Kitchen? Cleaning things? Vacuum cleaner?"

Meekly Jack showed her where everything was then hastily retreated out on to the veranda, feeling slightly embarrassed about the state of his living quarters.

Finally, the screech of the vacuum cleaner subsided and he wandered back inside to the kitchen to make himself some coffee. Winnie was bent over the glass topped table in the sitting room spraying and wiping all the marks of plates and glasses, bits of golden fur from the dog and fingerprints away.

Jack had always disliked glass topped tables, they showed every mark of the inhabitant. Whorls of glass bottoms, dust from outside, fingerprints…

He stopped and sucked in his breath. The smell of the cleaning materials. Madeleine's old house, her obsession with wiping things down.

'*Then after he came, she was wiping, wiping, wiping. This she had not done before.*"

Jack sat outside with his coffee. He remembered Gift, the barman at the hotel had said she always wore gloves. Madeleine, as he now knew was her name, had always worn gloves and always wiped down her glass of wine at the hotel and the top of the bar where she had been sitting.

This he now understood. If she was in some kind of programme, she would not want to leave any fingerprints anywhere. Was she frightened of something? No-one knew who she was, she had a different name. What on earth would make her so obsessed with wiping surfaces?

According to Eunice she had then had a visitor. After that she became almost fanatical about every surface being wiped clean all over the house. Then she had found Eunice another job.

Jack worked it all through. So, who was the mystery man who had visited her and why had she become obsessed with wiping every surface clean?

He doubted Madeleine would give a damn about whoever the visitor was, spook or otherwise, handler or whatever.

However, she might have been concerned about this one particular visitor, enough to eliminate any sign of him when he left.

He took a tentative sip of his coffee. Why had Madeleine decided to find Eunice another job after the visit of this man?

Because, he speculated, this man had not made only one visit, he had come back, perhaps more than once and she didn't want Eunice to know about it…or anyone else.

Perhaps it was why she had turned her gaze from the water hole where she must have watched the animals come to drink, before the visitor first arrived, maybe content with her daily rides, crossword puzzles and monthly trips to town ending with a glass of wine at the bar Gift worked behind. Then after the man had arrived, she had turned her gaze towards the road, watching and waiting for him to return.

Maybe, after months, Jack speculated, she finally realised this man was not coming back again and had taken her own life in despair?

Therefore, he concluded, to do such a thing she must have been in love with this man, or at least have been extremely fond of him.

However, there was one other person on the farm who would have seen the comings and goings of any visitors – Nico, the groom.

He flicked through his phone until he found the number of the hotel he had stayed at in Wolmaransstad. He asked to be put through to the bar.

Gift, the barman, answered. "Yes, this is Gift here speaking."

"Hey, Gift, it's me Mr Yak. You probably won't remember me, but I hope you do. I spoke to your cousin who worked for Mrs Hartley some years ago, then I met her where she is working."

"Good afternoon, Mr Yak, I remember you, yes."

Jack cleared his throat. "I need your help again, Gift. The man who looked after the horses on the farm, his name was Nico. I would like to speak with him again?"

Jack heard the clink of glasses. "Then, Mr Yak, if you are here, you would have driven a long way for no reason. There are no horses on the farm now and Nico left some weeks ago. He has gone back to his family in Zimbabwe. It is a long way to go also."

Jack's heart sank. Another dead end. He thanked Gift for his time and rang off.

Jack parked outside Hugo's hotel and strolled into the noisy bar and found himself a seat. Hugo hurried over a look of great surprise on his face, as he shook his hand.

"Well, hello Jack, good trip to India? I thought you would be gone for months?"

Jack grinned, knowing he hadn't fooled Hugo for a second. "Nah, you know I'm a fast worker, got my story on tourism. I have to say India, although beautiful in parts is way too crowded for me. The hotels are stupendous but to get to them you have to weave your way through the abject poverty, the beggars, the traffic, the pollution and, well, the heat is something else. I know we have all that here in South Africa to some extent, but not on that scale. Also, I'm done with the curry. I don't like highly spiced foods, never have. British grub for me will do."

He grinned at Hugo. "I met some ancient old colonials who stayed on after independence, that was interesting. Anyway, job done. I'm back. How are things with you Hugo?"

Hugo leaned towards him as he wiped down the bar. "You're not fooling me for a minute, Jack" he hissed, "but I'll go along with it. You must have a reason for hiding out and then suddenly re-appearing before a year was up when you're supposed to be out of the country." He stepped back and said more loudly. "Beer?"

Piet's dog padded her way into the bar and greeted Jack as though he had indeed been gone for a year. "Hello, Hope! Where's the boss?"

Piet ambled over to him. "Hello Jack, good to see you again. What a surprise, thought you would be out of the country for months, so long. How was the trip?" He shook his hand enthusiastically then thumped him on the back almost knocking him off his bar stool.

"What the *fok* are you doing in here, Jack," he said quietly. "This wasn't the plan, my friend. But you have a reason and I want to hear about it. Meet me at my cottage in half an hour, okay?"

Piet and his dog left the bar and Jack looked around. The usual crowd, including Daniel Van Heerden who was sitting in his normal place, watching him, before turning back to his drinking companion his finger tap tapping on the bar counter.

Jack pretended to study his notes in the little book he carried in his shirt pocket, then glanced up and noticed Daniel was deep in conversation with a young, tanned man who looked like a safari guide.

247

But Jack could tell the safari guide didn't have Daniel's full and undivided attention.

*****

Jack glanced at his watch, put his notebook back in his pocket, drained his beer and made to leave, seemingly to hurry to his next appointment.

Piet was waiting for him. "What the *fok* are you doing here Jack!"

Jack lowered himself into a chair. "Can't do things the way people want me to do things, mate. Have to do it my own way. Harry has agreed. Now I have a theory on Madeleine. Her funny gloves and her odd behaviour. Notwithstanding she obviously had a major issue with depression."

Piet stood and listened. He walked around the cottage as he thought it all through. "Okay, it seems to make sense, I agree, my friend, but not a lot of sense. There are too many things missing in this puzzle."

He took off his cap and scratched his head. "Someone followed Lara from the auction sale of Madeleine's few possessions, right? Then the puzzle box was stolen, but found, minus the blue book. Everything leads back to the late Sir David Cooper. But there is no doubt he is dead, the burning plane, the death certificate. However, Madeleine Cooper is another story altogether, from what you have just told me."

Jack nodded. Piet continued. "Both of us agree this Daniel Van Heerden has a big question mark over him. What are you thinking here, Jack, that Van Heerden might have been the man who visited her on the farm?"

"Yes. This Van Heerden suddenly pitches up in Hazyview, at Hugo's bar. Never seen him here before, now he's here every week. I'm thinking not only are we watching him. I think he's watching us. He doesn't want to be a shadowy presence, although he might have been in the beginning. He wants to be close to us to see what we are trying to find out about the puzzle box and him."

Piet nodded. "Bertie checked him out, he was legit. But then we found out he had never been to Rhodes University, or at least the bar I made the name up for. Makes me think Bertie needs to do a little more digging."

248

Bertie tapped away at his keyboard; something had been bothering him about this Daniel Van Heerden. He had been feeding in mountains of other information from his own government and also his exclusive club of members around the world, on many other issues. But in the back of his mind was always the uneasy feeling he had missed something about Van Heerden. A common enough name in South Africa. Piet Joubert had asked him to do him a favour and Bertie knew he owed him.

Once more he opened up Van Heerden's file and studied it. What was wrong with it? What had he missed?

He took off his glasses and rubbed his nose and behind his ears where the glasses had left their mark. He checked everything in the file once more. Then he went back to Van Heerden's identity number.

He put his head in his hands then peered through his fingers and looked again. Maybe it was time he retired, after all, how could he have missed it?

But he had. He picked up the phone and called Piet.

"Hey, Bertie, how's it going my friend? You have news for me?"

There was a short silence.

"You there Bertie, you called me remember?"

"I think, Piet, it's time for me to find a shack somewhere near a river and retire. Spend the rest of my days fishing and watching the sun go down. I'm losing my touch, man…"

Piet frowned. Bertie was always so upbeat. What had gone wrong in his world of secrets? "It's Van Heerden, my friend, isn't it? You missed something, right?"

"Yup. The mind can play tricks. Your eyes follow something and assume it's what it is. I got it wrong, Piet. I'm sorry."

Bertie cleared his throat. "He was in the system, with his identity number, his tax payments, everything was in order, everything stacked up. I checked him out. But something was bothering me, so I double checked.

"Thing is, Piet, he died thirty years ago. His identity number was wrong, I missed it."

*****

Piet put the phone down. His instincts had been right. Daniel Van Heerden was not who he said he was.

But whoever he was his past was catching up with him. This so-called Van Heerden had stolen the identity of a dead man.

Chapter Fifty-Seven

Jack stood when he saw Piet and Hope trudging up to the veranda. Hope went straight for the stream to see what she could find. Piet sat heavily in a chair and sighed.

Jack went to fetch him a beer and one for himself. "So, Piet, what's up. Why are you looking so gloomy?"

Piet took off his battered cap and put it on the table then ran his hands through his hair. "I'm not gloomy, my friend. This is my thinking face. Something interesting, very interesting, has developed."

"Daniel Van Heerden is dead."

Jack stared at him a look of utter disbelief on his face. "What! What happened to him?"

Piet wiped the foam from his lip with the back of his hand. "He died thirty years ago, Jack. Bertie did a bit more poking around and discovered he'd missed something."

Jack looked incredulous. "But how can that be? I know it's a common enough name in this country but surely Home Affairs would have picked up someone else was using a dead man's identity?"

"Not necessarily. It's true everyone must carry their identity book with them at all times in case you're stopped at a road block, or for speeding and such like. But it's probable this man who now does not have a name, made photocopies of the original ID and carried it around with him in case he was stopped.

"He's an Afrikaner. Every policeman in this country speaks Afrikaans. If he was stopped, he would have told them, in their own language, he had lost it, or it had been stolen and he'd applied for a new one. It would be impossible for a cop to see if the copied ID was genuine or not."

Jack frowned. "But whoever this man is he would have needed the original to open bank accounts, buy or rent a place, buy a car and all the other things you need it for?"

Piet laughed. "Oh, he had the original all right, had to have to do all those things you just mentioned. No-one scrutinises an ID book, they take the number down and put it on whatever forms needs filling out and that's that. Sometimes a copy of the ID book is required, but it wouldn't have been a problem for our mystery man. It would only have been a problem for him if he had committed some crime. Then he would definitely be in the system and easy to track down. But he wasn't was he. Bertie would have found something like that...."

Jack interrupted him. "But where the hell did he get the ID book from in the first place?"

"This man is clever Jack. He lived in Joburg. Let me tell you my friend, you can get anything you need and want in that city – it's full of dodgy people, *skollies*, who can obtain anything for you for the right price. This is what he did. Of course, it won't be the original, it would be a copy but slightly adjusted shall we say."

Jack scribbled in his notebook and paused. "But your mate Bertie checked him out. Said he filed his taxes every year, was an English History Professor etc. How did this man manage to do all this and not get found out?"

"Like I said, so long. You can get anything and everything in Joburg on the black market, for the right price. There are plenty people in this country walking around with documents they're not entitled to. People steal identities...shady accountants file tax returns, again, of course, for a price."

Jack ran his finger across his drying lips. "Okay then, if he's not Daniel Van Heerden, we need to find out his real name. My gut feel still tells me this man is somehow connected to Lara and the puzzle box. I think he went to Cloud's End looking for it. Which means he knew Madeleine Cooper, or Marlene Hartley, as she was then known."

Almost talking to himself Jack continued with his train of thought. "I'm betting on the fact he was the man who visited the farm. The man Eunice told me about.

"But see here, Piet what the hell is the connection between a so-called Afrikaans History Professor previously living in Joburg and born in Bloemfontein, according to him, and Sir David Cooper, a highly respected member of Her Majesty's Government. A British aristocrat who died in a plane crash in Kenya?"

Piet took a long swallow of his beer. "This, my friend, is what we are going to find out. I still have contacts all over the place, I'm going to use them. First port of call will be Rhodes University and we'll track things back from there. Bertie is going to continue with his digging. He'll come up with something."

He adjusted his dog's collar and continued. "Then we flush this so-called Daniel out into the open and find out exactly who he is and what his connections with Sir David and Madeleine Cooper was. Because you're right Jack there is a definite connection although I'm buggered if I know what it is."

Jack rubbed his hands together. "Let's get to it then, Piet. I can feel our story maybe coming together. I need to make a few phone calls myself. So, no point in sitting around here drinking beer when there's work to be done. I'll see you later at Hugo's."

Piet whistled for his dog who was back at the river, she completely ignored him until she heard the car start up, then she bounded inside and showered the entire interior including the windows with a huge spray of water.

Piet rolled his eyes in despair, climbed into the driving seat and took off, wiping the dust, dog spray and bits of fur from his window with his sleeve.

*****

Jack phoned Harry and brought him up to date on what they had now surmised. "The story is gathering speed, Harry, I'm going with all my instincts here at the moment. Any feedback on the funeral? Good send off?"

He could hear a couple arguing angrily as they passed Harry who again must have been crouching in a doorway looking furtive.

"Big turn-out Jack, she was highly thought of, my aunt. It taught me a hard lesson. I'm too much of a reporter myself, always interested in other people's stories when I should be taking more care of my own family and their stories. I sent a junior reporter posing as one of her nephews twice removed. Her little dog even attended the funeral in the company of a rather fierce looking chap called Hamish.

"You'll be happy to know we found a huge bouquet of furry looking pinkish flowers called Proteas and left them for her from you. Prefer daffodils and roses myself.

"Keep up the good work Jack, sorry about the situation with Lara, but it might still work out when all this is over. Cheerio, must dash, train to catch."

Jack poured himself a glass of wine and lifted it in salute to Clair Davenport, a most remarkable woman by all accounts. He wished he could have met her.

His phone vibrated next to him. *Hamish.*

"Ah, Mr Taylor, it has been a sad day for us. Including little Joe, Clair's dog, who is sitting next to me looking most sad. Clair's message for you is rather brief. She told me to tell you '*There is no digit missing.*' Makes no sense to me, but it must have to her for her to be so insistent I tell you. I think she thought you would work it out."

Jack was disappointed. He was hoping for more. "Thank you, Hamish, thank you for calling me."

Hamish cleared his throat. "I guessed the furry pink flowers with the odd shape were from you. I have put them on the table in her suite, they are very beautiful. Goodbye, Mr Taylor. I hope you find what you are looking for, as I am sure Clair will."

Jack put the phone down feeling his throat tighten with unexpected emotion. He looked up at the deep blue sky and hoped with all his heart she was out there somewhere. If she was, he was quite sure she would be helping someone make sure no dodgy people were trying to get into heaven before they were cleared by her. He liked that thought, it made him smile, although he knew it was impossible – or perhaps not.

One minute you were here and then in the blink of an eye you were gone - forever. No shape of you left in the world you had lived in. No trace of a smile, the sound of your voice, nor the whisper of a word. Just gone.

A small bird swooped down towards him, he recognised it as some kind of sunbird he'd seen in the bush. Its iridescent colours of green, deep blue, purple and yellow catching the last of the sunlight. The bird hovered above him then perched on the table in front of him. Jack held his breath as it tipped its delicate beak into his glass of wine then flew rapidly away.

"Goodbye Clair – go well," he whispered to the still evening air.

He remembered the message on the back of the photograph of the puzzle box.

So, you have found your way into my box, discovered my past perhaps? Now what will you do... apart from being extremely careful? There's a digit missing somewhere. You'll never find it.'

What was Clair trying to tell him?

He had another call to make, a difficult one. But he hoped Hugo would not ask too many questions. It was a big ask, given the fact he wouldn't be able to tell Hugo why he was going to request him to do what he wanted him to do.

There was still no word from Lara.

Chapter Fifty-Eight

Jack strolled into the bar, it was Thursday, apparently Daniel so-called Van Heerden was always there on a Thursday night. Daniel was sitting in his normal place at the corner of the bar where he was watching everyone who came and went.

Jack lifted his hand in acknowledgement and reached for a discarded newspaper on the bar knowing Daniel, or whoever he turned out to be, was watching him.

Piet joined him at the bar, ordering a coffee and looking hungrily towards any snack Hugo might send his way, a bit like his dog. He shook Jack's hand.

"All fixed up then Jack?"

"Yup, wasn't easy, Hugo didn't like it at all. But Queen and country and all that. He begrudgingly agreed to help. I can tell you he didn't like it one bit."

Jack and Piet spent an hour together talking about everything going on in the country, politics, corruption, crime, murders.

They both watched Daniel, as he chatted to his friends, tapping away at his glass. Then he stood up and said goodbye to everyone, lifting his arm in acknowledgement to Jack and Piet but not coming over to them as he normally did.

A few moments later Hugo passed a paper bag over the counter. "Thought Hope might like a late-night snack, Piet."

They made their way to Piet's cottage and carefully lifted the glass from its paper container.

Piet grinned. "See here, my friend, we have the fingerprints of the so-called Daniel. This is his glass. Now let me see what I can find out from these prints, so long."

Piet disappeared for a few moments then returned with the tools of his trade. "Let's see what we have here…"

Piet carefully powdered over the outside of the glass, then sat back. "Something a bit odd. I don't have a full hand. Something a bit smudged with the little finger. But enough for Bertie to get stuck in and find out who these fingerprints belong to."

He took some shots of the powdery glass. "I'll send them through to him, just now."

Jack looked innocent. "Just now? Or perhaps tomorrow or next week - give me a clue here?"

Chapter Fifty-Nine
England

John Smith bent to tend to his roses. He had retired and was now in his late seventies. He looked up at the cloud free sky of an English spring and found it was not enough to lift his spirits. Savagely he plunged his fork into the soft brown earth of England.

He had recruited David Cooper into the service all those years ago. He remembered it quite clearly for being the biggest triumph of his career - and also the greatest mistake and inevitably his own fall from grace.

David had been exceptional. Fluent in so many languages, tough, unemotional – perfect for the job.

There were a few occasions which could be classified as "spying" where David was useful, always reporting back to Her Majesty's Government. But where he excelled was the deals he did with various governments. Awarding contracts worth millions, negotiating for the best price and closing the trade deals.

There was never a sniff of scandal in his life. His marriage to Madeleine was a bit of a front, John knew. He'd had a hand in manipulating it himself.

However, it had emerged some of those so called "goods" didn't quite go where they were expected to go. One could say they lost their way through a middleman and ended up in the wrong hands, depending on which side of the fence you were on.

A clerical error, spotted by one of the more diligent forensic accountants revealed something. The accountant and Sir David's secretary, Harold, followed the paper trail where possible, reaching their own conclusions, then presented them to John Smith.

"We have a fox in the hen house, sir," the auditor mumbled. "A most unlikely fox. But a fox nevertheless."

John had looked up with a frown of irritation on his face. "Don't talk in bloody riddles, man. What fox? What hen house?"

"Sir David Cooper, sir. Something I spotted. At first, I thought it was a clerical error. I followed it through, checked back on some of the deals he concluded over the past few years. A pattern formed. I followed the trail. I'm afraid not only has he betrayed us here, but he has betrayed his country as well."

Cooper's position as Britain's Head of Trade and Industry and his impressive track record, had not protected him. It had been one mistake, a clerical error – his spectacular career was over.

John Smith stabbed at the roots of a weed with uncontrolled fury. Who would have thought?

Sir David Cooper had been cutting his own deals. Making sure certain tenders and contracts went to the companies he wanted them to go to. There was always a middleman, and the middlemen had made David Cooper very rich indeed.

With his unique flair for languages, David had waited in all those countries, knowing it would eventually bring out the middleman.

John Smith knew all about the cartels, from different countries, who met in high-end hotels and cut deals. They had preferential access to business and would decide who got which contract, and for what amount. The deals for arms and munitions didn't always get to their intended destination. There were cuts, kickbacks and a percentage of benefits once the deal was done. Everyone made money, one way or another. Sir David Cooper included.

John threw his spade down on the ground. He needed a drink. Years ago, he had tried to work out what had driven David to betray his country. But to this day he hadn't reached any conclusions. David had become extremely wealthy at Her Majesty's expense. Where he had stashed his money was another question still unanswered. No doubt it was hidden behind numerous shell companies in various countries where it could never be discovered; and so far, it never had been.

His South African wife, Madeleine, had worked for the apartheid government in a senior position. South Africa was no different to other governments who had found themselves in the spotlight when the rest of the world decided they were in the wrong.

David's marriage had been government approved; such status was recognised as a benefit in diplomatic life. There would be arms deals going down and David would have been an integral part of it. His link with his South African wife, and her senior position in the old government would have been invaluable for trade relations with the new regime, giving David the valuable contacts, he needed to get ahead of the competition.

After years of sanctions, the South African government anticipated golden opportunities which had been denied to them for so long. The country was rich in minerals, gold and diamonds which could be traded for arms and munitions, and other commodities. They were ready to deal.

The Foreign Office had scrutinised Madeleine's background and run checks on her. There was nothing there to make them sit up and take note. She had shown none of the unpredictable traits waiting in the wings. But, as things turned out, she had become a real and dangerous threat to the British government.

John poured himself a large gin and tonic and returned to the garden.

He took a long pull from his glass, fished out the lemon and sucked it as he twirled the ice in his now half-empty glass.

The bitter taste of the lemon was not as bitter as the taste David Cooper had left in his mouth.

John and his forensic accountants, plus Harold his private secretary, had spent many hours poring over the figures, comparing notes. Checking dates and times of various deals David had done, where he had been at the time and who with. At some point he had disappeared for a month in the Far East, telling his secretary, Harold, he needed a few weeks break before he flew on to Hong Kong.

There was no mistake.

Sir David Cooper had betrayed them all.

The Prime Minister at the time had been John Major. Another election was coming up later in the year and Tony Blair had been tipped to be his successor.

The meeting at Number 10 had been attended by senior members of MI6, the Prime Minister himself, the Foreign Secretary and John Smith, Head of International Trade and Industry for Great Britain.

The stage had been set to bring in Sir David Cooper. Their agent in Kenya, where Sir David was then posted, was alerted to the fact there was a problem without going into specifics. Neither person was known to the other – it was how the MI6 worked. They always found a local resident who moved in the same circles as senior Embassy staff to keep an eye on things. Listening for anything interesting. Any unsuitable behaviour or relationships would be observed and reported back. Officially they didn't exist in the many countries where Britain had an Embassy or High Commission.

The Prime Minister had emphasised to them all that there was an election coming up. A scandal, a betrayal like this, would seriously throw a bomb in the laps of the voters who he hoped would be voting for him and another term of office for the Conservatives.

The Prime Minister had stood to indicate the meeting was over. "Bring him in, and his wife," he had said angrily. "Then bury him somewhere remote. I want no scandal. No media until the elections are over. Once this happens, whatever the result, an official investigation into the deals brokered by Sir David will be opened and he will be required to attend such an investigation and appear before the Board of Trade and Industry and explain himself, with a great deal of difficulty, I suspect. Given the facts we now have in front of us.

"Put his wife somewhere remote as well, but not with him. Ensure she speaks to no-one until the investigation is over. She may know nothing. But we have no guarantees of that do we? Are we clear on this?"

John Smith pushed the memory aside and looked out over his tranquil lawns as he watched the sun set over another day.

Despite everything, despite the sour taste it left, he had been unable to forget David Cooper. He had mentally stripped David of his title. He was the one man out of all the people he had recruited over the years, who he thought incapable of betraying his country. With his background and flawless education, it seemed impossible.

He remembered him as a young man when he recruited him. Tough, unemotional; a loner.

He had been the first one to get the news that David Cooper had died in a plane crash in a remote part of the Kenyan bush. Part of him was highly relieved. The sordid scandal would now be buried forever. No scandal, no threat to the Government. An official statement would be made and the whole unpalatable situation would go away.

But a part of John still wondered if it had been an accident, a suicide, or perhaps MI6 had their own ways of silencing what would have become an outrageous and dangerous scandal.

Madeleine Cooper had then become a real problem. It had been decided she would be removed from Kenya and returned to her own country, South Africa, and placed in a protection programme. Not to protect her, but to protect Her Majesty's government from what would be the biggest scandal since Kim Philby had been unmasked as a

Russian spy. The woman had been perceived to be unstable, a dangerous combination given the circumstances.

After David's death the Embassy had moved in swiftly to eliminate any evidence from David's house in Nanyuki. Madeleine had been uncooperative with their questions. Spaced out on some medication. It was the gardener who had been questioned and told them the memsahib had kept a writing book. The housekeeper had told him this.

They never found it.

John had done what was expected of him, the honourable thing. He had resigned and moved to the country. He was now out of the loop. Doors closed in his face. He was no longer a part of the establishment of which he had once served so proudly.

John finished his drink and threw the remaining ice cubes on the lawn, watching them melt as the sun faded into the twilight.

Something still bothered him about David Cooper. He knew who to call, but he was tired now. It could wait another day. After twenty years another day would make no difference at all. The watcher as he liked to call the unofficial agent in the field, was still the same one.

Daphne Forsyth-Phillips.

*****

John Smith died during the night. His whispered words to the person he wanted to speak to, but had put off for so many years, were lost before they could reach the cool winds of an African night.

MI6 moved swiftly on learning of John's death via his solicitor. They went through his home, his papers, took his computer and anything else they considered could be damaging to the government.

They were taking no chances – they never did.

Chapter Sixty

Jack peered up at the grey sky and the fine film of rain sweeping across his garden. He went back inside and shrugged on his sweater. There was a definite feel of winter in the air and he was looking forward to the cooler months ahead.

He had arranged to meet Piet in a coffee shop in town to discuss the story so far, which seemed to be going nowhere. Maybe Bertie had come up with the real identity of the man calling himself Van Heerden.

Piet waved him over. The place was busy with people taking shelter from the chilly wet weather outside.

"Hey Jack, how are you?"

Jack sat and ordered a large cup of coffee. "Frustrated is what I am, Piet. We seem to be grinding to a halt with everything. All the leads have dried up. Did you hear from your mate Bertie?"

"*Ja*, the prints weren't in the system. It was a good try but obviously our friend Van Heerden has never put a foot wrong as far as the authorities are concerned. There was no match. I checked with Rhodes University. Dozens of Van Heerdens there, given it's a fairly common name. Did a bit of digging asked a few questions, said I was looking for my old professor of history. The auntie in admin confirmed he had died thirty years ago. So, it was the end of that lead as well."

Jack stared at the slow-moving traffic outside. The pedestrians with their umbrellas up wearing warm clothes and he grinned. It was positively balmy out there as far as he was concerned. In the UK they would be setting out the striped deckchairs in the parks of London.

"So, Piet, here is the million-dollar question. Why would someone steal and obviously pay a lot of money for someone else's identity? Van Heerden being a South African would have had his own identity book. He doesn't have a criminal record, not even a traffic fine by all accounts. So why doesn't he use his own?"

Piet drained his coffee cup and smacked his lips. "Because, my friend, he is hiding from something or someone."

Jack frowned. "Not making a good job of it then, is he. If he was hiding out, he wouldn't be hanging around Hugo's pub, would he?"

Piet picked a bit of dog fur off his jacket. "Sometimes the best hiding place is right out there in the open, so long, behaving like everyone else. Anyways, Professor Daniel Van Heerden is dead. So, no point in hiding out is there?"

They stared at each other, saying nothing. "Listen, Piet. How about you come back to my place. I've tacked a big piece of paper to the wall in the spare room. The photographs are there and all my notes. Apart from our assumption Van Heerden has some kind of tenuous connection to Lara's box and the diary and possibly knew Madeleine Cooper, there is a pattern forming but I can't figure it out. Maybe you can pick up something I've missed?"

Piet paid for the coffee and they both stood. "I have some things to do at the hotel, Jack, but I can drop by around four if you like? Show you where you're going wrong?" He grinned. "Make sure you have the cocktails and snacks ready, hey!"

Chapter Sixty-One

Jack leaned against the cupboard in the spare room, his arms folded, ankles crossed, as he studied his work tacked to the wall. The whole story was there, he knew it. But something was throwing it out of kilter. If he could work out what it was it would start to make a bit more sense.

He heard Piet's car pull up outside and went out to meet him. Hope rushed up to him, circling his legs joyfully. Jack bent to pat her damp fur. "Keep off the furniture Hope, you hear me?"

Piet opened the back door of the car and hauled out a covered tray. "Knew there was bugger all chance of any snacks, Jack, so I've brought my own, managed to get a couple of steak and mushroom pies as well."

He took the tray through to the kitchen and peeled back the tin foil covering the food. He scowled and looked at his dog who was hiding under the table. "Hm, I see someone has been snacking on the journey here. Recognise those teeth marks anywhere." He threw a half-eaten sausage roll under the table. "Might as well finish it, Hope. *Jeez*, don't you ever get tired of eating?"

Jack brought out two plates and they piled them high before going into the spare room.

Piet reached into his pocket and put on his glasses, then studied the chart as he chewed thoughtfully. "You have all the components here, my friend, but there is nothing linking it all together. Something is missing."

Jack nodded and brushed the crumbs from his shirt. "Yes, there's something not stacking up. This Van Heerden weaves his way all through the things we have speculated on. Thing is I can't get the connection between an Afrikaans professor and Sir David Cooper. It's the bit which is missing as far as I can work out."

Piet reached for his beer and took a sip, his eyes travelling back and forth across the chart. "Unless…" he said softly.

"Unless what?"

"See here, Jack. There is no doubt Sir David Cooper was British through and through. But we have nothing on Van Heerden, not so? So, who the hell is he?"

"Right," Jack interrupted. "Look Piet, this is going to seem like an odd question, but I have to ask it. So far, Van Heerden does not check out. He's already slipped up a couple of times with his background. Are you one hundred percent sure he *is* Afrikaans?"

Piet looked at him, an incredulous expression on his face. "*Jeez, Jack,* I might not know a few things, but I can recognise a fellow Afrikaner when I see or hear one. He's as Afrikaans as I am!"

Jack chewed his lip. "The thing is this Piet. In the UK you can work out where someone is from by their accent. It's fairly easy if you're English. When it's impossible to define where someone was born or brought up is if they have no accent at all. People educated at Cambridge, Oxford or Eton, for instance, or any other public school, have one single accent – a posh one, if you like. How does it work with your language? Can you tell where someone is from by their accent?"

Piet chewed his lip and thought about the question for a moment. "To some extent, yes. Someone born and brought up on a farm in the Free State would speak slightly different from say, someone born and brought up in Pretoria. Also, if they were privately educated, they would sound a little different. But not as clearly as in your country. Where Afrikaans is different is that we use the same colloquialisms no matter where we come from in the country or what type of education or background we have had. Where are you going with this one Jack, you're losing me, so long?"

"Bear with me, mate. This Van Heerden, if you met him for the first time and he spoke to you in Afrikaans. Would you be able to work out his background?"

"Like I said, to some extent I would, yes. Van Heerden is definitely educated but I couldn't tell you which part of the country he comes from – he's not a farm boy from the Free State, that I can tell you."

Jack stared at his chart until he found the note he was looking for. "Listen, Piet, and this is a long shot. The reason Sir David Cooper had such a brilliant career in the world of international trade was because he had a gift for languages. I'm thinking he spoke several of them, with the correct dialects where necessary and the right colloquialisms. Afrikaans, as you know, is a language derived from the Dutch and adapted over time until it became what it is today.

"Sir David Cooper spoke several European languages, not difficult if you have a gift for words. Most southern European languages are Latin based. So, if you know Latin, it's pretty easy to understand most of them. He also spoke German which is not Latin based. Dutch is a similar language, therefore, Piet, my friend, it's not much of a stretch to believe Sir David could speak Afrikaans?"

Piet stared at him, dumfounded for a moment. "Surely, you're not suggesting what I think you're suggesting?"

Jack held his hands up. "Obviously this man is not Sir David, that's impossible as we both know. But I'm thinking he was a close friend of his. Maybe at Cambridge together. Maybe both of them had a flair for languages and that's where they forged their bond. It's the missing link we've been looking for. It was the Afrikaans part which kept getting in the way. Eliminate this and the picture becomes clearer. We know our mystery Afrikaans speaking man knew Madeleine. Eunice said they spoke Afrikaans to each other. She was born here. It was her second language."

Jack tapped his chart. "What I'm saying is I don't think he is any more Afrikaans than I am. I'm saying he's English, or Kenyan, and knew Sir David well, as he did Madeleine. He stole Van Heerden's identity and assumed his persona and learned his language. Effectively he disappeared, the question is – why?"

Piet nodded slowly, thinking things through. "Maybe they cooked up some crooked deal in Kenya together and got caught. Sir David commits suicide and this other *oke* skips the country – this would make sense wouldn't it, Jack? It would explain why he's hiding out with a new identity. If he and Cooper were close and lived in Kenya, he would have known Madeleine, not so? He waits until he thinks it's safe then goes and visits his old buddy's wife in Wolmaransstad."

Piet was warming to Jack's theory. "Madeleine would have been isolated in her protection programme. Probably welcomed him with open arms. Became close to him, lovers maybe. Not impossible.

"Then perhaps he gets a bit spooked by something and decides not to go back. Maybe because he couldn't find the puzzle box he was searching for. Then, being the smart guy he is, he hears about the death of Madeleine, goes back to the farm for a final search for the box. But Lara beats him to it? What do you think?"

Jack nodded slowly. "Yes, it's possible. Sir David Cooper was brought up in the Far East. The box is from the Far East, so it was his. He must have shown his wife how to open it. When he died, she panicked about something.

"She hid her diary inside it and posted it off to South Africa, along with the silver box. My question is how would her unexpected visitor know what to look for and how would he know how to open it, if he should have found it? More to the point how the hell would he have known how to find her. Where she lived?"

Piet shrugged. "No idea. Maybe at Cambridge David showed his buddy how the box worked, that's one answer. What is clear is his friend, or whoever he was, thought there was something of value inside it. When Sir David died, he knew he had to get hold of it to protect his friend. That's all I can come up with at the moment. Maybe David told him he thought Madeleine was using his box to hide her diary, perhaps he saw her writing in it at some point and it made him nervous about what she was writing."

Piet took a deep breath. "Or maybe, Jack, he didn't have a clue what was in it but, wanted to protect his friend and himself, in case there was something incriminating inside which might threaten him and his new identity. He went after the box and maybe, if he had found it, he would have put an axe through it and gained access to it that way?"

Jack pursed his lips. "But he did know how to open it, didn't he Piet. He took the diary."

Piet shook his head as he worked all the information through his mind. "*Eish,* my friend, you Brits are quite smart, hey. I think I need to sit down and have another beer."

They went back to the kitchen. Jack handed Piet a beer and they went through to the sitting room. Hope was stretched out on the sofa, snoring softly.

Piet sat down and shivered. "Don't you have any heating in here Jack? It's *bleddy* freezing.

Jack laughed. "Hardly freezing, mate. Don't ever go to the UK in the winter. You'll never survive."

Piet glared at him. "Why would I go to the UK, my friend, where people steal our identity documents, our language and pretend to be one of us? Labradors are English aren't they, popular dogs there? Even they nick things when no-one is looking. *Nah*, not going to the

UK that's for sure. Now, what are we going to do next? You're doing the thing with your foot Jack, makes me nervous."

Jack tried to stop his foot from jiggling, excitement coursing through his veins. "Actually, Labradors are not English dogs, they come originally from Newfoundland…but let's not get into that.

"Get hold of your chum, Bertie. See if he can run through who came into the country around the time Sir David Cooper died, also check around the time Madeleine Cooper came back to the country, with her brand-new passport and her brand-new name, maybe we can find a link there?"

Jack paused. "Something is bothering me about the note on the photograph of the puzzle box – *'there's a digit missing'* why then would Clair mention that there isn't a digit missing in her last message to me?

"See here Piet, it's not the first time a posh bloke has done something wrong, then disappeared. Lord Lucan is a good example. After he had allegedly murdered the children's nanny, thinking it was his wife, he disappeared into the London night and was never seen again. Whether it was friends or relatives who helped him escape, was never revealed. There were sightings of him everywhere. But it seemed, according to the media, he ended up in South Africa, hiding out with another rather dodgy aristocrat from his set."

Jack frowned. "The thing is, he was never found, and declared dead in 2016. They live in a different world, Piet. One I hope, for all the titles and wealth, I never have to live in."

Piet watched him carefully.

"All I'm saying, Piet, is those public-school types stick together. Must be the going to boarding school when you're a mere child of eight or ten. The isolation of being separated from your home and family. I think a bond is formed with those boys. A bond which excuses things that go wrong later in life."

Jack rubbed his eyes. "I was a weekly boarder, at Eton, went back to my parent's home every weekend and during holidays. That's quite different from being a little boy up-rooted from overseas and living in a foreign country, maybe only seeing their parents once or twice a year. Quite damaging I would think.

"I think these guys protect each other, perhaps understand each other and then, unlike most other children, they keep in touch. They excuse each other's behaviour and blame it on being abandoned by

269

those they loved. A bit like the Masons, they're secretive, help each other out."

Piet shifted in his chair. "*Ag*, Jack, this band of brothers you are talking about was not exclusive to you and everyone else. We had the *Broederbond* here. Same thing, watching out for each other. It seems to me nothing has changed in the world. We learn nothing from history. There will always be the secret clubs, the chosen few. The ones who will only deal with each other and have shifty handshakes."

Piet reached for his battered cap. "Not worth losing any sleep over, my friend. If we knew what kind of deals were going down, which government, or individual, was betraying this or that government for money, well, you wouldn't get out of bed in the morning."

Piet gave a cavernous yawn. "I'm off duty tonight. My Zulu is watching over the hotel. Okay if I doss down here tonight? I need to think things through, work out what to do next?"

He glanced at his dog. "Would prefer the spare room, if it's okay with you? Don't fancy spending the night with Hope here on the sofa, not after all the food she's eaten. Sometimes her manners let her down, especially when she's asleep…"

Piet stood. "Oh, before I forget. The hotel has been booked out for five days, next week. Some ANC conference. All the top boys will be there bristling with bodyguards, demanding this and that. I'll be busy sorting everything out, making sure no-one takes a pot shot at any of our esteemed government members. I hear the president himself will be addressing his comrades.

"I'm already having a problem with Shaka. He insists he won't wear his security uniform. It's a tribal thing. He has demanded he be allowed to wear his traditional Zulu warrior outfit."

Piet rolled his eyes. "All I need is for him to come creeping out of the bushes as night falls, rattling his shield – those bodyguards will take him out in seconds, and I'll have to look for a new head of security!"

Jack laughed, trying to imagine the scene. "Okay, well I'll press on with the investigation and see you before you leave tomorrow."

Chapter Sixty-Two

The letter had arrived by courier, a few weeks ago, addressed to Professor Daniel Van Heerden. He had signed for it, given the guy a tip then retreated into his study.

He watched the heavy traffic snaking along the motorways as commuters made their way home after a long day in the city of Johannesburg. The endless lines of red blinking brake lights necklacing the city.

He had torn open the strip of the sturdy envelope. She had only ever contacted him by phone, on the last Thursday of every month, at exactly the same time. But she had never sent him what he saw in front of him now. He recognised her handwriting immediately.

I didn't call you as usual for a good reason.

I fear the time has come when the truth must be told.

You did what you had to do, and I helped you with this. I have no regrets.

There is a journalist called, Jack Taylor. He lives in a place called Hazyview. Do you know it? I met him, by chance, here in Nairobi. He seems like a decent sort, not your normal hard-nosed journalist looking to ruin someone's life. He's following a story and is digging deep.

He knows about Madeleine and her visitor. He knows there's a connection there. He has joined all the dots and now he is absolutely focussed on finding out what happened, and he has the box.

Why not tell him your story and to hell with the consequences. What have you got to lose now after all this time?

You have left a legacy, a story. You will be judged of course, but I think Jack might give it a different angle.

It's time to tell the truth.

The life we knew has gone. Kenya is still the most beautiful place I know, but even I am becoming tired of all the politics, the bickering

271

and the social life is not quite the same. It's still good but we don't know the people we are dealing with. Those halcyon days are long gone, and we are left with our memories of how it all was.

So here I sit with my beloved cats, and dear Bashir, and my life goes on.

I have no children, as you well know, no-one to leave my possessions to. So, this is what I have decided. In my Will I have instructed Bashir will stay on in my house until the last of my beloved cats dies. I have left him and his brother, Saul, my beach house in Watamu and enough money to live on.

The rest of my estate should go to you, to do what you will with. The problem though would be the paperwork and the logistics, of course. Therefore, I have decided to leave it to the Catholic Church. They have a steady stream of nuns who come here from all over the world to do their good works, it could be a haven of some sorts, a home where they wouldn't have to pay any rent.

I was invited to meet eight of them and talk about life in Kenya. I was appalled to see how frugally they lived and in such spartan quarters where they paid a considerable rent. Dinner, needless to say was basic to say the least. Me and eight nuns...can you believe it! I thought about them often afterwards. Not a glamourous dinner party, I have to say.

Kenya has given me a glorious and happy life. I want to give something back to those good hard-working nuns. I want them to feel safe and happy in my house.

This is why I beg you now, to speak to Jack. Find him before he finds you – and he will.

Will you do this for me?
Daphne.

Daniel folded the letter over and looked into the distance seeing nothing. The night was still, the light forming patterns on the leaves of the trees. All this would go on long after he was gone, as it had gone on for generations before him. All the stories, all the lies, all the intrigue.

He too had had enough. Daphne was right.

Since Daphne had told him Madeleine had died, he had scanned the local newspaper on line, published daily in Wolmaransstad, for news of the winding up of the estate of Marlene Hartley, or Madeleine Cooper, and the property called Cloud's End.

There was to be an auction on the property and he had wanted to make sure he would be there for it. The day before the auction there was to be some items for sale which would be open to the public.

He left Johannesburg and made his way to Wolmaransstad.

He had searched the property before but had not found the one thing he was looking for. The one thing he knew he must have whatever the price might be.

The Chinese puzzle box.

But he had not been quick enough. A young woman had picked it up, examined it briefly and made her way to the cashier to pay for it.

He had followed the woman to Hazyview and checked into the same hotel.

Then he sat and watched and waited.

Checking out of the hotel two days later, having observed the woman, the tall man with the unruly hair and the stocky hotel security chief, he had driven to a modest guest house some half an hour or so away, and checked in for an indefinite period to plan what he would do next.

Chapter Sixty-Three

Jack had driven to Nelspruit for his monthly shop. Much as he liked Hazyview he sometimes felt the need for the buzz of a bigger town.

A smiling African, employed by the supermarket, offered to wheel his trolley to his car. Jack took him up on the offer then tipped him and climbed into the driving seat. Time to head back home.

He pulled out on to the motorway and put his foot down, his thoughts kept returning to the person calling himself Daniel Van Heerden. So occupied was he, he pulled over to another lane without indicating, much to the indignation of a fellow driver.

The driver of the car glared at him and gave him the international finger as he swerved around him. Jack grinned, everyone always in such a hurry these days. He returned the gesture then almost collided with the car in front of him which had braked suddenly.

Of course! The missing digit, which they had failed to find had been right in front of him. A digit didn't only mean a number – a digit could be a finger or toe.

He pulled over as soon as he saw the opportunity and using the steering wheel, he stretched his back. He picked up his phone and called Piet.

"Hey, Piet, listen. I'm on my way back to Hazyview. I had a driver who I seriously pissed off with my driving skills. He gave me the finger."

Piet laughed. "Nothing unusual about that, bet he had Joburg number plates. They have no patience with anything, or anyone, my friend. But why are you telling me this?"

Jack watched the cars whizzing past. "Because, mate, a digit can be a number – but it can also be a finger or toe…

"Remember the message '*there's a digit missing*' it's not a number, it's part of a finger is my guess. Remember when you dusted Van Heerden's glass you said one of the prints were blurred, smudged? This, Piet, was because there was no fingerprint for one of his fingers. His little finger if I recall?"

There was a pause from Piet's end of the phone. "It's true, hey. When he tapped his little finger on the side of the glass, an irritating habit, there should have been no sound at all. But there was. I'm thinking it's a prosthetic then?"

"Let's check this out Piet. I'll ask Hugo to have another run at it. He won't like it, but I think he'll do it - for Queen and country, and all that stuff."

Piet grunted. Jack pulled out into the traffic again.

Tap tap tap. It had annoyed Jack and he couldn't understand why. But now he did. A missing finger wouldn't make a sound but as Piet had said, a prosthetic would.

Not as if it would make any difference as there was no match for the fingerprints in the system anyway.

He would have to find another way of discovering how this so-called Daniel Van Heerden had lost his little finger or maybe part of it. Unless a complete finger was missing from a hand no-one would probably notice. So why have a prosthetic made to cover up such a small detail?

Because, he decided, if the man was on the run from something it would be the one thing which would give him away to whoever was looking for him. If indeed anyone was.

It was obvious the man who had visited Madeleine Cooper had been the man they knew as Van Heerden. But what was the real relationship between those two?

What was it with the woman that she had an obsession about wiping down surfaces? Van Heerden didn't have a criminal record and nor did Madeleine. She seemed to have lived the life of a nun out there on the farm.

Trying to find answers to his questions was like trying to un-knot a delicate silver chain. When he thought he had almost achieved it, up popped another knot.

He pulled into his drive and turned off the ignition. Something kept niggling away in his mind and each time he rejected it as impossible.

He knew from all his years of investigative journalism, digging deep into the underbelly of the world of crime, nothing was ever as it seemed. The trick was, in his experience, to make it look like it was.

Chapter Sixty-Four

As he was unpacking his shopping, his phone rumbled on the table. Lara.

"Hey, Jack, how is everything going?"

He smiled into the phone. "Are you ever going to come back here, Lara?"

He heard her take a deep breath. He knew what was coming.

"Jack, I loved everything about you. I loved South Africa. But things have changed a bit here. Look, there's only one way I can tell you this. You know I worked for Christies and Sotheby's before I went out on my own? Well, the thing is, I've been offered a fabulous job with a programme called The Antiques Roadshow. Do you know it?"

"I've heard of it yes," he murmured.

"I want to do this, Jack. I'll always remember you and dancing in the rain. The beauty of the country you've chosen to live in, the diversity of it. But my roots are here, my career is here – it's too good an opportunity to turn down. You were right about visiting a place and falling in love with it. But now I realise visiting a place and actually living there are two different things entirely."

Jack took a deep breath. "I understand, Lara. You have to do what's right for you. If you ever want a place far away, somewhere different, you'll always be welcome to visit me here."

"I'm sorry Jack, really, I am... but your life there, it's not something I could get used to. After a few months I know I would want to be back in the mainstream of things – and that's here. Please look after my box. It's yours now. A gift from me for the wonderful time I had with you."

"Go well then, Lara. I hope you find what you're looking for. Thank you for the box. I shall treasure it."

Jack put the phone down. He looked down at the gurgling stream and knew they would never sit there with their glasses of wine balancing on the rocks cooling as the fiery heat of a blood red sun sank below the hills, throwing shadows across the garden.

He was disappointed, that was more than true. But he knew his relationships with women had always been fraught with difficulties. His lifestyle, the weeks spent away following leads for his stories, well, it didn't exactly lend itself to any long-term relationships.

He hadn't been in love with Lara – but he had been hopeful it might happen.

No point in dwelling on what might have been.

It was over.

Chapter Sixty-Five

Jack was sitting, the smoke hazily rising from his *braai*. Squirrels darted across the lawns amidst the shadows falling over the garden in front of him. He could hear the lazy movement of the stream, the occasional splash as a fish made itself known then sank once more into the clear cool water.

The evening was still as the heat of the day seeped away. He went inside and brought out the Chinese puzzle box and put it on the table in front of him. He knew it was the key to everything. The problem was he didn't have the key.

All the information he now had led to one person. He had thought about the endless possibilities, but given the official information, he had reached a dead end. Inserting other possibilities into the life of Madeleine Cooper, relatives, sisters, lovers had led him nowhere.

Chopin's *Nocturnes* played softly in the background as he turned the slab of marinated ribs over, deep in thought. He knew he would get no more information from Daphne. She had told him as much as she wanted him to know. He knew she had tried to side swipe him with the odd bit of information she had given him. He was sure she knew a lot more about Sir David Cooper than she had told him.

Now it was getting dark. In the distance he saw the headlights of a car making its way along the dirt road towards his cottage. A trail of dust in its wake illuminated by the rear lights of the vehicle.

He stood up. All his instincts told him this was not going to be Piet. He lifted the ribs from the hot coals and put them to one side then tightened his grip on the tongs.

The car pulled up in front of his cottage, dousing its lights – then there was silence.

Jack frowned waiting for his visitor to reveal himself. He reached for his phone, keeping it close to him. Piet's number on speed dial.

The security lights in the garden kicked in, bathing his cottage and garden in a golden light.

Briefly the interior light of the visitor's car was lit then extinguished. The man walking towards him, illuminated by the lights in the garden, was tall, straight backed and clean shaven.

He made his way towards Jack. He stopped briefly when he saw him standing there waiting. He held out his hand.

"I feel it's time to introduce myself?"

Without any doubt Jack knew he was looking into the compelling blue eyes of Sir David Cooper.

Chapter Sixty-Six

Jack had had many moments in his life when his breath had been taken away by what he had seen or heard with various cold cases he had covered. But he knew this one would top them all.

He invited Sir David to take a seat. "Gin and tonic? I noticed that was your drink of choice at Hugo's?"

Jack brought the drinks through. He took a sip of his and looked at the man in front of him. The man who had purportedly been dead for twenty years. There he sat, Sir David Cooper, looking exactly as one might have predicted from the one photograph Jack had of the young man by the river in England and speaking with an impeccable English accent.

Jack had to ask an important question, so he could be sure.

"You have a tattoo at the base of your spine. I'd like to see it, to be absolutely sure."

"I give you my word. I am Sir David Cooper."

"Yes, but given your history from stealing someone else's identity. I would like to see your tattoo, as verification."

David stood up, wrestling his shirt from his trousers he turned his back on Jack. There at the base of his spine was the tattoo Daphne had told him about.

Jack smiled, satisfied. "Odd place to have a tattoo if you don't mind me saying. Why have it put there where you can't see it?"

David tucked his shirt in and sat down. "I am not a fan of tattoos. It wasn't my choice to have one." He lifted his hand; the top of his little finger was missing. "I wasn't planning on losing this bit of my anatomy either."

Jack raised his eyebrows. "So, what does the Chinese tattoo mean and what happened to your finger?"

David leaned forward and reached for his glass, his eyes not leaving Jack's face. "It says *traitor*. They cut off the top of my finger as a warning. I passed out when they chopped it off. No anaesthetic.

It's their way of dealing with things which don't quite go the way they anticipated.

"When I came round there was blood everywhere, as you can imagine. The hotel summoned a doctor who patched me up. I knew then I was flying too close to the wind. I stayed in the hotel for a month. That's how long it took to heal."

Jack listened carefully still not quite believing this was Sir David Cooper sitting in front of him. But the tattoo was irrevocable proof that it was.

David continued. "Reporting back to London was something I did regularly, as one would expect. The loss of the top of a finger would have garnered many questions, which I knew I wouldn't be able to answer. So, I had the prosthetic made. In China things can be done quickly…"

Jack knocked back his gin and tonic trying to imagine the man opposite him lying in a pool of blood in a hotel in China somewhere.

Someone who had been branded as a traitor.

Jack cleared his throat. "I want Piet here."

Sir David took a sip of his drink. "I would feel more comfortable if this was between the two of us, Jack."

Jack stared at him. "Sorry, no deal. I want Piet here."

He rubbed the side of his face. "You and I are part of the same establishment, David. I also went to Cambridge. But I chose not to become part of the old boy network, wearer of the old school tie, a member of private and exclusive clubs, using my old school chums to scale up the ladder to become a politician, a Prime Minister, head of global conglomerates, a diplomat. I wanted to go out on my own. Believe in myself and what I was capable of doing."

David raised his eyebrow. "Go on, Jack, I'm listening."

"Over the years the British Government has depended on its old boy network, history has told us some of those old boys let the side down badly, as I am now presuming you did?"

Sir David narrowed his eyes. "You are quite correct in your analysis. But you don't know anything about me."

Jack continued. "Actually, I know quite a lot about you. Someone died in a plane accident in Kenya and it wasn't you. I want to know who it was and how you got away with taking another person's identity, and the reason why you had the need to disappear.

"However, not everyone accepted your death. I know the British Government did and everyone else you knew. But Daphne knew all about it didn't she? She knows you're still alive."

Sir David Cooper took another sip of his drink. "Yes, she does. I do have something to tell, and I have chosen to tell it to you. There were times, over the past decades where I thought of taking my own life – fall on my sword if you will, like any English gentleman should." He straightened his back. "You think you know all about me but actually you know nothing about me whatsoever."

David closed his eyes and pinched the bridge of his nose briefly. Then looked up again at Jack. "It was Daphne, who has persuaded me to talk to you. I'm doing it for her, not for myself. There's also a child involved, although hardly a child any longer."

Jack studied the man in front of him, with his faultless British accent. He seemed perfectly relaxed, despite the extraordinary circumstances they both found themselves in. There was a coldness about him. He showed no emotion whatsoever and Jack remembered Daphne's words.

'He was the loneliest person I have ever met in my life.'

Jack leaned forward in his chair. "I need Piet here. You can trust him. You, no doubt, will epitomise what he thinks of, as he calls them *'posh English okes'* - but I can tell you right now, Sir David, this conversation will go no further until Piet joins us."

Without waiting for an answer, Jack reached for his phone.

"Piet? You need to get over here to my place. Daniel Van Heerden is sitting opposite me enjoying a gin and tonic and there's no tap tap tapping on his glass."

Chapter Sixty-Seven

Piet's car roared up the drive. Both man and dog alighted and made their way quickly towards Jack and his visitor.

David stood up and extended his hand. "I'm sorry about the subterfuge but it has been necessary, officer. My name is Sir David Cooper."

Piet looked at him. He ignored David's extended hand.

"*Ja*, you got me there. Not sure what mess you got yourself into in life, but your Afrikaans and accent are excellent. Had me fooled, but not all the time. You slipped up with your university, my friend, and a few other things, hey. You lied to me. For someone who has been dead for over twenty years you brush up good. You look different, what happened to the beard and glasses, so long?"

David looked uncomfortable but said nothing.

Piet sat down and pointed to the Chinese puzzle box. "So, this is yours, hey? Thought as much. You broke into the hotel grounds and stole it. Removed the diary then threw what was left in the bush." He turned to Jack. "Need a beer, Jack."

Jack stood and made his way to the kitchen. David leaned forward. "You're angry – but you haven't heard my story – how things happened. You're a policeman. You need to hear my side of the story before you judge me."

Piet turned back to David. "You stole someone else's identity. Identity theft is a crime. "He gestured to the box sitting on the table. "Breaking and entering and stealing are also crimes here."

David leaned towards him. "The box belongs to me. I would not call it stealing. If something belongs to you?"

"If the box means so much to you, why did you steal it and then chuck it in the bush – I'm not buying that, I'm afraid."

"Because I worked out that you would go looking for it once you realised it was missing, and find it." David gave him a faint smile.

"This box means everything to me. It's the only tenuous link with my past. I found the diary, of course, and destroyed it."

Jack returned with Piet's drink. He had seen his friend in many moods over the years but never as angry as he looked now. But he was an investigative journalist, and his biggest story was sitting right in front of him, ready to talk. He wasn't prepared to let the man go and perhaps disappear once again in this vast country.

Jack sat and crossed his legs, holding his ankle steady with his hand. "You want us to hear your story. Daphne wants the same thing. May I suggest you stay here? I have a spare room. No-one knows, except for Piet and Hugo, that I live here, that you are here?"

Piet tried to hide his surprise at the suggestion. But he understood what Jack was up to. They had the man cornered and no way was Jack going to let him out of his sight.

David pinched the top of his nose again, and sighed. "Thank you. It's good of you to offer me a bed for the night. I'll tell you what you want to know."

Jack stood up. "How about I throw some more meat on the *braai*, I'll open a bottle or two of wine. Let's be civilised gentlemen here. You have a story to tell, and we want to hear it."

He glanced at Piet's impassive face. "All I ask is you give me the keys to your car, so I don't find in the morning you've done a runner. Deal?"

David smiled at him. "A deal on a handshake – that's what gentlemen used to do in a world which has long gone. I don't need to give you my keys. But I shall if this is what you wish."

Jack looked at him then extended his hand for the keys.

David leaned forward, gave Jack his car keys, then picked up his Chinese puzzle box, running his hands over it with practiced ease.

"This is the only possession I care about. The only thing that means anything to me. It belongs to a time long gone now. A time when I was happy...before everything changed.

"Before I killed Madeleine."

284

Chapter Sixty-Eight
Kenya – 1998.

Sir David Cooper had known it was only a matter of time before he would be caught. Daphne had confirmed this with her phone call.

By chance he had been staying for a few days at Daphne's remote beach house in Watamu, on the Kenyan coast. Large wooden doors huddling amongst the palm trees hid the entrance to the house. He often snatched a day or two there. Far away from anyone. Especially Madeleine who was becoming alarmingly unpredictable with her moods. It was here he had first encountered Mike Cavendish.

He had noticed the tall man wearing a khaki baseball hat, meandering along the deserted beach. His hair seemed to be tied back in some kind of ponytail. Every morning and every evening he wandered along in his ragged shorts, with no shirt and carrying nothing but a *kikoi*, thrown around his shoulders. David wondered where he lived and what he was doing there. Perhaps he was a tourist.

Sometimes the man sat for hours staring out at the sea, watching the occasional wooden dhow with its stiff grey-white sails pass by with a simple lingering elegance, a timeless scene which had not changed for hundreds of years. The white of the seagulls' wings as they swooped and dipped, crying noisily behind the keel of the boat. Hoping the fishermen aboard would harvest the fish and toss away any they wouldn't take back to sell in the marketplace at the end of the day.

Although the man had no specific times when he would walk, or sit, on the beach, David was intrigued. That evening, an evening he would never forget, was an evening which changed his life. He took two beers from Daphne's fridge and made his own way down to the water's edge.

The man with the baseball hat was coming his way. David lifted his arm. "Hello, I've seen you walking along the beach – would you like a beer?"

The man shaded his eyes with his hand and stopped, looking startled. "I didn't think there was anyone else around. Most of the holiday homes are closed up this time of the year. But, yes, a beer sounds good." He held out his hand. "Mike Cavendish – of no fixed abode."

David laughed and handed him the bottle of beer. "David Cooper. I wish I could say the same. I'm staying at a friend's place for a few days. Cheers."

They both sat down on the soft warm sand. David leaned back on his elbows in the sand. "No fixed abode, eh? Sounds marvellous. Don't you have a home?" He gestured with his bottle at the empty beach. "I mean, you must sleep somewhere?"

Mike Cavendish shook his head. "Nope. I sleep on the beach. There are a couple of fishermen who know where to find me, they bring me fish. I don't need anything else. Been living like this for two years now."

David listened to him talk about his seemingly simple and uncomplicated life and felt a twinge of envy. Compared to his endless social life of cocktail parties, luncheons, dinners and a punishing business schedule, it sounded like heaven to him. But he knew there was a lot more to Mike Cavendish.

He was obviously English. Kenyan born maybe, educated and in his mid-forties. Something had gone wrong in his life, and he had chosen a different path. David wished he had been given the same chances, the same choices. But perhaps Mike's choice had not been his own.

"Listen Mike, as I said, I'm staying at a friend's place, you can't see it from here, it's rather private shall we say. Why not come up and have dinner with me. You must be a bit tired of fish, eating it every day. My friend has an excellent chef who is going on holiday tomorrow for a month. Saul makes a mean fillet steak with dauphinoise potatoes and a green salad. It's on the menu tonight, why not join me?"

Mike had turned and smiled at him. "Fillet and dauphinoise potatoes? Yup, I haven't had that for a while, I would relish something different. But I'm hardly dressed for dinner with a chef who will produce such *haute cuisine*?"

286

David laughed. "This is Kenya. Down here on the coast there is no dress code. Come as you are, I mean it. You must be living a life people only dream about – well for a while anyway."

They walked back to Daphne's house. David knew this man Mike Cavendish was not who he appeared to be. His accent, for one, gave him away. He knew about the real world he had turned his back on. Mike, he thought, was another product of a public school in England.

*****

Mike relieved the constraints of the *kikoi* now wrapped around his waist and sat back in his chair. The warm breeze enveloped his bare tanned chest and legs.

"Superb dinner, thank you. Sometimes you don't know what you miss until you try it again." He frowned. "Or perhaps some things are better not re-visited."

David watched him closely. It was obvious from the man's nomadic life he had become unused to alcohol. *In vino veritas.*

In wine, there is truth.

"Not wishing to intrude on your life, Mike, but how did you end up here, with nowhere to live? No family you've talked about?"

Mike dug his feet into the soft warm sand. "I had a life, of course I did. I married had a child. A child I love more than life itself. But I've let her down. My wife, ex-wife now, knew her way around town, knew which beds would give her what she craved – but not mine.

"Like all of us, I had my hopes and dreams. I lived in Nairobi. But I was away a lot. Shuffling tourists in and out of safari lodges. Life was good then, but obviously my wife didn't think so."

He ran his hand over his stomach and winced. After a few moments he continued. "My sister came over here to support me through the divorce, and look after my daughter. She took Cassie, that's her name, back to England to live with her family there. My wife was too busy with her own affairs to look after a young child of three. She eventually went to live in Australia with her new husband.

"I rarely saw my little girl. We grew apart after she left to live in the UK. I was taking jobs in Botswana, Tanzania, South Africa and here in Kenya. People in the safari business can be a nomadic bunch when you think about it, not belonging anywhere. Simply going where the work takes them."

David refilled Mike's glass. "So, then what happened to bring you here to this remote beach?"

Mike looked down at his feet "A choice was made for me, not my own. Two years ago, I was told I had a limited time left. The time left to me made me think. I wanted to be who I was. I would be leaving everyone behind, including my beloved daughter. What had I left her with? Certainly not money, of which I have none.

"I knew she wouldn't remember me... I didn't want her to see me ill, better that way perhaps? I wanted her to remember me when I was strong and unafraid.

"I was left with myself. That's how you see me now. I own nothing. I have two pairs of shorts, two shirts and a shack on the beach. Not much of a legacy to leave my daughter.

"When the time comes and the pain becomes unbearable, I shall walk into the sea and that will be that."

David shifted uncomfortably in his chair. "Sorry to hear this, old boy, I wish I could help..."

Mike stood up abruptly and held out his hand. "Wonderful dinner, please thank the chef. I'll be on my way then."

The moon had turned the placid sea into a carpet of wavering silver. David watched the lonely silhouette of his dinner guest as he returned to his shack, before being swallowed up by the night. He seemed like a nice guy. But life had turned against him.

David sat on the sprawling veranda of Daphne's house, a plan forming in his mind as he listened to the soft hissing of the surf, an enduring sound which would go on and on, as it had always done. Rich, poor, happy, sad, hopeless, betrayed — everyone had had their dreams at one time. The sea was constant and unforgiving, and cared for nothing, least of all the forgotten footprints of its fleeting visitors as the surf washed away their brief passage of time there.

Perhaps there was a way to help Mike Cavendish after all. But first he needed to get back to Nairobi.

288

Chapter Sixty-Nine

Madeleine was an increasing problem. She knew too much, and she was becoming even more unpredictable.

Earlier in her marriage she had asked him about the Chinese puzzle box and in a moment of nostalgia he had shown her how to open and close it.

He had watched her writing in her blue diary, with the Phoenix on the cover. Then he had not paid much attention to it, but now he wondered exactly how much she had observed, how much she had concluded on her own. What had she actually written in her diary?

He thought back to those years at their house in Nanyuki.

Marrying Madeleine had been a mistake. But they had made a deal with each other.

Initially she had sparkled next to his side as he travelled to various countries to negotiate his deals for the government. She was the perfect diplomat's wife, charming gracious and highly intelligent. He had found himself discussing various deals with her, telling her who the players were, and how they played – trusting her. But not with everything. Madeleine had been the one to make his travel arrangements when he didn't wish the Foreign Office to know where he was going.

This had been a grave mistake. When they moved to his new posting in Kenya she started to change. Madeleine from once being the compliant wife began to have violent mood changes, her behaviour became unpredictable. She didn't want to mix socially anymore, wanted to be alone all the time. This was when he moved them out to Nanyuki. To keep her, as she wanted, alone and away from everyone.

Madeleine raged at him for taking her from the land of her birth, for denying her any children, for not providing a permanent home for them both. He had tried to reason with her, understand her. But he didn't love her enough. Had never loved her, and so he eventually let her go into the wild confusion of her own mind.

Knowing how much she knew about him and his business, and concerned with her terrible rages, he had called one of Nairobi's most eminent physicians, to come to the house in Nanyuki to examine her. Approved by the embassy, of course. The doctor attended to all of the Embassy staff.

Sometime later the doctor had sat across from him in his study.

"I'm sorry, Sir David, but your wife is quite ill. Not physically, but mentally. Madeleine is, in my opinion, suffering from a form of psychological disorder. It's manifesting as some form of depression, but hard for me to pinpoint what exactly without keeping her under observation in a safe place. She's showing all the signs of it; avoiding social contact, limited emotional expression. She may have appeared to you interested, engaged and involved, but within herself she is emotionally withdrawn. Looking down on herself, if you like, from a different place."

David had listened carefully. "She would remember everything then, even though she felt she was watching things from afar? Is this what you're saying?"

The doctor closed his file. "Yes, that's what I'm saying." He cleared his throat. "I know your position here with the government in Nairobi, it's sensitive. I would advise you keep her here as far away from any social events you might attend. I will prescribe something to keep her calm. But someone must ensure she takes her medication, she needs help, Sir David. Professional help. As you are no doubt aware she has been on medication for years now, but we need to increase this."

The doctor held out his hand. "Madeleine lives in her own world now. Given who you are, it – how can I put this? Well, it would be in everyone's interests to keep her sedated. Madeleine is unpredictable and this could be dangerous. Not violent, I hasten to point out. But she is a threat to all you are doing for the British government. She knows a lot about you, Sir David. You must be cautious now.

"You know I will have to let the Foreign Office know about this. It's in your contract with them. It bypasses the doctor/patient confidentiality, one normally has. I'm sorry, but there it is."

The doctor had hesitated. "My advice would be to send her somewhere where she would be cared for. Obviously, it couldn't be here. You're too well-known and the government would never allow it. Bad for public relations."

"Are you suggesting, Doctor, Madeleine be put in some kind of institution overseas somewhere?"

"I'm afraid that is what I'm suggesting. She won't get better. The new medication will help, of course."

Then had come Daphne's urgent phone call.

Chapter Seventy

A week later David had flown his plane from Nairobi back to Mombasa, re-fuelled, then left it locked at the airport. Bashir's brother, Saul, who looked after Daphne's beach house, had left Daphne's battered old car at the airport before he left for his month's holiday with his family. The keys hidden in a shallow hole behind the front tyre.

David drove her car back to the beach cottage.

For the next two days David thought through the logistics of his meticulous plan. It was infallible.

Chapter Seventy-One

Mombasa airport that particular morning was busy. Small planes landing and taking off. Alongside the commercial flights taking back or bringing in tourists.

He unlocked the plane, stowed his bag behind his seat, checked his watch and patted the passport in his pocket. He put the battered, well worn, Panama hat on the seat next to him and adjusted his headphones. He filed his flight plan and waited for the all-clear from the tower to take off. With practiced ease he ran through the familiar pre-flight protocols with the panel of toggles, switches and dials. He could hear the blood pounding in his ears.

It was a perfect day for flying. The tower gave him the all-clear and he roared down the runway before lifting off and soaring into the clear blue sky as he headed in the direction of Tsavo.

He started his descent as he flew over the bush. Heading for the impressive rocky outcrop glaringly white against the brown parched bush.

Only seconds to go, he pushed down the side window and dropped the diplomatic passport through the opening. Then he closed his eyes as the plane smashed into the rocks before erupting in flames.

Chapter Seventy-Two

Daphne and Bashir drove down the dirt track towards her beach house. It was well hidden and couldn't be seen from the beach. The swaying palm trees rattled and clacked as she got out of the car.

He was waiting for her as she knew he would be.

"I don't know about you," she said unsteadily. "But I am in serious need of a large gin and tonic. The whole of Nairobi is talking about the plane crash in Tsavo and the death of Sir David Cooper. It's huge news. The Embassy have arranged for a service to be held the day after tomorrow, with indecent haste in my opinion. But no doubt they have their reasons?"

Bashir came through with two large gin and tonics on a silver tray, his face impassive as he looked at their guest. Daphne reached for hers with trembling hands. "Well, cheers, my dear. Here's to life. I think I need a cigarette."

She looked him over as he drank. "Now, tell me, how did you do it?"

Chapter Seventy-Three

David had waited two days after his return to Mombasa, before he saw Mike Cavendish making his way down the beach towards the beach house. Suddenly he had bent over, holding his stomach, clearly in great pain. Then sank slowly to his knees in the sand.

David ran down the beach then knelt down and put his hand on Mike's shoulder. "Can I help, old chap, are you in pain?"

Mike had gasped and nodded as he took deep breaths until the pain passed. "I'm alright. I need a few moments."

"Look come up to the house for a while. My friend has a well-stocked medicine cabinet. There must be something there which will help ease the pain."

He had helped Mike back to the house, brought the man a glass of brandy then searched the medicine chest for pain killers.

Mike rested his head against the chair and gave David a weak smile as he took the pills and swallowed them with a large gulp of the brandy, his eyes watering with pain.

"Not one of my better days, David. The pain is bad, I'm looking forward to walking into the sea and getting the whole thing over with. I can't do this anymore. The pain has become unbearable."

David sat down opposite him. "I want to help you. I know you don't think I can. But I've come up with something which is wholly dependent on one thing."

Mike looked at him wearily, his face grey and pinched with pain. "What would that be?"

"You said you were in the safari business, you moved tourists from lodge to lodge, right?"

"Yes."

"How did you do this? Was it by road?"

"No. I'm a pilot, I flew them in and out. Why do you ask?"

David decided there was no nice way of doing what he was going to suggest. "Look, you obviously don't know who I am, but I work for the British Government, have done for years. I work in many countries, flying the flag shall we say. Well, something has gone wrong. I have to get out of Kenya in a hurry."

Mike gave him a ghost of a smile. "Are you some kind of a spy then? The British government after you for something you've done wrong?"

David shook his head. "Spying? Working for the Foreign Office one sometimes has to do something like that. Yes, it's what all diplomats do, one way or another, depending who they are dealing with. Comes with the job description.

"The point is, I need to disappear. I think you can help me and in exchange I will ensure you leave your daughter a decent legacy. It's one of your biggest regrets, right. You have nothing to leave her?"

Mike nodded. "Nothing. Nothing at all. Not even any decent happy memories. She will have forgotten me by now. My sister takes good care of her though."

"I'm a wealthy man, Mike. You're dying, and obviously in great pain now. We can help each other. I have a plane parked at the airport here, it's fully re-fuelled.

"We're of a similar height and build. I wear a Panama hat as you have probably noticed, you could tuck your hair under it. Wearing my clothes no one would look twice at you. I'll give you the registration of the plane, the keys, my watch, with the family crest, my diplomatic passport and my pilot's licence. You need to drop the passport seconds before, well, you know. I don't need to explain the rest to you, but you know the bush as well as I do, as a pilot. Tsavo is fairly remote."

Mike was nodding resignedly. "At least it will be quick. But how will my daughter benefit?"

"I am prepared to pay four instalments of two hundred thousand pounds over a period of four years. I can't make one payment. The money needs to be moved discreetly from a shell company registered in the Bahamas. This money will be paid into a trust account for your daughter. Your sister will administrate this trust fund. I'll need her full name and bank details, of course. She'll have no idea who the money is from, but the paperwork will indicate the money is for your daughter's upbringing and education. When your daughter reaches the age of eighteen, she'll have full control over her trust fund.

"Your daughter, of course, will have questions, but neither you nor I will be able to give her the answers. There is one person who will have the answers and that's Daphne. We will have to trust her and her judgement, as to what your daughter needs to know and when."

David took a deep breath. "Your sister may assume it's from you, but she won't be aware of your death, obviously. This is crucial to the plan. You have my word if an opportunity presents itself and it may only be in a few years' time, your daughter will be told the money was from you. You say you haven't seen her for two years. She has no idea where you are, correct?"

Mike nodded again. "That's correct yes. Well, it's more like three years now. I haven't been in touch with my sister since I was diagnosed. I didn't know how to tell her, so I didn't. She will probably assume that I've left the country and found work somewhere else. She would have no reason to report me missing, although she will be deeply hurt. I haven't been in touch with my daughter. That my sister won't forgive me for."

"Okay, so no-one will be looking for you – correct?"

Mike leaned forward and winced with the effort, sucking in his breath, his face grey with the effort it took. Then he extended his hand. "It's a deal."

David smiled sadly. "It's the worst deal I have ever done in my life. A life in exchange for money."

"Your life too, David. To all intents and purposes, you'll be dead as well. The life you knew will be over too."

David nodded. "Yes, it will be," he said abruptly.

He pulled a piece of paper from his pocket. "Here is the registration of my plane and here are the keys. He pulled his old watch from his wrist and placed it on the table in front of him.

"Now, when do you want to do this?"

Mike picked up the piece of paper and the watch. "Tomorrow. I need to go back to my shack and remove the few things I have. My British passport still has a couple of years on it, but there's nothing I can do about it I'm afraid. I haven't kept up the hours on my pilot's licence either. If you tie your hair back, wear my baseball cap and my shabby clothes I don't think anyone would think you are anyone but me. After all, given my life I don't know anyone anyway. But you'll need to be seen wandering the beach – just in case."

Mike stood up, putting the watch and paper back on the table. "I'll come back when it's dark. We can do what's necessary. What about your dark hair though?"

"My friend Daphne has those packets of hair dye in her medicine cabinet. Shouldn't be too difficult if I follow the instructions, hardly long enough to tie back but I'll work something out. I'll stay out of view for a few days, walk along the beach now and again, then I'll disappear. Leave the country."

He paused. "You'll have to drive yourself to the airport in Daphne's old car. Park it and leave it there, take the keys with you. Saul will collect it when he returns. He has a duplicate set."

Mike stood up unsteadily. "You seem to have thought of everything, David. You knew I would agree to this?"

"Yes. I've seen a lot in my life. I know when a man has reached the end of his road and is tired of living with pain, physical or otherwise. Your daughter will be well taken care of. This is a promise. What's her name again?"

"Cassie. Her name is Cassie, Cassandra." He turned away but not before David had seen the tears in his eyes.

Mike fumbled for the silver chain and Maltese Cross he had worn around his neck since he was a teenager. "Cassie always loved this," he handed it to David.

"Should the right time and place present itself, I would like her to have it. Something for her to remember me by – if she remembers me at all. Will you do this for me?"

David took the only treasured possession Mike owned. "Of course, I will. I'm not sure what my life will be like after tomorrow...I'll ask Daphne to be the guardian of your final gift to your daughter. You can trust her to do as you've asked."

He watched Mike made his unsteady way along the soft white sand. He had made some unpalatable deals in his time, but this was one he had never imagined he would have to do.

But Mike had chosen his destiny and the way he wished to end his life. In the same position David doubted he would ever have been able to display such dignity and courage.

Chapter Seventy-Four

Daphne and Bashir, with David's money, had arranged everything.

Some weeks later the dhow had been waiting for him, to take him to Zanzibar. From there he had stepped aboard a private yacht. All organised by Daphne.

Arriving in Dar Es Salaam he had boarded the luxurious train called Roves Rail and made the epic journey from Dar Es Salaam to Johannesburg. Using Mike's British passport, he encountered no problems. He was Michael Cavendish, on holiday from the UK.

He had not mixed with other international passengers. Keeping to himself, dining alone in the sumptuous dining cars, appropriately dressed, then retiring to his suite. Not joining the other guests for after dinner nightcaps.

No-one recognised him with his blond hair, short beard and designer glasses.

The Edwardian train had clattered through the nights of that long journey. David's thoughts had been on Mike Cavendish and the legacy he had left him. Mike had given him a gift. The gift of a new life, a second chance. He would honour this, as he knew he must.

He had alighted in Johannesburg and disappeared into the city of gold to begin his new life.

Within two months he had acquired, at great cost, a new identity. Professor Daniel Van Heerden, a citizen of the Republic of South Africa.

But he had kept Mike's passport and expired pilot's licence.

Chapter Seventy-Five
South Africa

Last evening had ended abruptly when David told Jack and Piet he had killed Madeleine. This neither he nor Piet had expected to hear.

Jack had held up his hand trying to hide the shock on his face.

"Hold it there, David. Piet needs to get back to the hotel. Let's hear the rest of the story in the morning. I'm sure it can wait after all this time. I need to write up some notes."

Piet stood up and reached for his battered hat. He shook his head. "See you tomorrow, Jack. I'll be here around ten."

He gave David a cold hard look. "Make sure you're here, hey. Or I'll come looking for you…"

He walked slowly back to his car. He had been right Madeleine had not taken her own life.

Her husband had killed her.

*****

David took a hot shower. It had been a long night with Jack and Piet. He knew it was going to be the end of the life he had made for himself, provided for himself, created for himself.

He towelled himself dry then turned back the duvet on his bed. As he turned to switch off the light, he saw his Chinese puzzle box on the pedestal next to him. He once again ran his fingers over the familiar shape. Bringing back all his memories of running into the sea as a little boy, his amah, Ah Lan, following closely behind him watching over him as he splashed around in the calm warm water.

She had given him the box before he left for boarding school in the UK. Showing him how to open and close it. It had been his most treasured possession, his only possession apart from the tin trunk which contained his school uniforms and a long list of other things required for his new life at Eton. Ah Lan had hidden it beneath all his school clothes, knowing his mother would not have approved. But she had wanted to give him some sense of belonging to the life he was being forced to abandon.

He pulled the box over the duvet and with dexterity slid the panels back and forth. Inside the drawer with the tassel, he found his car keys.

For the first time in many years, he knew Jack Taylor was someone he could trust with everything that had happened. Piet had been hostile and he understood why. He had a policeman's blood running through his veins and David knew he wanted answers, just as Jack did.

He tried to hold back the emotions of his childhood which he had buried for so many years, but failed. He wrapped his arms around the box, with all its secrets. Thinking of all he had lost and all he had gained, which had never been enough. Never been enough for anything he cared about.

An emotion he had forgotten about found its way to his eyes and down his cheeks, as he thought about all that had been lost.

But he cared about Daphne. It had been the phone call from her which had been the catalyst for everything that happened afterwards.

"I've been told by someone at the Embassy to watch you, David. You're in a great deal of trouble. You need to get out of Kenya as quickly as possible, and disappear. Bashir and I will help you."

Chapter Seventy-Six

J ack, Piet and David re-grouped early the next morning."You want to know about Madeleine." David said his face devoid of any emotion.

Jack pushed his sunglasses up and nodded. "How were you able to track her for twenty years. Daphne?"

"Yes, Daphne. The Foreign Office trusted her, impeccable pedigree. Her cousin, I can't remember his name now, perhaps she didn't even tell me. He was the one who chose her to be the unofficial watcher on the ground. It's not unusual. A lot of governments do the same thing. Spies watching spies if you like. Most diplomats, whilst doing their appointed jobs, keep an eye open for unusual activities which might be a threat to their governments as does the watcher who they know nothing about.

"I met Daphne the first week I arrived in Nairobi. She was unlike anyone I had ever met before. Beautiful, yes, she was in her late forties then. There was something about her. She might have been married three times and lived in a fabulous old house in Muthaiga, but I saw something in her that I knew so well, recognised perhaps. She was playing her part, but she was lonely, despite her frantic social life.

"We were both looking for something more real." David looked at the two men before him, his gaze settled on Jack. "She warned me you were in Nairobi asking questions. You were staying at The Norfolk, right?"

Jack nodded.

David gave him a small smile. "Daphne came looking for you, asked reception to point you out. Surely you didn't think someone like Daphne would be wandering around a public bar at night, on her own, did you?"

Jack looked bemused. "I didn't think about it to tell you the truth. But, yes, I suppose knowing her as I do now, it was a bit unusual. So, she was trying to find out what I was looking for and how much I knew. Then she threw me a few bones of information and hoped I would go away."

"No, Jack, you're quite wrong there. She deduced you were a highly professional and astute journalist. She knew you wouldn't go quietly. That's why I'm here now."

Jack sat back in his chair. "Madeleine didn't notice the tip of your finger was missing, or you had a tattoo at the base of your spine? How did you explain that away?"

"As I said, I have a very good prosthetic. Madeleine found the bill from the Doctor. I told her I'd had an accident slicing ham, she didn't believe me, but that's what I told her. Madeleine and I had not shared a bedroom for years. The tattoo remained hidden from her. The marriage was finished – she wanted a divorce. I knew she would demand a large settlement and that perhaps, whatever she had been making notes about, she might use that against me, to ensure that settlement. She wasn't going to go quietly. She knew far too much."

David leaned back in his chair, he could see the stream, the sun glinting on its slowly moving surface.

Piet leaned forward. "So, with Daphne's help you were able to keep track of Madeleine, knew she was in some kind of protection programme, and you knew where she lived. Why did you wait so many years before making a visit to her to look for your box?"

David shrugged. "I was always concerned about the box and her diary, but over the years Madeleine did nothing with the information she had about me. As far as she was concerned, I was dead. But you have to remember she was extremely unpredictable, and it always worried me.

"Now I have destroyed her diary. I can see it wouldn't make sense to anyone, apart from the fact she had used her old secretarial skills and written everything in shorthand. But, of course, I recognised the letters, numbers and initials, it was easy for me to work out the time frame from there. The sensitive deals I had orchestrated were all there. The countries they took place in. The initials of the contacts I used. I underestimated Madeleine's intelligence.

"The British government must have heaved a huge sigh of relief when I died in a plane crash in Kenya. They were on to me; they were going to recall me. It would have been messy and embarrassing for the Foreign Office and indeed the government. I would have been facing a prison sentence."

Jack made a few notes in his notebook. "So, the bottom line is you gave government contracts worth millions and millions of pounds, to people they were not intended for, right?"

David rubbed his cheek. "It wasn't as simple as that, Jack. In a nutshell I made sure some of the contracts went to governments who were not going to use military equipment, arms and munitions against their own people. Yes, I made a great deal of money myself, through various middlemen, but it's the way the game is played. The Chinese deal went badly wrong. I trusted the wrong person, the wrong middleman, and paid for it with the loss of the top of my finger and the tattoo. I knew it would be impossible to do any more trade deals in China. As far as they were concerned, I had lost face.

"My then secretary, Harold, odious man that he was, but efficient, spotted something. I'm not sure what. He reported it to the auditors and the game was up. Daphne warned me they were onto me. I had to do something."

Jack took a sip of his coffee. "Daphne obviously knew all about your deals. Surely, she didn't approve of you working against the government, given that her contact was in a senior position with the Foreign Office. You used your position to betray them, or, to put it politely and to quote the Chinese – you were a traitor to your country."

David looked at him anger showing on his face. "You have that part wrong, Jack! How could I be a traitor to a country I never belonged to? A country I never wanted to live in? There was only one country I believed in, belonged to and, yes, loved.

"It was Malaysia where I was born and brought up." His voice shook slightly. "I didn't ask to go and live in Britain. I was sent there by my parents. I became a product of the old boy network, not a product of the country. So, no I was not a traitor to my country. I didn't betray them once. If there was a contract which I knew the Malaysian government were interested in acquiring, I made sure they got it. Daphne didn't approve or disapprove – she loved me, as I loved her."

Jack scratched his head with his pen and frowned. "When you first went to Cloud's End, obviously looking for your box and the diary you assumed must be in it – well, to put it mildly, Madeleine must have been shocked to see you if she thought you had been dead for years?"

"The years had passed Jack. I looked different; I spoke to her in Afrikaans. I was banking on the fact she might not recognise me – but, of course, she did. By that time, she was seriously disorientated, not in a good condition at all. I don't think she could process anything through her mind at that point, she just saw me in front of her.

"Madeleine asked me where I had been, as though I had been away for a few days and not years. I searched for the box everywhere, like a lot of seriously distressed mental health patients she was secretive. I never found it."

He leaned forward and clasped his hands in front of him. "The next morning, I watched her ferociously wiping down all the surfaces in the house, wearing a pair of white gloves. That's when I realised, she had somehow worked out I shouldn't have been there. She had to eliminate my fingerprints from everything. To protect me.

"Although I had never loved Madeleine, I think she loved me. I was distressed to see what I had put her through, how the way I had treated her had taken her life from her in many ways. My actions in Kenya had resulted in her being hidden away out in the bush somewhere. She didn't deserve it. No, she didn't deserve it. What I did was reprehensible."

Seeing David becoming emotional was making both Jack and Piet feel uncomfortable. It was a sad story in many ways, but one David Cooper had created for himself.

"You didn't go back and see Madeleine again then?" Piet asked.

"Yes." he said abruptly. "I wanted my box and the diary. One day I knew Madeleine would lose her mind altogether, and I had to make sure it didn't end up in the wrong hands I had to get hold of the diary which I worked out was inside the box."

Jack refilled their coffee cups. "I have to ask you this question."

David looked at him. "Go ahead."

"Apparently Madeleine liked to ride out over the bush. There was a sort of look-out point overlooking a water hole where the animals would come to drink. By all accounts she went there often over the years. Then she turned the chairs from the water hole, so they faced the main road between Kimberley and Johannesburg as though she were waiting for someone?"

David rubbed his eyes. "She was waiting for me. I told her I would come back. I promised her I would."

Jack bit the end of his pen. "When you didn't come back, she shot herself, right? Gave up hope in other words? A widow in waiting you could say…"

David looked at him briefly. "She gave up hope. I knew she was ill but even so, I blame myself for everything that happened to her. All of it was my fault.

"I did go back, some months later. Madeleine wasn't at the house, no-one was there. I went to the stables, there was no-one there either. The groom had probably gone into town. But one of the horses was missing. I guessed that Madeleine had gone down to the hide, the viewing platform in the bush. I drove down there and found her."

David rubbed his bloodshot eyes. "There was a sunbed there which she was lying on, but she wasn't asleep. When she saw me, she got up and picked up the gun which was lying on the table next to her. It's not unusual for women in South Africa, who live alone, to carry a weapon."

David looked at Piet, who nodded in acknowledgement of this fact.

David continued. "Madeleine was not in a good state, her eyes were wild, almost unseeing. I worked out from my last visit that she was no longer on any kind of medication."

He took a deep breath. "I may be many things in your eyes, but I have never been a violent person. She started to shout at me, demanding where her money was, berating me for the life she said I had taken from her.

"She was pointing the gun at me, telling me she would take my life as I had taken hers. I knew I had to get the gun away from her. So, I tackled her. The gun went off and she collapsed in my arms, the bullet went through her heart."

David looked off into the distance. "One of the worst moments of my life."

He took a few moments to compose himself. "I lay her down on the sunbed, the gun had fallen to the ground next to her. I hadn't touched it, so there would be no fingerprints.

"I left her there, you see. I didn't know what else to do. Her horse panicked when it heard the shot. I untied her and she took off back to the stables. I couldn't tell anyone what happened, it would have involved the police and that was the last thing I wanted, as you can imagine.

"I never loved Madeleine, but she was a good person. We were a good team. What happened to her still haunts me to this day. She married me so she could escape from the mundane life she was leading. I married her for my own reasons, I knew she would enhance my career. She was hand-picked by the Foreign Office. That's what they do. But Madeleine paid a much higher price than I did.

"Once again in my life I was doing what was expected of me."

"It was a terrible accident, you see," he said softly. "I have to live with that."

Chapter Seventy-Seven

David stood up. "Please excuse me, Jack, Piet. I'll see you tomorrow. I have one thing I would like to ask of you, whatever the outcome of all of this might be.

"I would like to spend a couple of days in the bush. I doubt very much I will get the opportunity again," he glanced at Piet. "Whatever you do with the information I have given you could still result in a prison sentence, either here or in the UK…"

Piet glared at him. "Yes, you are in serious trouble with the law, whether here or in the UK. I have a duty to report this to the police, you understand that, don't you?"

David nodded. "Yes, I know that, of course. But I'd like to make a deal with you both; you in particular Jack."

Piet glared at him again. "Another deal? No doubt in your favour, and who is going to have to pay the price this time?"

He stood up abruptly. "I need to get back to the hotel, make sure there are no more people with a criminal past walking about on my patch," he said, giving David a penetrating look.

David disappeared inside of the cottage.

They had pushed him hard with their questions. It was time to call it a day. He doubted David had ever spoken about his life, apart from to Daphne, or the fears he may have for what might possibly be a very bleak future indeed.

Jack turned to look at Piet. "So, what do you think? Pretty dynamic story isn't it – and we're not quite there yet."

Piet rubbed his eyes. He was tired. He was angry. He had to get back to the hotel.

"I think I need to think a lot about this, my friend. Take this *oke* out into the bush for a day or two. I think I know the kind of deal he wants to make…at least if you're with him he won't gap it."

Jack frowned. "Gap it?"

308

"*Ja*, he won't be able to do a runner, as you would say. Good plan, Jack, fill me in when you get back, hey? Record everything, he says on your phone. Don't worry, my friend I won't report him to the police, not yet. He has done some bad stuff, but I want to hear what else he has to say."

*****

Jack tapped his pen on the table. But what on earth was he going to do with this story given what he now knew?

Harry would have to wait. Jack realised the story wasn't at an end yet, and he needed that ending.

Chapter Seventy-Eight

A fter breakfast the next morning, David had once more composed himself. Although looking tired he sipped his coffee and waited for more questions from Jack. He seemed exhausted.

Jack disappeared into his cottage and came out shortly afterwards, holding up his car keys. "I've taken the liberty of booking two *rondavels* at one of the camps in the Kruger. I think we both need some time out there."

David smiled at him. "You're good Jack, very good. Take the subject of your investigation and put them somewhere else, a good tactic."

*****

The sun was setting bathing the bush in the colour of blood, the *braai* was smouldering in front of Jack's *rondavel*. He turned the steaks over and tried not to think too much about Lara.

In the distance they could hear the throaty call of the lions, could see the cavernous shadows of the silent elephants as they passed by the water hole.

Sir David Cooper sat alone on the little deck overlooking a water hole. He had said little on the short journey, knowing it would be his last.

Jack watched him as he carefully turned the steaks over again, the salad was ready, the garlic bread sizzling next to it. He recognised the loneliness and aloneness, of this man and respected his need to be that way. But he had given David enough time to put together his story. He wanted to hear the rest of it.

They finished eating. Jack threw another log on the fireplace and waited.

David pushed his safari boots off his feet and stretched his toes, then he turned to Jack. "You want to know how I spent the next twenty years, right?"

Jack nodded.

"As I've told you I set up various companies in the Bahama's. That's where all my money was invested. After Mike Cavendish died, I changed a few things. I set up a foundation, of sorts, The Cavendish Corporation. There were only two trustees, Daphne and me. Over the ensuing years we donated a considerable amount of money to various children's charities in the Far East and Africa, building schools, clinics, hospitals etc. Nothing big, but adequate enough to make a difference in many people's lives.

"I rented a place in Joburg and spent a great deal of time writing my memoires. It helped with the isolation and loneliness. Daphne flew out four or five times and we spent some time together. Just the two of us. Having had a life of great privilege she became enthusiastic about getting involved with the less fortunate."

Jack made a note in his little book. Memoires? Already his mind was working out a plan for those.

David continued. "There's a company in South Africa called The Gift of The Givers. I know you've heard of it; you sometimes write about what they do."

Jack nodded. He knew all about the non-government organisation, the medical doctor, with his private practice in Johannesburg, who headed it up but then had a moment of epiphany in his life. A fellow Muslim had told him he must heed the call and go out into the world and make a difference.

The doctor had created a global organisation, based in South Africa with no political, racial, religious allegiance or anything else. Where there was a humanitarian crisis, he and his team of volunteers went where they were needed. Somalia, Zimbabwe, Bosnia, Malawi, Nepal, Syria and other countries.

David stared at his hands then continued. "Whether it was a national disaster, a war-torn country in need of help, floods, famine or general mayhem – The Gift of The Givers stepped up. Not taking sides – only there doing what they could to help. Not representing the government of South Africa – not representing anyone but themselves."

David looked out over the bush, listening to its sounds, remembering. "I wanted to do something that meant something. I wanted to get involved. By this time, of course, Mike Cavendish's British passport had run out.

"I renewed it. Just two photographs were needed and a copy of his old passport. Bush pilots are an integral part of any emergency situation and I put in the hours to get my pilot's licence renewed as well.

"My new passport was issued and I had my pilot's licence back. I was more than ready to get involved in any way I could. The fact I spoke so many languages including French and Swahili, which are widely used in West and East Africa, well, I knew I could be useful."

Jack didn't interrupt him, but let David continue at his own pace with his own thoughts.

"I like to think I made a difference, not only with the money I regularly contributed, but to other people's lives which had been ripped apart by war and famine. It felt good. I was doing something which mattered. I was making a difference. I worked with them for eight years. Although I obviously didn't get involved in anything involving Kenya.

"All the money, Jack, which, you know I made on the side at the expense of the British Government, I gave back to many charities. I kept enough back to ensure I could lead a decent life but the rest I gave away. I was never a traitor or a crook. I have always remained true to myself – to what I believed in and not what I was expected to believe in. Madeleine's death was a terrible accident."

Jack threw another log on the fire sending bright orange sparks up into the night. "So, basically you have a valid British passport in the name of Michael Cavendish and you have a woman in Nairobi who clearly loves you, as you do her. Why don't you go back to Kenya and leave your past, good or bad, behind? Surely no-one will recognise you now, twenty years later. You could hang out at Daphne's beach house. No-one would ever know you were there and had returned? You said it was very private, hidden amongst the palm trees with big wooden gates, to keep prying eyes away."

David threw the dregs of his coffee on the fire where it hissed briefly before being consumed. He looked at Jack across the bright flames of the fire. "I can't go back. Because of your interest in what happened to me. That's why I can't even contemplate something like that. I'm not sure what you're going to do with the information you now have?"

312

David leaned back in his chair. "The British Government has a long memory. They have put considerable pressure on your editor Harry Bentley, and the other shareholders of your newspaper, to bury you and your story. They're nervous about the truth coming out with what you may now know.

"Daphne is well known to the Foreign Office. She is their eyes and ears on the ground in Kenya, as she has been for many years. I can't risk going back. One wrong move and I will put her entire life and reputation in jeopardy. The spooks are watching your Harry and his newspaper and everyone else you know. They will be relentless with their pursuit of the truth. Did Sir David Cooper die in that plane crash, or didn't he? They will trawl through my life and come up with some other possibilities. I can't do it, Jack.

"Someone may think they recognise me, perhaps speculate about it, the gossip could become rife. All the '*what ifs*' would swirl around the cocktail parties and clubs, along with the *hors d'oeuvres*, potato chips and dips. I won't put Daphne in that position – ever."

Jack's mind was churning with possibilities. He needed to speak to Harry. He needed to speak to Piet. But more than anything else he needed something from Sir David Cooper which he knew he would not get.

As though reading his mind David smiled at him. "The answer to that is a resounding no, Jack. I am a master at dealing with the media. It was an integral part of my job when I worked for your government. I know how your mind is working now. I will never give you what you want, my memoir, is that clear?"

Jack looked at him, an innocent smile on his face. "This may be so, but as you have illustrated over the years, you are indeed a master of illusion. But I know what you want, and you know what I want. I know you destroyed Madeleine's diary, but, you see, I have a copy of it. Translated from shorthand into English. Let's call it a day, David, and think things through, shall we?"

*****

Jack lay under his mosquito net, the fan above rippling the light cotton around his bed. Despite everything he liked David Cooper.

Inherently there was something good and decent about him, despite all the revelations. Yes, he had made mistakes. Madeleine, the memories of her, her death, was something only he could deal with.

313

But relationships were complicated, Jack knew that. Mistakes were made, emotions changed, people fell in love when they least expected it and fell out of love without understanding why. To Jack this was the rich tapestry of people's lives. Love – something no-one had ever had any answers to.

But Sir David Cooper had made a huge contribution with his money to good causes, asking for nothing in return. Only looking for a place to belong which clearly, he had never found.

He knew now he would never be able to write the story of what happened to David. Harry would agree with that. Both of them were up against too much.

But, Jack thought, as he closed his eyes, trying to stop his brain working. There was another way of doing this, another way of getting around it.

He had a copy of the diary – now he wanted David's memoirs.

Chapter Seventy-Nine

Jack and David returned to Jack's cottage the next day. Jack knew he needed to do some shopping, unsure of how long David would be staying. He hadn't mentioned any future plans to him. David was obviously waiting to hear what Jack was going to do with the story of his life. There were, it would appear, still a few deals left on the table.

After a light lunch David stood up. "I think I'll take a nap and then write the final chapters of my book…"

Jack's head jerked up with interest. "Go right ahead. I need to do a bit of a shop then I thought I'd drop in at the hotel and see Piet. See if he's in a better mood now the ANC conference is over. I'll leave you to it."

He looked directly at David. "You'll be here when I get back, right? Not going to disappear on me?"

David smiled. "I think you know too much about me for me to do that. I'll be here when you return. Where else could I go now?"

Jack drove off. David may well be finishing the last chapters of his memoirs and it sounded as if they were hand-written. But he doubted it was the end of the story.

There was one final chapter to be written and Jack was already composing it.

He hoped like hell David wasn't planning a dramatic exit and didn't have a gun stashed away in his leather safari bag.

He found Piet in his cottage at the hotel. "Hey, Jack, thought you had run off with the *bleddy* Englishman who doesn't seem to know his own name, so long."

Jack laughed pleased to see his friend again. "Nope, he's still at my cottage – well I hope he is."

Piet grunted. "Better be good, my friend, not feeling warm and fuzzy about someone who lied to me. He broke the law, and not just once, don't forget that, no matter what he's told you with his posh English accent. Doesn't cut any ice with me; *bleddy* Englishman. But I'll hear you out. We've spent a lot of time trying to figure out what happened to him? So, what else did he tell you out in the bush then?"

Jack played the conversations he had recorded on his phone.

Piet listened intently, not taking his eyes off Jack. He interrupted him a few times to ask a question, but otherwise he remained silent.

Jack sat back in his chair and reached for his beer, grinning widely. "It's a great story, Piet. Even if you don't like the man. Yes, he made mistakes, broke the law here and there. But he also contributed millions to various charities, and flew around Africa, avoiding Kenya, reaching out to people who had no hope. People forgotten by their own governments who sat back and did nothing. You have to give him credit for that."

Jack glanced at his friend. "He contributed a great deal of money to try and make a difference in the life of your own people, Piet."

Piet frowned. "Not sure what you're saying here, my friend. How? What did he do? Don't trust the man, don't believe some of things he has told us."

Jack paused, thinking carefully of how he should broach the subject.

"There are many disadvantaged people in this country, Piet, and some of them include your own Afrikaners, the ones with little or no education. They're living in squatter camps with no hope, no money and no future. They're called poor whites.

"You see them holding up pieces of cardboard at the traffic lights in the cities, begging for money or a job. The country they knew has gone, there is no place for them anymore, most of them can't speak English. You know about this, don't you?"

"Yes…" Piet said softly. "I know about this, of course I do. The forgotten ones. Once part of the land and now they have nowhere to go because they know no other language than their own, most of them barely educated."

Jack saw the pain in his friend's eyes. "Sir David Cooper found a piece of land in a place in the Free State. He poured thousands of pounds into making it a place where there was running water and electricity, clinics and schools, houses, simple ones yes, but houses where your people could live with pride in their country. Where they could have an essence of who they once were, and speak the language they knew. It was a grand gesture, Piet, whichever way you jump.

316

"The forgotten people, well, he made sure they would not be forgotten. David knew about losing his home, his family. It was the one thing he truly understood. Being abandoned. He knew how your people felt and he did something about it. The government did nothing to help them at all."

Piet drummed his fingers on the table still not entirely convinced Sir David Cooper was a good *oke* after all. But what Jack had just told him had surprised and moved him.

"Perhaps you're right Jack," he said softly, almost to himself. "I accept that people make mistakes. All the money this David person siphoned off his own government and stashed away in the Bahamas, he gave back, it's true, hey. Not saying he killed his wife, but he caused her death one way or another.

"But what you are telling me now, about the place in the Free State, well, I've heard about it, but no-one seemed to know who put up the money behind it, not the government that's for sure. So, it was David, hey?"

Piet stared into his beer. "That matters to me a lot," he said softly. "I could do nothing about improving those poor white's lives. But someone came along and did something about it. I'm not saying it was right to do what he did during his career. He broke the law, but I think he tried to make up for it. He did something for my people, I won't forget that."

Jack smiled at him. "So, what language will you speak to him in now? English or Afrikaans?"

Piet wiped his eyes. "I'm thinking, my friend, I will be speaking to him in Afrikaans…

"But Jack, what will you do with this story now? Harry won't touch it will he?"

"No, Harry won't touch it. But I have a plan which might work, if David will go along with it. He wants something and I want something."

Piet frowned. "Which is?"

"A deal." Jack told him his plan.

Piet nodded, a smile spreading across his face. "Good plan, my friend. Let's hope the Englishman is still at your cottage, otherwise you're stuffed, hey."

Piet glanced at his watch. "Better get back to work, my friend, and tell your English friend I'd like him to make a contribution to the cost of putting an electric fence around the hotel property. It cost Hugo a lot of money. I'll send him a bill, if he's still at your place. See you, Jack. Good story." Chuckling to himself he strode back to the hotel, Hope running along trying to catch up with him.

*****

Piet walked through the grounds of the hotel. He looked up at the sky and clouds, and the hills in the distance. Nothing had changed with the landscape; it was enduring and would go on forever.

He thought about Sir David Cooper's life. By comparison his own had been blessed. He lived in the country he loved, he had a good job, a woman he loved, a hopeless dog who he also loved, and Jack who he had become close to, despite the fact that he was English...

Chapter Eighty

Daphne Forsyth-Phillips lay back on the pillows on her bed, her cats stretched out around her. The phone next to her rang.

"Jack," she said struggling to sit up. "How are you? How is the story coming along?"

"Hello, Daphne. I think we can dispense with all the subterfuge, don't you? Your old friend is staying with me at my place in Hazyview. He's told me everything – absolutely everything. Let's not mention his name in case others are listening."

Daphne felt the colour drain from her face along with a huge feeling of relief. The time she had waited so long for had arrived.

"Oh, Jack. Please don't hurt him, he's been through enough. He's a good man, a decent man, who made a few mistakes, but his heart was always in the right place. He's given so much back to so many people."

Her voice broke. "If you write your story he'll be finished. All his good work, our good work, will have been for nothing. They'll take him away and put him in prison. I can't bear to think about it…"

Jack cleared his throat. "Listen Daphne. I'm not going to hurt either of you. I'm not going to write the story. I know, as you do, he has a limited time left. He told me. Perhaps a couple of years that's all. Some heart problem, maybe brought on by the trauma he went through as a little boy, I don't know.

"His career was built on making deals, whether they were good or bad. But we've made a deal. You're very much part of what happens next. I think you need to speak to him, okay?

"Here he is."

Chapter Eighty-One

The sea was calm and placid, the huge moon turning its surface to molten rippling silver. The palm trees clattered softly in the warm air, as she made her way down to the water's edge. The beach house was lit with lanterns, its dark arches illuminated. Crabs skittered across the sand in front of her then disappeared into secret holes. The sea hissed quietly beneath her bare feet.

The dhow, with a single lantern, made its final journey around the black rocks and into calmer waters close to the beach, then doused its light.

Six Siamese cats watched from the beach house, the light of the moon glinting on the bangles of the woman who stood there waiting. Her kaftan caressing her ankles, then clung to her as she walked out to meet the man who had disembarked. He carried nothing other than an old wooden carved box.

The two dark figures headed towards each other until they became one, silhouetted against the light of the moon.

Chapter Eighty-Two

Jack, true to his word, waited until he received the phone call from Daphne eighteen months later.

Sir David Cooper had died, with the woman he loved beside him. Daphne and Saul had buried him in the grounds of her beach home, with the only possession he had ever valued and loved. The Chinese puzzle box.

No-one would ever find David's final resting place. She had not registered his death. That would have been impossible.

David had given her a letter addressed to Mike Cavendish's daughter Cassie. The man who had given him a second chance, a chance he had not been given himself.

*****

Cassie turned on the light in her London home and opened it.

The silver chain and Maltese Cross slithered out of the envelope. "Daddy", she whispered, "Oh Daddy, I remember this."

A letter was also enclosed. Through her tears Mike Cavendish's daughter read it.

"I never met your father, Michael Cavendish. I wish I had done. I have met many people in my life, but your father stands out as one of the bravest. It took a lot of courage for him to do what he did. But he did it for you, Cassie. He loved you very much. He became ill. He knew he was dying but his thoughts were only about you. He didn't want you to see him as anything but the strong, young, father you had known.

He made sure you would be well looked after when he knew he couldn't do it himself.

He gave his life so that Sir David Cooper could go on and live his. The money came from David.

I have no doubt you will read all about it in The Telegraph, *and the book which will be published. Your name will not be mentioned.*
You see, Cassie, he protected you to the end.
He loved you as only a father loves his child.
Remember him well, won't you?
Daphne Forsyth-Phillips

Jack, hearing of David's death, immediately retrieved his memoirs from the safe at the hotel.

He would write the final chapter of the extraordinary life of Sir David Cooper. Of the people whose lives he had touched and what had happened to him after his apparent death in a plane crash in Tsavo.

They had made a deal. He and David. Jack had promised he would not write his story and had made a promise in exchange for David's memoirs and permission to use excerpts from Madeleine's diary.

David had kept a meticulous account of his life, all handwritten with dates and times. But he hadn't named names. Daphne was never mentioned, but it was clear through his writings that David had eventually found the love and affection he had craved since he was a little boy.

David had given Jack the publishing rights in exchange for the promise that he would not write about him until after his death. Jack had given him back the Chinese puzzle box full of his memories as a child in a faraway country where he had once been happy.

Harry, his editor, was beside himself with excitement.

"Oh, yes, this is going to be a big one. To hell with the spooks, the shareholders and everyone else, Jack. We're going to publish this story. Publish and be damned as they say in the trade. The story of Sir David Cooper and his extraordinary life. They won't be able to touch us if it's written by him. You wrote the final chapter – a masterpiece. We'll run it in our Sunday supplement before the book is published.

"Welcome back, Jack, you're still my man in Africa. Go write your columns and get me another story, you hear?"

David also made Jack promise that he would not write about his journey back to Kenya, to Mombasa. Protecting Daphne right until the end and leaving the readers with a mysterious question.

Where was Sir David Cooper now?

Jack remembered his last conversation with David, asking him where he would go after he left his cottage.

David had replied. "I want to go somewhere I belong. With someone I trust. Someone who will never turn their back on me."

Chapter Eighty-Three

The florist in Wolmaransstad looked at the order which had been placed for a wreath in the local graveyard. She frowned and called out to her assistant.

"Hey, my girl, this wreath is for someone called Marlene Hartley, but the message is for someone with a different name? *Shoo*, not sure what to make of it, is all."

Her assistant turned and smiled at her. "Names don't really matter in the end; people change their names. We'll put the wreath on her grave with the message that came with it. What is the name anyways?"

The florist peered at the name on the card. "It says: *To Madeleine from Jack.*"

Epilogue

The woman stood on the wooden deck of her modest home, built on traditional bamboo stilts with its attap roof woven from palm leaves. A paraffin lamp threw shadows around her simple furniture, hardly penetrating the thick jungle in front of her.

She was dressed in wide black trousers and a simple white short sleeved blouse with a mandarin collar. Her glossy hair was held back with a black ribbon. She watched the final moments of the torrential rain which came every afternoon during the monsoon season thundering through the coconut palms and the banana and papaya trees.

Then there was only the silence and the remnants of the rain dripping onto the banana leaves.

Ah Lan, sensed him before she felt his small familiar hand find hers.

She bent down and lifted him onto her hip. "Come, David. I have been waiting for you. You are home now."

He lay his head on her shoulder as he had always done, and wrapped his arms around her neck, inhaling the familiar scent of her. He closed his eyes.

She held him close and stroked his hair. "Remember the stories I told you about the ghost people?" she said softly. "We must go now and meet them. They have been waiting for us.

"Come, little one, you will be safe with me now. We will go together."

*****

If you enjoyed reading this book and would like to share that enjoyment with others, then please take the time to visit the place where you made your purchase and write a review.

Reviews are a great way to spread the word about worthy authors and will help them be rewarded for their hard work.

*****

You can also visit Samantha's Author Page on Amazon to find out more about her life and passions.

Also by Samantha Ford:

The Zanzibar Affair

A letter found in an old chest on the island of Zanzibar finally reveals the secret of Kate Hope's glamorous, but anguished past, and the reason for her sudden and unexplained disappearance.

Ten year's previously Kate's lover and business partner, Adam Hamilton, tormented by a terrifying secret he is willing to risk everything for, brutally ends his relationship with Kate.

A woman is found murdered in a remote part of Kenya bringing Tom Fletcher back to East Africa to unravel the web of mystery and intrigue surrounding Kate, the woman he loves but has not seen for over twenty years.

In Zanzibar, Tom meets Kate's daughter Molly. With her help he pieces together the last years of her mother's life and his extraordinary connection to it.

A page turning novel of love, passion, betrayal and death, with an unforgettable cast of characters, set against the spectacular backdrop of East and Southern Africa, New York and France.

Amazon Reviews

"This book will keep you guessing; that's a good thing. I could barely put it down and one night dreamed about it so much I woke up and read more. It's unbearably sad in some places and wonderfully happy in others. Fantastic!"

"This book takes you on a safari round Africa. It is a compelling story with so many twists. It is beautifully and hauntingly told. The details and descriptions made me feel the heat, smell the ocean and slap the mosquitoes. Thank you."

"I loved The Zanzibar affair. I felt I was there sensing the smells, the sea and the warmth of Africa. The way she weaves the characters into the story is quite fascinating, leaving the reader spellbound and wondering where it's going to end. Always with an unexpected twist. A fabulous storyline and book which I could hardly put down. Highly recommended."

The House Called Mbabati

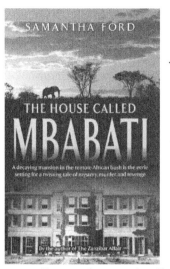

The Mother Superior crossed herself quickly. "May God have mercy on you, and forgive you both," she murmured as she locked the diary and faded letters in the drawer.

Deep in the heart of the East African bush stands a deserted mansion. Boarded up, on the top floor, is a magnificent Steinway Concert Grand, shrouded in decades of dust.

In an antique shop in London, an elderly nun recognises an old photograph of the mansion; she knows it well.

Seven thousand miles away, in Cape Town, a woman lies dying; she whispers one word to journalist Alex Patterson – Mbabati.

Sensing a good story, and intrigued with what he has discovered, Alex heads for East Africa in search of the old abandoned house. He is unprepared for what he discovers there; the hidden home of a once famous classical pianist whose career came to a shattering end; a grave with a blank headstone and an old retainer called Luke - the only one left alive who knows the true story about two sisters who disappeared without trace over twenty years ago.

Alex unravels a story which has fascinated the media and the police for decades. A twisting tale of love, passion, betrayal and murder; and the unbreakable bond between two extraordinary sisters who were prepared to sacrifice everything to hide the truth.

Mbabati is set against the magnificent and enduring landscape of the African bush - where nothing is ever quite as it seems.

Amazon Reviews

"It is a long time since I have been so absorbed by a novel about Africa. Reading it, I vacillated between willing it to last longer as I was enjoying it so much, and wanting to get through it to reveal the outcome.

There can be no greater praise for this novel than its endorsement by the late John Gordon Davis, to whom the novel is dedicated. Anyone who has read any of JGD's novels, in particular his classic 'Hold My Hand I'm Dying' will understand that Samantha Ford's novel is in the same league."

"What a wonderful story where you have a stormy love affair set in the heart of Africa. It twists and turns as the plot unfolds and you will surely shed a tear or two along the way. For those who have been on an African safari you will not put this book down. Such intelligent and beautiful writing."

"The book is captivating from beginning to end. It takes you on a riveting journey where the story develops and keeps you guessing. Loved it! Didn't want it to end!"

A Gathering of Dust

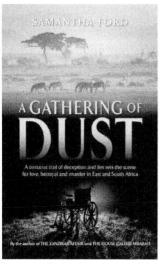

Through the mists of a remote and dangerous part of the South African coastline, a fisherman stumbles upon an abandoned car and an overturned wheelchair.

Thousands of miles away in London, an unidentified woman lies in a coma. When she recovers she has no memory of her past or where she comes from. As fragments of her memory begin to return, the woman has to confront the facts about herself as they begin to unfold. A disastrous love affair in the African bush: a missing husband: and a sinister shadowy figure who knows exactly who she is and where she comes from.

Tension builds as images and secrets begin to resurface from her lost past – rekindled memories that plunge her back into a world she finds she would rather not remember.

Set against the magnificent backdrop of East and Southern Africa. A Gathering of Dust is a fast-paced story of love, betrayal and murder scattered along a trail of deception and lies, with a single impossible truth, and an unthinkable ending.

Amazon Reviews

"What a writer this author is! So cleverly written and with twists and turns you never see coming. I am an avid reader and this authors books are the best I have read in a long time. Her books have everything, mystery, murder, romance, intrigue, suspense etc etc. Well worth a read."

"My husband knows when I am reading this author's books that there is little that will get my nose out of them. Her descriptives of even the simplest things create such a vivid picture. She has made me fall in love with Africa and her story lines are captivating and

intelligently thought out. I never want to finish one of her books only because I don't want them to end."

"Superb. Absolutely brilliant. I simply couldn't stop reading, turned TV off and just read and read, even ignoring my hubby. Can't wait to read the next book!!!"

"A gripping read, with many gut-wrenching twists and turns. I had trouble putting the book down to eat, sleep or work! Fabulous."

The Ambassador's Daughter

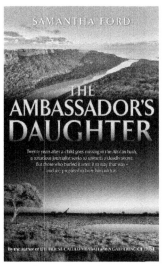

During a violent storm deep in the African bush, a child disappears.

Sara, the ex-British ambassador's daughter, and mother of the child, is arrested.

Twenty years later, journalist Jack Taylor, travels from London to the magnificent landscape of the Eastern Cape, in South Africa, where the unforgiving bush hides long-forgotten secrets of loss, hate, betrayal and revenge.

A staggering story awaits. A deadly secret threatens to destroy the lives of people who thought themselves now safe - a story which has fascinated the media for decades.

Only one person knows exactly what happened on that day - a nomadic shepherd called Eza - but can Jack find him?

Amazon Reviews

"This is simply the best book I've read in a very long time. This talented lady brings Africa alive. Wilbur Smith you have some competition..."

"A cracking good story with a totally unexpected twist at the end!"
John Gordon Davis – author of Hold My Hand I'm Dying

"Having read all Wilbur Smith's books, this author ranks up with the best of them. Best read I've had for years!" Peter C. Morgan

The Unexpected Guest

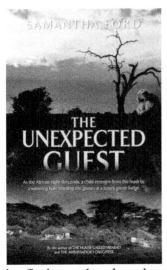

As darkness descends on the bush a child appears at a watering hole opposite a game lodge. The guests watch in horror as she collapses in front of them.

Jack Taylor, a London journalist now living in South Africa, is given the exclusive to investigate the child's mysterious past. A past the child is unable to help him with.

Jack's investigation takes him deep into the sinister world of international crime, and a journey to Zimbabwe where he finds an abandoned ranch watched over by someone with desperate secrets of his own, which he is unwilling to share.

Set against the magnificent backdrop of the South African bush. The Unexpected Guest is a fast-paced story with twisting unexpected possibilities, taking Jack down a trail of deception, lies, murder and tragedy until he discovers the bitter truth of what happened to the little girl and how she ended up alone on a dark night in the bush.

Amazon Reviews

"A wonderful story which kept me intrigued from the first page to the last, the characters are rich and unforgettable. The storyline twists and turns and you are unsure what is going to happen next. A truly outstanding read and loved every page. And the ending blew me away. Highly recommend a truly wonderfully written book."

"I may have mentioned before, I hate novels. The author, Samantha Ford has changed all of that. Now i am hooked and will be looking for the remainder of her novels on Africa as soon as I am done here.

Taking the reader to the African destinations is done to perfection. To an extent you also get to meet the African people. Some good and some not so good. This story could easily be true as it kept me spell bound with descriptions and actions. For one who hates fiction, I can't not give this a 5-Star rating. Well-deserved Samantha"

"It's not just a novel. It's an adventure. A journey we long for. Travelling down dirt roads you can feel the dust in your throat. The cool cocktails and beers quenching your parched throat. The excitement of human interactions. The raw emotions. You will laugh. Get riled up at injustice AND you will CRY. My soul this is not just a book. So real you will feel you have made friends with the characters. Samantha Ford may your light shine bright."

Printed in Great Britain
by Amazon

21913354R00199